Clothed or unclothed,
the vampire was stunning, something
he was obviously aware of.

JEANIENE FROST

THIS SIDE
OF THE
GRAVE

A Night Huntress Novel

AVON

An Imprint of HarperCollinsPublishers

This is a work of fiction. Names, characters, places, and incidents are products of the author's imagination or are used fictitiously and are not to be construed as real. Any resemblance to actual events, locales, organizations, or persons, living or dead, is entirely coincidental.

AVON BOOKS
An Imprint of HarperCollins*Publishers*
10 East 53rd Street
New York, New York 10022-5299

Copyright © 2011 by Jeaniene Frost
Excerpt from *One Grave at a Time* copyright © 2011 by Jeaniene Frost
ISBN 978-0-06-178318-0
www.avonbooks.com

First Avon Books paperback printing: March 2011

To Matthew, Melissa, and Ilona,
for too many reasons to list.

Acknowledgments

This might look long-winded but it actually doesn't scratch the surface to acknowledge all the vital persons involved in the Night Huntress series. For everyone I don't mention by name, please know it's not out of lack of appreciation, but simply lack of room instead.

As usual, I have to start off by thanking God for all the amazing opportunities I've been given. I remember when all I asked for was a book to be published. Luckily for me, You had much bigger plans.

Thanks so much to my wonderful editor, Erika Tsang, and the rest of the fabulous team at Avon Books. Nancy Yost, my agent, continues to be worth her weight in gold. A big shout-out goes to Tage, Erin, Kimberley, and Carol, for all you ladies do over at Frost Fans. Thanks so much also to the Night Huntress readers for your support of Cat, Bones, and the rest of their "twisted little fang family." I will never be able to articulate how much I appreciate you spreading the word about the series or contacting me with notes of encouragement. "You rule!" doesn't even begin to cover it.

Thanks to Miriam Struett and Angelika Szakácsi, winners of the Name That Kitty contest. I think Helsing (short for Van Helsing) is the perfect name for Cat's cat!

And, of course, endless love and thanks go to my husband and family, for more things than I could ever begin to list.

THIS SIDE
OF THE
GRAVE

One

THE VAMPIRE PULLED ON THE CHAINS restraining him to the cave wall. His eyes were bright green, their glow illuminating the darkness surrounding us.

"Do you really think these will hold me?" he asked, an English accent caressing the challenge.

"Sure do," I replied. Those manacles were installed and tested by a Master vampire, so they were strong enough. I should know. I'd once been stuck in them myself.

The vampire's smile revealed fangs in his white upper teeth. They hadn't been there several minutes ago, when he'd still looked human to the untrained eye.

"Right, then. What do you want, now that you have me helpless?"

He didn't sound like he felt helpless in the least. I pursed my lips and considered the question, letting my gaze sweep over him. Nothing interrupted my view, either, since he was naked. I'd long ago learned that weapons could be stored in various clothing items, but bare skin hid nothing.

Except now, it was also very distracting. The vampire's body was a pale, beautiful expanse of muscle, bone, and lean, elegant lines, all topped off by a gorgeous face with cheekbones so finely chiseled they could cut butter. Clothed or unclothed, the vampire was stunning, something he was obviously aware of. Those glowing green eyes looked into mine with a knowing stare.

"Need me to repeat the question?" he asked with a hint of wickedness.

I strove for nonchalance. "Who do you work for?"

His grin widened, letting me know my aloof act wasn't as convincing as I'd meant it to be. He even stretched as much as the chains allowed, his muscles rippling like waves on a pond.

"No one."

"Liar." I pulled out a silver knife and traced its tip lightly down his chest, not breaking his skin, just leaving a faint pink line that faded in seconds. Vampires might be able to heal with lightning quickness, but silver through the heart was lethal. Only a few inches of bone and muscle stood between this vampire's heart and my blade.

He glanced at the path my knife had traced. "Is that supposed to frighten me?"

I pretended to consider the question. "Well, I've cut a bloody swath through the undead world ever since I was sixteen. Even earned myself the nickname of the Red Reaper, so if I've got a knife next to your heart, then *yes*, you should be afraid."

His expression was still amused. "Right nasty wench you sound like, but I wager I could get free and have you on your back before you could stop me."

Cocky bastard. "Talk is cheap. Prove it."

His legs flashed out, knocking me off-balance. I sprang forward at once, but a hard, cool body flattened me to the cave floor in the next instant. An iron grip closed around my wrist, preventing me from raising the knife.

"Always pride before a fall," he murmured in satisfaction.

I tried to throw him off, but a ton of bricks would have been easier to dislodge. *Should've chained his arms* and *his legs before daring him like that*, I mentally berated myself.

That arrogant smirk returned as the vampire looked down at me. "Keep squirming, luv. Rubs me in all the right places, it does."

"How'd you get out of the clamps?" Over his shoulder, I saw a hole in the cave that used to be where the inch-thick titanium cuffs had dangled. Unbelievable. He'd ripped them right out of the wall.

A dark brow arched. "Knew just the right angle to pull. You don't install restraints without knowing how to get out of them. Only took a moment; and by then, I had you on your back. Just like I said I would."

If I still had a heartbeat, it would be racing by now, but I'd lost that—for the most part—when I'd changed from a half-breed into a full vampire several months ago. My eyes turned bright green as fangs slid out of my teeth.

"Showoff."

He leaned down until our faces were only an inch

apart. "Now, my lovely captive, with you trapped beneath me, what's to stop me from having my vile way
with you?"

The knife I still held dropped from my hand as I
wrapped my arms around his neck. "Nothing, I hope."

Bones, my vampire husband, gave a low, sinful
laugh. "That's the answer I wanted to hear, Kitten."

Being underground in a cave wouldn't make most
people's favorite last-minute accommodations list, but
it was heaven to me. The only sounds were the smooth
motions of the underground river. It was a relief not to
have to tune out the background noise from countless
conversations that were all too audible with a vampire's hearing. If it were up to me, Bones and I would
stay here for weeks.

But taking a time-out from our lives to get some
R&R wasn't in the cards for us. I'd learned that the
hard way. What I'd also learned was to grab moments
of escape when we could. Hence the stopover to rest
the dawn away in the same cave in which, seven years
ago, my relationship with Bones began. Back then, it
had been me in the chains, convinced I was about to
be eaten by an evil bloodsucker. Instead, I ended up
marrying that bloodsucker.

Helsing, my cat, gave a plaintive meow from the
corner of the small enclave, scratching at the stone
slab that served as a door.

"You don't get to explore," I told him. "You'd get lost."

He meowed again but began to lick his paw, giving
me baleful looks the whole time. He still hadn't
forgiven me for leaving him with a house sitter for
months. I didn't blame Helsing for his grudge, but if

he'd stayed with me, he might have gotten killed. Several people had.

"Rested enough, luv?" Bones asked.

"Um hmm," I murmured, stretching. I'd fallen asleep shortly after dawn, but it hadn't been the instant unconsciousness that had plagued me for my first weeks as a vampire. I'd grown out of that, to my relief.

"We'd best get moving, then," he said.

Right. We had places to be, as usual.

"The only thing I regret about stopping to catch some sleep here is the lack of a normal shower," I sighed.

Bones snorted in amusement. "Come now, the river's very refreshing."

At forty degrees, "refreshing" was a kind way to describe the cave's version of indoor plumbing. Bones moved the stone slab out of the way so we could exit the alcove, putting it back before my kitty could leap out, too.

"The trick is to jump in," he went on. "Taking it slow doesn't make it any easier."

I swallowed a laugh. That advice could also apply to navigating the undead world. *All right. One leap into a freezing river, coming up.*

Then it was time to get to the real reason why we'd come to Ohio. With luck, nothing was going on in my old home state except for a few random cases of fang-on-fang violence.

I doubted it, but I could still hope.

The afternoon sun was still high in the sky by the time Bones and I arrived at the fountain of the Easton mall. Well, a street away from it. We had to make sure that this wasn't a trap. Bones and I had a lot of enemies. Two recent vampire wars will do that, not to mention our former professions.

I didn't sense any excessive supernatural energy except a smaller tingle of power in the air that denoted one, maybe two younger vampires mixed in with the crowd. Still, neither Bones nor I moved until a hazy, indistinct form flew across the parking lot and into our rental car.

"Two vampires are at the fountain," Fabian, the ghost I'd sort of adopted, stated. His outline solidified until he looked more like a person and less like a thick particle cloud. "They didn't notice me."

Even though that was the goal, Fabian sounded almost sad at that last part. Unlike humans, vampires could see ghosts, but by and large they ignored them. Being dead didn't mean people automatically got along.

"Thanks, mate," Bones said. "Keep a lookout to make certain they don't have any unpleasant surprises waiting for us."

Fabian's features blurred until his entire body disappeared.

"We were only supposed to meet with one vampire," I mused. "What do you think of our contact having a buddy with him?"

Bones shrugged. "I think he'd better have a bloody good reason for it."

He got out of the car. I followed suit, giving the silver knives concealed by my sleeves a slight, reassuring pat. *Never leave home without them* was my motto. True, vampires were keen on protecting the secrecy of their race and this was a crowded, public place, but that didn't guarantee safety. The knives didn't, either, but they sure tipped the odds in our favor. So did the other two vampires parked farther down the street, ready to jump into action if this turned out to be something other than a fact-gathering chat.

Scents assailed me as I approached the courtyard fountain. Perfumes, body odor, and various chemicals were the strongest, but underneath was another layer I'd gotten better at deciphering: emotions. Fear, greed, desire, anger, love, sadness . . . all those manifested in scents that ranged from sweetly aromatic to bitterly rancid. Not surprisingly, unpleasant emotions had the harsher aromas. Case in point: The vampires seated on the concrete bench both had the rotten-fruit smell of fear emanating from them, even before Bones gave them a quelling glare.

"Which one of you is Scratch?" he asked in a crisp voice.

The one with gray streaks in his hair stood up. "I am."

"Then you can stay, but he"—Bones paused to give a short jerk of his head at the other, skinny vampire—"can leave."

"Wait!" Scratch's voice lowered and he moved closer to Bones. "That thing you're here to talk to me about? He might have some information on it."

Bones glanced at me. I lifted one shoulder in a half shrug. "May as well hear what our unexpected guest has to say," I commented.

"I'm Ed," the vampire spoke up, with a nervous look over Bones's shoulder at me. "Scratch didn't tell me he was meeting *you* guys here."

From Ed's expression, I guessed that between my

crimson hair, the large red diamond on my finger, Bones's English accent, and the tingling aura of power he emanated, Ed had figured out who we were.

"That's because he didn't know," Bones answered coolly. His emotions, accessible to me ever since the day Bones changed me, were now locked down behind the impenetrable wall he used in public. Still, anyone could pick up on the edge to his voice as he went on.

"I take it introductions aren't necessary?"

Scratch's gaze slid to me and then skipped away. "No," he muttered. "You're Bones, and that's the Reaper."

Bones's expression didn't soften, but I smiled in my best "I'm not going to kill you" way.

"Call me Cat, and why don't we find some shade where we can talk?"

The sun's rays weren't lethal to vampires as mythology claimed, but we *were* easily sunburned. Expending some of our supernatural energy just to heal from the strong summer rays was pointless. A French restaurant with outdoor seating was nearby, so the four of us found a table under an umbrella and sat down as if we were old friends catching up.

"You said your Master was killed a few years ago, and she left no one to look after the members of her line," Bones stated to Scratch, after the waitress took our drink orders. "A group of you banded together to watch out for one another. When did you first notice something odd was going on?"

"Several months ago, around fall last year," Scratch replied. "At first, we just thought some of the guys skipped town without telling anyone. We kept an eye on each other, but we weren't babysitters, y'know?

Then, when more of us went missing, people who'd normally say something before taking off . . . well. It got the rest of us worried."

I didn't doubt it. As young, Masterless vampires, Scratch and others like him were on the bottom of the pecking order in the undead world. I might have some issues with the feudalistic system vampires operated under, but when it came to protecting members of their line, most Master vampires were pretty damn vigilant. Even the evil ones.

"Then, more ghouls started showing in the area," Scratch went on.

I tensed. This was why Bones and I had come to Ohio. We'd also heard about a recent influx of ghouls in my old home state, and reports of missing vampires.

"Hey, it's an undead playground here," Scratch continued, oblivious to my uneasiness. "Lots of ley lines and fun vibrations, so we didn't think anything about all the flesh-eaters showing up. But some of 'em act real nasty to vampires. Harassing the Masterless ones, following them home, starting fights . . . it got us thinking maybe they were behind the disappearances. Problem is, no one gives a shit since we don't belong to anyone. I'm amazed *you're* interested, frankly."

"I have my reasons," Bones said in that same impassive tone. He didn't even glance at me. Centuries of feigning detachment made him an expert at it. Ed and Scratch would have no idea that the reason we were pumping them for information was to see if my World's Weirdest Vampire condition might be the reason that some ghouls were acting hostile—and why vampires were disappearing.

"If you're looking for money, we don't have much," Ed piped up. "Besides, I thought you retired from contract killing when you merged lines with that mega-Master Mencheres."

Bones arched a brow. "Try not to think too often, you'll only hurt yourself," he replied pleasantly.

Ed's face tightened, but he shut his mouth. I hid a smile. *Don't look a gift horse in the mouth—especially one that bites.*

"Do you have any proof that ghouls might be involved in your friends' disappearances?" I asked Scratch, getting back to the subject.

"No. Just seems more than coincidence that whenever one of them went missing, they were last seen at a place where some of those asshole ghouls were."

"What places?" I asked.

"Some bars, clubs—"

"Names," Bones pressed.

Scratch began to rattle off a list, but all of a sudden, his voice was drowned out under a deluge of others.

. . . four more hours until I get a break . . .

. . . remember to get the receipt for that? If it doesn't fit, I'm taking it back . . .

. . . if she looks at one *more pair of shoes, I'm going to scream . . .*

The sudden crash of intrusive conversation wasn't coming from the mall shoppers around us—I'd tuned that out even before we sat down. This was coming from inside my head. I jerked as if struck, my hand flying to my temple.

Oh shit. Not *again.*

Two

WHAT'S WRONG, KITTEN?" BONES ASKED at once.

Ed and Scratch also gave me concerned glances. I forced a smile while struggling to concentrate on them instead of the plethora of conversations that had suddenly taken up in my mind.

"Just, um, a little hot out here," I muttered. Damned if I was going to tell two strange vampires the real cause of my problem.

Bones's gaze traveled over my face, his dark brown eyes missing nothing, while those voices pitilessly continued to chatter on in my mind.

. . . no one saw me. Hope I can get the security tag off . . .

. . . I'll give him something to cry about soon . . .

. . . if she doesn't show up in five minutes, I'm eating without her . . .

"I, ah, need some air," I blurted before recognizing the stupidity in that excuse. One, we were already outdoors, and two, I was a vampire. I didn't *breathe* anymore, let alone have any health conditions I could blame my sudden weird behavior on.

Bones stood, taking my elbow and throwing a stiff "Stay here" over his shoulder at Ed and Scratch.

I walked quickly, trying to concentrate on the cool pressure of his hand more than where I was going. My head was lowered, because my eyes had probably turned bright green from agitation. *Shut up, shut up, shut up*, I chanted at the unwelcome crowd in my head.

The din in my mind seemed to amplify the noises from the people milling around us, until everything blurred into a sort of white noise. It grew, overwhelming my other senses, making it hard for me to focus on anything except the relentless voices coming at me from all sides. I struggled to push them back, to concentrate on anything except the sounds that seemed to grow with every second.

Something hard pressed against my front the same time that a straighter, harder barrier flattened my back. Underneath the now-thunderous chatter bombarding my mind, I heard a familiar English voice.

" . . . all right, luv. Force them back. Listen to me, not them . . ."

I tried to picture the countless voices in my head as a TV channel I just needed to turn down—with my willpower being the remote control. Fingers stroked my face, their touch an anchor I drew strength from. With great effort, I pulled my mind away from the melee, distancing myself from the noise that wanted to consume the rest of my senses. After several minutes of dogged concentration, that mental roar subsided into an annoying but manageable mumble. It was similar to the sounds from the shoppers around us, oblivious to the fact that they were in biting distance of creatures that weren't supposed to exist.

"I have *got* to stop drinking your blood," I said to Bones when I felt in control enough to open my eyes. A glance around showed that he'd backed me into a pillar in what probably looked like a passionate embrace, judging from the slanted glances thrown our way.

Bones sighed. "You'll be weaker."

"But sane," I added. And safer, too, because if hundreds of voices suddenly crashed into my mind during a battle, it might be distracting enough to get me killed.

I tugged at Bones's short dark curls until he pulled back to look at me. "You know this can't be leftovers from when I drank Mencheres's blood; it's happening more often, not less," I said softly. "I have to be getting this from you. And I can't handle it."

I'd thought changing from a half-breed into a full vampire meant an end to my uniqueness, but fate thought differently. I woke up on the other side of the grave in possession of two things unprecedented in vampire history—an occasional heartbeat and a craving for undead blood. The side effect of the latter meant I temporarily absorbed power from the blood I drank, much like vampires absorbed life from human blood. That was all well and good, but if I drank from a *Master* vampire, I also temporarily absorbed any special abilities that Master had. This was great when it came to enhanced strength, but not so great when it came to other abilities that were out of my depth to control. Like Bones's ability to read human minds.

"You don't give yourself enough credit, Kitten," he said, his voice low.

I shook my head. "There's a reason why it takes centuries for vampires to get special powers, and only if they're Masters. It's too much to deal with otherwise. If I keep drinking from you, what happened today will only get worse. You've obviously grown into the mind-reading power you inherited from Mencheres, so much so that I'm starting to pick it up from your blood, too."

And if Bones started manifesting any other abilities as a result of the power exchange he'd received from his co-ruler, I *really* wanted no part of them. I'd drunk from Mencheres once out of necessity, and it had fried me for over a week afterward. I shuddered at the memory. *Never again if I could help it.* The voices thrumming in the background of my mind seemed to agree.

"We'll sort that out later, but we need to go back now, if you're ready," Bones said, giving my face a last stroke.

"I'm okay. Let's head back, before they freak out and bolt."

Bones slowly uncurled his body from mine. The din in my head was now low enough that I noticed several females around us checking him out. I stamped even harder on those inner voices. The last thing I needed was to hear a flood of lusty imaginings involving my husband and other women to *really* sour my mood.

In fairness, I couldn't blame them. Even in his trademark black pants with a casual white pullover,

Bones stood out like a jewel among rocks with his finely molded features and tall, sculpted frame. Every move of his body sent ripples along those lean muscles, and his flawless crystal skin practically dared people to see if it felt as good as it looked—which it did. Even when we'd first met and I plotted to kill him, Bones's looks had turned my head. In that way, he was a perfect predator, enticing his prey to come close enough to bite.

"You're being eye-humped by about a dozen women as we speak, but I'm sure you already know that," I said in a wry tone.

His mouth brushed my neck with the lightest of kisses, making me shiver.

"I only bother about one woman's desires," he murmured, the breath from his words teasing my ear.

His body was close enough to graze mine, a tantalizing reminder of how thoroughly he could satisfy my every lustful inclination as well as a few I probably hadn't thought of. Still, even though heat began to fill me, we had disappearances to investigate. Any intimate investigations between the two of us would have to wait.

As if in agreement, the cadre of voices in my head rose again, cutting off the warm sensuality that his nearness brought out in me.

"I don't know how you stand hearing this racket in your mind every day," I muttered, shaking my head as if that could clear it.

He gave me an unfathomable look as he drew away. "When it's always there, it's easier to ignore it."

Maybe that was true. Maybe if I didn't have only my own thoughts in my head most of the time, picking up on other people's mental frequencies would seem less overwhelming. I didn't know.

Still, I didn't want to keep drinking Bones's blood to find out.

Ed and Scratch didn't comment about our abrupt departure when Bones and I sat back down with them. Their expressions were also suitably bland, but the furtive looks they darted my way spoke volumes. They were wondering what the hell happened.

"Thought I smelled someone I knew," I offered, downing the gin and tonic that had arrived with the other drinks while Bones and I were away.

It was an obvious lie, but Ed and Scratch made agreeable noises and pretended to believe it. The look Bones gave them didn't lend itself to further questions on the subject.

"Right then, any more names of places these nasty flesh-eaters tend to frequent?" Bones asked, as if there had been no interruption in conversation.

Scratch elbowed the other vampire. "No, but Ed has something to tell you."

Ed looked reluctant but then straightened his narrow shoulders.

"A buddy of mine, Shayne, called me last night and said our friend Harris got the shit kicked out of him from some ghouls at a club. Shayne was gonna go home with Harris to discourage any more beatings on him. Thing is, I've been callin' Shayne's cell all day, but he hasn't answered, which isn't like him. When I told Scratch, he told me to come here because he was meeting people who might be able to help."

"Do you know where Harris lives?" I asked at once.

"Yeah. It's not too far from here, actually."

"Yet you didn't go there yourself to check on him?" Bones asked with heavy skepticism.

Ed gave Bones a weary look. "No, and I still won't unless I can get several people to go with me. I don't want to be the *next* vampire no one ever hears from. Judge all you want, but I don't have a bunch of badass powers to protect myself if something did happen to Shayne and Harris—and the ghouls who made it happen are still there."

Sympathy welled up in me, dulling the voices still yammering on in my mind. Ed and Scratch were doing the best they could to look out for their friends under the very harsh circumstances of living in a world where they were close to second-class citizens. I knew from experience that it sucked to feel like no one had your back when the monsters came sniffing around. Of course, technically, Ed and Scratch were monsters, too.

Then again, so was I. In this case, that was a plus.

Bones looked at me and arched a brow.

"Let's do it," I said to the unspoken question.

He rose, giving his knuckles a quick, expert crack, and then threw several bills on the table.

"All right, then, mates. Let's see if Shayne's mobile just ran out of charge."

True to Ed's word, Harris's apartment was only twenty minutes away. I found it ironic that it was also only about a mile away from the apartment complex I'd lived in when I went to OSU, seemingly another lifetime ago. If Bones noticed the close proximity to my old place, he didn't comment on it. He seemed more focused on the exterior of the building, trying to pick up any vibes of danger within. We couldn't risk sending Fabian in first to check it out. The ghost had snuck into our trunk when we drove off, unnoticed by Ed or Scratch, but if we sent Fabian in ahead of us, that *would* draw their attention to our phantom friend.

Tingles of power rode on the air behind us in the narrow parking lot. Ed and Scratch jerked around, but Bones didn't flinch. Neither did I. That was Tiny and Band-Aid, our backup who'd followed us over from the mall.

"Tiny, Band-Aid, keep an eye on these two for a moment, will you?" Bones said to them before striding toward the complex. I went with him, shrugging into my long leather coat. It wasn't because I was cold; the late summer day was warm, but my coat held several pounds' worth of silver knives. Sure, I had knives tucked under my blouse, but those were the shorter, throwing variety meant for vampires. Only decapitation killed a ghoul, which meant I needed bigger blades if any sinister members of that species awaited us inside.

Bones inhaled once we reached the second floor. So did I. The front doors were all in a line facing the parking lot, with the fresh air chasing away most of the telltale scents of their occupants, but I caught a whiff of something inhuman coming from the second to last unit. Bones must have, too, because his steps quickened. I inhaled again, my nose wrinkling when we were almost at that door. Bones paused to give me a grim look.

The shades were drawn tight, preventing us from peering inside, but I already knew what we'd find. The scent of death was unmistakable.

"We're too late," I whispered. Seeing the broken lock on the door was almost redundant.

Bones pushed the door open, moving immediately to the side in case a flash of flying silver accompanied his entry. Nothing moved, however. The inside of the apartment was as quiet as a tomb.

And just like a tomb, it had bodies in it.

"I don't feel anyone, but stay sharp," Bones said as he stepped inside. I followed, checking the corners first, joining Bones in doing a sweep of the interior with as much caution as if we knew enemy forces were within. As we'd suspected, though, the place was empty of everyone except us—and two shriveled vampires on the floor of the tiny family room.

The damn voices in my mind began to rise again. There weren't as many people in the apartment complex as the mall, so it didn't affect me with the same sort of mental explosion, but it was like my mind was filled with the hum from a nest of angry bees. I rubbed my temple, as if that could tone them down, but of course, it didn't help.

Bones didn't catch the gesture. His attention was still focused on the two shriveled corpses near our feet.

"Looks like a dawn ambush," he noted, taking in their lack of shoes and how neither body was fully dressed. "Poor sods didn't have the chance to put up much of a fight."

The lack of disarray in the apartment was testament of that. When supernatural creatures fought to the death, things usually got a lot messier than a few overturned tables and some blood smeared on the carpet. Investigating the deaths of vampires was still somewhat unusual for me. Sure, I'd spent years working for a covert branch of Homeland Security tracking paranormal homicides, but in those circumstances, the vampires had usually been the perpetrators. Not the victims.

. . . if I don't pay the car payment, I'll have enough money for the mortgage . . .

. . . told that bastard I wouldn't put up with him being out all night again . . .

. . . so proud of her, she'll graduate with her class . . .

I rubbed my head once more as the voices got louder. This time, Bones saw it.

"Again?"

"I'm fine," I said, attempting a casual tone.

His stare turned pointed. "Bollocks."

"I've got it under control, it's nothing to worry about," I amended. That was true. Dead bodies took priority over the mental mutterings going off in my head.

From his expression, Bones wasn't buying my blasé act, but the clock was ticking on this crime scene. We had bodies to remove, evidence to erase, and killers to find.

Bones raised his voice. "Ed, get up here."

The skinny vampire's face pinched when he came inside and saw the bodies. "Aw, fuck," he groaned.

"Are these Shayne and Harris?" Bones asked, in a gentler tone than before.

Ed bent down, sniffing at each body. Vampires might never look a day older than whatever age they were when they were changed, but all that ended upon death. After death, a vampire's body rapidly composed to their true age, meaning that most of the time, there was nothing left but mummified remains inside of whatever clothes they died in. These two bodies were no exception.

Ed sat back on his haunches next to the denim-clad body. "That's them," he said in a thicker voice. Then he snarled, "Fucking ghouls."

"Why don't you go back outside now?" I said, giving Ed's arm a pat. There was nothing more he could do, but Bones and I still had things to take care of.

Ed gave another long look at Harris's and Shayne's corpses before he got up and walked out. I sighed. This was bad for so many reasons, and Ed's grief was only part of it.

"Why do you think they left the bodies?" I asked Bones quietly. "Ed and Scratch hadn't heard of bodies being found from the other disappearances. Think the killers got interrupted?"

Bones's gaze swept around the room. It didn't take long; the area only consisted of a tiny kitchen and a family room big enough for just one full-sized couch.

"No, luv," he said at last. "I think whoever did this had the time to take the bodies, but chose not to."

I swallowed. That could be the result of the same sort of arrogance I'd seen in the past from killers who left bodies behind because they thought they were too smart to get caught. But unfortunately, I didn't think that was the case. Instead, this looked like confirmation of a much bigger problem—killers who *wanted* us to know who they were. Only an idiot wouldn't label those ghouls as prime suspects after they'd beaten on Harris just the evening before he and Shayne were murdered. Those ghouls knew that by leaving the bodies here, they were practically signing their names on them.

Only one reason I could think of—whoever was behind this felt strong enough to come out from behind the curtain. This might as well be a public service announcement that the ghouls would start stepping up their attacks, and I didn't think it was a coincidence that they'd chosen to start displaying vampire bodies in the same area I grew up in. No, I took this as a statement of "You can't stop us, Reaper," and damned if I'd let that stand. Vampires might be disappearing in other areas, too, but here was where the perpetrators were calling us out by leaving the bodies. If we didn't draw a line in the sand here, then we'd be almost inviting things to get worse elsewhere.

"But there's not much anyone else is going to do about it, is there?" I asked in a sudden rush of frustration. "My old team won't get involved because they only step in when the undead attack humans. The vampire community will just shrug because Shayne and Harris were Masterless. Ed and Scratch can't take on a bunch of ghouls by themselves, and if *we* go after the killers and their leader is who I think he is . . . we'll be playing right into that bastard's hands."

Bones stared at me without blinking. "You know you're right about your old team, the vampire community, and how we can't openly go after those ghouls if Apollyon is involved."

Apollyon. An image of the centuries-old ghoul with his squat body and almost laughable comb-over flashed across my mind. Appearance-wise, Apollyon might look to be on the ass end of average, but in the past year, he'd managed to incite a hell of a lot of trouble. Bones almost died after ghouls attacked us in Paris several months ago, plus ghouls provided support to another Master vampire in his attempts to force me to return to him. All courtesy of Apollyon's inflamed rhetoric. Even though I hoped I was wrong, I just knew he was the one behind these attacks, too.

Of course, that meant all these terrible things were happening because of me.

"We can't let him or the others get away with this," I growled.

Bones's mouth curled into a predatory smile. "Kitten . . . I said we can't *openly* go after them."

THREE

A LARGE SHADOW PASSED ACROSS THE DOOR-
way, blocking out the sun as Tiny entered the
apartment. The vampire's nickname was ironic, because he was massive in a way that would make even
the mythical Conan feel insecure.

"Cops are coming," he said.

I'd heard the wail of sirens growing ever closer
over the past couple minutes. Guess one of the neighbors had gotten jittery at the sight of several sinister-
looking people milling around the driveway. They
obviously hadn't heard the death struggle taking place
several hours before or we wouldn't have been first on
the scene.

"You keep nosing around here, I'll handle them,"
I said to Bones. If we were lucky, Bones might recognize the scent from one of the murderers. In his
two hundred and twenty-plus years as a vampire, he'd

come across a lot of undead people, and scent was as unique as a fingerprint.

Still, I didn't hold out much hope that we'd solve these murders that easily. Bones might know a lot of undead people, but vampires and ghouls made up roughly five percent of the world's population. Even with Bones's extensive history, there were too many for Bones to know each pulseless one personally.

Bones glanced at Tiny, who followed me outside. I didn't reach for my cell phone, but that had been my first instinct. Using my government connections to chase cops away from crime scenes was habit to me after the years at my old job. This next part, however, was still relatively new.

"Hey," I called down when the police officers arrived and got out of their squad car. "Glad you're here, I was just about to call."

"Do you live here, ma'am? We received a report about suspicious persons loitering in the area," the blond cop said, eyeing Tiny in a wary manner. His partner's hand moved to his gun.

"Skin that piece again and I'll forget I'm not hungry," Tiny muttered, so low the cops couldn't hear him.

I stifled a laugh and addressed the police officers again. "I don't live here, but my friend's place was broken into. Can you check it out?"

The cops gave me a once-over as they came up the stairs to the second floor. I smiled in a harmless way and made sure my empty hands were well within eyesight. Of course, a thorough cop would wonder why I was wearing a long jacket during the warm summer afternoon.

When they were within a dozen feet of me, my gray eyes turned glowing green. I lasered that stare at them, letting the entrapping nosferatu power cloud their minds.

"There's nothing going on here," I said in a firm, pleasant voice. "Turn around and leave, the call was a false alarm."

"Nothing going on," the blond officer intoned.

"False alarm," his buddy repeated, his hand leaving his gun.

"That's right. Go on. Serve and protect somewhere else."

They both turned around and got back into their car without another word, driving off. Before I became a vampire, it would've taken twenty minutes and two phone calls to get the same result, unless Bones green-eyed the local cops into leaving. Vampire mind control sure made it easy to cut through the bureaucratic red tape when it came to crime scenes.

Bones appeared in the apartment doorway holding two slender, sheet-draped bundles. To any nosy neighbors, he might have been carrying wrapped horizontal blinds instead of what I knew they were—the remains of Shayne and Harris.

"Tiny, put these in your boot," Bones said.

Tiny glanced down at his feet in confusion. I snorted. "He means your trunk. British English can be so confusing at times."

"That's only because you Yanks keep renaming things," Bones replied with an arch look, handing off the corpses to Tiny. Then he leapt over the balcony, landing in the parking lot without a hitch in his stride as he walked over to Ed and Scratch. Both vampires regarded Bones gloomily.

"What're you doing with their bodies?" Ed asked.

"Burying them elsewhere," Bones replied.

Scratch ran a hand through his gray-streaked hair. "Suppose you'll be off now that you've learned what you wanted to know."

Scratch sounded resigned. I caught Bones's slight smile as I came down to the parking lot the normal way by taking the stairs.

"Get in the car, lads. We have some things to discuss."

I got behind the wheel with Bones riding shotgun as Ed and Scratch warily climbed into our backseat. From my rearview mirror I saw Tiny stuff the remains of the two vampires into his trunk, then he and Band-Aid were ready to go.

"Back to the mall?" I asked, pulling out of the driveway.

"That's fine, Kitten," he replied. His arm rested across the back of his seat as he settled himself in a lounging way while staring at Ed and Scratch.

"Would you try to bring your mates' killers to justice if you had assistance?" Bones asked them.

A scoff came from Ed. "Of course. Shayne didn't deserve to go out like that. Didn't know Harris very well, but he probably didn't, either."

"Damn straight," Scratch muttered.

I cast a sideways glance at Bones, wondering where he was going with this and still unable to plug into his emotions to get a hint. He tapped his chin thoughtfully.

"Would be dangerous, even with help."

Another scoff, this time from Scratch. "Living is dangerous when you're Masterless, unless you're one of the lucky strong ones, but I don't expect you'd know much about that."

A smile ghosted across Bones's lips. "I know a thing or two about dangerous living, in fact, but as you seem not to fancy being Masterless, what say you to joining my line?"

My gaze flew to Bones before flicking to the rear-view mirror. Both Ed and Scratch looked stunned. So was I. What Bones was offering was akin to adopting them.

"Think before you answer," Bones went on. "Once sworn, you can't change your mind and get your freedom back unless you formally ask for it and I decide to grant that request."

Ed let out a soft whistle. "You're serious, aren't you?"

"As death," Bones lightly replied.

"I heard you're a mean bastard," Scratch said after a long pause. "But I've also heard you're a fair one. I can deal with mean and fair. Beats being on my own trying to fight off every asshole who thinks killing Masterless vampires is an easy way to make a name for himself."

My brows went up at this blunt analysis, but Bones didn't look the least bit offended. "What about you, Ed?"

"Why are you offering this?" Ed wondered, looking at Bones with narrowed eyes. "You know from our power levels that we'll never be Masters. You can't be hard up for our measly ten percent tithe, either, so what's in it for you?"

Bones matched Ed's stare. "For starters, I want to catch these ghouls, and you'd help me with that. You also must have heard that recent wars killed several members of my line. You were loyal to your mates even after your Master died and you had no obligation to them. Then you were smart enough not to walk into a potential trap without backup. I could use more smart blokes whose loyalty to me, my wife, and my co-ruler would be without exception."

Ed met my gaze briefly in the rearview mirror before looking back at Bones. "All right," he said, each word measured. "I'm in."

Bones pulled out a silver knife. I snapped my attention back to the road before I caused a wreck with my frequent glances around the car. Besides, I knew Bones wasn't about to start stabbing Ed and Scratch. He was just making this official.

"By my blood," Bones said, scoring a line in his palm, "I declare you, Ed, and you, Scratch, to be members of my line. If I betray this oath, let my blood be my penalty."

Then Bones passed the knife to Ed, his cut healing before the first drops of blood splashed against his dark pants. I didn't need to look back to know that Ed made a slice into his palm; the tantalizing new scent of blood told me that.

"By my blood, I acknowledge you, Bones, as my Master," Ed rasped. "If I betray this oath, let my blood be my penalty."

Scratch repeated the words to the accompaniment of another mouthwatering scent filling the car. Aside from my discomfort with the whole "master" aspect that came with vampire lineage, I now had the tightening in my stomach to think about. I hadn't fed since last night and my next meal might be tricky to get since I had to find someone aside from Bones to drink from. Normal vampires had plenty of options when it came to feeding. The power in their gaze meant they could snack off humans without their donors remembering it had happened, or vampires exchanged room and board with specially selected humans in return for blood.

I didn't have those conveniences. Mind control didn't work on other vampires, and no undead households I knew of had a stable of *vampires* available to feed from. Plus, we were still trying to keep my strange diet—and its side effects—from becoming common knowledge. So I couldn't just ask the next vampire I saw if I could take a bite out of him or her.

Scratch passed the blood-smeared knife back to Bones once he was finished swearing his fealty. I resisted a sudden urge to lick the blade and concentrated on the road, making a mental rundown of ways I could get blood. Juan, a member of my old team, was undead just a year, so he was a possibility. Maybe I could get him to ship some of his blood to me, though Juan would wonder why I wanted it. None of them knew about my odd diet yet.

Bones's best friend, Spade, knew what I fed off of and I'd had his blood before, but I didn't want to make it a habit. Spade was a Master vampire, so that meant he was too strong. Most of Bones's friends were too strong, in fact.

Dammit. Not drinking from Bones without starving would be more difficult than I'd imagined.

"For now, don't tell anyone of our association," Bones said to Ed and Scratch, centering my attention back on the present situation. "Go about your business as if we'd never met. Here's a number where you can reach me. At the first sight of those ghouls, you ring me straightaway, but do *not* confront them. Understood?"

"Got it" and "Sure" were the responses. I wondered if they did understand. I did, and wasn't thrilled.

I dropped the vampires off close to the Easton fountain where we'd met them, waiting until I'd driven a couple miles away before I slanted a glance at Bones.

"You're using them as bait."

Bones met my gaze, his dark brown stare concealing nothing. "Yes."

"God," I muttered. "You're not letting them tell anyone that they've just been upgraded from being Masterless to belonging to a powerful vampire so those ghouls will still consider them easy meat. That's deliberately putting them in danger."

"No more than they were before, as they said themselves. But now if they're harmed, I'll have rights under our laws to investigate," he replied with annoying logic. "Believe me, pet, I'm hoping nothing happens to them and their usefulness comes from pointing me in those ghouls' direction. But if Apollyon is behind these attacks, we need a way to get to him without looking like we're being mindlessly antagonistic. Otherwise . . ."

Bones didn't have to finish the sentence. *Otherwise, Apollyon will have more fuel for the rumors that I'm seeking to be some sort of vampiric Stalin*, I mentally finished. Right, because *that's* what I put on my To Do list every morning. *Brush teeth. Wash hair. Rule undead world with an iron fist.*

"I don't know why ghouls would listen to Apollyon

about me being a threat anyway," I muttered. "I might have a wacky diet as a vampire, but Apollyon can't tell people that I'll combine ghoul and vampire powers anymore. Changing over took care of that paranoid rant from him."

Bones's stare was sympathetic, but unyielding. "Kitten, you've been a vampire for less than a year. During that time, you've blown the head off a Master vampire through pyrokinesis and frozen dozens of vampires into a stupor through telekinesis. Your abilities, plus your occasional heartbeat, are bound to frighten some people."

"But they're not *my* abilities!" I burst. "Okay, the intermittent heartbeat is mine, but all the rest were borrowed powers. I don't even have them anymore, and if I hadn't drunk from Vlad and Mencheres, I never would have gotten them in the first place."

"No one knows how you got them, or that you lose them after a while," Bones noted.

"Maybe we should tell them." But even as I said it, I knew better.

He let out what might have been a sigh. "If Apollyon knew the source of your abilities, he could argue that you could manifest any power you wanted merely by drinking from a vampire who had it. Better he just thinks you're extraordinarily gifted based on your own merits."

In other words, no matter how we tried to dress it up, I still came across as a dangerous freak. I took in a deep breath in the hopes that the familiar gesture would calm me. It didn't. All it did was bring the scent of blood into my lungs, clenching my stomach in an almost painful way.

"Too bad your co-ruler's visions still aren't back to full strength. That would take the guesswork out of whether or not this is Apollyon's doing."

Bones gave a shrug in concurrence. "Mencheres has had a few more glimpses into the future, but nothing relating to this, and he still can't command his visions at will yet. With luck, his full powers will return soon."

But until then, we were on our own. "So we stick to not telling anyone how I absorb power from blood, and to using Ed and Scratch to lead us to these ghouls to see if Apollyon is behind them."

"That's right, luv."

I closed my eyes. I might not like the plan, but at the moment, it was our best option.

"That just leaves one more thing," I said, opening my eyes to give Bones a wan smile. "Finding someone other than you for me to feed from."

Four

I DIDN'T RECOGNIZE THE GUARDS WHO RAN onto the helicopter pad to escort me and Bones into the compound run by my former boss and uncle, Don Williams. Then again, I hadn't been back here since last year. Maybe I should've called first. Announcing myself to the control tower once I was inside their air space wasn't really giving notice, but Don needed to know about the trouble brewing. That sort of information merited a face-to-face update, in my opinion. Plus Juan was here, and I hoped he was open to the idea of letting me take some of his blood.

Of course, if I were being entirely truthful, I'd admit the impromptu helicopter trip to eastern Tennessee was about more than information or even eating. Business had made Don cancel our last few attempts at getting together, so it had been months since I'd seen my uncle. We might have had a rocky start to our relationship, but I'd missed him. This trip was a chance to kill three birds with one stone, which Don should appreciate. He was all about multitasking.

We had reached the double doors of the roof when Bones stopped walking so abruptly, one of the guards collided into him.

"Bloody hell," Bones muttered.

My head whipped around, but nothing unusual was going on except the guard looking embarrassed about plowing into Bones's back. Then pity and resolve skittered across my subconscious. I tensed. Those weren't my emotions.

"What?" I asked Bones.

His expression became so controlled that fear flared in me. The guards next to us exchanged baffled glances, but if they knew what the problem was, I couldn't tell. I couldn't hear anyone's thoughts but my own at the moment.

Bones took my hand. His mouth opened, but before he could speak, the roof doors swung outward and a muscular vampire with short brown hair strode toward us.

"Cat, what are you doing here?" Tate demanded.

I ignored the question from my former first officer, keeping my attention on Bones. "*What?*" I asked a second time.

His hand tightened on mine. "Your uncle is very sick, Kitten."

Something cold slid up my spine. I glanced at Tate. From the grim set of his shoulders, Bones was right.

"Where is he? And why wasn't I *called*?"

Tate's mouth twisted. "Don's here, in Medical, and you weren't called because he didn't want you to know."

Tate didn't sound like he approved of that decision, but anger flared in me.

"So the plan was not to tell me unless there was a funeral to attend? Nice, Tate!"

I shoved by him, pulling my hand out of Bones's grip to dash into the building. Medical was on the second sub-level, one floor above the training facility and two floors above where we used to house captive vampires. I stabbed at the down button on the elevator, tapping my foot in impatience. A few startled looks were thrown my way from the guards, but I didn't care that my eyes were glowing or that fangs pressed against my lips. If those guards didn't know about vampires before, Tate could deal with altering their memories so they wouldn't remember later.

"How the hell'd you know about Don?" I heard Tate demand of Bones.

"From the scurry of activity going on to make him presentable for her" was Bones's short reply. "Mind reading, remember?"

The elevator doors opened and I went inside, not caring to listen to anything else. Normally I'd be worried about leaving Bones alone with Tate since the two of them mixed like oil and water. But now, all my thoughts were on my uncle. What was wrong with him? And *why* would he forbid anyone to tell me about it?

I almost ran out of the elevator when it opened on the second floor, dashing down the hallway and through the doors marked MEDICAL. I ignored the staff I passed along the way, not needing them to tell me where my uncle was. Don's coughing and muttering to someone in the last room on the right told me that.

I slowed when I reached the door, not wanting to burst in if my normally debonair uncle wasn't dressed.

"Don?" I called out, feeling hesitant now that only a few feet separated us.

"Give me a moment, Cat" was his response, sounding hoarse but not like he was in imminent danger of dying. Relief swept through me. Maybe Don had caught swine flu or something equally nasty, but now he was recovering.

A nurse I didn't recognize came out of his room, giving me a look that required no mind-reading skills to interpret.

"He's getting dressed," she said in a crisp tone while the ammonialike scent of annoyance drifted from her.

"I take it he's not supposed to be up doing that?" I asked her.

"No, but that's not stopping him," she replied bluntly.

"I can hear you, Anne," my uncle snapped.

She gave me another pointed look before lowering her voice to a whisper. "Don't let him overexert himself."

A round of coughing prefaced my uncle muttering, "I can still hear you." My brows rose. Whatever was wrong with Don's health, his ears were sharp as ever.

After another series of fumbling sounds, my uncle opened the door. He had on a slightly wrinkled pullover shirt paired with gray pants that matched the color of his eyes. For a second, I just blinked, realizing this was the first time I'd seen Don with his hair mussed and wearing something other than a suit and tie.

"Cat. I'm afraid you've caught me a bit by surprise."

The irony in his voice was familiar, even if his appearance wasn't. In the months since I'd seen my uncle, he seemed to have aged ten years. The lines

around his mouth and eyes were pronounced, his gray
hair was nearly white, and his impeccable posture was
slightly stooped. I swallowed the lump that worked its
way into my throat.

"You know me," I managed. "Always a pain in the
ass."

Don reached out to squeeze my shoulder. "No
you're not. Not even when you're trying to be."

The way he said that, combined with the sadness
that flitted across his expression, almost made me lose
it. Right then I knew that his condition was terminal.
Otherwise, Don would've told me with sardonic affection that yes, I *was* a colossal pain in the ass and
always would be. Not held on to my shoulder with a
grip that trembled even as he managed to flash me a
smile.

All the things I'd dismissed before came back in
sharp focus. Don's recurring cough the past several
times I'd spoken to him, brushed off as "just a cold."
The plans canceled at the last minute, rescheduled
just to be canceled again . . .

I wrapped my arms around him, feeling the weight
loss that his clothes concealed, taking in a deep breath
that filled my lungs with the scent of antiseptics,
sweat, and sickness. More tears burned my eyes that
I blinked back. *Whatever's wrong with him, vampire
blood will cure it*, I reminded myself, trying to get a
grip on my emotions. Don was probably just being
stubborn and refusing to drink any, even though he
of all people knew the amazing healing powers of
undead blood.

Well, I'd get him to rethink that stupid decision.

"So, I hear you didn't want me to know you were

sick," I said, managing to sound mildly chiding instead of hysterically worried. Point for me.

"You've had enough to deal with lately," Don replied.

I let go of him and swept my gaze around the room. His bed was one of those adjustable ones where the head and foot could be raised, but it lacked the normal hospital rails on either side of it. An open laptop was perched on a rolling tray nearby, alongside several stacked folders, his cell phone, pagers, and an in-house office phone.

"How typical of you not to stop working even though you looked like death warmed over," I said in a half-joking, half-censuring way.

My uncle gave me a baleful look. "I might look like death warmed over, but now you *are* death warmed over, remember?"

I would've smiled at his quip, but I was too worried by the grayish tone to his skin and the slow, painful way he moved as he took a step away from me. My uncle always had a commanding presence no matter the circumstances, but now, he seemed frail. That scared me more than facing enemy forces while unarmed.

"What's wrong that's got you here?" I asked, again controlling the fear that made my voice higher than normal.

"I have a bad flu," Don replied, his words roughened by a cough.

"Don't lie to her."

Bones's voice flowed into the room, and a few booted strides later, so did he. His dark brown gaze focused on Don, who visibly stiffened.

"Your abilities don't give you the right to—"

"My bloodline does," I interrupted Don, clenching my hands into fists. "You're my family. That means I have a right to know." *And if you don't tell me, I'll just green-eye your nurse until* she *does*, I mentally added.

Don was silent for a long moment, looking between me and Bones. Finally, his shoulder lifted in a faint shrug.

"I have lung cancer." His smile was strained, but his trademark dry wit still rose to the occasion. "Appears those warnings on cigarette packages are correct."

Everything in me tensed as soon as he said the C word. "But I've never seen you smoke," I blurted, stunned into denial.

"I quit before we met, but for thirty years before that, I had a pack-a-day habit."

Lung cancer. Advanced, too, for him to look this way and allow himself to stay in the compound's medical facility. To say Don was a workaholic was to put it mildly. In all the time I'd known him, my uncle hadn't taken time off for vacations, holidays, or birthdays, let alone sick days. Then amidst my stunned absorption of this news, a businesslike mentality swept over me, mercifully blocking out the grief that made me feel like I'd just been shot in the gut.

"I assume your doctors are going to operate? Or do chemo? Both? What treatment plan have they given you?"

He sighed. "It's too advanced for surgery or chemo, Cat. My treatment plan is to make the most of the time I have left."

No. The word resounded in my head as loudly as those

unwelcome conversations had earlier. Then I uncurled my hands from the tight fists I had clenched at my sides, trying to make my voice very composed. Weeping and panic wouldn't help, but calm logic would.

"Maybe your condition is past what traditional medicine can treat, but you have other options. Vampire blood will heal your lungs from sustaining further damage, maybe even put the cancer into remission—"

"No," Don interrupted.

"Dammit!" I exclaimed. So much for the calm, rational approach. "You're letting bigotry get in the way of your common sense. Your brother was an asshole before he became a vampire, Don. Changing into one didn't make *me* evil, and drinking vampire blood to help your condition won't make *you* evil."

"I know," he said, surprising me. "I began drinking vampire blood shortly after I was first diagnosed seven years ago. You made that possible with the captive vampires you brought back from missions when you were working for me. You're right, it did put the cancer in remission, but time catches up with everyone, and it has, at last, caught up with me."

Seven *years*! My mind reeled. "You hid this the whole time we've known each other? *Why?*"

Don's sigh rattled in his throat. "I didn't trust you when you first joined the team, as you remember. Then, I didn't want to distract you from your job. After you discovered you were my niece . . . well. Things happened. You've had a lot to deal with the past couple years, more than most people have had in their entire lives. I was going to tell you about it, but I wanted to give myself time to sort some things out first."

I knew my mouth hung open, but I couldn't seem to summon the willpower to close it. Bones came to me and took my hand, wordlessly squeezing it.

"You must have had an important reason for coming here without calling," Don said. "What's going on?"

I couldn't believe he expected me to just change the subject, as if the topic of his impending death wasn't worth further discussion.

"Chemo, surgery, and vampire blood might not be able to help you, but *I* still can." The words spilled out recklessly. "I'm a vampire now and I can make you one, too. You won't owe me any of that normal fealty crap, and changing over will cure everything—"

"No."

The single word was soft but emphatic. My instant, sputtering argument faded as Don was seized with a wracking cough.

"But you can't . . . you can't just *die*," I whispered.

He straightened, controlling his cough. The same fierce will that had ordered Tate to shoot me the day we met was still in his gray eyes.

"Yes I can. It's called being human."

I swallowed hard. The same argument I'd once used with Bones to rationalize why a relationship between us couldn't work had just been flung back in my face. Now I knew the frustration Bones must've felt at that time, because I had a sudden urge to shake Don until the blind stubbornness rattled right out of his head.

But since I couldn't do that, I'd try another tactic. "You're indispensable to this operation. If you were gone, I wouldn't be the only one who would suffer. Think of the team—"

"They have Tate," Don interrupted me. "He's taken

over this department for the past three months and he's doing an excellent job."

"Tate's needed out in the field, not for management," I argued even as I reeled at this new bit of information. "You only have one other vampire and a ghoul on the team aside from Tate. That's not enough when going after the undead. Plus, some serious shit is brewing with ghouls right now."

A cough made Don pause before replying. "We may have another vampire on the team soon."

Must be Cooper. He was the next in line to lose his pulse. Seems a lot of changes had happened. Even if I wasn't a member of the team anymore, I'd thought being a friend and family meant *some*one would keep me in the loop. Boy, was I wrong.

"Christ Almighty," Bones muttered.

Don shot him a look. "We'll talk about that later. Now, tell me what trouble is brewing with the ghouls, Cat."

My uncle's expression said that continuing to discuss the obvious reasons why he should save his life would only be pointless right now. I tried to pull myself together enough to focus on why we'd come, but I felt like the floor had just opened up underneath me.

"You remember last year that a ghoul leader, Apollyon, was all worked up about me possibly changing into a vampire-ghoul hybrid? Well, he hasn't calmed down . . ."

Several minutes later, I'd given Don all the details as we knew them. He tugged on his eyebrow as he listened. When I was finished, he let out a heavy sigh.

"Those vampires reporting back to you are a good

start, but I don't think it's enough. If hostilities increase between vampires and ghouls, humans will bear the brunt of the fallout. We need someone to infiltrate Apollyon's group. Find out everything we're only guessing at now."

I let out a grunt. "That would be great, but there's a problem. Any ghouls we'd trust enough to spy would be known associates of Bones and would be killed on the spot. Finding someone tough and reliable that Apollyon wouldn't recognize will be hard . . ."

My voice trailed off even as Bones raised a brow. Don gave me a short nod.

"Dave."

I closed my eyes, hating the thought of my friend in such a situation, but Don was right. Dave was smart, tough, experienced, and already dead. Bones had raised Dave as a ghoul over two years ago after Dave had been killed on a mission, but few people in the undead world had ever met Dave. He'd been too busy as a member of Don's team to hang out at many fang or flesh-eater parties.

"We'll ask him," I settled on. "Let him decide if he wants to do it. Going undercover is always dangerous, but going undercover to infiltrate a group of murderous undead zealots is too dicey to make it an order."

"Go get him," Don said. "He's in the Wreck Room."

I met my uncle's intractable gaze with an equally stubborn one of my own. "I'll go get him and we'll deal with the ghoul situation, but I'm not giving up on you. Think about my offer. About all the positive changes you can make in the world if you're still *alive*."

He gave me a faint smile. "I was always going to

die, Cat. Whether in a few months or a few years, it's inevitable. You should have already accepted that, but you haven't. You've thought with the mind of a vampire since the day we met. Your fangs are new, but that's the only difference I see since you changed over."

I bit my lip, refusing to acknowledge that he might be right. "I'll go get Dave."

Five

I WALKED OUT OF DON'S ROOM WITH BONES following me, trying to concentrate on anything but my uncle's sad, stubborn gaze. Click-click-click went my shoes on the tile. *Lung cancer.* Click-click-click, bringing me closer to the elevator. *Past the point of surgery, chemotherapy, or vampire blood.* Click-click-click. *Known for seven years.*

Once inside the elevator, however, my control cracked and tears blurred my vision. Aside from my mother, Don was the only real family I had left. My grandparents had been murdered several years ago and my father was serving a whole new definition of "hard time" for repeatedly trying to kill me. Even though our relationship was nowhere near normal, over the past few years, Don had become the closest thing to a father I'd ever had.

And soon he'd be gone. Forever.

Bones folded me into his arms. With his height, my

face was pressed to his collarbone, his leather jacket cool against my cheek while his hand smoothed over my hair. I held on to him, sinking into the oasis of his embrace, feeling his strength not just in the muscled wall of his body, but also in the power that enveloped me like a thick cloud as he dropped the shields from his aura.

Then I pushed him away, clearing the pink from my vision with several blinks. If I let myself dwell on this now, I wouldn't be able to handle the very important tasks ahead of us. I wasn't giving up on Don, but I had to pull myself together and concentrate on what needed to be done. This wasn't the time for me to fall all to pieces.

"I'm okay," I said to Bones, holding out a hand when he would have spoken. "Let's just get Dave. One crisis at a time, right?"

The elevator doors opened to reveal a darkly handsome vampire on the other side, black hair in a loose ponytail and normally playful expression subdued.

"Hey, Juan," I said, managing a limp smile.

"*Querida*," he murmured, opening his arms. Even though I was upset with him, I went into them, giving him a brief hug.

"*Lo siento*," he whispered when I let him go.

"Yeah, I'm sorry, too," I replied bleakly. "You, Tate, Dave—*all* of you should have told me."

"Don made us promise not to. He didn't want to worry you."

I was too upset to laugh at the irony of that. "Too late now."

"Bones, *mi amigo, cómo es usted*?" Juan said next. Bones answered in the same language, but I was too distracted to bother translating their Spanish as I headed for the Wreck Room. Despite my vow not to think about Don's condition, a part of me was still busy plotting ways to save him. *Maybe the vampire blood Don used to treat his cancer just wasn't strong enough. If he started ingesting a* Master *vampire's blood—like Bones's or Mencheres's—maybe his results would be different.*

Farther down the hall, the double doors to the training area opened and Tate walked out. He headed straight for me, but I didn't even look at him as I strode down the hall toward the same room he'd just left.

Tate caught my arm when we drew level with each other. "Cat, there's something I need to—"

"Save it," I replied, shoving his hand off. "You couldn't run fast enough to tell me when you thought Bones was cheating on me last year, but when it came to Don and something that was actually *true*, then you're all about respectful silence."

"That's not—" he began, reaching out once more.

Bones grabbed Tate before his hand could brush my skin, appearing faster than if he'd materialized from the air around us.

"If you fancy keeping this," he said in a growl while his fingers tightened on Tate's arm, "don't try touching her again."

Any other time I would've objected, knowing Bones never bluffed and he *would* rip Tate's arm off, but today I didn't care. Out of everyone's silence about my uncle's health, Tate's hurt the most. Yes, things had been strained between us ever since Bones came back into my life, but for a long time before that, Tate had been my closest friend. Facing death together on countless missions had forged strong bonds between us, but this was the last straw for me.

"Better yet, try touching me again and *I'll* rip your arm off," I snapped, stepping around him to continue down the hall. "I've put up with a lot from you despite your animosity to Bones and refusal to accept that you and I will never *be* more than friends. But after this, we're done, so stay away from me."

Behind me, Juan cleared his throat. "Ah, *querida* . . ."

"Don't bother defending him," I replied, yanking open the heavy doors of the area we'd dubbed the Wreck Room due to how intense training got. "I'm not—"

My voice trailed off while my eyes bugged. There, in the middle of the room, was a brunette vampire running through what looked to be a new obstacle course, easily dodging the cement blocks that swung at her.

"What?" I gasped.

The vampire didn't hear me. Tate muttered something that sounded like "I tried to warn you," but I didn't turn around. *She's wearing a uniform*, my mind hazily noted, immediately followed by *Why the HELL is she wearing a* uniform?

"Mom!" I shouted at her. "What are you *doing* here?"

Her head whipped around—and then she was knocked off her feet by the next swinging cement boulder. Even from the distance, I caught the aggravated look my mother threw me as she jumped back up.

"Sloppy, Crawfield!" Cooper barked at her from his position overseeing the obstacle course.

"Catherine's here," she replied, pointing.

He swung around, a guilty look crossing his mocha features. My shock dissolved enough for me to march inside, barely noticing Bones mutter under his breath that they were bloody lucky my temper no longer manifested itself in fire.

He was right. If it had been just six months before, fire would be shooting from my hands from this new shock to my already volatile emotions. Three months before and I would've ground all the activity in the Wreck Room to a halt with a furious squeeze of my mind. But with those borrowed abilities now gone, all I could do was lash out with my voice.

"You have got to be *kidding* me," I snapped to the room at large. "I thought it was crappy no one told me about Don's condition, but who knew you guys had even *more* secrets up your sleeve!"

"Everyone, take ten," Dave called out. The dozens of team members stopped whatever grueling activity they'd been involved in to file out of the room— taking the door opposite the one I was closest to, I noticed.

In minutes, the training room was empty of everyone but Cooper, Dave, Tate, Bones, Juan, and my mother, who was the only one aside from Bones who didn't have a shamefaced expression.

"Catherine, stop overreacting," she said in a chiding way as she walked over to me. "After all, I'm not doing anything you haven't done for over a decade."

"And I've almost gotten killed more times than I can count," I shot back, resisting the urge to shake her.

Her blue stare hardened. "I did get killed," she replied flatly. "Hiding from the evil in this world did nothing to protect me. Not then and not the other times before it, either."

Guilt stabbed through me at her words, taking the edge off my anger. Aside from the night she met my father, every other time she'd been abused by vampires or ghouls had been because of me. Monsters didn't fight fair, and when they came after me, they'd also come after those closest to me. The last vampire I'd tangled with thought forcibly changing my mother over would be just the thing to teach me a lesson. I was only sorry I couldn't kill him more than once.

"Quite a difference between hiding from danger and dashing headlong into its arms," Bones noted in a more reasonable tone than I'd used. "Can't undo the wrong that was done to you by getting in over your head, Justina."

"You're right, I'm beyond fixing," she said, bleakness flashing across features that looked like she was in her thirties instead of forty-six. "But other people aren't," she went on. "I can't change what I am, but killing that vampire months ago showed me I can at least use it to make sure others don't end up this way."

It's like listening to me when I was younger, I thought in disbelief. For so long, I'd hated what I was and took out my ignorance and loathing on other vampires, thinking it would balance the scales against my father. If not for Bones showing me that evil was a decision, not a species, I might still be trapped in that vicious cycle of self-destruction.

And this was twice in one day that I'd been on the receiving end of the same stubborn arguments I'd once used myself. I cast a quick, pleading glance

upward. *Any time you want to lay off the paybacks,
God, that'd be great.*

"You could kill hundreds of rogue vampires and
ghouls, but it still won't make the pain go away," I
finally said, my sense of déjà vu growing as I repeated
some of the same things Bones told me back then.
"Believe me, I know. Only accepting yourself will
make the hurt diminish, and that means accepting
even the parts you don't like or didn't choose."

My mother looked away, blinking back a sudden
pink shine in her eyes. "Really? Rodney accepted me.
Look where that got him."

"Rodney didn't just accept you, he loved you,"
Bones said quietly. "Else he wouldn't have died trying
to save you."

She whirled until her back was to us, but even though
her spine was straight, I saw her shoulders tremble. I
wanted to hug her, but I knew sympathy would only
be salt in the wound. A hug wouldn't bring back the
only man she'd had a real relationship with.

"I'm going after every filthy bloodsucker I can," she
said after a long moment, seemingly oblivious to the
fact that she'd insulted herself by the "filthy bloodsucker" comment. When she turned around, her gaze
was devoid of pink and lit up with vampiric green instead. "You have no control over that. The only thing
you *can* control is whether I do it with the support of
your old team, if I make it through their version of
basic training, or on my own."

"Even with their support, you'll still probably get
killed. You don't know how dangerous it is." I let out
a sigh of sheer frustration. "Please, don't *do* this."

Her jaw tightened until it creaked. "I'm doing it."

"God, you're just as stubborn as Don!" I said, fed up.

"Just as stubborn as someone else I know, too," Tate muttered under his breath.

"Stuff it, Tate," I snapped.

"Kitten." Bones placed a hand on my arm. Waves of calm seemed to wash over my subconscious, soothing my twisted emotions like salve applied to a burn. "Some things can't be taught, only learned. But there is a matter we *can* change; stopping these ghoul radicals. If their numbers grow, every vampire will be in danger, including your mum."

Right. That problem wouldn't wait for me to try to talk sense into my senselessly obstinate family. I had to focus on priorities. First: Stop the lethal, fascist propaganda in the ghoul community that had already left a trail of Masterless vampire bodies. Then I could move on to trying to talk my mother and uncle out of their newfound death wishes.

Something cynical in me wondered if the ghoul zealots might turn out to be easier.

I stared at my former team members. "You guys are so on my shit list, both for hiding this and for concealing Don's condition from me, but we've got bigger problems. Come with me so I can bring you up to speed. Mom." I shook my head. "We'll talk later."

She redid her dark hair into a tighter ponytail as she walked away. "Much later. I have training for the next several hours."

Six

Don sat on the bed, an oxygen mask lying on the table next to him. From the faint lines around his face, he'd had it on before we came in. I would've told him to keep using it, but of course, that logic would only fall on deaf ears. I shut the door behind the six of us and then proceeded to outline the situation with the ghouls as we knew it.

"As I told Cat, we need a person on the inside," Don stated once I was finished. "It's important enough that I'm asking you, Dave, to take an extended leave from the team to infiltrate these zealots. Our country has enough problems as it is with human terrorists. We can't afford to let undead ones grow in power. The results could be catastrophic."

Dave ran a hand through his hair. "Fuckin' right. I'll do it."

I knew that would be his answer. Dave had never

backed down from a dangerous assignment. Not even after he'd been killed on one.

Satisfaction flitted across my subconscious for an instant before it was gone. I cast a glance at Bones just in time to catch his faint smile before it, too, disappeared. Then realization hit me.

He'd intended this all along. Bones knew what Don would do if we told him about the ghouls, and he also knew I'd have balked if he'd been the one to suggest that Dave be the undercover operative. Hell, I already didn't like using Scratch and Ed as bait, and we'd just met them.

No wonder he'd been so keen on coming here when I broached the subject of dropping in on my uncle. I'd wanted to wait until tomorrow, but Bones said we should go at once. I'd just thought it was because he wanted to be back in Ohio quickly if Scratch and Ed happened to run into those ghouls tonight, but he'd had another plan altogether.

"You and I are having a talk later," I told him in a low, measured voice.

A dark brow arched, but Bones didn't pretend ignorance as to what the topic would be.

"Why are you the focal point of this ghoul's rhetoric again, Cat?" Tate asked, his indigo gaze flicking between me and Bones. "I thought Apollyon's paranoia with you ended when you became a full vampire."

I shifted, uncomfortable. This was a subject I'd hoped to avoid, but if Dave was risking his life and my old team was handicapped by losing one of its members on an extended assignment, they deserved to know.

"Okay, so I have kind of an eating disorder . . ." I began before laying out the details of my unusual diet and its subsequent side effects.

Silence descended on the room. My uncle looked too shocked to even cough while the rest of the guys stared at me with varying degrees of astonishment.

"You eat *vampires* and absorb their powers?" Juan blurted. "*Madre de Dios!*"

"And I thought you won the freak award as a half-breed, Commander," Cooper murmured. Then he shot a look at Bones. "Though I guess he keeps you well fed."

Dave slowly shook his head. "You always had to do things different, Cat. Guess this shouldn't be the exception."

Tate still hadn't spoken, but his gaze raked me. "Looks like we're not the only ones who kept secrets," he said at last.

"That's not *even* the same," I replied sharply.

"Of course not," he said in a tone that screamed *bullshit*.

"We've been keeping what causes my abilities under wraps because we didn't want to give Apollyon another tool to incite paranoia with," I said in exasperation. "Under normal circumstances, I don't think anyone would care that I feed from undead blood versus human, but clearly some ghouls aren't thinking normally now. Why add fuel to that fire?"

Silence met this question, but it was more rhetorical than anything I expected an answer on.

"Now that we all know the plan, Bones and I are heading out," I went on. "We need to get back in case our vampire spies call, not to mention I left my cat in a cave with only a ghost to watch over him."

"We can't leave yet," Bones stated.

I gave him a cagey look. What else did he have up his sleeve? "Why?"

His mouth curled. "Because you're still hungry, Kitten."

Oh, right. In the midst of everything that had happened the past couple hours, I'd forgotten about that. I cleared my throat, awkwardness setting in. What was the proper etiquette for asking a friend if I could drink his *blood*?

"Um, Juan, would you be willing to—"

"Drink from me," Tate cut me off. Emerald pinpointed in his gaze. "That's what you were about to ask him, wasn't it?"

"Not you," I said even as Bones stiffened like a rattler poised to strike. "I told you before, I'm all out of patience with you."

Something like a snort escaped him. "I'm not offering for personal reasons. After I watched you leave with the Prince of Darkness instead of me when you thought Bones cheated on you, I finally got it. You don't want me and you never will. Not even if Bones was out of the picture."

My eyes widened even as Bones muttered, "Thought you'd *never* bloody learn." Cooper and Juan pretended to suddenly go deaf, but my uncle cast a thoughtful look at Tate.

"Then why do you want Cat to take your blood?" Don asked.

Tate squared his shoulders. "Because I'm the leader

of this team, so if anyone's blood is getting spilled, it's mine."

The strangest form of nostalgia washed over me. *This* was the Tate who'd cracked my cold standoffish-ness when I first joined the team several years ago. A strong individual who never hesitated putting himself on the front lines, either for his friends or for his unit. Not the pigheaded, caustic person who'd repeatedly tried to drive a wedge between me and Bones. The friendship I'd just vowed was dead between us gave a small gasp of life.

"I'm not biting you. A needle and a bag, that's how we'll do it," I settled on saying.

Tate shrugged. "Suit yourself."

Don pressed a button. "Anne, can you bring in a syringe, catheter, and an empty bag?"

The nurse replied with an affirmative and had the items procured within two minutes flat. Tate stuck himself, waving Anne off, and soon the plastic bag began to fill with crimson liquid.

My stomach let out a rumble that I was sure every person in the room could hear, to my embarrassment.

"Gonna tell us why you're not drinking from him?" Tate asked, jerking his head toward Bones.

"He's too strong. I'm picking up more abilities than I can handle," I replied, trying not to stare in a fixated way at the bag that was now half full.

"And someone like me is nice and weak." Tate let out a snort.

Even though Tate deserved to be taken down several notches for all the shit he'd pulled the past couple years, I couldn't bring myself to rub salt in the wound.

"You're not weak; you're just a young vampire. If you were Bones's age, I'm sure you'd be way too strong for me to drink from."

Bones's amusement flitted across my subconscious even as Tate muttered, "FYI, pity makes it worse, so next time, don't try to cheer me up."

I threw up my hands. Men. They were impossible to reason with.

"How were you intending for Dave to make contact while he's undercover?" Bones asked Don, changing the subject.

My uncle frowned. "The usual way. Calling in whenever he can safely manage."

"Too risky, that," Bones stated. "His mobile could be monitored, texts and e-mails copied . . . you need a communications method the ghouls won't suspect whilst he's still gaining their trust."

"And what method is that?" Don asked, skepticism heavy in his voice.

Bones's smile was sly. "Ghostly courier."

"Of course!" I exclaimed, all of a sudden feeling better about Dave's chances. "The other ghouls, if they notice Fabian at all, will just ignore him. Plus, Ohio's full of ley lines, so he can travel fast if there's trouble and Dave needs to be extracted."

Don look intrigued. "Will the ghost be agreeable to this?"

"We'll ask, but I bet he says yes." My spirits lifted the more I considered this. "Fabian told me that above everything else, he misses feeling useful. Being noncorporeal limits a lot of things he can participate in, you know?"

Fabian had also missed companionship, which is how he'd ended up with me and Bones. Loneliness wasn't limited to the living, after all.

"Why can't we just have Fabian spy on the ghouls and report back, instead of sending Dave in as a plant with Fabian as the relay?" Cooper asked.

I pursed my lips. Much as that option appealed to me because it represented the least amount of danger, it wasn't practical.

"Ghosts are usually ignored, but for Fabian to glean the same amount of intel that Dave could while posing as a new recruit, he'd have to practically piggyback those ghouls. If they put two and two together about the same ghost always being around, they could feed us misinformation through him."

Sometimes the old-fashioned way was the best choice, even if it meant a greater risk.

Tate pulled the needle out of his arm, and the small hole healed before he'd handed over the now full bag.

"There's someone else who might be useful with this operation," he said slowly. "A freelance reporter who keeps exposing classified paranormal information to the public."

"How can a reporter help track a group of ghoul zealots? I doubt they advertise their anti-vampire rallies in the newspaper."

"This guy's got good instincts," Tate replied with a touch of grimness. "So good that we now have an employee whose sole job is to find ways to discredit him every time his Ugly Truth e-zine goes up with way too many things the public isn't ready to know."

I wasn't convinced a reporter would help. Especially one who blitzed the Internet with supernaturally sensitive information, but far be it for me to leave any stone unturned.

"So you're going to apprehend this modern-day Morpheus and talk him into aiding our cause?"

Tate's mouth curled. "No, Cat. You are, because for starters, he happens to be in Ohio."

SEVEΠ

Ï GAZED AT THE ΠARROW ROAD ÏΠ FRONT OF us, thick trees on either side giving the area a naturally secluded feel.

"Of all the places, figures he'd come here," I muttered. "If we're even let in the door, I'll be amazed."

Bones slanted a grin my way as he steered the car off the road onto a gravel drive. An open gate about a mile ahead was the only indicator that this road led to something other than a dead end.

"We'll get in. Trust me."

Once we were through the chain-link gate, a large warehouse came into view. From the outside, it looked abandoned, windows boarded up and only a few scraps of trash in the empty parking lot. If I didn't have supernatural hearing, I wouldn't have caught the music wafting out from the soundproofed walls, but snatches of songs rode on the wind as unseen doors periodically opened.

Bones drove around to the back. Once behind the warehouse, another parking area came into view, this one packed with cars. Because of its unusual clientele, the real entrance to the club was here, the decrepit warehouse image in front set up only to discourage motorists accidentally passing by.

"Why don't we just hang out here until he comes out of the club?" I asked. "If we go inside, we might be recognized."

I'd left my wedding ring at the hotel we checked into, but I hadn't dyed my hair or done anything else to disguise my appearance. And Bones's looks meant he stood out no matter what color his hair was.

He shrugged. "It's better if we are recognized. We'll only be in Ohio a few more days, but if we're seen frequenting pubs, there's less chance those ghouls will think we're on to them. They'd expect us to stay hidden if we were."

He had a point. *I'd* expected us to stay hidden, after all.

"Besides." Something cold glittered in Bones's eyes even though his voice remained light. "If they think we're unaware of any danger, some of them might be thick enough to try taking us on. I'd only need to keep one alive to verify that it's Apollyon behind these attacks."

I shifted in my seat. Put me in a straight-up fight and I had no qualms about getting lethal, but when it came to the sort of interrogation Bones was talking about, I wished there was a better way. There wasn't, of course. Not when it came to the undead, and if things had to get messy to stop a potential ghoul uprising . . . well, just call me Hannibal Lecter. With cleavage.

Headlights flashed in the rearview mirror as another car entered the parking lot. Tiny and Band-Aid would keep an eye out here. That meant there would be no surprise ambush later when we were coming out of the club, which made me more relaxed.

Bones parked and I got out, brushing a few specks of lint off my charcoal-colored skirt. It was tighter than I preferred, plus low enough to expose my navel and several inches of my stomach with my midriff halter top, but the goal was to look more interested in fun than fighting. The knee-high boots might be expected to contain a blade or two, but only a very careful person would notice the texture of my heels as something other than wood. Or the faint outlines on my back underneath my top as something more than a strapless bra.

Bones was also dressed as though entertainment were his only motivation. His long-sleeved top was made entirely of black mesh, his crystal skin exposed more than it was covered with the material. Leather pants hung low on his hips, tight enough to hint at his assets, but with enough give that they wouldn't hinder his movements. The all-black ensemble combined with his dark hair only made his pale skin even more striking by comparison, drawing the eye to the muscled flesh those hundreds of tiny holes revealed.

He caught my lingering gaze where the peep show of his skin ended and the front of his pants began— and flashed me a wicked grin.

"Hold that thought, luv. With luck, we'll be back in our hotel room breaking in the Jacuzzi before dawn."

If I'd have still been human, I might have blushed. Logic said I should be past the stage where it was obvious that I was mentally stripping and molesting my own *husband*. We weren't in the earliest bloom of our relationship anymore, after all. But when Bones approached, his dark eyes glittering with hints of green, gooseflesh still rippled across my skin as though this were a first date. Then everything in me tensed with expectation when he stood as close as possible without touching, only his breath hitting my skin as he spoke near my ear.

"Have I told you how lovely you look tonight?"

A wave of heat rolled over my subconscious, as if my nerve endings had just been brushed with the warmest of caresses. My hands slowly fisted while I resisted the urge to touch him, enjoying the building tension between us. Yes, this was different from the first giddy stage of attraction I'd felt for him, but that didn't diminish his effect on me. Instead, the desire I felt was richer, stronger, and far more intoxicating when combined with the hold Bones had over my heart.

His scent deepened, that blend of burnt sugar and musk tantalizing me with the evidence that he felt the same way I did. Last night, after leaving the compound, I'd been too emotionally bruised over Don's condition and my mother's new deadly aspirations to be in an amorous mood. Plus, we had to fill in Fabian, relocate from the cave, and take the ghost back to Dave in Tennessee before returning to Ohio again. That left little time to do more than grab a few hours' sleep before heading out for tonight's activities.

Now, however, I wished we would have spent another hour or so back at our hotel room before leaving for this club. His comment about the Jacuzzi tub made some explicit images dance in my mind. Like how devastating Bones would look wearing nothing but suds—and then nothing but my body.

Another thought teased its way into my mind. *Why wait? The backseat of our car is only a few feet away . . .*

"You know, in addition to your mind-reading abilities, I may have absorbed some sluttiness from your blood," I said, giving my head a little shake. Had to be. I normally wouldn't think of getting it on in a parking lot when we had a reporter to snag inside *and* two undead friends just a few dozen feet away.

Soft laughter tickled my neck while the invisible caress of his aura intensified. "Be still my nonbeating heart."

The sinfulness in his tone said he'd be only too open to the idea of delaying our appearance inside the club—and blistering Tiny and Band-Aid's ears—should I suggest that backseat option. I took a step away, deciding it was in the best interest of my rapidly dwindling propriety not to touch him until we were safely inside the club.

Though possibilities lurked there, too . . .

"Let's, um, go find our reporter friend," I said, the words hitching as a breeze made his scent wash over me in a swell of lust-fragranced air. I couldn't resist a quick, longing glance at the car before I gave myself a mental slap. *Mind out of the gutter, Trampzilla! People to see, bad ghouls to stop, remember?*

Bones took in a long breath, making me wonder if the air was also tinged with my arousal. Probably. Scent was a more obvious indicator of desire for vampires than a man with a hard-on tenting his pants was for humans.

"Right," he said, the single word edged with a hint of roughness. Then he folded his aura in, the invisible energy around him decreasing until only the faint tingles of an average vampire remained. At the same time, my link to his emotions ceased, as abrupt as a cell phone dropping a call. Only very old vampires or Masters had the ability to camouflage their power levels, which made them even more dangerous. Bones might want us to eventually be recognized, but it seemed we were going in low-profile to start.

We walked up to the entrance of Bite. The line of humans waiting to get in was smaller than usual, but I chalked that up to it being Wednesday night instead of a weekend. We didn't wait at the back, our lack of pulses the same as being on the VIP list here. But once we were close enough for the tall, brawny female bouncer to notice us, she held out her hand.

"Stay right there. Verses is pissed at you two."

Bones gave the vampire his most charming smile. "Now, Trixie, he can't still be sore over that trifling incident."

Her mouth opened in disbelief, showing off her gold-plated incisors. "Trifling? You guys demolished the parking lot!"

"At least fetch him so he can tell us to sod off himself, if that's how he feels about it," Bones replied, still with that same effortless smile.

Trixie let out an exasperated noise, but she barked out a comment telling someone I couldn't see to get the owner. After a few moments, a large black ghoul appeared, a thoroughly unwelcoming expression on his face.

"You've got a lot of nerve coming back here—" Verses began.

"Come now, mate, that wasn't our fault and you know it," Bones interrupted, clapping him on the back. "Could've happened to anyone, but we're only here now to do a bit of drinking and dancing."

If possible, the ghoul's mocha features darkened even more. "Don't think because we've been friends for eighty years that I'm dumb enough to believe that. This place is meant to be a time-out for all our species. No violence on the premises, and the parking lot is *still* the premises!"

"I'm really sorry about what happened before, but we won't even bend a drink straw the wrong way this time," I chimed in, giving Verses my most winning smile.

"Indeed," Bones added, his own grin widening. "On my honor, mate."

"And on your credit card, if anything so much as gets dented," Verses shot back before letting out a grunt. "Fine. Come in, but don't make me regret it."

At first glance, even people who couldn't feel the vibrations that the undead patrons gave off could guess that Bite wasn't a typical club. For one, the random bursts of lights across the ceiling were far more muted than in a normal club, plus the interior was darker than what legal guidelines would allow. The music also wasn't painfully loud to my ears, another concession to the heightened senses vampires and ghouls had.

But the most notable difference was that the bars weren't the only places where patrons could get drinks. In booths, on the dance floor, and even in corners, couples held each other in embraces that, upon closer look, were more predatory than passionate. The scent of blood flavored the air with a faint, coppery tang, probably tickling Bones's taste buds but doing nothing for mine because it was human blood, not vampire.

"How long do you want to wait before we split up?" I murmured to Bones once we were away from Verses. If Bite's owner did still happen to be watching us, we couldn't have him getting suspicious if we immediately separated after we'd stressed that we were here just for recreation.

"Let's start with a few drinks. Then perhaps you can go powder your nose and take the long way back. After that, I'll find someone to take a nip from, and I'll be quite picky about my choice," he replied in equally soft tones.

Sounded like a plan to me. After all, both of us would recognize the reporter on sight, if he was here. I let Bones lead me to the bar, glad that so far, only my thoughts rattled around in my mind. I hoped with the high percentage of patrons in this club being undead, if I did start picking up on any stray thoughts, I wouldn't feel overwhelmed like at the mall. Guess there were benefits to frequenting places filled with my own kind instead of having mostly humans around me.

My own kind. How strange that I felt that way now. I'd spent the first sixteen years of my life not knowing about my mixed heritage, then the next six years hating vampires until I met Bones. Now, at twenty-nine, I'd been a full vampire for less than a year, but I almost couldn't remember what it had been like to

think of myself as human. I hadn't felt that way since
my mother first told me why I was different from everyone else.

"Gin and tonic, plus a whiskey, neat," Bones told
the bartender.

Oddly enough, that made me smile. Some things
didn't change, after all.

Eight

I WAS ON MY WAY BACK FROM MY THIRD TRIP to the bathroom, thinking my nose couldn't *be* less shiny and being glad public toilets were no longer a necessary evil for me, when a shout jerked my head around.

"Let me go!"

Even above the music and the other noises, the words were distinct. I switched directions and headed toward the source of that cry, realizing it came from the booths in the far corner where I'd first met Bones. A cluster of vampires gathered in a circle, their backs to me. They had someone in the middle of them, and from the sounds of it, whoever it was wasn't happy.

"Get your hands off me!" came another yell, too shrill for me to tell if I recognized who was speaking.

"You know the rules. Take it off the premises," the DJ boomed out. He didn't sound too concerned about what would happen after that, I noticed.

I reached the vampires just as they shoved the screaming man out of my line of sight. From the frantic internal thumping in his chest, he was human.

"What's going on, guys?" My voice was casual and I kept my hands off the silver strapped to my upper back. After all, I'd promised Verses we wouldn't break his rules this time.

One of the vampires gave me a hostile glare. "None of your business, Redhead."

Bones came into the area, obviously having heard the disruption and my involvement in it. He smiled at the group of vampires, but that wasn't what made them stop to give him their full attention. It was the power Bones unleashed when he dropped his shields and the full weight of his aura blasted out like a geyser, swirling the air around him with invisible currents.

"I believe my wife asked you a question," he noted in a deceptively light tone.

It was very unfeminist of me, but the expressions of wariness that settled on their faces had me biting my cheeks to keep from laughing. *Just realized having several of your buddies around doesn't mean you have the upper hand, huh, boys?*

"The human's a spy," the one who'd snapped at me said to Bones in a much more respectful manner. "I've seen him coming in here before, asking questions about our kind . . . now we caught him taking pictures. You know we can't have that."

I still couldn't see him behind the wall of vampires, but I was betting this was the reporter we were looking for. And as soon as they took him off the premises, he was in deep shit. Vampires and ghouls would do anything to ensure that all but a few, select humans were happily unaware they shared the planet with creatures that were supposed to be myth.

"Give him to me," I said, thinking fast. "I'll wipe his mind and destroy all his gadgets. No harm, no foul."

"But I'm hungry," one of them protested.

Oh yeah, the damage control they'd intended was far more permanent. "Lots of people here would be happy to help you with that, but you're *not* getting him," I said, my words soft but steely.

The apparent leader of the group ignored me as he pulled out a cigarette, sticking it between his teeth.

"No need to fight. You want him? I'll bargain," he said to Bones.

I was past my initial amusement over how these vampires were so focused on Bones that I seemed to be invisible to them. Plus, Bones *had* said it would be better if we were recognized. Well, let this serve as my introduction.

"I have an idea. How about we arm wrestle? Winner gets the human."

That switched their attention to me. Laughter broke out from the group and the leader's gaze actually became pink with tears of mirth.

"You've got to be joking," he managed.

I gave him a sweet smile. "Not at all."

His gaze flicked to Bones. "You're not going to let her do this, are you?"

Bones snorted. "*Let* her? Mate, if you think you can control a woman, you must be single—and a thousand pounds says she beats your arse."

"We can use this," I went on, walking over to a high-top table that butted against the half wall separating the booth area from the dance floor. "Come on. Moonlight's burning."

A small crowd started to form. I didn't look at them, reserving my attention for the leader as I cocked a brow in invitation. I could have suggested we take this off the premises. Upped the stakes to a brawl instead of a simple test of strength, but though I wasn't about to be dismissed as arm candy, I wasn't looking to make new enemies, either.

The vampire handed his cigarette to one of his friends before coming over. He rolled up his right sleeve with a confident glance at my very average build. If he was measuring my aura to gauge my power level, he'd find nothing intimidating there, either. Bones told me I felt like a new vampire, which was as much of a disguise as my heartbeat had been when I was half human. In comparison, the vampire was almost as tall as Bones, but with black hair and a burly build that spoke of thick muscle underneath a layer of firmly packed fat. His appearance wasn't what I paid the most attention to, however. It was his aura, dating him at around a buck fifty, and he carried his big form with easy grace.

Not an unbeatable opponent, but not one to half-ass my efforts with, either. I set my elbow on the table, not needing to do any more prep because my halter top didn't have sleeves. All around us, bets were being placed. It amused me to hear my low odds.

The vampire's hand curled around mine as he placed his arm on the table, having to bend a little due to his greater height. His grip was firm but not punishing, raising my opinion of him a notch. A schmuck would've ground my fingers in his fist trying to make a point.

From the corner of my eye, I saw Verses shoulder his way to the front of the other onlookers. He was probably wishing he hadn't let us in after all.

"Count of three?" I suggested to the vampire.

Blue eyes tinged with emerald met mine. "Why not?"

Calls of "Show her what you're made of, Nitro!" and "Knock her on her pretty ass!" rang out when I began to count, never taking my eyes from my opponent. As soon as the word *three* left my lips, that previously steady grip tightened and Nitro hammered his hand downward, going for the quick win with a blast of inhuman strength.

Except our arms stayed in their same vertical position. Nitro's biceps bulged almost as much as his gaze when his efforts didn't move my arm so much as an inch. I flashed him a smile as I held my position, mentally counting to ten before I began to edge his arm in a slow, steady arc downward. After all, I didn't want to embarrass him by slamming his hand on the table before he'd even realized what happened. It wasn't Nitro's fault he had no idea I'd been born with unusual strength, or that I still had some of Bones's power in me from drinking his blood. Poor burly vampire didn't stand a chance.

Murmurs rose from the crowd, drowning out even the music as Nitro's arm inched closer to the table. Lines formed in his face and a harsh grunt escaped him as he put more effort into holding me off. I let him raise his arm up a few inches—the male ego was such a *fragile* thing, after all—before sending it down onto the table with a thunk hard enough to crack the Formica.

We'll have to pay for that before we leave, I thought amidst the burst of surprised exclamations from the watchers around us.

Nitro stared at his arm in disbelief. Then his gaze swung back up to me even as I disentangled my grip and shook the temporary numbness out of my hand. He'd really gone all out those last few seconds.

"How the *hell* did you get to be so strong?" he demanded. "You can't be more'n a year undead!"

"Good guess," I remarked. "It'll be a year this fall, actually, but I'll tell you a secret—I had vampire strength long before that."

His brows drew together in a frown. Then comprehension dawned and Nitro laughed. "Red hair, beautiful, and badass. *You* must be the Reaper."

I grinned. "Call me Cat."

He glanced at Bones next, drawing the obvious connection as to who he had to be. Bones didn't notice; he was too busy collecting his winnings. Comments like "Ah, that's splendid," and "Better luck next time, lads" came from him. By the time he sauntered over, he had a thick stack of bills in his hands. Most vampires were slow on catching what they considered the "new" credit card trend and still carried cash.

"Leave it to you to find a way to make a profit off this," I noted in amusement.

His mouth curled. "Fortune favors the bold."

Nitro shook his head as he looked back at us. "Guess it's time for me to pay up, too." Then he walked over to where his friends stood, pulling the reporter out from behind the wall of vampires. He gave him a light shove that nevertheless had him landing in an ungainly heap near my feet.

"All yours, Reaper," he drawled.

I ticked my hand off my brow in a jaunty salute. "Pleasure doing business with you, Nitro."

That earned me a laugh. "Next time, I'll know better than to fall for your innocent little female act."

"Don't feel bad, mate," Bones replied. "She fooled me with the same thing the first time we met, right up until I saw her kill a vampire seven times her age."

Then Bones went over to the nearest bar and slapped his bundle of cash onto it. "Drinks are on me until this runs out," he announced, to a rousing round of applause. I caught his wink to Verses next and the ghoul's wry shake of his head. It probably didn't come close to making up for the damage we'd caused the last time we were here, but it was a start.

With another chuckle, Nitro and his group walked away to place their drink orders. Around us, the onlookers faded as people went back to dancing, drinking, or whatever it was they'd been doing before this all started. I looked down at the man who was slowly getting up from the floor, sandy-brown hair mussed from his earlier struggles.

Yep, this was who we'd come here for.

"Hi, Timmie," I said in a low voice.

His head whipped up, revealing a face with five o'clock shadow on his jaw and faint lines around his eyes and mouth. He looked different from the gangly boy who'd been my neighbor seven years ago when I was a college student by day and a vampire hunter by night. In addition to the stubble on his face, the laugh lines, and his hair being longer, his frame had also filled out to a stockier, more muscular physique. *Getting older looks good on him*, I mused.

"How do you . . . ?" he began. Then his voice died away while his eyes widened.

"Cathy?" he managed. He looked me up and down, his shocked expression changing into a smile that wreathed his face. "Cathy! I *knew* you weren't dead!"

Nine

Timmie continued to stare at me with a mixture of glee and disbelief. I smiled back, happy to see hints of the boy I'd been friends with amidst the differences in the man in front of me. When Tate told me Timmie was the troublesome reporter we needed to collect tonight, I'd been stunned, but pleased at the thought of seeing him again.

"I can't believe it," Timmie marveled. "You look *exactly* the same, except, uh, you didn't use to dress like that before," he added as goggled at my outfit. Then he made as if to hug me, but stopped when he noticed the man striding up to my side.

"You!" Timmy burst out, losing the smile while he blanched. "God, Cathy, you're still *with* him?"

I smothered a laugh at the incredulity in his tone. "Yep. Married him, too."

Bones gave Timmie a grin that managed to be predatory even though he didn't flash any fang. "She does indeed look very fetching, but if you continue with that particular line of thought, I'll neuter you for real this time."

Timmie's cheeks reddened. "I—I didn't . . . I mean, I wouldn't . . ." Then his eyes narrowed. "Wait a minute. You don't look any different, either, except your hair's dark now. *Neither* of you look a day older than the last time I saw you."

Fear wafted from him as he looked back and forth between me and Bones, putting it all together with what he'd learned about this club. I watched him closely as I waited. The Timmie I'd known had been open-minded and kind, albeit ignorant about the undead like everyone else. How much of who he used to be was still left in the person in front of me? Had the years changed not just his appearance, but his tolerance as well?

"I'm right about all of it, aren't I?" he asked at last, very softly. "Some of these people . . . they're not human."

"No, they're not," I answered in a steady tone.

His face paled even more as he looked around at the people by the nearest bar. On the surface, nothing about them looked different from patrons gathered around any other bar, especially since Timmie couldn't see the handful of ghosts circling over the last seat on the left. But every so often, emerald would glint from a person's gaze. Or someone would move with a quickness that Timmie's subconscious would register even if his eyes couldn't follow.

Finally his shoulders squared as he looked back at me and Bones. "You two aren't human, either." A statement, not a question.

"No," I said gently. "We're not."

He shook his head like he was trying to clear it. "Those guys, the ones who grabbed me . . . they were gonna eat me?"

No use lying about that, either. "Oh yeah. Definitely."

He glanced at Bones. "But you won't."

Bones arched a brow as if disputing that. I elbowed him while I said, "No, Timmie, he won't. Neither of us will hurt you."

"Tim," he replied, then gave me a wry smile. "No one's called me Timmie in years."

I smiled back. "Sure. And it's Cat, by the way."

"Cat." That wry smile remained. "Guess it suits you better than Cathy."

"No," Bones said.

Timmie's—*Tim's*—smile faded. I glanced at Bones in confusion. "No what? You think I look like a Cathy?"

"No to what he's about to ask you," Bones replied. "You already owe her for saving you from those other blokes. Don't thank her by asking for another large favor."

Tim clapped his arms around his head. "My God, you can really hear . . . ? Well, stop it!"

Bones laughed outright. I had to admit Timmie did look funny clutching his head, but I didn't join in Bones's chuckles.

"Try wrapping tinfoil around your nog next, see if that works better," he suggested devilishly.

I gave Bones a sharp look, sorry he couldn't read *my* mind anymore to hear my mental reprimand. "Stop it. I might have been tempted to do the same

thing myself when I knew certain people could eaves-
drop in my head."

Tim let his arms down. "I don't care what he says,
you gotta help me," he got out in a rush.

Bones rolled his eyes and then gave Tim a glare
that would have struck most people mute out of terror.
"Right thick, aren't you? Let's see if I can't explain
my position better outside."

Off the premises, where violence was allowed?
"Don't even think about it," I drew out warningly.

"Not for that," he replied, though his mouth
twitched in a way that said the thought *had* crossed
his mind. "Believe me, Kitten, you'll have wasted
your time saving him before if others hear what he's
about to ask you."

That didn't sound promising. But I needed
Timmie—dammit, Tim!—for something, too, so I'd
hear out his request. Didn't guarantee I'd agree to
whatever he wanted, but I'd listen.

"Okay. Let's go outside and talk."

Timmie gave Bones and me a speculative glance.
"Before we go, I gotta know: If mind-reading abilities
are real, there's something else I wondered if fiction
got right about vampires—"

"Ask me if I sparkle and I'll kill you where you
stand," Bones cut him off with utmost seriousness.

"Not that." Timmie's mouth quirked before his expression became serious and, oddly, hopeful. "When I
go back to my apartment, is it true that, uh, your kind
can't come inside?"

I hated to destroy his sense of safety, but believing
that would only be dangerous for him.

"Sorry, that's a myth. Vampires don't need to be

invited to go anywhere they want to." I didn't add that
we'd already been in his apartment earlier, finding out
from his roommate where Timmie would be tonight.
Not that the young man remembered Bones and me
questioning him once we'd given him a few flashes
of our gaze, but I thought that was more information
than Timmie could handle at the moment.

He was silent. "Shit," Timmie said at last, with
heartfelt emphasis.

I nodded. Sometimes, that word summed things up
better than I ever could.

"Let's go, before people start to wonder what we're
blathering on about," Bones said, inclining his head
toward the door.

We walked past the crowded parking lot toward the
empty one ahead. It was far enough away from the real
entrance of Bite that no one should be able to overhear
us, aside from Tiny and Band-Aid, who still kept watch
in their car. I couldn't hear his thoughts, but Timmie's
scent was a mix of excitement, fear, and determination.
Whatever he wanted to ask meant a great deal to him.

"Look, if your girlfriend vanished after sniffing
around looking for proof about vampires, chances are
she's dead," Bones stated once we reached the chain-
link gate.

I winced at his bluntness. Timmie also looked
shaken, but then he raised his chin. "Nadia's not my
girlfriend, and I don't believe she's dead. You don't
know her. She's my best freelance reporter because
she can charm *any*one into doing what she wants."

Bones snorted. "I don't care if she was Helen of
Troy and Scheherazade combined, obviously some-

one caught her and wasn't pleased about her snooping. The fact that she wasn't sent back to you afterward with her memory erased and a new desire to quit reporting doesn't bode well for her."

I winced again, but Bones was probably right. There was a reason the world didn't know about the undead, and that was because vampires and ghouls were zealous about keeping their existence a secret. Some of them too zealous, like the vampires that had been about to make Timmie a nighttime snack.

"We could check around," I said, giving Bones a slight shake of my head when he looked like he was about to object. Yes, we had a lot of urgent matters on our plate, but Timmie's pleading expression made me unable to say no.

"Discreetly, of course," I added. "We'll start by asking Verses if he remembers seeing her, then show her picture to your people, Mencheres, some of your allies . . . maybe one of them will know where she is."

I didn't hold out much hope for Nadia turning up alive, but at least this way, Timmie could feel like he wasn't abandoning someone he cared about. From the look on his face, the fact that Nadia hadn't been his girlfriend wasn't due to a lack of interest on Timmie's part.

"Really?" he said. Then Timmie grabbed me in a hug. "Thank you, Cathy!"

We were *never* going to get each other's names right.

"I'm not promising that we can find her, but we'll look," I said, giving him a light squeeze back.

Timmie let me go, flashing a crooked smile at Bones. "Aren't you going to threaten to pull my nuts off for that?"

A dark brow arched. "Not at the moment."

"Cathy, what happened seven years ago?" Timmie asked. "Why did the feds claim you were shot trying to escape after being arrested for killing the governor and your whole family? I knew that was bullshit. You could never kill anyone."

Something between a laugh and a snort escaped Bones. I shifted uncomfortably. Here's hoping I never had to explain to Timmie the reason behind my nickname of the Red Reaper.

"Well, the part about the killing the governor . . . that was true, but he totally had it coming. He was involved in some very bad shit and my grandparents were murdered because of him. Then this secret unit of the government recruited me to work for them—"

"Men in black!" Timmie interrupted triumphantly. "I *knew* they existed. Those creeps have been sabotaging my stories about the paranormal for years!"

I stopped myself before I rolled my eyes. "Uh, *yeah*, but why are you surprised by that? They couldn't just sit on their hands while you scared the hell out of people telling them things they're not ready to hear."

Timmie bristled. "I can't believe you'd say that. The public has a right to know—"

"Bollocks," Bones interrupted crisply. "Governments might lie to their people for selfish reasons most of the time, but this one they're spot-on about. Think there wouldn't be worldwide hysteria if the masses knew they shared this planet with creatures from their bedtime stories? A nuclear bomb would cause less devastation."

"We could handle it," Timmie said, his chin jutting out further.

Bones let out a derisive noise. "The day your kind stops killing each other over skin color or which god someone prays to, I might believe that."

I cleared my throat, defensiveness for my former species rising within me. "Considering what's going on with vampires and ghouls at the moment, I'd say humans don't have a monopoly on lethal bigotry."

"Yes, but it's been six hundred years since our kind last clashed over such matters," Bones muttered.

"Really? What happened six hundred years ago?" Timmie asked, echoing the same question that popped into my mind.

Bones's expression cleared, becoming inscrutable. I knew him well enough to know such a reaction meant he'd just spilled something he hadn't meant to, though I didn't know what the big deal was. Six hundred years *was* a long time. Whatever happened back then should have no bearing on the potential trouble stirring between vampires and ghouls today . . .

Premonition slid a cold path up my spine. The past few days, hearing my mother and uncle parrot the same ill-founded arguments I'd once used had reminded me time and again of when I'd first met Bones. Something teased the edge of my mind from that time. A long-forgotten memory of what Bones said the second night we met, when he thought another vampire sent me after him because he couldn't believe I was a half-breed.

Suppose I believe you're the offspring of a human and a vampire. Almost unheard of, but we'll get back to that . . .

"Bones, whatever happened to the other half-breed? You said half-breeds were *almost* unheard of, and Gregor mentioned at least one before me, right?"

He let out a slow hiss, something he didn't do unless he was upset or aroused, and these were *not* titillating circumstances.

"Kitten, now's really not the time—"

"My ass," I cut him off, voice hardening as my suspicions were confirmed. "Talk."

Timmie cast an interested look between the two of us, but didn't say anything. Bones ran a hand through his hair in a frustrated way before meeting my gaze.

"Let's take a drive. Need to bring your mate home anyway."

So he was being *very* cautious about being overheard. No way would we drive straight to Timmie's apartment and drop him off before we explained how we needed his help with the ghouls. I gave a short nod before gesturing to Timmie.

"Come on, our car's this way."

"I brought my own," he began, stopping at the glare Bones threw him. "But I can always come back and get it later," Timmie lamely finished.

"Wise choice," Bones commented. "After you, mate."

Ten

WE WERE SEVERAL MILES AWAY, CRUISING down Interstate 70 with Bones's usual disregard for the speed limit, before he spoke again.

"Once before, in the fourteen hundreds, a woman was widely known to be half vampire. There might have been others in history, but they managed to remain anonymous. She didn't. Her name was Jeanne d'Arc, but you'll know her better as Joan of Arc."

For a second, I thought Bones was kidding, even though he wasn't the type to pull silly pranks. Then that same stunned part of my brain acknowledged he stared ahead at the road with a deadly serious expression, so this wasn't a joke.

"Joan of Arc?" I repeated. "*Saint* Joan? *She's* the only other known half-breed?" *Talk about a hard act to follow!*

"This was before my time, but I'll repeat the story as Mencheres told it to me. Back in her day, Joan was well-known to humans for her battle skills and religious convictions. To vampires, she was also outed as a half-breed after one saw her actions on the battlefield. Apollyon seized upon her unusual status to sow seeds of rebellion among ghouls in Europe. He claimed Joan could be the most powerful undead creature in the world if her vampire abilities were combined with those of a ghoul, and if so, Joan would unite all vampires against ghouls."

"In other words, the same shit he's spouted about me." My initial surprise vanished under a wash of anger. "I don't suppose she intended to do any of that, either."

"Apollyon didn't have a shred of proof at the time—and none has been found since—but there were still those fearful or gullible enough to be swayed. Ghouls began withdrawing from undead society, attacking Masterless vampires. Then they openly attacked smaller vampire lines, picking off the weakest and less connected first. Rumors began to swirl that they were amassing an army for a full-scale attack on all vampires. A species showdown seemed inevitable, but once Joan was executed by the Church, a truce was negotiated between vampires and ghouls. Apollyon has been relatively quiet since . . . until recently."

Right, when another half-breed came on the scene for him to use as a scapegoat for his genocidal tendencies. And now the same scenario looked to be happening all over again with the recent attacks on Masterless vampires.

Timmie's mouth hung open in almost comedic fashion, but I only felt anger coursing through me.

"It wasn't just the Church who made sure Joan was burned at the stake, was it?"

Bones closed his eyes briefly. "No, luv. Even after her death, some of Apollyon's ghouls were still afraid of her. They dug up her bones and ground them into powder to make certain Joan could never be brought back."

"And the vampires let her burn," I said. My voice rose. "She was their sacrificial lamb, her death the price for their truce."

His gaze was so dark and bottomless that I almost felt swallowed by those brown orbs. "Yes and no. Joan was offered a choice to become a full vampire instead of facing the stake. She chose to die instead."

The strangest sort of grief snaked through me. Even though Joan had been dead centuries before I was born, a small part of me still felt like I'd lost a friend. She was the only other person who'd known what it was like to live as I had—fitting into neither the human world nor the vampire one. She'd been punished for her unwanted uniqueness like me, too, but even if she'd chosen vampirism over death, Joan's persecution from Apollyon might not have ended. Not if all half-breeds who changed over ended up as strange as me. I was as much of a full vampire as I was ever going to get, but because of my oddities, the ghoul leader was still trying to use me as kindling for the fires of war.

Right then I determined to kill Apollyon. We hadn't wanted to do that to avoid strengthening his cause by turning him into a martyr, but even if I had to make it look like an excruciatingly painful accident, that ghoul was going down. It wasn't enough to stop him or discredit him. He'd only bide his time until another half-breed popped up in history and then use that person as a poster child to rally fear-bought support in another quest for power. I would *not* let that happen.

"No wonder you're so wigged about Apollyon being behind these recent attacks," I said quietly. "And you should have told me all this before."

"That creep is still alive?" Timmie blurted, sounding aghast.

"I *was* going to tell you, Kitten." His mouth twisted. "Though I admit to a great abhorrence for the subject, as you can imagine."

I certainly could. It let me know just how high the stakes were if Apollyon was back to his old tricks—and everything pointed to that being the case. If we didn't stop him before things reached a tipping point, the vampire nation might just offer Apollyon the same deal that had prevented war last time: the life of the half-breed.

Or in my case, the life of the freaky, mostly dead vampire with the occasional heartbeat and really weird diet. I wouldn't be given another alternative like Joan, considering I'd already changed over. If the vampire nation made that deal, the world wasn't big enough for me to hide in. Not with how ninety-five percent of all vampires would suddenly be screaming for my head to prevent an all-out species clash.

And Bones would die defending me from his kind, no matter if our situation was hopeless. I knew that, because I'd do the same for him. Now his ruthlessness with Ed, Scratch, and even Dave, whom Bones considered a friend, made a lot more sense. Stopping Apollyon from inciting war between the species wasn't good enough. We had to stop him before things even got *close* to that point. If not, I was toast, and Bones along with me.

"Well, then." My voice was very calm. The situation was so serious that it pushed me past my usual nerves. "We'll just have to work that much faster, won't we?"

"Is there anything I can do to help?"

Timmie's voice was a hoarse croak, but I turned to him with a grateful, though somewhat forced, smile.

"I'm so glad you asked."

City lights blurred by as Bones whizzed down the freeway. I had my arms around his waist more for comfort than fear of falling off the motorcycle. Even though I wasn't afraid of riding them anymore—being dead tended to cure a *lot* of phobias—I still didn't think I'd ever grow as fond of them as Bones was. Plus, you wouldn't catch me riding one without a helmet like he did. Not with all the bugs that congregated in the warm summer air. Ew.

We'd spent the past ten days fruitlessly club hopping, hoping we'd seem so clueless and relaxed that some rabble-rousing ghouls wouldn't be able to resist attacking us. No such luck, as it turned out. Ed and Scratch hadn't seen any of those ghouls recently, either. Timmie, who'd agreed to help us, also hadn't come up with any promising leads through his sources yet. Dave, trolling the places Ed and Scratch said the ghouls had frequented, had likewise struck out while he masqueraded as a ghoul looking for a nice bunch of bigots to hang with. So far, the score was Apollyon, one; us, zero.

The logical part of me knew this was to be expected. That Apollyon was too smart to be lured in so easily, but I was still frustrated. Every day I spent chasing that zealot's minions was one less day I had to convince my uncle and mother not to do the equivalent of riding hell-for-leather into death, as both of them seemed determined to do. For once, couldn't the bad guys be a *little* accommodating?

Obviously not, so it was time to switch tactics. Maybe Bones's and my presence in Ohio had made Apollyon's ghouls move on to another city. Maybe they were waiting to attack us until they had more forces in place. Who knew? All that was apparent was our current strategy wasn't working, and we didn't have the time to wait and see if another ten days of the same activities would net better results.

I'd had an idea for a potential Plan B: trotting out in public several times without Bones. Mencheres could always claim to need his co-ruler for some fabricated, urgent business so Bones would have an excuse for not being there. Bones had flatly refused to go for it, however. Too dangerous, he'd stated, and it was either drop the subject, or do what I'd sworn never to do again—go behind his back and take the risk anyway.

That had been my modus operandi several times in the past, but no matter how it seemed like the only way to handle things at the time, it had always backfired. I was determined to show I'd learned from my mistakes, but the rebellious part of me knew if I wasn't his wife, Bones would agree that using me as bait was our best option. Still, we'd promised to fight our battles together instead of one of us—usually me—dashing off into the fray while leaving the other person on the sidelines, and I intended to keep that promise.

Stopping the bad guys would be hard, yet sometimes, making a relationship between two strong-willed people work seemed like an equally challenging goal. Of course, if Bones had a meek personality and I could easily bulldoze over him, I wouldn't love him like I did. The same unyielding determination that frustrated me now was what had drawn me to Bones in the first place. He'd said much the same thing about me once. Guess we were both masochists in addition to being stubborn.

I jerked out of my musings when Bones turned off the highway. With how fast he drove, it hadn't taken us long to get to the Chicago suburbs where Mencheres was staying so his girlfriend could be close to her family. It was still strange to think of the mega-Master vampire in a relationship, but Mencheres was fangs over heels for Kira. She seemed to be a nice person, too, instead of a homicidal bitch like his former wife. Otherwise, the world should fear. When Mencheres fell for a woman, he fell hard. If Kira asked for her own continent as a birthday present, Mencheres would probably have one conquered for her before she blew out her candles.

After going down a few windy roads and announcing ourselves at the security camera by the gate, we pulled up in front of Mencheres's home. The three-story house was far less grand than his other residences, being able to sleep a mere fifteen instead of fifty. But once again, this scaled-down residence was due to Kira's influence.

"This isn't a house; it's a hotel," she'd commented about the place Mencheres initially picked out, and the former pharaoh acquiesced to living somewhere smaller without a single word of protest.

"See?" I'd whispered to Bones, nudging him with a grin. "He never argues with her. Isn't that sweet?"

A snort preceded his response. "Keep dreaming, pet."

Bones put the Ducati in park just as the front door opened and Gorgon, a Nordic version of Alfred to Mencheres's Batman, came out. I took off my helmet, pulling out my iPod earphones at the same time—hey, I hadn't needed to pay attention to traffic as a passenger—only to have something aside from Norah Jones's latest CD assail my ears.

Gorgon's features were perfectly composed, as if there wasn't a symphony of moans and groans coming from one of the upper rooms of the house behind him.

"Bones, Cat. Mencheres is regrettably detained at the moment, but please, come in."

It was only my new vampiric control that allowed me to keep a straight face, but Bones just laughed.

"He clearly hasn't gotten his bedroom sound-proofed yet, so we're quite aware he's not regretting his 'detainment' in the least."

A crashing sound followed by an extended feminine squeal made me look up at the house in bewilderment. What was he *doing* to her?

Gorgon blinked even as Bones's chuckle grew wicked. "I don't know, but I'll be sure to ask him later."

Oops. Must've said that out loud. I cleared my throat, once again fighting to appear nonchalant, despite what all of us could still hear in graphic detail.

"Um, what *lovely* gardens in the back," I stammered. "I don't think we got a chance to check them out the last time we were here, Bones."

"We'll be back in round an hour," he told Gorgon,

raising his voice so more than the blond vampire could hear him. From the continued noises upstairs, I doubted Mencheres got the message, but I didn't stay around long enough to find out. I walked into the field behind the house, popping my iPod speakers back into my ears. With my pace and a few clicks of the volume, soon I could hear nothing but Norah crooning on about young blood and ghosts going home. Much better than listening to Bones's co-ruler and his girlfriend getting their freak on.

Bones caught up to me in a few long strides, not saying a word, though his twitching lips spoke volumes about how my discomfort amused him. Nothing embarrassed him, of course. Working as a gigolo for London's wealthy, bored wives had killed any shame in him long before becoming a vampire killed his humanity. This wasn't the first time I'd overheard people having sex, having preternatural hearing since I was a child. But this was *Mencheres*, the solemn, somewhat scary vampire whose extensive powers unnerved me ever since I'd first met him. So it was another shade of weird entirely, hearing him hoot and holler like, well, a normal person.

"At least he'll be in a good mood when we finally speak to him," I told Bones without taking my earpieces out.

He pulled me to him in response, his mouth covering mine before I could even formulate a word. A long, hungry kiss seemed to ignite flares along my nerve endings as his tongue caressed mine with deep strokes and tantalizing flicks. Lust filled my senses from my connection to him and my own response, a double punch to my emotions that made me arch against him despite my surprise.

"We'll be in a good mood, too," he murmured after taking the earphones out, then began to undo my jeans while his mouth burned a sensual trail down my neck.

My head fell back even as I sputtered out a protest. "You can't be serious. Someone could see."

The house was only about a hundred yards away from where we stood. Sure, it was dark out and the grass around us was high, but not that high! Anyone undead looking in this direction would be able to see what we were doing, not to mention they'd be able to hear us.

Bones's laugh was dark and decadent. "Of course I'm serious. Why do you think I said we wouldn't be back for an hour?"

His mouth slid up to mine again, kissing me with even more passion while working my jeans down enough to reach inside. It only took a few strokes of those knowing, skillful fingers for me to forget about our surroundings and sink to the ground with him, pulling at his pants with an impatience that bordered on urgency.

I hadn't really wanted to see the gardens, anyway.

Eleven

An hour and a half later, I sat on the sofa in the living room, petting a mastiff that thought he belonged on my lap instead of by my feet. If the dog weighed fifty pounds less, I would've let him, but he was bigger than I was.

Kira came into the room after a few minutes, her amber hair still wet from what had probably been a hasty shower. As a new vampire, she didn't blush at what had obviously kept them from greeting us when we first arrived, but she was almost effusive in her offers to get us something to drink. Bones took a whiskey but I politely declined while hiding a smile. Good to know I wasn't the only one who lacked the blasé attitude most vampires seemed to have about their sexual activities.

"Mencheres will be right down," Kira said for the second time, tucking a strand of hair behind her ear as she glanced up at the staircase.

"How's the Enforcer training going?" I asked her.

She brightened. The process that would eventually turn her into the vampiric version of a cop was Kira's favorite subject.

"Good." Then she laughed. "Though it would go better if Mencheres didn't keep telekinetically flinging people across the room every time they punched me a little too hard. He says it's an accidental slip of his power, but I'll have to ban him from my combat practice, or I'll never get past the first stage."

Those poor bastards are lucky they still have their heads, I thought, even as I returned her smile. Mencheres batting them around a room was almost a love tap compared to what he'd do if he really thought Kira was being roughed up too much by her trainers.

"Bones, Cat. My apologies for keeping you waiting."

Mencheres came into the room, his black hair also damp. He had on a long white garment that on a woman I'd call a shapeless dress, but on him somehow looked like a masculine form of leisure wear. He actually managed to sound sincere about keeping us waiting, too, even though I knew he wasn't sorry in the least. Not that I minded. In fact, I was pretty happy about their earlier delay, considering what it resulted in.

"Grandsire."

Bones rose, giving Mencheres a hug in greeting. I did, too, though with less affection than my husband. Recent events had Bones forgiving Mencheres for his sins of omission regarding my past, but I hadn't quite gotten over *all* my grudge against him.

Though if I were honest, I'd admit that even if I had, Mencheres would still creep me out a bit. Despite

Bones calling him Grandsire because Mencheres changed over the vampire who later turned Bones, appearance-wise, Mencheres looked like he was only in his early twenties. Appearances, however, were deceiving. Mencheres had been around longer than most civilizations existed, and his abilities were truly scary. I should know; I'd briefly absorbed some of those abilities after drinking his blood to aid my friends in a fight. It had knocked me out for a week straight afterward, my body fried from power overload. So some residual wariness around Mencheres wasn't too unreasonable, in my opinion.

"Please, sit." Mencheres gestured to the couch we'd recently vacated, playing the part of gracious host. His dog scooted closer as soon as I sat back down, putting his head in my lap for easier scratching access. Mencheres took a seat next to Kira, trailing his hand over her arm before returning his attention to us.

"I assume you're here because you have new information regarding Apollyon?"

Some part of me was amused at how staid and proper all of us must look right now, perched on our opposing couches with our very somber expressions. Just a group of vampires discussing a supernaturally dangerous situation with all the solemnity and gothic dignity it deserved, recent sexual indulgences notwithstanding.

"Only thing new is there is nothing new," Bones growled, taking a long swallow of his whiskey before continuing. "We're on our way to New Orleans to speak with Marie. With luck, we'll be able to convince her that Apollyon is as much of a threat to rational members of the ghoul nation as he is to us."

Mencheres nodded thoughtfully. "Marie Laveau would indeed be a powerful ally for whoever can sway her loyalties."

That was an understatement. The voodoo queen wasn't just the master of a large line of ghouls; she also ruled over an entire city, a feat no other undead person I knew of had accomplished. Therefore, the thought of anyone "swaying" her allegiances made me let out a snort.

"Marie's first loyalty is to herself, and if I were a betting woman, I'd say she's already made up her mind whether she's backing Apollyon or not. Our only shot is the fact that war would be bad for everyone involved, not just vampires. If Marie didn't always insist on face-to-face meetings, we could save time by just asking her over the phone. Or texting her."

Then the mental image of potentially getting a text from Marie reading "i kill u" made me laugh. Marie didn't mince words once she'd determined a course of action, so I wouldn't put such a thing past her.

Bones gave me an inquiring look, but I waved a hand.

"Never mind. Just my warped sense of humor. So, Mencheres, I don't suppose you've had any recent visions about where Apollyon's base of operations is, hmm? Or whether he'll whip the ghouls into the same hysterical frenzy as last time?"

He opened his mouth, but Kira beat him to it, her aura sparking and eyes flashing green. "Don't pressure him. He already feels guilty that he can't see anything about this."

I bit back the laugh that rose in my throat, feeling a similar wave of amusement sweep over Bones even though nothing changed in his expression. Kira's hackles rising in protectiveness for a vampire who could kill all of us without even getting up from his seat was just too funny. So was the quelling look Mencheres shot us before murmuring something soothing to her, obviously picking up on Bones's humor through their shared power connection, if not mine as well.

"You're right, Kira. Mencheres, I'm sorry," I said, managing to make my voice contrite despite my ribs aching with suppressed laughter. "Um, anyway, we wanted to give you guys a heads-up about where we're headed and why. You know, in case we're never heard from again."

I said the last part jokingly, but the grim reality was that it was true. Marie Laveau normally promised safe passage to and from any meetings with her, but with her being the *ghoul* queen of New Orleans, these circumstances with Apollyon made things a little different. She might decide it was in the best interest of her species to go back on her word just this once, and make our trip to the Big Easy a one-way journey.

"We will go with you," Mencheres stated.

"No," Bones replied softly. "You'll stay here protecting our line in case anything does happen. That way, our people will remain safe."

The faintest smile ghosted across Mencheres's lips. Bones had just repeated the same argument the Egyptian vampire used on him two months ago, when it had been Mencheres refusing Bones's help in a dangerous situation.

"Very well," he said, with a graceful tilt of his head. "I shall stay. Perhaps Spade can accompany you in my stead."

"There's a problem with that," I pointed out. "One, I know Bones's best friend, and Spade won't want Denise to go if it's dangerous, which it will be. Two, I know my best friend, and hell no will Denise agree to stay behind. Plus, all we need is for Apollyon to find out that Denise is now a shapeshifter for him to *really* have something to go batshit over."

I didn't add that if anyone found out what was in Denise's demonically altered blood, she would have even less of a chance at survival than I would if the vampire nation decided to offer me up to Apollyon. While Mencheres already knew and I didn't think Kira was untrustworthy, I didn't know how many other undead ears were in this house in addition to Gorgon.

"What about Vlad?" Kira asked. "He's tough and scary."

"Not the show hound," Bones grumbled, while at the same time I said, "Good idea."

His brows rose as he turned to me. I cleared my throat, squirming a little under that lasered brown gaze.

"Well, it is," I replied, straightening. "Just because you don't like him doesn't mean he's not our best bet, and while he might refuse to do it if it was just you going, odds are he'll say yes because I'll be there."

Bones's mouth twisted in a way that told me that wasn't the best argument I could've used. "Because we're friends," I quickly added. "Vlad's big on being there for his friends."

"I don't question Tepesh's taste in regarding you as a friend. Just yours for feeling the same way about him," Bones muttered.

I couldn't resist a slight grin. "Maybe because he reminds me of someone I love."

Bones snorted in disagreement, but out of the corner of my eye, I caught something he didn't—Mencheres's wink at me. It startled me so much that I whipped my head around to stare at him, but by the time I did, the vampire's expression was as smooth and impenetrable as a pond at midnight.

"Tepesh doesn't need to go with us," Bones said at last. "His presence could be construed as a threat by Marie since she knows damn well he and I don't fancy each other. If he's in a nearby city, however, that would be close enough for him to provide assistance, should we require it."

Considering Vlad could fly, if it wasn't close enough, then we were screwed anyway. But I didn't say that out loud. Everyone here already knew it.

TWELVE

THE RITZ-CARLTON HOTEL WAS LOCATED on the very edge of the French Quarter, facing Canal Street. Its exterior was a beautiful combination of modern architecture and old-style Southern influence, with white plaster and carved lion gargoyles adorning the building. As we checked in, the staff was polite to the point of obsequiousness, making me want to tell them to relax; I wasn't that hard to please. Only when I'd stayed at Vlad's house had my ass been so thoroughly kissed, and the management here didn't have a reputation for expressing displeasure with their people by impaling them on long wooden poles. At least, not that I knew of.

Once inside the elevator leading up to our floor, however, I understood the reason for the employees' over-the-top graciousness. If the fur-clad woman next to me had her nose any higher in the air, she'd get altitude sickness—and really, who wore a full-length fur coat in the *summer*time, anyway? The man with her, her husband, I deduced from their matching rings, also looked like a stick took up permanent residence in his ass. She gave me a cool glance, her gaze traveling over my windblown hair and somewhat unkempt appearance with a disdain that took me right back to my days as a small-town outcast. Hey, for riding straight through from Chicago to New Orleans on a motorcycle, I looked pretty damn good. Nary a bug in my teeth or anything.

A slight sniff accompanied her turning away to whisper, "Clientele here seems to have slipped," to her husband, loud enough that even without supernatural hearing, I would've heard her. My teeth ground together while I reminded myself that mesmerizing her into believing her ass had just grown by five sizes was *not* a mature thing to do.

The elevator doors opened in the next moment, thankfully on the couple's floor. As they exited, Bones gave the husband a bland smile.

"She's rogering the plumber every Thursday while you're at the club. Did you really think your loo needed repairs four times this past month?"

The woman let out a shocked gasp even as her husband's face became mottled.

"You told me he was laying pipe, Lucinda!"

Bones grunted. "Right you are, mate."

The doors closed just as the woman began to sputter out an indignant, yet unconvincing, denial. My jaw still swung open at the whole exchange.

"Bones!" I finally managed.

"Serves the sow right for what she was thinking about you, and he was no better" was his unrepentant reply. "Now they'll have something else to occupy their time aside from looking down their noses at people."

Part of me was horrified at what he'd done, while another, less charitable part cackled shamelessly. God, the look on that woman's face! She'd had "busted" written all over her formerly haughty expression.

"Not like I broke some poor, innocent bloke's heart, either," Bones went on. "He's shagging his barrister. Pair of them deserve each other."

"This just reinforces my opinion that I don't want mind-reading powers," I said, shaking my head. "I never need to pick up on things like that from other people's heads."

The elevator doors opened again, our floor this time. Bones's hand rested lightly on my back as we walked to our room. Once inside, my jaw dropped again. This wasn't a hotel room; it was the size of a house. I slowly looked around at the gorgeous hardwood floors, Oriental rugs, elegant antique furnishings, a dining room complete with crystal chandelier, ornate family room with gilded fireplace, floor-to-ceiling glass doors that afforded a view of the Mississippi River and the outdoor courtyard—and I hadn't even gotten to the bedroom yet. The other time we'd come to New Orleans, we'd stayed at Bones's town house in the Quarter, but we knew that would be the first place anyone looked for us, so checking into a hotel seemed safer.

Though a lot more expensive, judging from all the finery around me.

"Did we win the lottery and you forgot to tell me?"

He flashed me a grin as he tossed his jacket onto a nearby chair. "Know one of the advantages of being mates with a vampire who used to get regular visions of the future? Two words, luv. Investment advice."

I laughed even as I shrugged out of my own leather coat. "Now I have another reason to hope Mencheres's visions get back to full strength."

"Even so." He sauntered over, brushing my hair back from my face. "We have time to wash up and change, but don't get too comfortable. We're going out."

My brows furrowed. "I thought we weren't seeing Marie until tomorrow night."

"We're not." Bones brushed the barest of kisses across my lips. "Tonight, we have other plans."

I looked at the river several stories below me, wondering if this was some sort of joke. The bridge I stood atop of—under construction and therefore empty of commuters—swayed slightly in the breeze, or maybe that was just a result of me clutching the beam next to me too hard.

"Say again?" I called down to Bones. He stood at the bottom of the bridge, having flown there after dropping me off on the overhanging beam with only one word of explanation that I *must* have misheard.

"Jump," he repeated. No, I hadn't misheard him before.

I glanced back at the swirling waters of the Mississippi below. "If this is your way of saying you want a divorce . . ."

"You couldn't drown if you tried," he countered in amusement. "You haven't breathed for necessity in almost a year. Now quit dithering and jump. It's the best way for you to learn how to fly."

"Sounds like a really good way for me to learn how to *fall* while *screaming* instead."

He grabbed two of the metal support beams under my section and rattled them. The subsequent vibrations were so strong that I let out a yelp while my grip on the rod next to me increased until it creaked. Damn him. He knew I didn't like heights.

"Ghouls can't fly, which gives vampires who can a large advantage over them," he called up. "I want you able to fly before we meet Marie tomorrow night, just in case we need to make a quick escape. You've flown twice before, which means you have the ability. You just need to sharpen it."

"I didn't fly, I just jumped very high," I corrected him, still holding on for dear afterlife. "I don't even know how I did it."

"Your instincts kicked in under duress. Falling from this height should make you experience similar duress, allowing those instincts to take over again," he replied with more calm than was fair. "Come on, Kitten, jump. Or I'll throw you off."

"You throw me off this bridge, Bones, and you'll have a *lot* of celibacy in your future!"

His lips curled in a way that said he wasn't worried. "Only means I'd have to work harder to change your mind, and you know how I love my work. Now quit stalling. If you're still up there in five minutes, I'm tossing you off."

I slowly uncurled my death grip from the beam. He'd do just what he said, and if I knew Bones, he'd already started the countdown. While common sense said he was right about his reasons for me learning to fly—plus, true, jumping couldn't kill me even if I belly flopped into the Mississippi—I still cursed him as I edged away from the beam.

"Sneaky, manipulating, merciless bloodsucker . . ."

A chuckle drifted up to me. "Pillow talk already? You'll have me hard before we're even back in our room."

"Well, I hope your hard self enjoys flogging the bishop tonight!" I snapped.

His laughter only increased. "Really, luv, I'm impressed. Wherever did you learn such a salty expression?"

I was a few feet away from the beam I'd held on to, nothing nearby to grasp anymore and only my balance keeping me from tumbling into the dark waters below. Jeez, it really was a long way down.

"From Spade. He was helping Denise brush up on her English slang."

"Ah, of course. Only three minutes left now, Kitten."

I looked out at the city's lights winking across the other side of the bridge, trying to steady my nerves. Even in the dark, I could see the buildings lining the water clearly. Every now and then, spectral forms caught my eye, ghosts seamlessly moving in and out of them and other structures as they went about their phantomy business. New Orleans truly was one of the most haunted places in the world, with more sentient ghosts than anywhere else I'd ever seen. Hell, this was where we'd adopted Fabian from.

"Final minute, luv. No more stalling," Bones said relentlessly.

Bastard. I straightened my shoulders, took in a deep breath for courage, and then sprang off the ledge of the bridge as if it were a diving board. Instantly my eyes watered with the sting of air whipping at them. Even though I knew this wouldn't kill me, a rush of panic still filled me as nothing happened except me falling faster toward the river. Almost madly, I began to windmill my arms, as if by doing that they'd suddenly sprout feathers and wing me away. This strategy of his wasn't working! I wasn't flying; I was falling like a dropped brick. God, I'd hit that water any moment . . .

My whole body braced for impact when I felt a whoosh and distance abruptly began to grow between me and the river. For a split second, I thought Bones had caught me, deciding at the last moment not to let me crash into the water after all. But just as quickly, I realized I didn't feel the hard pressure of his arms. No, I felt nothing but the oddest sensation of air cushioning me, like invisible jets had magically appeared to propel me upward. A glance down proved I was now dozens of feet above the river, moving upward with every passing moment, nothing supporting me except those pulsating currents of air.

A wild grin split my face. *Holy shit, I was doing it! I was actually flying!* That former panic at once turned to elation. I was flying and it was the most *amazing* feeling. Far, far superior to the occasional dreams I'd had where I could soar without explanation or practice. The air continued to feel different, too. Like it had form that I could mold and manipulate. No longer empty space, but a canvas of opportunities and exhilaration instead.

I looked around, trying to spot where Bones was, when just as suddenly as I'd risen, I began to fall. My arms started doing that mad flapping again, but this time, nothing happened. A dull resignation filled me as I saw the distance disappear between me and the river. *Good thing Bones has my leather jacket* was my last thought before I landed into the river with a tremendous splash.

The jolt went through my body like a roundhouse kick. My momentum plunged me several feet under water and I came up spitting out the mouthful I'd accidentally sucked in when I gasped at the impact. Bones's face was the first thing I saw when I resurfaced. He hovered a few feet above me like a beautiful apparition, staring at me with a grin.

"Told you jumping off that bridge would flare up your instincts enough for you to fly."

I gave a pointed look at the less-than-aromatic river I was floating in. "Yeah, but I'm still in the water, so it didn't work as well as you thought it would."

His grin widened. "Never said it wouldn't take practice before you learned how to keep from crashing."

I lunged for him, determined to plunge him into the water with me, but he neatly avoided my grab, chuckling. Then he hauled me out of the river by my shoulders. An expertly controlled glide later— *showoff*—and I was back on the top of the bridge, soaking the metal ledge with my waterlogged clothes.

"All right. Again," Bones stated.

I glanced down at the river and then back at him, noticing he was far enough away to avoid any other attempts I might make at grabbing him. *Before we're done tonight*, I promised him silently, *you're taking a dip in that water with me.* Necessity might have prompted him to insist on this extreme form of flying lesson, but his smirk said Bones was getting a kick out of seeing me splat into the river while I struggled to find my vampiric wings.

"I'd forgotten how much you used to enjoy giving me a hard time in training. Take every cheap shot, every low blow, right?"

His grin became more wicked, confirming my guess. "Be harder to stress you into flying now that you've already jumped once. Might have to throw you off to get your blood up enough this time."

"Don't even *think* about it," I warned him.

A brow arched. "That a dare, Kitten?"

He was somehow on the other side of me, moving with a lightning quickness that left me no defense. I felt an instant's strong grasp, a push—and then I was tumbling end over end toward the river, my curses flowing as fast as the wind and rapidly approaching water.

"Goddammit, I'm going to get you for this! You just wait until I get my hands on you—"

"Sticks and stones, luv," I heard him call out in reply. Then I smashed into the river, cutting off more of my furious rampage. I came up sputtering again, seeing Bones hovering over me, this time without even bothering to hold back his laughter.

"You look like a drowned rat. Perhaps you should try less flapping and more concentrating next time."

"You are *so* going to pay," I swore, lunging at him.

"If you want your revenge, come and get it," he taunted, flying just out of my reach as I continued to swim toward him.

My gaze narrowed. He wanted to play games, huh? Well, maybe I'd forgotten how much he enjoyed being a hard-ass in training, but *he'd* obviously forgotten that I was a fast learner. *You've flown twice before, which means you have the ability. You just need to sharpen it*, he'd said just a short while ago.

Oh, I'd sharpen it. Right now.

I channeled all my plans for paybacks into picturing the air above me as a ladder I could climb, if I could make it solid in my mind. Bones continued to fly in tight circles above me, asking how I enjoyed my evening bath and pondering that it must not be true that cats didn't like water. I ignored those witticisms, continuing to picture the air as something that was malleable.

Energy began to push against my skin, building until it thrummed with the same steadiness that my heartbeat once pulsed inside me. *Remember how the air felt before. It's* not *empty space. It's something you can shape and mold, propelling you up and after him, if you just concentrate hard enough . . .*

When I felt the air above me pulsating in time to the energy in my body, I vaulted straight up out of the water. Bones was in the middle of his next pass over me and I barreled after him even though he yanked himself backward at the last second. That exultant feeling returned, like a shock of adrenaline to my system, as I felt the air bend to my will, allowing me the momentum and support to catch him with an aerial tackle that flipped both of us around.

And then, with a victorious snicker, I tightened my grip and tumbled us into the river, his answering laugh the last thing I heard before the water closed over us.

Thirteen

"Now I know why you chose a room located all by itself on the roof," I remarked as Bones dropped us down in a graceful landing on the outside courtyard of our suite. After several hours of practicing, I probably could've managed to land myself, but I might have taken out some of the wrought-iron furniture in the process.

"Comes in right handy now," he said, with a meaningful glance at his ripped pants and shirt, casualties of my midair grab on him before. Between that, our wet clothes, and our dripping hair, we'd give any snooty patrons of the hotel a heart attack if we took the normal way in through the lobby.

I smirked. "Told you I'd get you back."

His laugh was its own caress on my senses. Even wet and smelling like a stinky river, Bones still managed to entice me. His clothes might be ripped and his leather jacket dripping water, but he made that look sexy. Maybe because being waterlogged meant his pants and shirt clung to all the lines of his body with explicit snugness, highlighting the lean muscles and hard planes like they'd been molded onto him.

He leaned down. "Dare I hope that vengeance was sufficient enough to make you forget your other vow of retribution?"

My hands trailed over his chest, pausing near his nipples, which were rigid due to his wet clothes—or because he knew how those tight buds practically screamed to be touched. Without conscious thought, I licked my lips.

"And let you go back on your promise to work hard to change my mind?" I couldn't keep the husky catch from my voice. "That wouldn't be smart of me, would it?"

He moved closer, pressing his chest more firmly against my hands until I could feel all the play of his muscles as his arms rose to encircle me.

"No, not smart at all," he murmured, his breath landing on exactly the right spot near my ear.

I closed my eyes, savoring the sensations rising in me. Then I pushed him away and began digging in my pants. Just a short distance away from us was a bedroom. That's where we needed to be, and the sooner the better.

"Hope the room card didn't fall out . . . ah, thank God for button pockets," I said, pulling out my card. This outdoor courtyard had key card entry access, though I'd bet it hadn't been used as the first way into the room before.

But when I went to the exterior door, Bones following closely enough for his energy to throb along my back, nothing happened when I pressed the card to the slot. I did it again, double-checking that the arrow was in the right position. It was, but still no green light.

"Try yours," I said, frowning.

After a few moments, Bones had his card out and in the correct position, but several tries later, the door still didn't open.

"Getting them wet must've shorted the magnetic strip," he said, shrugging. "Wait here. I'll go back through the lobby and let you in once I've gotten new cards."

"Dressed like that?" I asked with a laugh. "I should let you just because I'll crack up imagining the looks on people's faces, but I'll go. I might be just as wet as you, but at least my clothes aren't ripped half off, and my jacket's dry because you left it by the bridge before I pulled you into the river."

"I don't care what any of those toffs think," he replied dismissively.

No matter that I'd done far more questionable things myself in recent months, shades of my rigid upbringing insisted that one did *not* appear with indecent gaps in their clothing in public if one could avoid it. I tried another tactic.

"Come on, have mercy on any older women who might be in the lobby. You don't want to give them heart attacks if they catch a glimpse of your goods," I teased, trailing my fingers down the front of his torn pants.

His hand closed around mine, bringing it flush up against the goods in question. Things low inside me clenched in response, drawing a short moan. God, feeling him grow thick and hard in my grip almost ended my control right there. It was all I could do not to drop to my knees and replace my hand with my mouth.

"I'm leaving," I said, the words hoarse from the willpower it took for me to pull my hand away. "I won't be long."

His eyes were bright green, matching the hunger in his expression, fangs tantalizing me from underneath those perfectly sculpted lips.

"Hurry."

I jumped off the roof without even looking to make sure someone wasn't below me until I'd almost reached the ground. Good thing it was almost four in the morning, late even for most of this city's residents to be out and about.

Then I rounded the corner and went into the Ritz, giving a brief nod to the doorman. One short elevator ride later and I was in the lobby, pretending not to notice the surprised looks the employees gave my wet hair and shoes. I pulled out my driver's license—fake, but registered to the same last name Bones booked this room under—and explained my room key was somehow not working. While I waited for my new cards, a man checked in, holding a sleeping little girl in one arm while awkwardly signing his forms with the other. From his hushed voice, it was obvious he was hoping to have her in bed before she woke, and after hearing his weary comment about airport delays, it was also obvious he was just as tired.

I got my new cards at the same time the employee finished checking the man in, so we waited for the elevator together. He blinked a little at the drips of water that pooled at my feet when we stepped into the elevator, but said nothing.

"Tripped and fell in a big puddle," I whispered.

"Ah" was his equally quiet reply. At least he didn't give me the same kind of stink eye that the fur-wearing, plumber-banging older woman had.

We'd gone up about ten floors when all of a sudden a booming noise preceded the elevator shuddering like we were caught in an earthquake. The man staggered and I grabbed him so he wouldn't accidentally drop the little girl, who awoke with a cry. I had a split second of confusion before dread slid up my spine. Supernatural energy filled the air, coming from the top of the elevator, where moments ago, it sounded as if a boulder had dropped on us.

Except boulders didn't drop from nice hotels onto elevators, and they also didn't make ominous growling noises.

Oh shit, I thought, right before I heard the first cable snap.

"Get in the corner!" I ordered, shoving the man when he just stood there.

"What's going on?" he shouted. His little girl began to wail. The elevator shuddered again, this time accompanied by a horrible whipping noise that sounded like another cable being ripped away. At the same time, pounding began on the roof of the car. I ignored that, plunging my hands into the seam in the elevator doors hard enough to bloody my fingers before shoving them apart. A slab of concrete and steel met my vision, no open spaces to escape through. The elevator was suspended between floors, but not for long, judging from the latest snapping sound.

"Oh God, what *is* that?" the man screamed.

Metal, plaster, and glass rained down on us as a

hole appeared in the roof where none had been before. A ghoul's face came into view, a savage smile lighting his features as he spotted me.

"Reaper," he hissed.

I pushed the man aside just in time to knock him away from the ghoul's grasping hands as he lunged for me.

"Get down!" I yelled, trying to fight off the ghoul while standing under the hole he'd torn open. If the ghoul got inside, both father and daughter would be dead in seconds, and that's only if they were lucky enough for the elevator not to drop before then.

Pain slashed across my arms and face, red immediately coloring my gaze. *He's got a knife. A* silver *knife,* I realized, judging from the burn it left on my skin. I tried to avoid that flashing blade while still keeping the ghoul from dropping into the elevator. Another snapping noise and the car dropped a few feet before coming to an abrupt stop, metal groaning under the strain of a last brake kicking in to hold the elevator up.

But one good thing had come out of the elevator's fall. Now, shiny steel doors took up part of the concrete and metal wall. The car had dropped halfway to the opening of a new floor.

"Pull those doors open and get out now!" I shouted, a crimson-filled glance revealing that the man was crouched in the same spot as before, clutching his daughter while gaping up at us.

He still couldn't seem to tear his gaze away. Dammit, he was in shock, and it wouldn't be long before either the ghoul got into the elevator or the strain of two supernaturals fighting proved too much for the last emergency brake. I braced my arms on the support railings lining the car, using them for leverage as I flipped upside down and then kicked the ghoul with everything I had. The railings broke, landing me on my ass with enough force to make the elevator shake dangerously again, but for the moment, the ghoul was gone from the hole in the roof.

I wrenched those doors open and yanked the sobbing little girl from her father's arms, shoving her through the space. She landed on the adjoining floor with a cry that filled me with joy, because while she might be bruised, she was now also safe. Before I could shove her father through the same opening, however, a roar filled the air as the ghoul jumped through the hole in the roof and landed in the elevator with us.

The elevator shook hard enough that I felt sure it would drop. I didn't have time to reach in my coat for my weapons, but ran headlong into the ghoul, knocking him away from the man. Amidst the screeching of metal, the man's screams, and the solid thumps of the ghoul and me crashing around the elevator locked in a death struggle, I heard something else. An enraged English snarl.

"Come here you bloody *bastards*!"

I had a split second of dizzying relief. Bones was here, so the father and I would make it out of this. If I wasn't worried about keeping the ghoul away from the huddled man—a careless stomp or swipe from the flesh-eater would snap his neck like a twig—I could've gone for my weapons and evened the odds a little. But my relief vanished in the next instant as a loud cracking noise preceded the ground dropping beneath my feet.

Oh Jesus. The elevator was falling!

Everything around me shook with terrible vibrations as the velocity lifted us up a few inches before gravity had my feet back on the floor. The ghoul flashed me a hate-filled grin even as the man screamed so loudly it briefly drowned out the noises from the free-falling elevator. The ghoul and I could survive the crash, though no doubt the ghoul would try his damnedest to make sure my survival didn't last much beyond that. The father, however, would be dead in moments.

The ghoul lunged at me, ripping his silver knife through the air toward my heart. I didn't raise my arms to block him, but moved to the left at the last second. That blade buried into my chest, spearing through my flesh with flames of anguish, but not piercing my heart. At the same time, I shoved the ghoul down and to the side, aiming for the flashes of light that appeared between the partially open elevator doors as we fell with even greater speed.

A crunching sound accompanied the ghoul's entire body going limp as the rapidly passing floors and tight space acted as a crude guillotine. I didn't waste a moment to savor my victory, but pulled the knife out of my chest and grabbed the man, tucking as much of his head into my bloody torso as I could. Then, still bent over him, I vaulted myself upward with all my strength.

White-hot agony slicing through my body made me barely register the crescendo of noise that followed. Dust, glass, and blood filled my gaze, making it almost impossible for me to see. *Up* was my primary thought, followed closely by *Don't him let go!* Several hard objects slammed into me and I blinked furiously, trying to clear my gaze while keeping my grip on the man. Those bone-crunching jolts could be more ghouls trying to kill me, or parts of the elevator shaft I crashed into as I blindly propelled us away from the explosion of debris as the elevator smashed on impact below.

"Kitten!"

Bones's shout gave me a frame of reference. Then shadows became solid objects as my gaze cleared with nosferatu quickness. Red still colored my vision, but I didn't need to see in more colors than that to know that I'd gotten us out of the elevator with probably only a second to spare. My back still flamed as it healed, but at least I could straighten now, even if it did feel like I'd just had my spine readjusted with a bulldozer.

"I'm okay," I called out, not seeing Bones, but judging he was fighting from the sounds above. Last thing he needed was to be distracted wondering if I'd bought the farm in the crash. My upward velocity began to slow while I looked for anywhere safe to set the man.

There. A small lip between the floors marking where the elevator would stop, if it wasn't in pieces below. I adjusted my hold on the man, carrying him with one arm while reaching for that tiny ledge with the other. I grabbed it, dangling both of us a couple stories above the wreckage of the elevator. He was limp, but his heart still beat, thankfully. I kept my grasp on him and the narrow ledge while I swung a leg up, wedging my foot between the split in the doors that protected those waiting for an elevator from the dangers of the shaft on the other side. Then, gritting my teeth at the awkward position, I kicked out, pushing those steel walls open.

When they were big enough for the man's bulk to fit through, I swung him up, gently pushing his prone form through the opening. No one was around, but it wouldn't be long until someone found him. With the thunderous noise of the elevator crashing, the hotel would have all hands on deck as quickly as possible to see if anyone was injured. Being propelled through the top of the elevator left broken bones and slashes all over him, even with my body taking the brunt of the abuse. But he was alive, and so was his little girl. That was the best I could do for them.

Then I stood on tippy toes and forced the doors closed again. As soon as they were shut, I leapt from narrow ledge to the remains of the dangling elevator cable, moving swiftly now that I didn't have the man to protect and my injuries had finished healing.

"Where do you think you're going?" Bones's voice hissed before more noise boomed through the shaft and light debris rained down on me. Then a body sailed at me from above, outdistancing its detached head by about a dozen feet. Neither piece was Bones, so I sent up a quick prayer of thanks while swinging to the left to avoid it hitting me. I didn't call out to him again, not wanting to alert my presence to any more ghouls who might be waiting in this shaft. With Bones's furious energy filling up the space, it was hard to feel if anyone else undead was here.

I climbed even faster, not wanting to try flying again yet. First, I might be healed, but I felt weaker from using my body to make an elevator escape hatch large enough for two people to fit though, and I still hadn't mastered the art of not crashing when I flew.

If I barreled into Bones while he was in the midst of a fight, that could have awful consequences. Even if I couldn't hear the sounds of battle, which I could, I'd still know that he was locked in combat. Seething, deadly purpose washed over my subconscious, mixed with flashes of pain followed closely by exhilaration. Whatever was going on, Bones was winning, because I felt no fear emanating from him.

Another series of loud thumps later and then his voice drifted down from the top of the shaft.

"Kitten?"

"I'm almost there," I called out, doubling my efforts. I reached the top level where Bones was less than a minute later, heaving myself through the man-shaped hole in the wall that had bloodstains around it. Probably made by the headless ghoul right before his free fall through the shaft. That must've been the boom I'd heard before his body came sailing by.

Bones's back was to me. His coat was gone, which showed that his clothes were even more ripped than the last time I'd seen him, and he was on his knees restraining a ghoul underneath him. Their faces were close together while the man's legs kicked out on either side of Bones's hips in a macabre parody of passion. Despite the stress of the past several minutes—or maybe because of it—I burst out laughing.

"Do you two need a few minutes alone?" I managed.

"Oh, we'll have time alone very soon. Won't we, mate?" Bones drew out in a voice that dripped with menace. "Kitten, I need both hands for this bloke, so put your arms around my neck and hold on."

I did, locking my arms firmly under his chin. Bones bent his head to press a single kiss to them before the air thickened with power and he flung himself upward, flying us through the damaged service hallway and out of the hotel.

Less than thirty minutes later, we flew toward a two-story house that was located about a mile off the main road bordering a dense swamp. Frankly, I didn't know how Bones found the place, but he never hesitated in his direction. I could see about half a dozen people standing in guard formation outside the house, and they all looked up at us as we drew closer.

Bones didn't bother with his usual graceful landing. He set us down hard enough to leave a crack in the driveway. The guards formed a loose circle around us, their weapons drawn but not firing, clearly waiting for instructions. That came in the form of the front door swinging open and a lean, bearded vampire striding out. His long brown hair swung with his rapid steps, while blue flames swirled up his arms, somehow not singeing a stitch of his clothes.

Then the vampire stopped as he saw us.

"Bones. Cat." A sardonic smile quirked Vlad Tepesh's mouth as he took in Bones's partially clad state, the grip he had around the ghoul's throat, and my own bloodstained clothes. "How nice of you to drop in."

Fourteen

I LET GO OF BONES, ALLOWING HIM GREATER range of motion to handle the ghoul. He was probably glad not to have me throttling him anymore, even though he didn't need to breathe.

"This sod has answers I require," Bones stated crisply to Vlad as he flung the ghoul face-first onto the concrete drive, jumping on his back before he could even attempt to scramble away.

I gave Vlad a small wave as Bones proceeded to make more dents in the driveway using the ghoul's face. "We, ah, got jumped by ghouls at our hotel and he's the last one left alive," I said by way of explanation.

"They attacked you inside the city?" Vlad gave the ghoul an intrigued look, not appearing concerned with the damage inflicted on the driveway even though I made a mental note to cut him a check. "Marie didn't go back on her word of safe passage, did she?"

"That's my first question," Bones said, grinding the ghoul's face against a jagged edge of concrete. "Did the queen of New Orleans send you?"

"Fuck you," the ghoul spat.

Why did he have to say that? Now things were going to get *really* unpleasant.

"Do you want to do this the bloody way, or the fast one?" Vlad asked, looking them over with cool detachment as Bones resumed making a hole in the driveway with the ghoul's face.

"Can't say I care how I get my answers, as long as I do," Bones replied curtly, banging the ghoul's face again for emphasis.

"Hmm. Hold him, but not too close."

Bones grasped the ghoul's arm in a grip that steel wouldn't break, but jumped off his back. Vlad walked over to the ghoul and ruffled his hair, almost a friendly gesture. Then he returned to my side. In the few short steps that took, flames began licking up the ghoul's legs, blackening his clothes and skin. The ghoul screamed. I couldn't suppress a grimace of remembrance. I'd been burned before, and it hurt worse than even being stabbed with silver.

"Feeling more talkative now?" Vlad asked, barely discernible above the ghoul's shrieks. "You continue to stay silent and I'll cook your frank and beans next."

The ghoul yanked at his arm in a frantic attempt to get away, but as I'd suspected, Bones's grip didn't even budge. What did surprise me was the ghoul throwing the rest of his body in the opposite direction so hard that more than his shirt ripped.

Bones didn't share any of my qualms about suddenly holding an arm that wasn't attached to a body anymore. He just grabbed the ghoul by his other arm and began thumping him over the head with the loose limb. I'd heard Bones threaten to beat someone with their own limb before, but I'd always assumed that was a figure of speech. Apparently not.

"Did Marie send you?" Bones snarled, keeping away from the flames climbing higher up the ghoul's legs. *There go the frank and beans*, I thought with a wince.

"Majestic knows nothing of this—aarrrghhh!"

"He's being cooperative now, ease up on the flaming," I said to Vlad.

The man whose history inspired the world's most famous vampire novel gave me a jaded look.

"You call that cooperative? I call it barely getting his attention."

"Vlad . . ." I drew out.

"Spoilsport," he muttered.

The fire ebbed on the ghoul's lower body at the same rate as it disappeared from Vlad's hands. I shivered, remembering what having that power felt like after drinking Vlad's blood. If I were honest, I'd admit it had been tantalizing and terrifying. To suddenly have all your anger flow out of you in streams of fire had been as overwhelming to my senses as my newfound ability to fly. Trouble was, just like all the powers I borrowed through blood, I couldn't control it. I might have blown an enemy to fiery smithereens, but I'd also set Bones on fire by accident.

"You make me burn you again and I'll forget that I care about her opinion," Vlad said to the ghoul so casually, he might have been commenting on the weather.

"Marie didn't send you after Cat?" Bones asked, giving the ghoul a final whap with his severed arm before throwing the shriveling limb aside.

The ghoul's blue eyes met mine. He might look no older than me in human years, but to be strong enough to keep from babbling out his name, rank, and serial number as soon as Bones began working on him, he had to be old.

"Majestic did not know our intent," he said, calling Marie by the ostentatious name she preferred.

Bones cast a look at the sky. "It'll be dawn soon. If I'm not in bed with my wife by then because I'm still dealing with your worthless arse, I'll be in a very foul mood. So you'd best reconsider lying to me. Else I'll send her inside and do things to you that you'll be too horrified to want to live through."

I actually blanched at the coldness in Bones's tone, not to mention the whole "send her inside" part, but Vlad's mouth curled in what looked like grudging appreciation.

"Majestic did not know," the ghoul repeated, more emphatically this time. "We planned to leave the city afterward to avoid her wrath for striking a guest without her permission."

"Oh, she'd be right brassed off at you, if you're telling the truth," Bones agreed. Then his grip tightened ominously. "But I'm still not convinced. If you're not doing her bidding, who sent you?"

"We sent ourselves," the ghoul rasped.

"Kitten." Bones's voice was so flat it was terrifying. "Go inside."

"Now wait a minute," I began, even as the ghoul shouted, "It's true! We cannot allow Apollyon to incite our species to war!"

My brows rose at that. I'd assumed if Marie hadn't sent him, he must be one of Apollyon's ghouls, but it didn't sound like he was a fan.

"Who's we?" Bones asked, tracing his fingers almost delicately over the ghoul's regenerating skin where Vlad had burned him. Even that light touch generated a harsh gasp from the flesh-eater before he spoke.

"Those like me who know Apollyon seeks war for his own gain, not for any benefit to our species." The ghoul tossed a hard look my way. "Apollyon was denied his coup centuries ago when the other half-breed was killed, so now he forbids his supporters from harming her. If we're to stop him before his madness infects too many of my people, she must die."

Bones crashed the ghoul's skull into the driveway hard enough for a hunk of it to fly off, clattering like a grisly mini Frisbee not far from my feet. I looked away, rubbing my temple with a sudden weariness that had nothing to do with the approaching dawn. It shouldn't surprise me that more than the vampire nation might seek my death to avoid war, but I hadn't anticipated things to progress this far so soon. I'd also assumed Apollyon wanted me dead. Silly me should have realized my death didn't fit into his grand scheme of species dominance. No wonder his ghouls avoided Bones and me when we were out trolling in Ohio. We were the safest vampires in the state, if Apollyon had forbidden his people from harming me.

"Why is Apollyon so convinced ghouls would win in a war against vampires, anyway?" I asked, still rubbing my temple. "No offense, but from what I've seen, fangers have some distinct advantages over flesh-eaters."

The ghoul still seemed a little dazed from the recent blow to his head, but he managed to answer me.

"Ghouls are harder to kill than vampires with your fragility to silver. But most importantly, since her sire is dead, Majestic no longer has loyalty to the vampire world. Should the ghoul nation go to war, she will now side with her people instead of vampires."

Vlad let out a short laugh. "Your brains must not have fully regenerated if you think one ghoul alone can win the war."

"I don't know if Majestic's aid can cause us to win," the ghoul replied, sounding as weary as I felt in that moment. "Apollyon believes it can. But my brethren believe both sides would suffer unimaginable losses if we warred, and after that, how could anyone be considered a winner?"

A part of me empathized with the ghoul. He understood what a lot of people didn't—that if you had to nearly destroy everyone on both sides to win a war, then it wasn't a victory. He wasn't blindly driven by a lust for power like Apollyon; in fact, in his own twisted way, this ghoul and the others from the hotel had been trying to save lives. I might not care for their strategy, but their motivations were far better than those of other hit men who'd been after me.

"Aside from your dead mates back at the hotel, how many others make up this vigilante group of yours?" Bones asked, his expression still hard as ever. A glance at Vlad revealed equal coldness. Looked like I was the only one feeling sorry for my would-be assassin.

The ghoul smiled. With the still-healing rent in his head, it wasn't a pretty sight. "We were assigned to small groups, never knowing anyone outside our immediate division so that if one of us were captured, we couldn't betray our brothers."

Great. Someone smart had masterminded this cadre of killers out for my head. Maybe I should add shopping for tombstones to my To Do list. Was it Kennedy who said if an assassin was willing to give his or her life for a kill, there was no real way to defend against it? If so, he'd sadly had his own theory proved, too.

"How did you know where we were?" Bones went on.

The ghoul's gaze slid to me again. "We heard you were meeting with Majestic. We watched the airport, the docks, train station, and bridges. There are only a limited number of ways into New Orleans. We followed you to the hotel when you rode in. Without your helmet, you were recognizable, even if she was not."

"Told you helmets were safer," I couldn't help but mutter.

Bones gave me a look before hauling the ghoul up to his feet. "Right, then. If you've nothing else useful to tell me—"

"Let him go," I said to Bones, who'd already hooked an arm around the ghoul's neck with obvious deadly intent. "There's no reason to kill him."

His arm quit tightening, but both brows rose. "You're putting me on?"

"No." I came closer, giving the ghoul a measured look. "We don't want war, either. That's why we're going to stop Apollyon before things get to that point, but we'll do it without offering up my head. Maybe you can find those other groups and tell them we're on the same side."

Then I returned my attention to Bones. "Killing him isn't going to help anything. While I'd be glad if I never saw him again, in his own way, he was just trying to protect his people."

Bones let go of the ghoul with a muttered "Move and you're dead," before closing the last few feet that separated us. His hands settled gently on my shoulders.

"Look, luv, you can sympathize with the plonker's motivations all you want, but the fact remains that—"

I smelled smoke right before hearing the "pop," like a firecracker had gone off. Splatters of something thick coated my back even as a thud reverberated behind me. I whirled around to gape at what was left of the ghoul. His body pitched forward on the driveway, nothing but a smoldering mess left where his head had been.

Much slower, I turned around to see Vlad examining his fingernails, as if his hands weren't still ablaze in the flames that had blasted the ghoul's head off moments before.

"What the hell was *that*?" I gasped.

"Premature inflamulation," he replied. "Happens sometimes. Very embarrassing, I don't like to talk about it."

A snort of amusement came from my right. I swung in that direction to see Bones bestow the most approving look on Vlad he'd ever given him. Then his expression sobered as he met my gaze.

"This is some sort of joke to you two?" I asked sharply, waving at the ghoul's still smoking body. "We had a chance to *maybe* spread some goodwill among people who hate Apollyon as much as we do. You know, my enemy's enemy is my friend and all that? But no, you guys think a barbecue is a better way to go about it!"

"If you'd let him free, he wouldn't have told stories praising your generosity," Vlad replied, his coppery green gaze remorseless. "He would've gone back to his zealot friends with the happy news that you're a sentimental fool, inciting them to redouble their efforts to kill you. Quit applying human rules to undead power plays, Cat. You won't like the results."

Bones said nothing, but a glance at his face confirmed that he agreed with every word. My fists clenched as angry despair welled up in me. Dammit, why did it always have to come down to taking the bloodiest road or risking death and defeat? Couldn't problems for once be worked out by *negotiation*, instead of just seeing who could kill the most opponents?

"It won't always be this way," Bones said quietly, sensing the source of my frustration. "You're still very new to this world, but once sods like Apollyon see they can't break you, they'll move on to easier game."

Vlad gave a shrug in concurrence. "I'm rarely challenged anymore, even though I have my fair share of enemies. When you respond harshly enough the first few times, it makes other adversaries less eager to test your mettle later."

I blew air out in a tight sigh without asking the question logic stated neither of them could answer anyway. *How many enemies do I have to kill before the rest of them decide it's not worth it to take me on?* And the more frightening questions—what sort of person would I be by the time I reached that point? Would I even recognize myself anymore? Was survival really worth giving up so many pieces of my soul?

Bones came nearer, taking my face between his strong, pale hands and gazing at me as if I was the only person around for miles.

"Do you think me an evil man? A wretched bloke you'd have been better off never having met?"

"Of course not," I said at once, hurt that he'd even wonder such a thing. "I love you, Bones. You're the best thing that ever happened to me, and I'm not half as honorable as you are."

A slight scoff sounded behind me. I ignored that, concentrating on the dark brown eyes boring into mine.

"Yet you know I'm a killer. So if you believe I'm a good man despite that, then you know *you* can still be a good person even though, sometimes, circumstances will require you to act harsher than you'd prefer."

"Eh, I'll be inside," Vlad said with another soft scoff. "For some reason, I feel the urge to watch *Hitman* followed by *Mr. and Mrs. Smith*."

I ignored that as well, still staring into Bones's eyes and feeling the steady thrum of power coming from his hands. Yes, Bones was a killer, but that wasn't what I saw when I looked at him. I saw the person who'd taught me how to accept myself when no one else wanted me to. Who loved me without any of the fears or conditions I'd first put on our relationship, and who'd risked death several times for my life, my mother's, my friends, and countless other people he'd never even met when he took on an undead white slavery ring. All of that had just been in the past decade, too. I'd probably never know all the things Bones had done for others in the time before he met me, or the centuries before I was even born.

Killer, yes, but that was the smallest part of him in my eyes. I was a killer, too, but he gave me hope that I could learn to make it the smallest part of me, even if it *was* necessary in the world I'd chosen to live in.

"As long as you're with me, I can handle it," I said, reaching up to touch his face. "I can handle anything with you."

"I'll always be with you, Kitten. Always," Bones rasped before his lips closed over mine.

Even though he was inside the house, I could still hear Vlad's sardonic mutter of "Where's a tissue when I need one?"

I turned my face away from Bones after a long moment, ending our kiss, and called out, "If you're not too busy watching *Hitman*, I hear *Dracula 2000* is a good movie."

"Vicious," came Vlad's reply, amusement clear in his tone. "Just make sure you hold on to that ruthless attitude until Apollyon's been defeated, *Catherine*."

I couldn't help my grin at his emphasis on the name I was born with but rarely went by anymore. Bones rolled his eyes, putting his arm around my waist as we walked into the house.

"If it's not too much trouble, Tepesh, we could use some new clothes, blood, and a place to sleep. I don't fancy retuning to New Orleans until it's time to meet with Marie, in case more of this ghoul's mates are hanging about."

Vlad came out of a room down the hall. "I only arrived yesterday, so this house doesn't have much, but it does have all of those things. Maximus."

The tawny-haired vampire I remembered from my stay at Vlad's home in Romania came out, bowing once to Vlad before gesturing to Bones and me.

"Please, come with me."

FIFTEEN

SEEING THE SPECTRAL FORMS TWINING around the whitewashed crypts inside of Saint Louis Cemetery Number One made me miss Fabian. Who knew I'd get so attached to a ghost? But just because Fabian was transparent didn't mean he wasn't also a great friend. Most of the ghosts in the cemetery weren't sentient like he was. They were just shades of their former selves, no thought, no feelings, just repeating the same actions over and over like a snapshot on a Mobius strip. Occasionally, I saw some spooks that clearly had all their ectoplasmic marbles like Fabian did. They gave Bones and me looks ranging from curious to disdainful as we waited outside the cemetery gates. They were locked, a warning to visitors that no one but the dead or wannabe dead should be inside the graveyard's walls at night.

I doubted we'd be attacked by any ghouls so close to Marie Laveau's preferred meeting place, but Bones was rigid enough to shatter as I ran a hand along his arm.

"My poor cat's going to hate me for disappearing on him again," I remarked just to break the tension. We'd left Helsing back in Ohio since it would be animal cruelty to try and tote him on the back of the Ducati. I'd intended to leave him at a nice pet resort, but oddly enough, Ed and Scratch insisted on watching him. Seems they considered kitty-sitting Helsing as the least they could do to demonstrate their new loyalty to Bones as their Master. Considering what had happened at the Ritz, I was glad that we hadn't attempted to take my cat with us to New Orleans. If the hotel management had figured out that we'd been part of the elevator destruction yesterday, they might have seized Helsing and turned him over to the pound in retaliation.

Tate already placed a few calls to have the ghouls' bodies from the elevator shaft shipped to him instead of the local morgue. Nothing made cops ask a lot of questions like having corpses dated to be decades or even centuries old turn up at a crime scene. Tate handled everything with perfect competence, but speaking to him instead of Don about crime scene containment was just another reminder of how serious my uncle's condition was.

I shifted impatiently. I couldn't spend time with my uncle until this situation with Apollyon was resolved, and Don didn't have a lot of time left. Then there was my mother's bright idea of painting a bull's-eye on her ass by joining the team. *Family.* Villains had nothing on the stress my relatives could cause me.

Speaking of that, where was the ghoul who always

accompanied Marie's guests into the cemetery to see her? He should've been here ten minutes ago.

As if I'd summoned him, a familiar dark-skinned ghoul rounded the bend on the opposite corner, looking almost taken aback to see us waiting by the gates.

"Jacques," Bones greeted the ghoul, casting a pointed look at the clock on his cell phone. "Didn't interrupt you from having a bit of fun, did we?"

The ghoul's face cleared by the time Bones finished speaking, until it was smooth as polished obsidian instead of registering surprise.

"Majestic did not know you'd returned to the city. She assumed your absence meant you'd canceled your meeting tonight."

The barest smile flittered across Bones's mouth. "We only just arrived a few minutes ago."

Yep, and not by plane, boat, train, or automobile, either. Not after the now-headless ghoul told us his cronies were watching all those venues. Bones flew us in under his own power about ten minutes ago, landing on the roof of Saint Louis Cathedral in Jackson Square before we hopped down and walked the couple blocks to the cemetery. He hadn't wanted me to try my wings again for this jaunt into the city. Something about conserving my energy for later. Under other circumstances, I'd think he meant that in a naughty way, but I knew he was referring to possibly fighting for our lives later, if things went awry. I knew which activity I'd rather be conserving my energy for, if I had control over my own life, but that hadn't happened much lately.

"I will notify Majestic," Jacques said, staying on the other side of the street. He pulled out his cell, speaking quietly into it, his words indiscernible amidst the other noises of the nearby French Quarter. Jazz Fest was getting under way in the next day or so, but from the swell of extra tourists, the city was starting the party early.

"Why'd he even come by, if he didn't think we'd be here?" I whispered to Bones.

"Because Marie would make sure nothing was left to chance" was his equally soft reply.

That sounded like the infamous voodoo queen. She might look like a cross between Mrs. Butterworth and Angela Bassett, emitting matronliness or a take-no-prisoners attitude depending on her mood, but Marie Laveau was nothing if not meticulous. Figures I'd be seeing her again under the same circumstances that we'd first met—me trying to find out if she'd back an asshole in his claims against me. This time, however, the stakes were much higher than determining who I was married to according to vampire law. I'd ended up settling that matter rather decisively by blowing my ex-husband's head off. If only I could do the same to Apollyon soon, I'd consider meetings with Marie as a good-luck omen.

"She will be here in twenty minutes," Jacques announced, coming back over to us. Bones let out a snort.

"I should think so, after the trouble we've gone through to speak with her."

Jacques didn't reply to that. He hadn't been much of a talker the last time I'd met him, either. After waiting the stated amount of time, Jacques opened the gates to the cemetery and I went inside, knowing where we were headed but willing to let him take the lead. The ghoul started to close the gate after me, but Bones's hand shot out to stop him.

"I'm going with her."

He frowned. "Majestic said she will meet with the Reaper first and you afterward."

Bones smiled, an easy stretch of his mouth that made his features even more startlingly gorgeous, but his voice didn't match his playboy good looks.

"Perhaps you misheard me. *I'm going with her*, and if you think to stop me, I'll soon be decorating one of these gate spikes with your head."

Jacques was at least twice the width of Bones and just as tall, so to an onlooker, if they fought, it would be a no-brainer who'd win. But the ghoul couldn't match the power seething off Bones as he dropped his shields. It poured from him and fanned out to encompass the cemetery, making the sentient ghosts give him a more interested glance as it brushed across them.

"This way," Jacques said at last, turning his back on us.

We picked our way around the crumbling crypts and refurbished tombs as Jacques led us toward Marie Laveau's vault. I knew this cemetery was a popular tourist attraction, but I didn't see myself coming here just for fun. The air was thicker with all the residual energy from the ghosts, making me feel like I walked through invisible cobwebs with every step. The cemetery might not be large, but because of New Orleans's history of extremely high mortality rates in comparison to their burial space, each crypt we passed housed the remains of dozens if not hundreds of residents—some of whom watched us as we passed by.

It also had a different vibe than the time capsule feel of the French Quarter. There, in the backdrop of streets suited for horses instead of cars and gas lanterns illuminating the sidewalks, it somehow didn't seem odd to see a transparent person adorned in clothes from a different century mingling among the living residents. Here, however, melancholy hung in almost palpable waves, making me imagine that every crypt I passed or foot of ground I trod upon sighed in regret over a life never to be experienced again.

Jacques stopped by the white oblong crypt bearing Marie Laveau's name, date of supposed death, and a faint inscription in French that I couldn't read. He said something in what sounded like Creole, and at the base where several offerings were left to the voodoo queen, a grating noise emanated. Then a few of the old, decrepit-looking stones slid smoothly back to reveal a dark hole within.

Marie might be calculating and meticulous, but she also had a sense of humor, making people travel under her crypt for meetings with her.

Jacques jumped down into the hole without hesitation. Bones flashed a look at me before doing the same. I followed after a second or two, giving him time to move so I didn't land on him, and squished down into an inch of brackish-smelling water. Impressive mechanical hideaway, yes, but nothing stayed totally dry underground in New Orleans, and this area was flooded most of the time. Marie must have a better pump system down here than the Army Corps of Engineers.

Above us, the slabs creaked again as they closed, plunging the tunnel into what would have been complete blackness to anyone without supernatural vision. Bones and I both had that, so I wasn't worried about something jumping out at us unseen. We also both had boots on, so disgusting things squishing through my toes as we followed down the tunnel wasn't a concern as well. Still, when I glanced at the tight walls around us, I was unable to suppress a shiver. I'd seen what Marie had installed for a booby trap in this tunnel, and let's just say it involved enough blades to turn anyone trespassing into red-splattered coleslaw.

After about forty yards, Jacques opened the metal door at the end that revealed a narrow flight of stairs. Again Bones went up first, me following behind him. At the top of the stairs was a small, windowless room that might be located in a nearby home, or we might possibly be inside one of the larger national crypts in the cemetery. I had no idea, and I was sure that was how Marie wanted it.

"Majestic," Bones greeted the woman seated on a plush recliner chair, nodding his head respectfully.

But when I came out from behind him and saw Marie more clearly, my polite hello vanished under a burst of laughter. On the floor right next to her smart little heels was a pale container of plastic-wrapped poultry, and I didn't have to look at the label to guess what kind.

"A headless chicken," I said once I'd gotten my laughter under control. "Very cool."

Bones arched a brow at me, not knowing that upon first meeting the ghoul queen of New Orleans, I'd commented that I was sure she'd be holding a headless chicken considering her fearsome voodoo reputation. Apparently, she'd remembered that, yet another example of the sly humor lurking underneath her whole Queen of the Damned demeanor.

"It was the best I could do under short notice," Marie replied with an elegant shrug. Her voice was like acoustical caramel, that Southern Creole accent sweetening each word. Her shawl shifted as she sat up, inky curls brushing her shoulders with the movement. Then her eyes narrowed as she fixed her gaze on Bones.

"Did Jacques not relay my instructions for you to wait while I met with Cat alone first?"

Bones didn't lose any of his easy posture, but I felt tension that wasn't my own brush over my emotions.

"I'm certain you heard of the incident at the Ritz yesterday, and I'm also certain you know the attack was aimed at her. So you'll forgive me, Majestic, if I'm overprotective of my wife's safety at present."

"Yes, I heard." Not a hint of emotion flickered across her features. "I can assume the bodies recovered from the hotel were those of your attackers?"

"All but one," Bones replied. "We took him with us when we left."

Now we had Marie's full attention. She leaned forward, her dark gaze intense. "Tell me you brought this person with you."

"Sorry, he's dead now," Bones stated impassively.

"You killed him?" Marie didn't look pleased, and I didn't think it was because she'd wished a long, happy life on the other ghoul. In fact, if the man were still alive, he might be grateful that Vlad spared him whatever Marie had in store. From her reputation, she was hell on anyone who violated her safe-passage rules.

"Vlad did," I said before Bones could answer. "He didn't know all the details." Partly true, anyway.

"I'll speak with him about that later," Marie murmured, almost to herself.

I gave the single empty chair across from her a glance. "You mind?"

She waved a hand. "Please."

"Bones?" I inquired, assuming I'd just sit on his lap.

"I'll stand, Kitten."

I settled myself in the chair. So far, things were going better than I expected. Marie hadn't pitched a fit about Bones being here or the ghoul being dead. Maybe she thought Apollyon was as much of a threat as we did.

"You may remain, but you will stay silent while I speak with Cat, or I will remove you," Marie said to Bones in a tone that dared him to argue.

My hopes plummeted with that single sentence. Bones folded his arms across his chest and leaned back against the wall, looking for all the world like he was completely relaxed. I couldn't feel his emotions—he'd locked them down tight upon entering the tunnel—but I bet his little half smile concealed a slew of uncharitable thoughts toward Marie. I couldn't help but admire his blasé performance. I could never fake nonchalance that well when I was pissed.

I cleared my throat in the sudden uneasy silence. "So . . . how 'bout them Saints, huh?"

Marie's sharp gaze didn't leave mine. "The last time I saw you, you were still a half-breed. Tell me, Cat, how do you find being a full vampire?"

"It's great," I said, knowing she had something up her sleeve with this, but pretending it was a casual question. "I haven't missed getting my period even *once*, and hey, no more counting calories. What's not to love, right?"

She smiled at me, revealing pretty white teeth that contrasted nicely with her matte red lipstick. "You forgot to mention your ability to kill your first husband with a fireball."

My answering smile froze on my face. I'd expected us to talk about Apollyon, not Gregor. He'd been the vampire whose blood was combined with a ghoul's heart to raise Marie from the dead almost a hundred and fifty years ago, but Marie had wanted him dead, too, so I didn't anticipate recriminations from her for killing him.

Marie's a valuable ally, don't lose your temper and give her an excuse to side with Apollyon, I reminded myself. *Look at Bones. He almost seems bored even though he's got to be as ticked as you over Marie bringing up Gregor.*

"Because he cheated in his duel with Bones, the Guardian Council of Vampires cleared me of any wrongdoing," I said, proud that my voice was very calm.

Marie leaned back in her chair, idly stroking the fabric. Part of me wondered where the secret door was in this room. That chair wasn't a permanent fixture or it would be mildewed from the damp air, not to mention I didn't believe Marie would leave herself without an alternate means of escape.

"Cheating, that doesn't surprise me," she commented. "Gregor's arrogance always was his Achilles' heel. Like bringing you to Paris when you were sixteen. I told him to come here instead. That his hometown would be the first place anyone would look for him, should his actions be discovered, but he didn't listen."

Everything in me froze. I didn't dare glance at Bones again. The flash of rage that skipped across my subconscious before he recloaked his emotions told me he was *thisclose* to losing it at this revelation.

"So." I couldn't keep the edge from my tone if my life depended on it. "Gregor told you about his kidnapping plans for me back then?"

She continued to stroke her armrest, as though the tension in the room hadn't become thick enough to cut. "Gregor told me many things. He trusted my loyalty to him as my only living sire. I don't betray those I've sworn loyalty to. This shouldn't surprise you. I told you last year that if Gregor's claims of marriage to you were proved, I'd back his side."

"You also told me a neat story about how you murdered your husband when he pushed you too far," I replied sharply. "Well, I'd say tricking me into marrying him as a teenager, murdering my friend, forcibly changing my mother into a vampire, and trying to murder Bones by cheating in their duel all fell under the 'too far' category for me. Too bad for Gregor the vision he had of me when I was sixteen didn't show the part about me using all those neat powers he wanted to control to kill him."

"Underestimating you was Gregor's mistake." Marie didn't move a muscle, but all of a sudden, I felt like a mouse staring at a hungry owl. "It won't be mine. But"—a shrug—"no one can hide from death forever. *No one*, not even our kind. Death travels the world and passes through even the thickest walls we protect ourselves with. You should remember that."

Was that a threat? "Not to be rude, Majestic, but it sounds like you're telling me to watch my back with you."

Marie grunted. "When you truly understand what it means, you'll know how to defeat Apollyon."

At last, we were getting on topic. I'd already figured out that I'd need to kill the ghoul to stop him, but if Marie wanted to feel like she was being all cool and cryptic with the advice, I'd play along.

"Okay. I'll remember that."

She smiled, genial and somehow terrifying at the same time. "You should. If you don't, he'll win."

"You could always just spell it out and save us all some time," I said, unable to keep all the exasperation out of my voice. Did being dead for over a century turn everyone into riddle masters instead of people who could just *say* what they meant?

"I won't join your cause against Apollyon. Last year, my sire could have ordered me to, but with Gregor dead, my loyalty is to my people alone."

Anger rose in me. "Even at the expense of countless thousands dying over reasons as stupid as who has fangs versus flat teeth?" I gave her café-latte skin a pointed look. "I would think you'd be smarter than to side with a senseless bigot."

"It has nothing to do with bigotry," she replied sharply. "But Apollyon's reach has grown. If I openly oppose him, I will be seen as a betrayer of my race. Even ghouls who disagree with Apollyon may side with him out of species loyalty. It will be civil war. During this, am I to believe the vampire nation will not swoop in to crush us while we are weak from infighting?" Marie gave me a thin smile. "I am not so trusting."

"Oh come on," I huffed. "Vampires have no dreams of subjugating ghouls. You know that's just a smoke screen Apollyon's using."

"There are some among your race who would take advantage of ghouls just as ruthlessly as Apollyon is seeking to do with vampires. If you're not smart enough to heed my words and outwit him on your own, then you deserve to lose," she replied with brutal bluntness before leaning forward and reaching behind her chair.

Everything in me tensed, ready to spring for the knives in my boots, but all she did was pull out an empty wineglass. That previous tension began to ebb. Jacques had served us drinks last time I was here, even though for the life of me I didn't know how he'd managed to procure a cold gin and tonic in this dank underground area. But instead of calling out to him, Marie set the glass on the armrest of her chair without a word. Then she flicked open a ring on her finger, revealing that it hid a tiny sharp point, and sliced it across her wrist before holding the wineglass underneath the cut.

Oh fuck no, I thought, keeping myself from bolting out of my chair with every last bit of willpower in me.

Her gaze drilled into mine as dark purplish liquid began to fill the glass.

"Reaper," she said coolly. "Won't you have something to drink?"

Sixteen

Once more, I couldn't even risk glancing at Bones to see if he looked as appalled as I felt. *Play it cool, she could be bluffing*, I chanted to myself, managing not to flinch when she held out that half-full glass to me.

"What an unusual offer, but you know I prefer gin and tonic," I said, praying my heart didn't start beating out of sheer panic. If she did know about my twisted feeding habits, who would have told her? And did that person somehow screw it up and report back that I drank *ghoul* blood for nourishment instead of vampire?

"Over a dozen years ago, Gregor told me of his vision about a young half-breed who would one day wield the power of pyrokinesis," Marie said. "After his sire, Tenoch, perished, only one other vampire existed who could manifest fire and bend it to his will, and as you know, Vlad Tepesh was no ally of Gregor's.

Gregor assumed you'd come into this power about a century after you'd been changed into a vampire, and he intended to have you under his control long before that. Yet you killed him using fire within a month of your turning."

I didn't move, afraid that my slightest gesture would betray me. "Everyone knows that," I said as calmly as I could. "Beginner's luck."

A sharp laugh came from her. "Then, curiously, you weren't reported to use fire again, even when you were in dire circumstances. You *were* reported to have used telekinesis against a group of vampires in Monaco a few months ago. So that's two incredible powers, all manifested less than a year after your changing. More beginner's luck?"

"I'm a lucky girl," I said, thinking if I were still part human, I'd be puking from stress right now.

Marie glanced at the glass of blood in her hand before meeting my gaze. "Let's find out," she said, her Southern accent changing until it sounded like hundreds of voices suddenly spoke through her, and none of them friendly.

Bones moved at the same time I did, but an icy blast of power knocked me back into my seat hard enough to topple me over. I came up with knives in both hands, only to have them ripped from my grasp by what felt like razor-sharp claws. In disbelief I saw Bones suspended in midair, shadows swirling around him, his mouth open in a roar that still didn't drown out the horrible keening noises that filled the room.

Marie hadn't moved from her position, that glass of blood still resting on the side of her chair. I started toward her again, only to be met by a wall of ghosts that shot up from the ground, their features indistinct due to their sheer numbers. When I tried to push past them, it felt like they slashed my body with thousands of razors, but worse than that, my energy drained away as abruptly as it had at dawn when I was first changed. Pain radiated in me from my boots to my eyebrows. I looked down, expecting to be covered in blood, but only a faint smudge of dirt marred my front even though I felt like I'd pass out.

"Stop," I gasped to Marie.

She shrugged. "Make me. Call forth fire, or knock this drink from my hand with your mind, and I will."

Bitch! Rage filled me as Bones was flung against the wall by those malevolent shadows. He wasn't shouting anymore. He looked, frighteningly, like he was trying to speak but couldn't. His features twisted as he struggled, more searing pain flashing through me, but not mine this time. How could these ghosts be able to inflict so much damage? Fabian couldn't even poltergeist up a limp version of a handshake!

My gaze narrowed as I looked at Marie. It had to be her power enabling the ghosts to do this, what with how her voice sounded like a microphone to the grave and the icy, vibrating waves pouring off her. Even though I hadn't manifested as much as a spark recently, I still tried to turn my anger into flames, picturing Marie, that fluffy chair, and even the package of chicken by her feet bursting into a fiery inferno. *Burn. Burn.*

Nothing. Not even a hint of smoke leaked out of my hands, let alone any fire. I tried focusing on the wineglass next, picturing it shattering and splashing her blood all over her. More hard thwacks came from my left, audible even above that awful high-pitched moaning the ghosts made. A glance revealed they had Bones's arms and legs extended straight out, those shadows appearing and then disappearing from his flesh. Fragments of agony sliced across my consciousness, made more intense by the brief periods of blankness between them. Dammit, Bones was trying to shield me from his pain, even in the midst of being pureed from the inside out by those spectral freaks.

I looked away, tears spilling out my eyes, to concentrate back on that blood-filled glass. It hadn't been too many months since I'd drank Mencheres's blood. *Some* of his power still had to be left in me! *Break, glass, break!* Or just fall from her hand, at least.

More of those lightning-quick flashes of pain flitted across my emotions, the periods between them growing shorter. I couldn't stop myself from glancing at Bones again. His back was arched, eyes closed, muscles contorting every time one of those shadows dove into him. The agony leaking through to me from him was nothing compared to the searing pain that ripped through my heart seeing him that way.

I tore my gaze away and glared at the glass with enough loathing that it should have exploded into sand. It didn't. Not even a shiver of movement disturbed it. Maybe it was because I hadn't drunk nearly as much of Mencheres's blood as I did with Vlad that one time. Maybe because I'd stopped drinking Bones's blood, I was now weaker and less able to summon any residual telekinesis power left in me. Ultimately, the reason didn't matter. All I knew was that the man I loved was being tormented, and even though I was in the *same fucking room*, I couldn't help him.

I wasn't surprised when a dull thrum slowly began to sound in my chest. Marie's eyebrows rose, but she looked more curious than startled. Hatred surged through me at how calmly she sat there, directing all this mayhem as though it were a puppet show. I'd whipped out two knives from my boots and flung them at her before even planning the action, only to let out a scream of frustration when they were batted away by the wall of ghosts without even grazing her.

I threw myself against that spectral barrier next, determined to make her pay, but no matter how many times I bashed against that writhing wall of other-worldly bodyguards, I couldn't force my way past them. Worse, it seemed to weaken me, replacing my rage with the same dizzying lethargy I'd only felt the day Bones drained all my blood to change me. After what seemed like hours but was probably only minutes, I couldn't even stand. Despair choked me as my legs gave out. The unearthly keening in the room seemed to grow louder in triumph.

"You can't win against them," Marie stated, her voice still echoing in that creepy way. "These aren't ghosts. They're Remnants, slivers of the most primal emotions left over after someone crosses over to the other side. Every time you touch them, they feed from your energy and pain just like a vampire feeds from blood, and they grow stronger."

Almost in a daze, I stared at the concrete floor. Nothing marred it except cracks and mildew stains, but I'd seen something similar to these Remnants when Mencheres raised wraiths in retaliation for a vicious spell against him. Even though those had looked like ghosts, too, they were utterly lethal, cutting through dozens of vampires like a hot knife through butter.

And these Remnants seemed just as strong.

"Did you work the spell before we got here?" I forced myself to ask, even though talking seemed to suck the last bits of strength from me. "Where'd you hide the symbols?"

Her laugh resounded around the room. "I need no spell. I don't practice black magic; I *am* black magic."

Normally I'd say something caustic about how pride always went before a fall, but considering I was the barely conscious one on the ground, I didn't think the insult would have the same effect.

"What are you waiting for, Reaper?" Marie asked calmly, glancing at Bones. "If they continue to feed from him for much longer, eventually they will kill him. If you want him freed from the Remnants, unleash these great abilities of yours. Show me fire, or move this glass even an *inch*, and I will send them back to their graves."

I stared at her, my heart still sputtering out sporadic beats due to my fear and fury, noting every speck of her appearance as though the details could help me defeat her. Those large dark eyes, smooth ageless skin, and full wide mouth framed by black hair that barely brushed the lace shawl covering her tailored navy dress. Everything about Marie looked modern and normal right down to her sensible yet stylish heels, but this woman was the most dangerous adversary I'd ever encountered. I'd thought only Mencheres could wield enough power to clean my and Bones's clock without even getting up from his seat, but here was Marie, doing that very thing. Her ability to control these Remnants must be what Apollyon was counting on to make the difference in a war between ghouls and vampires, and I had to admit; it was a damn frightening sight.

I looked at Bones. His face was still contorted, pain blasting across my subconscious like rounds from a machine gun, but though his mouth moved, not a word came from him. Not only could Marie direct the Remnants to hold him against the wall, but she could also make them keep him from speaking. Rage gave a flare of energy to my limbs, making me drag myself to my feet as I faced her.

"We both know if I had any of those abilities left in me, I'd be decorating the walls with your bloody, smoldering remains right now," I said, wishing I had the stamina to sound more threatening. "I only picked up those powers for a short time when I drank from Vlad and Mencheres."

Satisfaction flitted across her features before they became smooth again. "Like a Mambo," she said, drawing out the unfamiliar word. "In my sect of voodoo, select Mambos drank from blood sprinkled with Zombi's essence to absorb the god's powers over the dead—temporarily. When I was changed into a ghoul, those powers became permanent, and increased more than anyone could imagine."

"Get those things off Bones and you can tell me all about it," I gritted out. Marie had confirmation of her suspicions about my power source, but we were still alive, so she must want something from us. I didn't need a Magic 8 Ball to know if she wanted us dead, we'd be nothing but shriveling heaps in this dingy room by now.

Her hazelnut gaze met mine, no mercy in their depths as she held out the glass filled with her blood. "Drink this or he dies."

I looked into her eyes and knew, down to my soul, that she wasn't bluffing. No matter that I feared what would happen when I drank from that glass, I'd drain it dry to save Bones.

A swipe of my hand indicated the wall of Remnants between us. "Let me through."

Her brow ticked up, and then a path appeared amidst the mass of transparent bodies. I went through that chasm, refusing to look at Bones in case by gesture or mime he'd try to tell me not to do what I was about to. *It won't affect you, won't affect you*, I repeated like a litany as I took the glass from Marie's outstretched hand and then tipped it to my mouth, swallowing deeply.

Relief swept through me at the bitter, cloying taste, so different from vampire blood. If I didn't like it, then it couldn't have the same effect as vampire blood did, because that tasted like ambrosia to me. I let the glass drop from my hand once it was empty, feeling small, petty satisfaction to see it shatter upon impact. I was pissed enough at Marie to want to see her in tiny pieces on the floor, too, but right now, I'd settle for imagining the glittering shards of crystal were bits of her corpse.

"You got what you wanted. Now get them off him," I said, feeling stronger by the moment. The draining effect from my contact with the Remnants must be wearing off. Good. That meant Bones wouldn't suffer any lingering damage, either. I didn't know if spectral abuse could somehow screw with a vampire's natural ability to heal, but that must not be the case, so Bones should be fine as soon as those energy-munchers got the hell away.

I swung my head around to glare at the shadows still funneling through his body. They'd better pray once I finally bit the dust, I stayed all the way dead, or I'd come back and kick their asses for this—

Those shadows fell from Bones so abruptly that he dropped to the floor before catching himself, crumpling into a heap. I ran over to him, cradling him, biting my lip so hard I drew blood from my rage at how slowly he pushed himself upright. Then I lasered a glare at Marie. She watched us with the oddest look on her face, the Remnants who'd so recently tormented Bones now appearing around her.

"You can send your little friends back to their graves, or you can play with them all night. I don't care, but we're leaving," I told her curtly, noticing Bones looking between me and Marie with a sort of angry incredulity. The wall of Remnants surged toward Marie, until she was surrounded above, below, and on all sides by the twisting, diaphanous horde. *Still showing off her power*, I noted in contempt, *as if we hadn't gotten the message before*.

"I ordered them back to their graves the same time I had them release him," Marie said, each word holding only the sugary flavors of her accent instead of the echoing timbres of the grave.

"Bullshit," I snapped, feeling another wave of anger rip through me, followed by an almost overwhelming hunger. "They're still here, aren't they?"

"Kitten, your voice . . ." Bones said with disbelief.

Something slammed into me so hard that my

vision went black. I braced for pain, but strangely, it
didn't come. Sounds became muffled, disorganized. I
thought I heard Bones shouting, but couldn't focus on
what he was saying or even where he was anymore.
Air rushed by me in ever greater whooshes, reminding me of how it felt when I'd fallen from the bridge,
but I couldn't be falling. I was still in the room beneath the cemetery, wasn't I?

Flashes filled my vision; streaks of silver and white
going by so fast, they were almost indistinguishable.
I could see through them dimly, but it was as if I
was watching things from a long way off. A groan
came out of my mouth, part of me registering that it
sounded like it was filled with the voices of people
who'd died decades, centuries, even millennia ago. As
if in a dream, I watched Bones gently lower me to the
concrete floor and then punch Marie so hard that she
smashed against the far corner of the room.

"I'll grant you that one strike," she said, the words
seeming to echo in my mind, "but only one. Now, will
you listen to what you must do to help her, or will you
make me kill you and leave her at the mercy of the
grave?"

I could hear Bones reply and Marie answer, but
somehow their words were lost to me amidst the keen
of countless others, so much louder than when I'd
picked up on humans' thoughts. His touch wasn't lost,
though, when he knelt next to me and scooped me
up in his arms. The feel of his skin on mine was an
anchor I tried to focus on amidst the whirling chaos
that had overtaken me.

I was so cold. So empty. So HUNGRY.

As he carried me out of the room, Marie stopped

him, pressing her mouth to my ear. She murmured something, but it was only one voice among thousands, her words snatched away by the roar in my mind before I could fully register her question. Bones yanked me away, but I could still feel the burn of her lips against my skin. His long strides took me into the blackness of the tunnel, brushing by Jacques as though the ghoul wasn't even there. My fingers dragged along the damp walls as we passed, faintly bemused by the trails of light they seemed to leave. That light increased, pulling itself from the walls to reach toward me with seeking tentacles, but I wasn't afraid. I was sad. There were so many of them, poor things, and they were so *hungry* . . .

Grinding metal sounded ahead, then a thicker ray of silvery light shone at the end of the tunnel. Bones increased his pace, jumping straight up into it when we were bathed in its glow, and then everything around me exploded. The voices became deafening, the cold mind-numbing, the hunger insatiable. Those sensations increased, until it felt like I was struggling in the midst of a huge silken web to get away, but all the while my efforts only tightened the cage around me.

SEVENTEEN

THE FIRST THING THAT REGISTERED WAS THE scent of smoke, curling around my nostrils as if begging to be inhaled. The next realization was that my arms felt stiff and my wrists were sore. I opened my eyes, the bland grayness of a concrete ceiling above me, Bones's pale, naked flesh to my right.

"What?" I began, trying to sit up, only to have something pull on my arms. I tilted my head backward, shocked to see that I was manacled to a wall even as another glance revealed that Bones and I were on a narrow bed. My gaze flew to him once more, noting the cigarette he set down even as he exhaled a long plume of white.

"Why are you lying there *smoking* while I'm chained to a wall?" I demanded.

The look he gave me was a mixture of relief and cynicism. "Since it seems you don't remember anything about the past two days, let me assure you, luv—I earned that smoke."

Two *days*? The last thing I clearly remembered was Bones carrying me out of that underground room with Marie. That was two days ago? And during that time, it had somehow become necessary to chain me to a wall?

"Oh shit," I whispered, the memory of my voice sounding like the gateway to hell reverberating across my mind. "Marie's blood . . . I absorbed some of her powers, didn't I?"

He grunted even as he pulled a key out from under the bed. "Kitten, that's quite the understatement."

I thumped my head against the bed a couple times, more angry than afraid. Goddamn Marie. Why the hell had she insisted on me drinking her blood? Wasn't it enough that she'd figured out where I got my abilities from? Guess not. She had to add to my problems by forcing me to drink from her. Now in addition to freaking people out once it became known that I could absorb vampire powers through feeding, Marie made sure to have proof that I could do the same thing with ghouls. People would be *flocking* to Apollyon's side once these little tidbits were revealed.

"She must want war," I said, rubbing my wrists when Bones unlocked the manacles. "If she didn't, she would've just killed us. Once news of this hits, nothing but my public execution will calm things down with the ghouls."

"That's not going to happen," he said coolly.

I grunted. "I'm not in favor of dying, either, but when people hear about this, Apollyon's going to be fighting off converts with a stick—"

"I meant Marie's not telling anyone, though you're also right that I won't let any of that zealot's sods touch you."

I sat all the way up, wondering briefly at the dampness beneath me but more focused on what he'd just said.

"Marie won't tell anyone?" I repeated. "That doesn't make sense. Why else would she have used such drastic measures to make me drink her blood, if she didn't think it could benefit her in some way? And what other way could it benefit her except to tell everyone that I can absorb powers from vampires *and* ghouls? I don't think she did it just so I can be her new voodoo buddy."

His mouth twisted. "I don't think so, either, but the last thing she said to me was if we revealed to anyone that you were able to siphon powers from ghouls, or that you'd drunk her blood, she'd kill the pair of us. Said she'd *know* it if we told anyone, too. Must mean she already has some ghostly buggers spying on us. Makes me want to hire an expert to banish every filmy-fleshed one of them I come across, and double goes with the Remnants."

"Don't say that." Thank God Fabian was with Dave or the ghost would've been inconsolable at hearing Bones speak so coldly about his kind. "They're not the same as Fabian or other ghosts," I went on, my voice catching at a fresh surge of memory. "Marie said that, but I could also feel them. They're not conscious of right, wrong, what they're doing, any of that. Those Remnants are just . . . like huge gaping holes of need that gravitate toward whatever energy source they're pointed at. They couldn't help what they did to you—"

"Sweet bleedin' Christ," Bones interrupted. "Try not to let this turn you into a Ghost Whisperer, hmm? Adopting Fabian is one thing, but we're already turning away spooks by the dozen. If you want another pet, we'll get you more cats."

"Speaking of my cat," I began.

"He's here," Bones said, rising from the bed. "Not in this room, for obvious reasons, but Ed dropped him off yesterday."

I let my gaze travel over his nudity because, one, who wouldn't? And two, it was almost habit for me to admire him every time he rose from the bed. But something caught my eye when I lingered over his muscled thighs, making disbelief snake through me. A glance at the dampness under me as I scooted aside only confirmed it, not to mention the matching pink smudges on my own thighs.

"Bones, are you serious?" I gasped. "You couldn't wait to have sex with me until I was *conscious*?" Sure, he was a very sexual person. Almost insatiable, some might claim, and I'd be tempted to agree, but this was crossing a line—

He began to laugh in a way that was more ironic than amused. "You may not want to have this conversation until you're a bit less . . . agitated," he said, seeming to choose his words with care.

I crossed my arms over my chest, not tapping my foot only because it was still on the bed.

"You're not going to try that whole lame male 'I had to do it or I'd explode' excuse, are you? Because it's bullshit for humans, but even more so for a vampire, especially one as old as you."

His brow arched in challenge. "Really think I'd

shag you if you were out cold? Didn't we cover this a long time ago, before we even started dating?"

I gave a pointed glance down at the pink stains on the bed, evidence of his climax due to the blood-to-water ratio in vampire bodies. "So you made those . . . by yourself?" *And rubbed some on me for good measure?* I mentally added, but didn't say out loud.

"No, luv, you were most definitely part of those, but you weren't unconscious," he replied evenly. "You were crazed with hunger from the effects of Marie's blood, and I don't mean hunger in the nutritional sense."

Oh. My cheeks actually tingled with the urge to blush. That hadn't occurred to me, even though one of the last things I remembered with clarity was a feeling of incredible hunger. Guess I'd misjudged what kind of hunger.

I strained my mind more, trying to think past that moment in the graveyard. After a short wait, a scattershot of images danced across my memory. *Bones's pale body rising over mine, his mouth open in a moan . . . crimson drops of blood on his skin that I licked away before biting him again . . . his hair, so dark against my thighs when he lowered his head between them . . . the restraints digging into my wrists while waves of pleasure and need crested within me . . .*

Yeah, I'd been involved, all right. And bitey, too, it seemed. "Well, um . . . sorry for accusing you of, ah . . ."

"Taking advantage of my own wife while she was out cold?" he supplied.

I winced. "I'm starting to get little glimpses of what happened—though why'd you chain me to a wall?

Don't tell me that Marie's blood temporarily turned me into a bondage junkie, too."

If so, that begged the question of what exactly the voodoo queen was into for kicks, if I'd absorbed *that* from her, too . . .

Bones actually took in a breath before he spoke. "Kitten, let it alone for now. It'll only upset you, and it wasn't your fault."

"What?" I burst out, dread replacing the lingering warmth those sensual images had evoked.

He sat down, taking my hand, his fingers stroking over my knuckles. The fact that he was being comforting made me even more nervous about what he was about to say.

"In the rituals Marie was famous for back in the eighteen hundreds, she'd take her followers into the woods off Lake Pontchartrain," he said, still sounding like he was cherry-picking his words. "There they'd chant, watch Marie do tricks with a pet snake, and drink from a vat of wine sprinkled with her blood. Due to Marie's position as priestess of the voodoo god Zombi, her blood was supposed to give the participants some of Zombi's power over the dead, a side effect being uncontrollable lust, if you consider all the orgies that took place."

Relief surged in me. "But that's great news! Then I *don't* have the ability to siphon ghoul powers like I do vampire ones, because Marie's blood could affect anyone that way—"

"Those rituals were a sham," he cut me off. "They gave people the excuse to pretend any depravities they indulged in weren't their own doing, but none of them ever really received Zombi's power over the dead from her blood. What happened with you was the real thing, however. Marie said she'd never seen it before, except very rarely with other voodoo priestesses."

"Mambos," I supplied glumly, my relief turning to ashes as I remembered Marie's earlier words. *I am black magic*, she'd said about turning from a Mambo into a ghoul, so it stood to reason that her blood was potent magic, too. "So is that why you had to chain me up? Because absorbing Marie's powers turned me into a *violent* tramp? No wonder you said you'd earned that smoke."

It made even the powers I'd absorbed from Vlad and Mencheres seem like a mild inconvenience by comparison. Shoot a little fire from my hands when I was upset? No big deal, and hey, came in handy at times. Accidentally smash several pieces of furniture in our house through telekinesis? Well, we'd needed a new couch and TV anyway, and that also had helped out against the bad guys at a critical time. But this? Not useful at all, unless Bones had a deep sadomasochist streak.

"The good news is, she said this sort of blind hunger shouldn't happen to you again," Bones responded. "That it was just the initial, overwhelming response to the gate opening between you and the dead. Similar to the blood craze new vampires experience, but that you'd be able to control future twinges once you were yourself, as you clearly are."

That *was* good news, but he'd avoided answering my question, I noticed. "Chains?" I prodded, my voice hardening so he'd know I wasn't about to drop the subject.

"All right, luv, if you won't let it go," he drew out.

"As I said, you were crazed with hunger, and a lot bloody stronger than you normally are. Didn't seem to recognize anyone, either, which meant you weren't being particular about who you sought to assuage that hunger with. Had to chain you up because otherwise, you tried to find someone else to ease your needs if I wasn't servicing you, and I did have to pause to feed a few times."

My jaw dropped at "weren't being particular" and hung lower at each subsequent word, until I was vaguely surprised it wasn't resting in my lap by the time he finished. I grabbed the sheet, pulling it around myself in a sudden rush of scalding shame.

"Oh. My. God. *Please* tell me I didn't—"

"You didn't," Bones said, with a trace of a grim smile. "Though you did give a lucky bloke in the Quarter quite a thorough fondling by the time I caught up with you after you broke free from me in the cemetery. Still wasn't a hundred percent at that point, and I hadn't expected you to be so strong. I was able to fly us back to Tepesh's after I'd fed, but by then, you were well and truly lost to the hunger. Marie warned me you'd be that way, and I must admit, she didn't exaggerate."

I'd had to be dragged away from sexually assaulting a *tourist*? Why oh why hadn't I listened when Bones told me not to pursue this subject? But now that I knew this much, I had to know the rest.

"So, I attempted to rape a tourist and turned you into a sex slave for two days." My voice was neutral because the embarrassment was so deep, it transcended reaction. "Anything else I should get a heads-up about? Like, who else to expect a restraining order from? Are we still at Vlad's? Don't tell me you had to drag me off of him, too?"

Bones made a sound like a delicate cough. "No, and we're not at Tepesh's anymore. It was a temporary residence, so it didn't have the means to restrain a vampire in it. Marie offered to take us in, but as you can imagine, I wanted far away from her. Mencheres had a place with a vampire holding cell in West Virginia. He chartered a plane to Louisiana and helped contain you while we traveled here."

His voice changed ever so slightly when he said "contain," making me almost screech as I demanded, "What *exactly* did Mencheres do?"

"Held you immobile with his power while I shagged you in the back of the plane," he replied bluntly, a half shrug seeming to say, *You wanted to know.* "Couldn't risk you breaking free and crashing the aircraft, and attempting to drive to West Virginia with you in that condition wouldn't have been wise."

Mencheres. Bones's co-ruler, grandsire, Master vampire of incredible power, and the ally who unnerved me the most, had telekinetically held me down so Bones could boink me into submission en route to a vampire holding cell? Sweet holy Jesus, let me have hallucinated hearing that!

"Get me some silver," I managed to croak. "I'm going to kill myself."

"Don't fret, he faced the other way the whole time," Bones said unperturbedly. "Aside from knowing it would've bothered you to have him watch, Kira also wouldn't have fancied that."

"*Kira* was there, too?" Good God, I barely knew her! And she'd been just a row or two away while all this was going on? If I still had the ability, I would've passed out from humiliation.

"Told you you'd feel better if you didn't know the details," Bones replied with a pointed look.

"I'll never doubt your word again." *Or set foot out of this room, if Mencheres and Kira were still here.*

He dragged me into his arms even though I was stiff from mortification.

"You needn't be so ashamed. All you did was shag your husband; who's to be shocked by that? Can't say it's an experience I'd care to repeat, but that's only because you weren't really yourself." His lips brushed my ear. "Otherwise, chaining you up for over a day and a half of uninhibited rogering sounds terribly appealing."

I knew he was trying to cheer me up, but I was still staggered over hearing I'd assaulted a tourist, gotten crazy every time Bones wasn't plowing away at me, and as the *coup de grâce*, Mencheres had—in a manner of speaking—participated in Bones and me having sex. *And here I swore I'd never have a threesome*, the thought occurred to me amidst my lingering incredulity.

"Thought you said it was two days," I muttered, finally registering the last part of what he'd said.

"You've been asleep for round nine hours now. Wasn't sure if you'd still be caught up in the same hunger when you woke, so I didn't take your restraints off."

I didn't blame him. God, I wouldn't have blamed Bones if he'd duct-taped a vibrator to me and just took care of the whole sordid nightmare that way.

"You know what they say about being careful what you wish for? I used to wish there was something we could do, you know, intimately together that you hadn't already done before, but I didn't think it would ever happen." I gave him a limp smile. "Though I doubt you've ever been forced to nonstop bang a woman hyped up on the undead voodoo version of Spanish fly, have you?"

His chuckle was soft. "Can't say that I have, Kitten."

"Yeah, well, consider me an original."

This time, when his lips brushed across my skin, it lasted more than a moment.

"I always have."

How he could be affectionate with me right after this latest cluster fuck—literally!—was beyond my comprehension. I should thank my lucky stars that while this scenario was an eleven out of ten on *my* perversity scale, Bones's former human life as a gigolo combined with his promiscuous past as a vampire meant this probably only rated a three for him. Thank God he'd been there, too. I would have been horrified to cheat on Bones if I'd been hit with Marie's blood-induced slut whammy when he wasn't around.

The idea made me shudder. I was already fuming at Marie over letting those Remnants loose on Bones; if she'd have damaged our marriage as well—and though Bones would understand given the circumstances, it wouldn't be something he'd ever forget—then I'd truly despise her.

The question that overshadowed even my searing embarrassment over my actions the past two days was why Marie had forced me to drink her blood. If not to use it as fuel for Apollyon's warmongering, why would she want to see if I could absorb *her* powers? Marie was too calculating to have forced me into doing that just to satisfy her curiosity over whether ghoul blood would affect me the same way vampire blood did. She could have made me drink from another ghoul aside from herself to get the same proof.

What was she up to? And should that be of greater concern than what Apollyon was doing?

"If you've, ah, been occupied dealing with me for most of the past two days, there might have been some developments," I said, swinging my legs off the bed. "Let's hope there has been, and that it's good news."

Eighteen

To my dismay, the first two people I saw when I came upstairs later were Mencheres and Kira. They sat next to each other in what I guessed was the living room, my cat sedately curled in Kira's lap.

Both of them looked up, so it was too late for me to run. For once, I was grateful for Mencheres's trademark stoicism as I met his impenetrable expression. If he'd waggled his eyebrows knowingly, or crossed his wrists in a mime of bondage, I might have jumped right out the nearest window.

"Let me say right off that if I could avoid you two for the next decade, I would," I got out in a rush. "But since I can't indulge in a little modesty-salvaging me time right now, I'll just offer my sincerest apologies and hope we never mention what happened again. In fact, you know that amnesia spell you put on me when I was sixteen, Mencheres? I'd love another one."

"You erased her memory when she was a teenager?" Kira asked in surprise.

"That's a story for another time," he smoothly answered her before turning that charcoal gaze back to me. "Unfortunately, Cat, my ability to erase your memory was predicated on your half-human status. Vampire memories can't be altered. At least, not that I'm aware of."

"Just my luck," I muttered. "Well, then let's go with Plan A: Pretend it never happened."

"Pretend what never happened?" Kira replied with deliberate emphasis even as she gave me a purposefully blank look.

I flashed her a grateful smile. "Exactly."

Something hazy caught the corner of my eye. I turned to see Fabian floating in the doorway, watching me with a mixture of happiness and wariness.

"Hey," I said in surprise. "Aren't you supposed to be with Dave? He's not here, too, is he?"

"He's still in Ohio." Fabian came nearer, almost twitching in either excitement or agitation. "Are you well, Cat? Can I . . . do anything for you?"

There went that tingling in my cheeks again before I reminded myself that Fabian couldn't mean anything suggestive by his question. He wasn't *solid*, which was a definite requirement for what I'd needed before, my smutty lack of preference as to who provided it notwithstanding.

"I'm fine," I said, trying to cover my lingering embarrassment with a businesslike mentality. "But why'd you leave Dave? Did something happen?" Maybe Dave had to stop trying to infiltrate Apollyon's ghouls because of something going on with Don or the team?

Fabian seemed to shift uncomfortably even though his feet didn't touch the floor. "I thought you needed me," he mumbled. "So I found you. Dave still hadn't come across the ghouls and it seemed okay to leave him—"

"What do you mean, you found me?" I interrupted, trying to make my voice calm instead of accusing. Fabian already looked like he might burst into tears, if that was even possible for a ghost. Still, if anything had happened to Dave because he hadn't been able to send Fabian for help . . .

"He means you seem to be a spook magnet now," Bones supplied, coming into the room. "Dozens of ghosts followed you from New Orleans to Tepesh's and then even here. I suspect Mencheres has been sending them away lately, or you'd have woken up with some perched next to you in the cell below."

Mencheres gave a concurring shrug even as Fabian looked more miserable. "So you just . . . found your way to me with no one telling you where I was?" I asked the ghost in disbelief.

He nodded, almost boyish in his dejection despite the fact that Fabian had been forty-five when he died. "Don't be angry. Dave tried to call you but it went to voice mail, and I just *felt* like you were reaching out to me. I rode a few ley lines, not sure where I was going, but somehow I ended up here."

Ley lines. Spook highways, Bones had called them once. I still didn't fully understand how they worked, but I knew ghosts used them to get places very fast because they contained some sort of magnetic energy they could ride on. Like bullet trains for the dead, but invisible.

And these ley lines had led Fabian to me because he felt like I was "reaching out" to him. Him, and a bunch of other ghosts, from what Bones had said. Marie's blood was the gift that kept on giving, it seemed, and each new revelation about its effects only mired me deeper into trouble.

If I'm a ghost magnet, it won't take long before more than ghosts find me, I thought with dismay. Aside from how I didn't like that some of them might be Marie's spies, this presented another problem, too. For the lethal cadre of ghouls out to stop Apollyon by killing me before tensions reached a boiling point, I'd just made myself a much easier target. Nothing said, "She's over here!" quite like a line of ghosts following after me wherever I went.

"Fabian, I'm not mad at you," I said in a soothing way, because he was flitting around in obvious agitation and it *hadn't* been his fault. How could he know I now had the ghostly version of a dog whistle going off in my veins? "But I'm going to need your help. Are those other ghosts still nearby now?"

He glanced at the windows, which, due to the glare from the lights inside and the darkness outside, were harder for me to see through. Especially since I was looking for people who were transparent, anyway.

"Yes."

And being so close, they could hear everything I said. No point in having Fabian relay a message for me.

"Alrighty, then . . ." I sighed, leaving the room to look for the front door. After living with Fabian for almost a year, I knew that showing ghosts the same respect I'd show a living—or undead—person went a long way toward winning brownie points with a species that was routinely ignored.

Bones followed me, pointing to the left with a resigned look on his face. At least he didn't argue about what he'd obviously guessed I was about to do. I went out the front door and saw the many diaphanous forms twirling around the trees at the end of the driveway. I couldn't see any other houses nearby, but having been in several of Mencheres's homes, I recognized this as one of his typical, large, off-the-beaten-path locations. In fact, with the steep hills, occasional rocks jutting through the landscape, and woods nearby, it reminded me of my home in the Blue Ridge. Like Bones and I, Mencheres didn't want to increase his chances of having nosy neighbors get in on his business.

"Hi," I said to the group. A flurry of activity commenced as at least two dozen hazy apparitions stopped what they were doing and zoomed over to the front porch, hovering around it like the coolest Halloween decorations ever. I was amazed at the range of eras the ghosts represented, like a snapshot of history in a glance. Out of outfits I could recognize, I saw one had on what looked like a Union army uniform while another wore Confederate gray and saffron. One was shirtless with buckskin leggings, another was a woman in full Victorian gear, two wore sailors' gear, another was in a twenties flapper dress, a few looked straight out of a fifties movie, and a few more might have been cowboys. Only two looked like they were from my time, judging from the cut and style of their clothes.

All we need is some spooky music, a full moon, and a few bats for this to be perfect, I thought irreverently.

"Hi," I repeated, trying to meet each ghostly gaze at least once so they'd all feel included in my speech. "My friend Fabian tells me that some of you might have just . . . ended up here even though you're not sure why or how," I went on. "Normally I'd say that's fine. The more the merrier, but I've got some stuff going on that makes you guys hanging out, um, potentially problematic for me."

I was starting to doubt the wisdom behind this idea, seeing some of the ghosts exchange confused glances with each other. Fabian rested his hand over mine, the outline of his nonexistent flesh merging with my skin in the closest he could come to an encouraging pat. I squared my shoulders. I'd come this far, might as well plunge ahead and see if the power I hadn't wanted to absorb from Marie could be used to help me now.

"So while I'd love to see you all again in the future, right now, I need you guys to *go*," I said, putting force into the words to make them more than a request. "Please don't follow me, even if you feel like you should. I also need you not to repeat anything I just said, or anything that you might have overheard before. I know you'll do this for me, because ghosts are an honorable species, and—" Oh crap, I was just babbling now, and this wasn't working. None of them even moved. "—and it would really help me out," I finished lamely.

Ghost Whisperer, my ass, an inner voice seemed to mock me.

Nothing but silence from the spectres. Silence, and complete immobility. My hopes sank. Whatever I'd absorbed from Marie's power over the dead, it didn't appear to be the ability to make ghosts leave if they didn't want to. Either I didn't know how to channel her powers properly when it came to regular spooks versus Remnants, or maybe there was a special code word she knew that I didn't—

All at once, the ghosts simply vanished into thin air. I'd seen Fabian do the same several times, but it looked a lot more eerie when it was dozens of them dematerializing simultaneously. Even their energy faded from the air, leaving behind only the soft caress of the evening breeze to waft along my skin.

Nineteen

"Quite impressive," Bones said from behind me.

I turned around to smile at him, relieved that it worked, only to notice that Fabian, too, was now gone.

"Fabian!" I exclaimed.

He materialized in front of me moments later, an expectant look on his face.

"What can I do for you?"

Guilt stabbed through me. If he was making that offer of his own free will, it would be fine, but Marie's blood changed the balance between us. Friends shouldn't be able to compel their friends into doing things whether they wanted to or not.

"Fabian, you don't *have* to do anything for me," I told him. "You can make up your own mind about what you want to do or not do."

"Whatever you say," he replied, still looking at me expectantly.

A stifled snort came from Bones. Okay, so this wasn't as easy as it looked. Damn Marie for making me drink her voodoo juju blood.

"I order you to do only what you want to do," I tried again, more strongly this time.

Now a slight frown stitched between his brows. "I've made you angry. Tell me what to do to make you happy again."

I threw up my hands even as Bones's snort became a full-blown laugh. "Kitten, I'm sure there's a way to fix this in the future, but right now, we've more pressing concerns," he said once he'd controlled his chuckles. "Ask our mate what can help repel ghosts. Can't have you stopping to do that same speech every few hours, and while New Orleans might be one of the world's most haunted cities, it's not the home of *every* spook on the planet."

I shook off my guilt and frustration over Fabian's sudden lack of willpower enough to absorb Bones's point. New Orleans did have an unusually high ghost population, which I'd always attributed to its history of disease, war, malaria, natural disasters, and native predators. But Bones was right. If Marie's blood called to ghosts—and obviously it did, judging from my new popularity with the living-impaired—then the Big Easy should have tons more spooks than it did. Here's hoping the dampener to Marie's spectral siren song wasn't just a natural geographical perk, like an overabundance of alligators. That would be cause for even more notice than a huge posse of ghosts trailing me everywhere.

Even though Fabian would have heard Bones, he didn't offer up any information on the topic. Just continued to look at me with an eager expression. I sighed, thinking Ghost Dominatrix probably fit me better than Ghost Whisperer with my new condition.

"Fabian, if I wanted to try to keep ghosts from following me everywhere, what could I use?"

He looked worried. "You want to get rid of me?"

"No, of course not," I replied, mentally cursing Marie once more. "You'll always have a home with us; I told you that. This is only for a short time until the situation with Apollyon is fixed. You need to get back to Dave in the meantime, anyway. He's in danger without you."

I assuaged my conscience by reminding myself that Fabian had agreed to accompany Dave before, when he had control over his own actions. This wasn't ordering him to do something against his will; it was just sticking to the plan.

I still felt like a heel.

"Ah, I understand," Fabian said, smiling again as he stroked one of his sideburns in contemplation. "I can think of two things that, when combined, are hard for many ghosts to be near because they make the air feel bad. One of those is garlic. Not just a few cloves, but many."

My mouth sagged at the irony. The plant most fabled to repel vampires was actually part of a *ghost's* kryptonite?

"The other is the plant some people smoke," Fabian went on. "When large quantities of that and garlic are present in close proximity, most ghosts can barely stand to be near it."

"You mean tobacco." Wow, guess cigarettes weren't healthy for anyone, living or dead.

"Not that plant," Fabian said, frowning. "The other one that makes people act silly when they smoke it."

"*Weed?*" I burst out. "You're telling me *marijuana* is part two of the ghost repellent formula?"

I couldn't be more shocked, but Fabian nodded serenely. "Yes. If you have a lot of garlic and marijuana on you at all times, it should help keep most ghosts away from you, though I am strong enough to withstand it," he added with obvious pride.

I couldn't stop shaking my head. Who would ever guess that garlic plus ganja equaled ghosts-be-gone? On reflection, I *had* smelled a lot of pot and garlic while in New Orleans, but I thought the latter was from the Cajun and Creole cooking, and the former was just a reflection of the city's party atmosphere. Who knew it was Marie's way of keeping the ghost population from becoming so large that vampires and ghouls would have to realize something was going on? She must have a pot and garlic field surrounding wherever her house was.

"Smashing, I'll get right on procuring both of those," Bones said, appearing not at all thrown by the idea. "Kitten, tell him he's to report to Mencheres from now on. Shouldn't be us anymore, not with all the herbs you'll soon be sporting. He says he's strong enough, but we can't risk the possibility of delaying an important message from him."

I repeated that to Fabian, still feeling weird over how he seemed to wait for me to say the same thing before reacting to it. Now I knew how Sigourney Weaver's character must have felt in *Galaxy Quest*. "Computer, do we *have* a beryllium sphere on board?" I muttered under my breath.

"What's that?" Bones asked.

"Nothing."

"I will return to Dave now. It shouldn't be hard to locate him. He said he wouldn't change hotels again until I came back," Fabian said.

I stared at him, wishing I could give him a hug goodbye and once more hating how everything I said hijacked his free will. "This won't be for long," I told him, brushing my hand over his face even though it went right through him.

An incandescent palm covered my hand, no weight or pressure in the gesture.

"I will not fail you," Fabian said, and then he disappeared from sight.

I stared at the spot where he'd been with a sort of grim resolve. Damned if I'd fail him, either. I *would* find a way to give Fabian his free will back, beat Apollyon without martyring myself—which would also get the ghoul hit men off my tail—and then talk some sense into my senselessly stubborn family.

I just had no idea how I'd do all those things.

"Don't fret, Kitten," Bones said quietly. "In addition to knowing how to keep most ghosts from flocking to you, we might have had another spot of good luck. I checked my mobile, and Timmie texted me this morning. Thinks a large nest of Apollyon's ghouls might be gathered in Memphis, according to curious events his sources reported to him."

That *was* good news. It just sucked that we needed to nab one of Apollyon's minions now more than ever, but according to the headless ghoul from the hotel, they'd vamoose at the first sight of me. Too bad I couldn't clone myself and have Fake Cat be a decoy somewhere else, making the ghouls feel safe, while the real me snuck up behind them. That would solve a lot of problems, but as cloning had only been accomplished scientifically with sheep, to my knowledge, I was shit out of luck.

Still, a modification of the same thing wasn't totally far-fetched. Maybe one of Don's scientists could design a replica of my face and we'd slap it on a woman of similar height and build. It worked in movies, after all . . .

"Of course!" I said, feeling a renewed surge of optimism as another idea struck me. "We'll call Dave and tell him where Timmie's got a nibble on the ghouls, plus I have to tell him Fabian's on his way back. We'll send Ed and Scratch to Memphis, too. Between the three of them, someone has to run into A-hole's minions before too long. Then we need to test out this garlic and weed combination to make sure it's enough to keep the majority of ghosts at bay. Once we know that, we're heading to Memphis, too."

His brow arched. "You sound like you have a plan, luv."

"Yes I do," I said, the wheels continuing to spin in my mind. "Part one involves me drinking your blood again. I'll need all the power I can get. As for part two . . . well, I'll need to make a couple phone calls."

TWENTY

BARON CHARLES DEMORTIMER, WHO WENT by Spade so he'd never forget that he was once referred to by the tool an overseer had assigned him, was Bones's best friend. They'd known each other over two centuries, ever since they were human prisoners at a New South Wales penal colony. Right now, I was pretty sure their long history was the only reason Spade hadn't gone for my throat at first sight of me. The look he threw me when Bones glanced away said loud and clear that he was fantasizing about throttling me.

"I'm so glad you called!" Denise, my best friend, said as she hugged me. "I'm thrilled to finally be able to help you out for once."

Over her shoulder, Spade glowered at me again when Bones turned away to see if they'd brought any more bags with them. I ignored that, squeezing Denise in return while marveling at her new strength.

It reinforced my opinion that this was our best course of action, even though it might take Spade a few years to forgive me for suggesting it. He and Denise had just gotten married recently, and he was very protective of her.

So was I, and if Denise were still human, she wouldn't be here now. But she wasn't really human anymore. A demon made sure of that when he branded Denise with his essence a few months back. Now that the demon was dead, what he'd done to her could never be undone, which made Denise perhaps the most indestructible person on the planet. Hell, if I cut her head off right now, the only result would be a big mess on the floor until another one grew back.

That wasn't the only incredible thing Denise could do, which was why I'd asked them to come. I linked arms with her as we went into the living room, letting out a short laugh as Denise said, "Not to be rude right off, Cat, but . . . why do you smell like you bathed in garlic?"

"Just be glad your nose isn't strong enough to get a whiff of the weed, too," I replied wryly. "It's a, uh, homemade remedy to keep a certain unwanted element away from me."

"You'll keep quite a lot of elements away from you with that particular aroma," Spade said, wrinkling his nose with such refined distaste that it was like getting a glimpse of him when he was an eighteenth-century nobleman.

"Yeah, well, good thing I'm not trying to pick up vampires anymore, what with my new stinky perfume," I said, hiding a smile. Spade must be *really* ticked at me. Normally his innate chivalrousness would have him replying with a gallant lie about how garlic was all the new rage for fragrances, or that the cloud of weed wafting from me really brought out the shine in my hair.

Bones gave him a look that said Spade's lack of warmth hadn't gone unnoticed by him, either. He poured two whiskeys from the decanter on the credenza, handing one to Spade with less graciousness than normal.

"Correct me if I'm wrong, mate, but I seem to remember my wife risking her life on your behalf twice just this year. So you can't be sore over her asking your wife for a favor that endangers her *not at all*, can you?"

"Of course it endangers her," Spade replied at once. "If even a drop of Denise's blood should spill in a place where other vampires might taste it—"

"Dammit, Spade, we talked about this," she interrupted him, her hazel eyes narrowing in way that warned of repercussions. "I'm going to live a very, very long time, and I refuse to spend that life in fear like I did before. If this even works, which it might not, you'll be with me the whole time, right? And stopping this crazy ghoul leader before he gets too many people riled up means more safety for everyone, *right*? So quit with the overprotectiveness. You wouldn't want me to act that way with you."

"This sounds familiar, doesn't it?" I whispered to Bones, feeling like I was watching actors play the parts of me and him.

He grunted. "Too right."

"If I thought Denise would be in danger, I wouldn't ask her," I said to Spade. Since she'd been branded, only demon bone through the eyes could kill Denise, and that was about as rare as a proverbial snowball in hell. "You want to keep her safe," I continued. "So do I, which is why Apollyon's got to be stopped. Even if I was staked with silver tomorrow, I don't think Apollyon will all of a sudden go away. He's waited six hundred years to try this power coup, and I'll bet he won't want to wait another six hundred or longer until another half-breed pops up again."

Spade said nothing for several moments, his tiger-colored gaze traveling over Denise, Bones, and me in turn. At last, he spread out his hands.

"You're all correct, of course. My apologies. It seems logic fails me when it comes to my wife's welfare."

Bones snorted. "I know how you feel. But don't fret. I'm sure Denise will remind you of any flaws in your logic as often as my wife reminds me of mine."

I couldn't help but laugh at the dryness in his tone. "Right back at you, honey. You're pretty good about pointing it out when I'm acting with my fears and not my brain. So I guess we've all been guilty of it."

The tension in the room drained away, resulting in a few moments of companionable silence. Then Denise cleared her throat.

"So . . . let's get started. I haven't eaten all day to try and gear up for this, and I'm starving. If this works, I'm rewarding myself with enough food to choke a horse."

So saying, she got up and stood a little way off from the couch. I went over to her, not really sure if I should say anything or if that would break her concentration. Mencheres and Kira had left, so the house was empty aside from us. No ghosts lingered in the vicinity, thanks to the illegal stink remedy on me and around the house, and the drapes were drawn even though the closest neighbor was a good two blocks away. We weren't taking any chances of being observed by anyone—unless you counted my cat, who groomed himself while throwing occasional glances our way.

Denise looked me over from top to bottom, her forehead creased with concentration. Then her scent changed, souring from her natural jasmine base to a harsher aroma of agitation. Her pulse sped up as well, breathing becoming shorter, sharper. The air around her thickened as her scent changed even more, now tinged with faint undertones of sulfur. Even though I'd seen this reaction in her before, I couldn't stifle a twinge of unease as her hazel eyes slowly filled with deep crimson.

Then Denise cried out, harsh and loud. Her skin seemed to ripple over her features in a misshapen, melted way, like wax held too close to flame. More moans came from her, the sounds almost animalistic in their intensity. She bent over, shudders wracking her body so viciously it looked like her muscles were being torn out of place. Unbidden, my hand rose to my mouth, stifling a gasp. Spade was right. I shouldn't have asked her to do this. What the hell had I been thinking?

Denise fell to her knees, her hair falling over her face as a horrible shout wrenched from her. Spade was at her side even before I was, taking her in his arms and whispering to her. I touched her shoulder, heaping recriminations on myself.

"Stop, Denise, it's not worth it. We'll find another way—"

My voice broke off as her head whipped up suddenly, her eyes now gunmetal gray instead of crimson or hazel, dark brown hair changed to red and framing the same face I saw looking back at me from the mirror.

"Bugger me dead, you did it," Bones whistled.

A slow grin spread across Denise's face—except it wasn't her face anymore. It was mine.

"That was *so* much easier than the last time!" she said, giving Spade a quick kiss before jumping to her feet. Even her body now looked exactly like mine, I noted with amazement. She'd grown inches taller and filled out in the butt and breast area, all in the space of about three minutes.

"Darling, are you all right?" Spade asked, rising and looking her over with far more objectivity than I felt. Staring at a mirror image of myself on my best friend was just . . . odd, even though this was what we'd hoped would happen. The demon's essence hadn't just made her virtually unkillable. It had also turned Denise into a shapeshifter like he'd been.

She smoothed her hand down Spade's chest. "Don't worry, I'm fine. Looks and sounds much worse than it is, really. Now, where's the kitchen? Did I mention I was *starving*?"

I'd just gotten out of the shower when Bones shut the bedroom door behind him, his gaze somber. After dinner, which all of us ate so Denise didn't feel like the odd person out, we'd finalized the details of our plan. Everyone agreed it was our best way to hopefully head Apollyon off at the pass, but Spade wasn't the only one who had misgivings about his spouse's safety. I was nervous for Bones, as he was for me, but we both knew *not* acting posed the greater danger. Still, now that we were alone, I felt his disquiet in the emotions grazing mine. His natural heady, burnt sugar scent was more reminiscent of kitchen accident than crème brûlée right now.

I stopped towel-drying my hair and went over to him, sliding my arms around his neck as I laid my head on his chest. Soon, I'd have to reapply the garlic-and-pot packets all over me, but for now, I could hold him without those smelly impediments.

"It'll be okay," I said, my words puffing onto the fabric of his shirt. "This will work."

Hard arms encircled my back as he pulled me closer. "I know. Just don't fancy being separated from you."

I let out a small snort. "I don't like it, either, but Denise is the ultimate decoy. You saw her. She's now my twin, right down to my cup size. If you saw her out at a bar, even you would swear it was me."

"Not as soon as I got close," he replied, head lowering until his mouth brushed my jaw. "Forget the heartbeat; she doesn't smell like you, her voice isn't yours, her posture is different, and she looks at people differently than you do."

"How do I look at people?" I asked, bemused. All the other things he'd listed made sense, but few except Bones knew me well enough to notice those differences. Denise's heartbeat was the biggest concern, but we had a way around that which would work for all but someone right up next to her—and I didn't think Spade would let anyone get that close.

Bones pulled back, staring into my eyes even as his fingers traced my face. "You have the gaze of a fighter. Noticed it right off when we met. You looked at me . . . and I could tell you were mentally assessing my strengths and weaknesses before anything else. At the time I thought it was odd, because that stare didn't match the green girl who tripped over her words when she asked me if I wanted to fuck."

Laughter bubbled from my throat. "I was trying to lure you outside so I could kill you, but unlike every other vampire I'd met up to that point, you weren't co-operating. Should've known right then that you'd be trouble."

His lips curled, a hint of green appearing in his gaze. "Ah, but that only made me more tempting to you. You couldn't resist the challenge. That's why you came looking for me the very next night, and why you agreed to let me train you even though you still plotted to kill me those first few weeks."

He was right. Back then, believing all vampires were evil bloodsuckers, I'd been determined to kill Bones despite the fact that he was much stronger than me. And he was right that the lure of defeating such a powerful vampire appealed to my sense of challenge. Or recklessness, depending on who you asked.

"What about you?" I breathed, standing on tiptoe to brush his mouth with mine. "If I'd have fallen back with my legs open like all the other women you came across, you'd have given me the night of my life, and then for-gotten my name before breakfast. But I was immune to your charms and prettiness. Must've shocked you." I couldn't stop my grin as I lightly nipped his lower lip. "So I'm not the only one who couldn't resist a challenge."

"You weren't immune to my charms for long, as I recall," he responded, a brow arching with sinful meaning.

"I admit to being stubborn when it came to resisting your appeal." Spoken as I unwound my towel to let it drop to the floor. "But I'd have to be all the way dead not to want you."

His eyes were now completely green, and fangs gleamed out from his upper teeth. I loved the way his gaze raked over me. Like it was the first time he'd seen me this way, and he couldn't stop himself from staring. I knew my body, was well aware of its flaws, but Bones made me forget those when he looked at me. Under the hunger in his gaze and the swell of his lust cresting against my subconscious, I felt beautiful, strong, and sexy. Free to do anything without fear or shame.

His hands slid down my bare skin, power caressing my senses at the same time. I opened my mouth as his head dipped, feeling those inner sparks ignite with his kiss. They increased as his tongue stroked along mine with deliberate, intimate thoroughness. He'd use the same slow, deep strokes when his mouth was somewhere else, and the thought made my loins clench with anticipation. Bones only rushed things when I wanted him to; when impatience made my need so sharp that I couldn't endure the delicious way he drew out foreplay. Tonight, though, I wanted *him* to be the one who felt drugged with passion, and if I let him keep kissing me, I'd soon be past the point of enough mental capacity to do that.

"Get on the bed," I said, tearing my mouth away.

He carried me there, trailing more dizzying kisses

down my neck at the same time, but I resisted when he started to lay me onto the mattress.

"Just you," I said, untangling myself from his arms.

He cast a meaningful glance at the thick bulge in his pants before looking back at me. "Not becoming a tease, are you?"

I felt the rub of fangs against my tongue, two pointed reminders of the heat flaring inside me, but I pushed my desire back. That was tough to do with Bones propped on his elbows, legs casually yet invitingly splayed, inky shirt unbuttoned to reveal a V of crystal flesh in extravagant contrast to the dark fabric. For a minute I stared at him, letting his beauty fill my eyes.

"Angels wish they were as gorgeous as you," I said with conviction.

"I'm very far from angelic, but thank you for the compliment."

The words were light—his expression wasn't. It was intense, his eyes flashing with emerald, and that bulge between his legs sent rip currents of lust through me. If I kept staring at him, letting my mind dwell on the fact that he felt even better than he looked, I'd fall on top of him and lose all thought amidst the bliss of his flesh merging into mine.

But I had an agenda, and right now, it didn't involve me jumping on him. We'd had so much stress, danger, and violence lately, with more coming on the horizon, that our circumstances didn't lend themselves to romance, but I didn't care. Sure, we could sit down, go over our battle strategy yet again, or smother each other with admonitions to be careful, but if I'd learned anything these past few years, it was to grab hold of moments of bliss when they came.

Or to make them myself, if circumstances weren't accommodating enough to throw one my way.

"After tomorrow, we won't see each other for a little while," I replied, voice low and throaty. "So I want to make sure that you have something to remember me by."

Twenty-one

I **REACHED OUT TO BONES WITH DELIBERATE** slowness, batting his hands away when he sought to pull me down again.

"No," I said, pushing him flat against the bed. "To-night, I'm in charge. Your only job is to lie back, relax, and"—memory of words he'd once said made a soft laugh escape me—"let me work."

His brow arched even as a wicked smile tugged at his mouth. "I'd tell you to be gentle, but we both know I wouldn't mean it."

No, he wouldn't, and that knowledge only fueled my desire. Bones might be a master at control, but once pushed past his limit, he made love the same way he fought; ferocious, unbridled, and inexhaustible. I couldn't count how many bed frames we'd ruined in our time together, and I hoped there were many more broken ones ahead of us in our future.

"Close your eyes," I told him. He did, and I pressed

on his lids lightly to punctuate my next point. "Keep them closed until I tell you otherwise."

That little smirk still hugged his mouth as he complied. "Fancy me calling you mistress as well? You could always punish me if I forget and address you as Kitten."

"No 'mistress,' and no more talking, either," I said, biting back my grin even though he couldn't see it.

Then, with far more slowness than I usually used, I unbuttoned his shirt, letting my knuckles brush his skin. Once that was off, I moved to his pants, controlling my urge to reach inside and instead treating his zipper to the same slow handling. With his pants undone, I dragged them down an inch at a time until they slid past his feet. Then, at last, I allowed myself to stare. Bones's body was a pale, smooth landscape of beauty, the only dark interruptions being the thin line of hair on his stomach that flared to a patch of darker curls cradling the only fat thing on him. His skin gleamed with a vampire's natural incandescence, emphasizing the hard muscles, lean lines, and enticing contours. His entire body invited touch, and I accepted that invitation.

My fingers grazed his chest, measuring his reaction in his deepening scent and the thrum of power in the air. His eyes remained closed, arms folded beneath his head for comfort—or maybe because he knew that showed off his chest to greater benefit. Probably the latter. Bones had mastered the art of seduction before this country even elected its first president. I continued trailing my fingers down his chest, enjoying the feel of him underneath their tips. He might be far more experienced at making someone weak with desire, but I had an edge, too. I knew everything he liked, and I was going to exploit that knowledge to my fullest advantage.

I splayed my hands along his ribs and moved them slowly up to his raised arms. His power tingled against my palms, sending pleasant vibrations through me. Then, I placed both hands on his chest and rubbed my thumbs across his nipples. They hardened to match the rest of his body.

"I love your hands," he sighed. "You think I look like an angel? Well, Kitten, your hands are my heaven and your eyes are my home."

The words warmed me, but his voice was its own temptation with its smooth English accent and sensual undercurrents. If I let him keep talking, he could entice me into doing whatever he wanted instead of what I'd planned.

"Shhh . . ." I drew out. Bones might not be able to see my smile, but he could probably feel it as I brushed my mouth over his in a feathery kiss.

"Mmm, my mistake," he murmured, stretching in a way that sent muscles rippling down his body.

I licked my lips, forcing down my urge to follow those ripples with my tongue. Instead, I let my hands wander at will, stroking and touching him from his face to his feet and back again. Honestly, I hadn't spent so much time just handling him before. Lust usually cut short such a thorough exploration since I lacked his patience and control. Tonight was different, though. Feeling him this way, lingering over the curves of his body and enjoying the low sounds of pleasure he made, was more than arousing; it was affirming. Bones was *mine*, and no matter what the future threw at us, we'd meet it together, come hell or high water.

He rolled onto his stomach when I directed him to, revealing those wide shoulders, the narrow curve of his waist, and the twin hard mounds of his buttocks. This time, it wasn't enough for me to merely caress him. I crouched over him, running my mouth down his spine and feeling his shiver underneath my lips.

The taste of his skin and his scent was like an aphrodisiac. I climbed on the bed, letting my hair tease his flesh as I continued to drag my mouth over him, licking and nibbling everywhere. He began to make low, guttural noises with every new inch of his back, ass, and legs that I gave the same thorough attention to.

"Sweet bleedin' hell, luv, this was a smashing idea."

His voice was strained, and his hands were now clenched into fists. I didn't comment on him speaking this time, but bit gently into a muscled cheek, not breaking his skin with my fangs, just applying pressure. Then my tongue crept out for a long lick while I pressed my bare breasts against the back of his thighs. His shudder reverberated underneath my mouth and along my subconscious as his arousal touched me even though his hands stayed where they were.

"*More.*"

The word was almost harsh in its vehemence. I smiled into his skin as I dragged my body lower down his legs.

"Don't worry, I'm not done yet."

I turned him back around, my lips trailing along his hip to the flatness of his stomach. His muscles bunched underneath my mouth in expectation, but

I only blew a teasing breath on the hardness jutting to his navel before sitting back. The bedroom was lit by candles on the nightstand and the dresser, natural light being easier on vampire eyes instead of the glare from electric bulbs, but now, those candles would serve a different purpose.

I scooted off the bed, stopping when Bones's hand shot out to land on my arm even though his eyes were still closed.

"Where do you think you're going?"

I pushed his hand off with a throaty laugh. "You're having a hard time being obedient, aren't you? If you don't behave, I won't do what I intended, and trust me, you'll wish I had."

That wicked curl was back on his mouth even as he dropped his arm. "My *sincerest* apologies, mistress, for my shameful disobedience. If you pray continue, I vow my complete submission."

Smart ass. Despite the promise, I knew Bones was about as submissive as Genghis Khan, but that was okay. I'd make what I knew was just his temporary compliance count.

I took one of the candles off the nightstand, considering Bones in the light of the flickering flame. His body was stretched out, arms once again behind his head, limbs completely relaxed even though he was still hard as a baseball bat in one very notable place. *All this bounty, mine to enjoy.* I licked my lips. Damned if I knew how I'd gotten so lucky, but that was a question for another time. Now was the time for action, not contemplation.

I moved closer until my legs pressed against the side of the bed. "Do you remember the first time you bit me here?" I asked, tracing my finger over the tight bud of his nipple.

"Yes." One word, hissed with all the weight of desire that I could feel through his emotions.

"It felt like your fangs were burning me." My voice was no more than a whisper from the shiver of remembrance, and I blew out the candle with an unsteady puff. "I can't duplicate that with you because you're not human," I went on. "The juice in my fangs won't feel the same, but maybe this will be close."

Then I poured some of the hot wax that pooled in the candle directly onto Bones's nipple.

His whole body arched while a strangled groan tore from his throat. I didn't wait for the wax to harden, but covered it with my mouth, biting into his skin and tonguing the searing mixture at the same time. His back arched again, strong hands tangling in my hair to press me closer with enough force to drive my fangs deeper into him. Pleasure blasted across my subconscious, inciting me to bite him again, pushing the wax aside in my mouth to swallow the heady vintage of his blood.

Then, before the wax cooled too much, I poured the remains from the candle onto his other nipple, rewarded by another guttural moan. I waited a second before switching my fangs there next, alternately licking and sucking the hard, heated peak. Once I'd swallowed another decadent mouthful of his blood— and possibly a few stray bits of wax—I leaned back, wiping my mouth of any spare drops and staring into his scorching green gaze.

His power throbbed beneath my hands, the scent of his lust heavy in the air. It mingled with the smoke and fragrance of my own arousal, creating an erotic ambiance. Without taking my eyes from him, I leaned forward, brushing my breast along his side as I reached to put the extinguished candle on the nightstand . . . and grab the other lit one.

Very slowly, I ran my free hand down his body, brushing aside the remaining bits of wax on his chest before following that thin line of dark hair to where it widened at his groin. Bones's eyes didn't close as my hand circled around him, but his lips parted, revealing those sharp twin fangs. I moistened my own lips as I looked down at the hard flesh in my hand. It overflowed my grip, pulsing with a different sort of power, the tip wet with the palest drop of pink as I stroked with firm, smooth pumps. Then I glanced at the candle in my other hand before meeting his unblinking gaze.

"Do it," he said, his voice so rough I almost didn't recognize it.

I blew the candle out with a soft puff that still left it smoldering, then poured the entire scalding contents onto the hard flesh in my hand.

His whole body jerked while flashes of pain and pleasure assaulted my subconscious. I mashed the top of the candle together to ensure that it was out before throwing it aside, ignoring the fleeting burn in my hand. Then, before the wax had a chance to cool, I fastened my lips around the head of his cock. A primal groan came from his throat when I pulled him in deeper, tonguing his flesh, taking as much as I could with two sharp, pointed fangs in the way. He felt like sculpted marble, flesh warmer from the contact with the wax that clung between my fingers. I stroked him as I continued to work his length into my mouth, sucking on his flesh like I wanted to rend the skin from him.

His hands clenched convulsively, tearing the sheets from the ripping noises. I didn't pause to check, but continued to flick my tongue along his flesh, brushing away the wax. Only pleasure flooded through our connection now since he'd already healed from the initial contact the wax caused. Even if I couldn't feel that through his emotions, I'd know it because my hand didn't sting anymore. Besides, I knew that on occasion, Bones liked a little pain with his passion. And after I became a vampire, I found out one of his favorite ways to receive it.

I lifted my gaze to stare up at him as I took him as deeply into my mouth as I could, my fangs pressing against the veined hardness beneath them. His eyes closed and his back arched—another invitation I took him up on.

I sank my fangs into him, reveling in the shudder that went through his body and the shout that seemed to erupt from his throat. The ambrosia of his blood teased my tongue as, very carefully, I rocked my mouth against him, taking his cock deeper without enlarging the punctures I'd made in it.

This had taken practice to perfect.

That blend of ecstasy and pain swarmed back over my emotions. He groaned, hips lifting in time to the rhythmic movement of my mouth. I pulled my fangs out to sink them in again at the base of his groin, only my vampiric lack of a gag reflex making it possible for me to enclose him completely. Then, I sucked once more, running my tongue along his length while swallowing the drops of blood that leaked past my fangs from the punctures.

"Turn around," Bones said hoarsely as his hands urged me up toward him.

I resisted, knowing what he wanted and also knowing I'd lose all sense if I let him do it.

"No. Just you, or I'll stop," I said, the words somewhat garbled, but punctuated with another slide of my fangs into his flesh.

He moved so that he was on his side, his body curled toward mine, hand reaching between my thighs. A choked moan escaped me as he rubbed my cleft, thumb circling my clitoris even as his fingers penetrated my depths.

"You're so wet," he muttered. "I want to drown in your taste and cover myself with your scent."

The graphic imagery made even more things inside me tighten, but I had a reason for not wanting him to go down on me, even if I couldn't recall it at the moment.

"No," I said again, taking him back inside my mouth and grazing his length with my fangs.

He groaned. "Soon. Don't stop, Kitten. Deeper. More."

I encased him to the hilt again, sucking even more strongly. His hand stayed where it was, fingers moving over my flesh with greater insistence, making my hips arch with each accompanying stroke. An ache began to build in me, a familiar tension that spoke of needs that couldn't be denied. Each rub wound me tighter, inflaming me. I continued to draw on the hard length of him, licking and biting the spots I knew he liked best, trying not to give in to the urge to feast on his blood. His hand moved faster, until cries spilled from my mouth even though they were muffled by his flesh.

"I can't wait anymore," Bones all but snarled.

I barely had time to pull my fangs out of his skin before he yanked me up, sliding down at the same time. His arms lashed around my waist, holding me in a viselike grip, mouth latching onto the soft, tingling flesh between my legs.

Pleasure slammed into me like a dam had burst. His fingers dug into my hips, molding me closer. Tongue and fangs and lips became a blur of sensations that whipped me with rapture, stealing all thought under the chaotic flood. The more I moved, the higher it took me.

Harsh cries took on the cadence of breathing, fed by a million nerve endings that urged me on for more. Had his hands not held me, I would have fallen from the tremors that started to rip through me. They culminated in an orgasm that felt torn out of me.

Some measure of coherence returned, enough to make me mildly embarrassed at how his head was now compressed several inches into the mattress. He finally released his grip and I fell back onto the bed. When he crouched over me, his eyes were still fierce, flaming green. A chopped inhalation escaped me when I saw traces of blood around his mouth. *Mine? Or his?*

"Bones—"

"Don't." Something lurked in his tone that shivered me. "Don't say anything, especially 'stop.' You're in for it now."

He gathered me to him, pulling me to my knees and turning me around. One pale arm curved around my waist, holding me firmly. In the next moment he thrust into me, sheathing himself in one rough stroke.

It made me cry out, as did the next one and the next, so hard and fast I felt tears leak from my eyes. He ran his mouth along my back before dragging it to my ear.

"Don't hold back." His steady tone belied his movements, driving into me with more force than I thought I could bear. "Scream for me."

"Too much." My reply was panted at his frantic pace.

"Like hell," he growled, licking my neck. "You pierced yourself on my fangs and you loved it. I feel your body, and you're not in pain. Let go, like you did before. Give in."

He bent me forward, his hands on my hips the only thing supporting me. True to his prior directive, I began to scream at the ceaseless, blistering passion of his body cleaving into mine harder than he ever had before. His grip immobilized me, accented voice muttering rough endearments between groans of his own as the intensity built to a staggering pitch. When it crested to the point of overwhelming me, he leaned down and buried his fangs into my neck, drinking my blood with strong, almost feral pulls of his mouth.

I collapsed onto the mattress, no strength, mindless, my release hitting me in pounding surges. It was so intense that I was only vaguely aware of Bones's shout before a deep spasm inside told me that he'd joined me in ecstasy. After a few moments that seemed to suspend in time, he fell next to me like someone cut his strings, both of us taking in a few ragged, if sporadic, breaths.

"If I have to beg, you are going to do that again,"

Bones finally said in a strained voice. "I can't feel my bloody legs."

Neither could I, but speaking was beyond my abilities at the moment. I could hear and think, but only hazily. Even with the lightning-fast regenerative abilities of being a vampire, I still felt twinges of soreness mixed in with the residual tingles from a really explosive orgasm. If I'd been human and Bones took me that hard, I wouldn't walk for a week. No, wait, make that a month.

"I think this'll definitely tide me over while we're apart," I said, managing to flop over onto my back. *And then some*, my glazed mind added.

Bones laughed, dragging me into his arms with far more strength and quickness than was fair, considering I still had trouble making my limbs operate.

"Oh, Kitten," he murmured as his lips dragged down my throat. "You didn't really think we were done, did you?"

He'll be the death of me was my thought, but I couldn't bring myself to utter a word of complaint. Or protest as his mouth slid past my neck and continued on a downward track.

After all, even if I was right, there were far worse things than death—and I couldn't think of a better way to go, anyway.

Twenty-two

THE PLANE TOUCHED DOWN RIGHT AS THE skies opened and heavy rain pelted the aircraft. Even though I was anxious to get started, a part of me lamented the fact that soon, I'd have to reapply my stinky phantom repellent again. Airport security would have taken issue with me trying to board a flight while covered in weed, and I didn't think my truthful explanation of "But I have to keep ghosts away!" would go over with them.

I collected my suitcase from the overhead bin— missing my usual weapons cache—and did the wait-stop-wait shuffle out of the plane with the other passengers. Once on the gangway, I could walk freely, and it didn't take me long to reach the passenger waiting area. A circular glance around didn't show the face I was looking for, and there was no telltale surge of supernatural energy in the air. Frowning, I glanced at my watch. No, I wasn't early. In fact, the plane was about fifteen minutes behind schedule. So where was Mencheres?

"Cat, welcome."

I whirled, blinking for a second at the tall, tawny-haired stranger—and then I laughed.

"God, that's amazing."

The slight hint of a smile on Mencheres's face was familiar, but not much else. His midnight-black hair and eyebrows were now golden blond, his charcoal-colored gaze azure blue, and instead of the normal, expensive-looking slacks and long-sleeved shirts he favored, Mencheres had on an Ed Hardy T-shirt and board shorts.

Most startling to me, however, was his aura. Or lack of one. Aside from his missing heartbeat, I'd almost swear he was human, because almost no preternatural energy stirred the air around us. Considering that being around Mencheres normally felt like flying a metal umbrella in a lightning storm, I was stunned at how thoroughly he'd managed to cloak his power level.

"And here I thought I was good at this cloak-and-dagger stuff," I went on, a vague gesture encompassing my newly raven hair, brown contacts, and artificially darkened skin courtesy of one of those tan-in-a-bottle creams. I'd even thickened and darkened my eyebrows and dyed the peach fuzz on my arms from golden-red to brown. A vampire had previously identified me because of a hint of red on my armpits, even though I'd shaved that morning. Fool me once and all that.

"I've had somewhat more practice than you," Mencheres replied with dry humor, taking my bag even though I could easily carry it. I didn't argue. He wasn't being chauvinistic; he just came from a different era. A *very* different era, considering the four-and-a-half-millennia gap in our ages.

We walked out of the airport without saying anything else, not wanting to draw attention to ourselves just in case this place was being watched by either Apollyon's ghouls or ones from the other sect. We couldn't be too careful, even though Bones had already been out the past three nights with Denise in Ohio. With her ability to shapeshift into an exact replica of me, I doubted anyone except him, Spade, Mencheres, or Kira had any idea that the real Red Reaper was in Memphis instead of hitting the bar and club scene with Bones.

Still, to further throw off suspicion, Kira wasn't joining Mencheres as we combed the Memphis area. She was going about her business as usual, making it easier to keep up the charade that Mencheres was still at home with her. I felt bad for being the reason they were in separate states so early in their relationship, but I also knew both of them understood the necessity. Kira had been a private investigator, so she knew all about stakeouts, and Mencheres had been playing catch-the-bad-guys since the time of the pyramids.

Once we were in the car, Mencheres handed me a bag from the backseat. I didn't even need to open it to know what it contained. The smell preceded its contents, but the two herbs had been as effective as Fabian promised. I'd only had a couple ghosts track me down in the past four days, and I sent them packing with a politely worded directive.

I kept the bag on my lap, telling myself I didn't need to start stuffing it down my clothes yet. Just putting off the inevitable, I knew, but *eau de garlique stoner* wasn't my favorite perfume. I flipped my dark glasses onto the top of my head, not needing them for concealment anymore, and settled more comfortably into the seat. I'd wait an hour or so before I called Bones. It was eleven o'clock at night; he was probably just arriving at whatever was the latest Ohio hotspot with Denise and Spade.

We were a few miles away from the airport when a blast of energy hit the car like an invisible bomb. I instinctively reached for my sleeves, forgetting I didn't have knives strapped to my arms, when I realized it was just Mencheres dropping his shields.

"Next time, how about a heads-up before you do that?" I said, exasperated. "Thought we were being attacked."

"My apologies," he replied at once, folding his aura back in until it no longer felt like an explosive. "I didn't mean to alarm you."

You've alarmed me ever since we first met, oh ancient spooky one was my sardonic thought, but I didn't say it out loud and he couldn't read it from my mind anymore. Just one of many reasons why I was glad I made the switch from half human to mostly dead.

Then, just as abruptly as his power had struck me moments ago, guilt slapped me. Mencheres's extraordinary power, age, and visions of the future had always creeped me out, but he couldn't help being the way he was. Just like I couldn't help being a half-breed before, or feeding from vampires and absorbing their powers now. On the weird scale, I probably outranked Mencheres, yet I was still letting my discomfort about his unusualness affect the way I thought of him.

If Bones lived a few more thousand years—and God knew I hoped he did—he might end up with many of Mencheres's unusual abilities, too. Mencheres shared his power legacy with Bones, giving him mind reading and a strength upgrade overnight, and we didn't know how many more things might crop up over time. How would I like it if people treated Bones suspiciously because his powers made him different from most other vampires? Even the thought made anger burn in me. Yeah, I knew how I'd like it; I'd want to kick their asses all over the place.

"I'm the one who owes *you* an apology," I said, staring at Mencheres's drastically altered profile. "Even before I was mad at you for not telling me that you'd wiped out a month of my life when I was sixteen, you always made me uneasy, and it was mostly because I was being a hypocrite."

He glanced over at me with the strangest expression on his face. "I'm afraid I don't understand, Cat."

"Apollyon's minions aren't the only ones who're guilty of being afraid of someone just because they're different," I replied softly. "You'd think with how I grew up, I would've known better, but I still ended up doing the same thing with you. I'm sorry, Mencheres. You deserved better than that."

The car decelerated as he pulled over to the side of the road, waiting until we were stopped before meeting my gaze fully.

"You owe me no apology." Each word was enunciated as though it were its own sentence. "By neither word nor deed have you ever exploited me for your own gain, and I cannot say the same about my actions with you."

Eight months ago, I might have snapped, "That's right, buddy!" but a lot of things had changed since then.

"I don't know what it's like to hold a huge supernatural line together for over four millennia. The most I did at my old job was lead a team of sixty soldiers for about five years. Even though there's no comparison between the two, I still had to make some 'greater good' decisions that were really tough, so while I was pissed at you over what you did, some part of me still understood. Besides"—I smiled wryly—"since your manipulating brought Bones and me together, it's kind of hard for me to justify still holding a grudge."

Mencheres took my hand and brushed it against his forehead in an oddly formal gesture. "You honor me with your forgiveness."

"And you can honor me by accepting my apology, because no matter what you did, I was still wrong, too," I countered.

He let go of my hand, an expression of amusement flitting over his features before they became impenetrable again.

"You are a very stubborn woman. Apology accepted."

"Thank you." Then I cracked a small, self-conscious smile. "Okay, enough with the intimate confessions, right? Let's go find some bigoted ghouls and pummel them into taking us to their leader."

Mencheres's faux azure gaze glinted with a hint of the frighteningly lethal ass kicker he was beneath his soft-spoken, proper demeanor.

"Yes," he said, drawing out the word. "Let's. Ed and Scratch have already arrived in the city. Vlad will meet us tonight at the town house I'm renting. Once we are all here, we will begin the hunt."

Of our group, Dave was the first to strike pay dirt in Memphis. A week after we arrived, he reported through Fabian that he'd made contact with some ghouls who had a definite bias against vampires. We weren't sure if they were directly affiliated with Apollyon, or just some knockoff bigots, but according to Dave, he'd spent a fun-filled evening listening to them rant about how ghouls and vampires should live separate, unmixed lives. That inter-dating/marrying was a contamination of the species, and only through separatism could real "strength and purity" be attained.

Sounded like the sort of bullshit Apollyon's minions would preach, considering he was like an undead version of a KKK Grand Dragon. Dave had a tentative meeting with the same group tomorrow night, and I wasn't going to interfere. No need to tip our hand by being impatient and grabbing the pawns if waiting meant we could get our hands on the king instead. I hoped after a couple more meetings, Dave would be trusted enough to be let deeper into the ghouls' twisted group.

As for Vlad, Mencheres, and me, we were batting zero. Timmie's sources pointed to some odd activity at bars, plus I'd run the information past Tate and he'd verified that the crime rate had ticked up in Memphis recently, also adding credence that this was the area Apollyon was most likely centered in. But even though we'd hit local bars looking for suspects in the past seven days, we'd come up with nothing but an appreciation for the many varied flavors of barbecue in the city. Or maybe that was just me. Feeding from the sealed bags containing Bones's blood keep me nourished, but I still liked to vary up my palate a bit.

My cell phone vibrated in the side pocket of my jeans. I pulled it out, recognizing the number before I answered it.

"Reaper." Ed's voice, lowered enough that it was hard for me to hear him.

"You got something?" I asked at once, straightening. He and Scratch were across town at another popular watering hole; hopefully one more fruitful than the dive Mencheres, Vlad, and I were in.

"Maybe," Ed said, still so low I had to strain. I'd tell him to text me if he was worried about being overheard, but as I found out before, that was one modern skill Ed hadn't mastered yet. "Some bone-munchers came in earlier," he went on. "They had a nasty vibe coming off them, too. I overheard one of 'em mentioning the Falcon drive-in, and about ten minutes ago, they all left."

A drive-in? "You mean theater, right?" I asked, just to be sure it wasn't slang for something else.

Ed snorted. "Of course. I looked it up before I called you. It's on Summer Avenue near I–40."

Ed might not be able to text, but luckily, MapQuest wasn't beyond him. "Good. You head on over there, but not for at least ten minutes in case you're being watched. I'll start out now."

"See ya there," he grunted, and hung up.

"We're in the wrong place," I announced to Mencheres and Vlad as I signaled the bartender. "Let's settle up and get out of here."

Vlad's brows rose. "Do elaborate," he drawled.

I lowered my voice. Texting might be quieter, but it was also senseless with both of them right there. "Ed's heard of some strange activity at the Falcon drive-in, as though the words *activity* and *drive-in* in the same sentence weren't strange enough."

Mencheres gave me a quizzical look. "Why?"

I was about to say, *Because they're obsolete*, but then I reminded myself that for someone as old as Mencheres, drive-ins would still seem like a new form of entertainment.

"Because progress is a merciless bitch" was what I settled on, followed by "The bad news is, if the place is still open, not abandoned, we'll have human bystanders to worry about if Ed's right and anything does go down."

"Drive-ins," Vlad said, his lip curling in a way that said he hadn't been a fan of them even when they were popular. "I suppose that's better than a regular theater. Less people at drive-ins, and if they're anything like I remember, most of the humans there won't be concentrating on anything but fornicating anyway."

His disdainful tone almost made me laugh. Who knew the reputed scourge of the underworld looked down his nose at drive-in nookie?

"Not everyone had their own castle to go back to when *they* were young and horny," I said, my lips twitching.

The look he threw me was more than cynical. "My youth was spent in constant war, not the pursuit of tender seductions."

Privately I thought *tender* was the last word I'd associate with Vlad, but we had places to be, ghouls to track down, and all that. I glanced at my watch. Ten forty-five. That helped, but it was a Friday night, so the drive-in would be as populated as it was going to get.

"Well, boys," I said, placing some bills on the table. "Let's go to the movies."

Twenty-three

THE DRIVE-IN WASN'T ABANDONED, AS THE cars lined up in front of the four large outdoor screens attested to. I heaved a sigh even as I crept around the back of the first projector. Of course we wouldn't be lucky enough for this place to be closed down. Hell, from the number of people here, either I'd underestimated the drive-in's appeal, or they were giving away free popcorn *and* condoms with each show.

I crouched low as I crept along the bushes, making my way toward the less populated screening of some horror movie, it looked like. With all the headlights, I'd stand out like a sore thumb if I straightened and just walked there, but we weren't about to all cruise in through the main entrance. Even with our power levels cloaked, if this was some sort of secret ghoul meeting place, three vampires showing up would be enough to stir trouble, no matter if they thought we were here just to watch some flicks.

Hence the sneaking around while we sought to find out if we were the only pulseless people here. We'd split up to cover more ground. I couldn't see or sense Vlad or Mencheres, so they were doing a good job at being stealthy. I hoped I was being equally furtive.

Then I stopped. That was odd. A van was too far off to the side of the viewing area of the closest screen to even see the movie. It didn't rock in a telltale way, either, leaving the possibility of being out of viewing range of the movie for a romantic reason doubtful. It still might be nothing insidious, true, but there was only one way to find out.

I crept closer, still keeping low and doing my damnedest not to crunch the fallen leaves I stepped on. When my cell phone vibrated with a noise that seemed like a screech to my tense nerves, I hit ignore even though I saw with a pang that it was Bones calling. I didn't have time to chat with him now, and aside from the noise that someone with undead ears might pick up on, I needed to keep my cell clear in case Vlad or Mencheres texted with anything important. Like "need help" or "run for it, we're outnumbered!"

Fifty yards away from the van, I heard voices that weren't from the movie or inside my head, thanks to being back on Bones's blood. I stopped, trying to feel the air with my senses to catch any supernatural vibes on it, plus taking in a deep breath to see if I caught the earthy scent of ghouls. Nothing.

I'd just have to get closer to find out for sure.

The van was parked near where a clump of bushes turned into a tree-lined hill. In the dark, with the slope and the lights from the movies glaring in the opposite direction, the area behind there would be practically invisible to anyone looking. Hell, I could see in the dark, but with the slant, glare, and bushes, it was still hard for me to tell if any people were in that area, or if all I was seeing were trees.

I was almost crawling now to avoid being seen and straining my ears for any sounds that weren't the movies, the people watching them, their thoughts, or the nearby highway. *There.* A male voice, definitely, followed by another one, both back in the wooded area where no regular moviegoers would have any reason to be. Could be a couple of vagrants just having a little chat, but I drew out two of my bigger knives anyway. Damned if I'd let myself get captured if it wasn't just an innocuous gathering of humans. I might be the only chick in the group, but that didn't make me the damsel in distress.

After another few minutes of quiet crawling, I could pick up the twinges of power in the air, too low to make me turn around, too high to be Vlad or Mencheres with how they were cloaking their auras. I got a tighter grip on my knives and continued forward, glad I didn't have a regular heartbeat anymore, or it would be racing. *Come out, come out, wherever you are.*

" . . . take more down. Show our brothers we mean business," someone muttered.

A particularly loud crescendo of music cut off the first part of whatever the other person replied, but I caught " . . . till every last bloodsucker's *dead*," and really didn't need to hear anything else.

I was close now, barely thirty feet away. Enough to see that there were four ghouls standing in a loose circle, one of them casually prodding the dirt with the toe of his boot. Two of them looked pretty normal, wearing denim pants and short-sleeved T-shirts in the warm summer evening. The other two were dressed like a bad imitation of Hell's Angels with their leather jackets, fingerless gloves, black jeans, and thick chain accessories.

Overcompensating for something, are you? was my contemptuous thought.

"Did you feel that?" one of them asked, glancing around.

The others didn't even have a chance to reply before power slammed through the air, feeling like a whip on my skin before it skipped over me to land on them. I stood up, still holding my knives even though none of the ghouls was able to put up a fight anymore. From their horrified expressions, they couldn't even move enough to scream.

"You do know how to make an entrance, Mencheres," I remarked.

The Egyptian vampire appeared from the opposite side of the ghouls while measured, crunching noises coming from behind me told me where Vlad was.

"There's a white van nearby, did any of you check it out?" I asked.

"Stinks of these ghouls, but it's empty," Vlad replied as he drew abreast.

I stared at the four ghouls, thinking if their eyes bugged any wider, they might pop out of their sockets. Bet they never expected party crashers like Mencheres to show up. Vlad and I could kill them easy enough, but only Mencheres could freeze them into complete immobility without even laying a finger on them.

"This group is too small to warrant meeting out here like this. More must be coming," I said, lowering my voice.

From the flash of emotion across two of the ghouls' faces, I'd guessed correctly.

"I've still got them," Mencheres said, backing away. "Let's hide."

I'd seen his power in action before, so I had no hesitation about turning my back on the ghouls and creeping deeper into the woods. Odds were, their buddies would approach from the other direction, and if they smelled vampire, hopefully they'd think it was from a recent kill the group had made.

Mencheres and Vlad melted away into the woods as well. Once I reached a good vantage point, crouched behind a rocky formation about forty yards away, I stared back at where we left the ghouls. Lots of trees were in my way, so I couldn't see them exactly, but it looked like the four ghouls still stood where we'd left them, not even talking, and sure as hell not running. I shook my head. Damn handy power Mencheres had—if you were strong enough to control it, which I hadn't been.

We didn't have too long to wait. Less than twenty minutes later, we heard another vehicle pull up very close to where the van was, from the sounds of it. Then the casual, genial chatter of its occupants as they congratulated each other on killing two young vampires that morning.

Son of a bitch. No need to wonder if these were the rest of the group!

I crept closer, because they made enough noise to cover the soft sounds I made. Clearly they sensed no danger. Dark satisfaction filled me as I heard one of them jokingly ask what the others were looking at.

"What's the matter, Brent?" a voice laughed. "Cat got your tongue?"

That was too priceless an opening for me to leave hanging.

"Not yet, but I can make an exception," I said, straightening to my full height as I strode toward them.

Mencheres's power beat me, whooshing past and cementing them in their places before they could even gasp at the vampires popping up from the woods. Even though I recognized the practicality, a part of me was disappointed. Fighting them would be a great way to release some of the stress that had been building, but it wouldn't be a real brawl unless they could hit back.

When I drew within touching distance of the group that had now grown by seven, something white caught my eye, distracting me from lamenting that Mencheres's power took all the sport out of capturing them.

"You're wearing *fangs* around your neck?" I blurted, snatching at the necklace that hung from one of the Hell's Angels wannabes. Sure enough, eight fangs were strung on a silver chain, and the sight of them pissed me off into temporary speechlessness.

Vlad didn't seem as perturbed. He appeared to the left of the group, wagging his fingers at them almost playfully. "Here I'd always found drive-ins boring, but you're going to make this one fun for me, aren't you? Mencheres, give them the ability to speak, though if any of you screams, it'll be the last sound you make."

No one needed to tell me that this was about to get messy, and there were too many of them for us to take back to our rented town house.

"We need to get all these people out of here," I said, adding, "something that *won't* make the eleven o'clock news," as an important afterthought. Sure, Mencheres could clear this entire outdoor theater complex in a matter of seconds. But people might pause to wonder why their car was suddenly flying through the air, or why every huge movie screen crumbled into a ball, and we didn't need that sort of publicity.

Mencheres gave me a pointed glance. "I know how to be discreet," he said, before vanishing in a blur of speed.

I contained my snort with the utmost difficultly. It wasn't that long ago that Mencheres demolished a section of Disneyland in front of stunned witnesses, or changed Kira into a vampire on a video that was later blasted all over the Internet. *Yeah, essence of discretion, those things were.*

"So, boys . . ."

I turned around to see Vlad striding along the jagged circle of ghouls, still held in place by Mencheres's power even though the other vampire was out of sight. He touched each of them, the reason not lost to me. Whatever Vlad touched, he could burn.

"Whoever tells me all about your little gang gets to live," he went on. "Whoever doesn't talk . . . well, you can figure out what'll happen, I'm sure."

Flames sprouted around his hands for emphasis. A few of the ghouls grimaced, figuring out who Vlad was. Only one male vampire was infamous for wielding fire, and Vlad's reputation would have been anything but soothing to them.

"There's still too many people nearby," I reminded him. Bonfiring some of the ghouls was bound to draw attention, even through the bushes and trees.

"Then Mencheres had better hurry," Vlad replied, his tone hardening. "These fellows still aren't talking, and having my commands ignored is what you might call a pet peeve of mine."

One of them made weird grunting noises, flapping his lips in the oddest way, but the others stayed silent. Vlad sighed.

"No one believes you're serious until bodies start to fall."

Then he moved so fast that I wasn't even sure what he was doing . . . until I saw the four new crimson necklaces some of the group was sporting. Their expressions went abruptly blank, eyes rolling back, but their bodies stayed upright and their heads stayed on, even though nothing but Mencheres's power kept them glued to their necks anymore.

I blinked at Vlad's efficient brutality, but it wasn't a shock. Bones would have done the same thing. I might dislike killing enemy combatants if they couldn't fight back, but these ghouls were involved in trying to stir up a clash between two species that would leave thousands dead at least if they were successful. That meant my personal preferences had to be set aside.

"Those guys got off lucky. The rest of you won't," I said quietly. "In case you haven't figured it out, that's Vlad Tepesh you're looking at, and as for me? I'm the Red Reaper, and I'll bet you've heard of me."

Two of them spat curses, the nastiest from the ghoul wearing the fang trophies. I didn't give Vlad a chance to act, but swiped my blade through the ghoul's throat before he could say anything else. Now he had two necklaces; one made of fangs, the other made of the last blood he'd ever shed.

The other ghoul who'd cursed me burst into flames that burned so fiercely, his screams were cut off in seconds. I glanced toward the cinema, hoping none of the moviegoers would decide to check out the sudden blaze of fire, if they saw it. But before I could drop my mental shields to better pick up on any "what's that light over there?" thoughts, the flames on the ghoul vanished, leaving only smoke curling up over his remains.

That's right, no worry of a forest fire with Vlad around. My own control over fire had been far less during the brief time I'd borrowed the ability from him.

My hip vibrated. I jumped, tense from the circumstances, before realizing that it was just my cell phone. I pulled it out, seeing Bones's number, and grimaced as I hit ignore again. Much as I wanted to talk to him, chatting or texting during a fiery interrogation was just not appropriate.

"As your numbers dwindle, so does my patience," Vlad said in a chillingly genial tone. "Still not going to tell me what I want to know? Eeny, meeny, miny . . ."

At "moe," the ghoul Vlad pointed at exploded like a firecracker, pelting flaming bits of things I didn't even want to identify over the two ghouls on either side of him. It took all my willpower not to look away. *Gross* didn't even begin to cover what that looked like. Instead of doing something completely girly, like saying, "Ewwww," I concentrated on what I'd overhead the ghouls talking about, and on how many lives would be destroyed if Apollyon's plans were allowed to move forth.

"You'll kill us anyway, no matter if we tell you what you want to know," a ghoul with scars on his neck finally said. The other ghoul, who looked to be in his teens, still flapped his mouth in that strange way, like he was miming a fish out of water. *What's the deal with that?* I wondered.

Vlad shrugged. "If your information proves to be useful, after a period of time, I'll let you go. Before that, you'll be my captive, but you'll be alive, which is more than your friends can say," he finished with a tip of his head toward the other corpses.

The ghoul grunted. "Why should I believe you'll really let me live?"

Vlad became very still, but his eyes blazed with a dangerous light. "Call me a liar *one* more time," he said, each word dripping with challenge.

Even though I wasn't the one being threatened, a shiver still passed through me. This was one of the times I was glad I was on Vlad's good side.

The younger ghoul flapped his lips again, mouth opening and closing even more frantically. I gave him an irritated look. Nobody liked a drama queen in the middle of an interrogation. But then my eyes narrowed, and I had him by the shirt before Vlad could speak.

"Open your mouth again," I said, because he'd shut it in what might have been surprise once I grabbed him.

"Don't do it," the scarred ghoul ordered.

I snapped out a sideways kick, breaking his knee without once taking my eyes off the ghoul I held. Slowly, with a gaze that I now recognized as pleading, the ghoul opened his mouth. Wide.

"Jesus, Mary, and Joseph," I breathed.

Twenty-four

I KEPT STARING INTO THE GHOUL'S MOUTH.
Only a scarred lump of tissue remained where his tongue should have been. This mutilation couldn't have happened after he was undead. Anything cut off him after that would grow back, same as with vampires. The scar tissue proved his lack of a tongue wasn't a congenital condition, either. So someone had cut it off, then turned him into a ghoul shortly thereafter, judging from the permanently raw look to the scar. If it had been healed for a while before he'd become undead, the area would have been much smoother.

And I didn't know many people who'd willingly consent to such a thing. Especially someone as young as this boy had been when all this happened.

But just to be sure . . .

I spun around, grabbing the other ghoul and shoving my knife into his mouth to hold it open.

"Did you have anything to do with that?" I asked,

digging the blade in. "Lie to me, and I swear to God I'll make Vlad puke with what I do to you."

"I didn't do that to him," the ghoul said quickly. His gaze flicked behind me. "I'm not lying. He was like that when he was put in our group."

"And who put him there?" I asked, digging the knife in until it must have been grazing his sinuses, but I didn't care. *Mutilation. Forced changing of a teenager.* He might not have done it, but he'd been a part of it.

"You know who," the ghoul rasped.

I didn't blink. "Say the name. Convince me that I should believe you."

My cell vibrated against my hip again, but I ignored it, not wanting to divert even an ounce of my attention away from the ghoul in front of me.

"Apollyon." The word was almost sighed. "He has several people like Dermot in his line. He takes kids who are young, not too bright, then mutes them and changes them. They make good muscle. Got nowhere else to go, can't talk, can't write real well, so we know they can't betray us."

I thought I'd been furious before, but that didn't compare to the rage filling me now. My hands trembled, the knife digging even higher into the ghoul's head. He screamed as much as he could with the blade in the way.

"Cat." Vlad's voice was low but resonant. "Stop. We need him alive."

I knew the wisdom in that. Knew that if I killed the ghoul, we wouldn't find out if he knew where Apollyon was, and that was vitally important information. But my mind felt frozen with the urge to destroy anyone who'd been a part of such a horrible practice, and my knife kept on its upward path into the ghoul's skull. Dermot couldn't have been more than seventeen when he was tortured, killed, and then forced into this existence. The ghoul in front of me knew that. Allowed it to continue. He had to pay.

"*Cat!*"

My hand trembled again . . . and then I yanked the knife out, twisting it in the process, savoring the scream the ghoul made. I moved away from him, taking in a deep, long breath to remind myself that I'd made the right decision. Information was more important than revenge. I chanted it in my mind like a litany until I began to feel stable.

"Aren't you supposed to be burning him to get more details?" I asked Vlad, my voice almost normal despite the anger still swelling in me.

Vlad gave me an unfathomable look, the faintest smile hovering on his lips. "If you live long enough, Reaper, one day you might scare even me."

"Girl's gotta have goals," I replied shortly. "And he's still not spilling where Apollyon is."

"No, he's not, is he?" Then Vlad made a series of odd motions with his hands, but no fire emanated from them.

"Are you having *performance* issues?" I asked in surprise.

"Bite your tongue," Vlad said, with a snort. "I was seeing if Dermot understood sign language, but from the look on his face, it seems not."

I glanced at the young ghoul, who'd been watching Vlad's hands with a sort of morbid fascination. *He picks kids who are young, not too bright* . . . the other ghoul had said about Apollyon. Did Dermot know that there was an entire language he could learn that required no verbal or written words? How trapped he must feel, forced into this life, and denied any real means to even communicate.

"You're going to be okay," I said to Dermot. "We're not going to hurt you, and you won't have to live with those other people anymore, I promise."

A little voice inside told me that Bones wasn't going to like what I intended, but I pushed it back. He might not like it, but he'd understand.

Noise from dozens of cars combined with multiple groans as abruptly, the dialog from the four movies—and the exterior lights—cut off. It didn't take more than a second of dropping my mental shields to catch the internal grumbling from the moviegoers over the sudden power failure at the drive-in.

Even if I hadn't heard that, the loud voice of some-one with a bullhorn began apologizing for the inconve-nience, promising rain check tickets for the next night. Must be the manager. From how calm he sounded, I guessed that Mencheres had had a little talk with him using the power in his gaze. Otherwise, I'd expect him to be far more glum about all the money driving out of the theater and the promise of refunds later.

Maybe I'd make an anonymous donation to this theater. The manager shouldn't have to take a finan-cial hit just because warmongering, murderous ghouls had chosen this place to hold their get-together.

"Someone's coming, and it's not Mencheres," Vlad said, jerking his head.

I drew out another knife as I headed in the direction he'd indicated, ducking to use the bushes as camouflage again. But when I was about twenty yards away, I caught familiar scents on the air, and my tenseness eased.

The sight of the vampires, one with gray streaks in his hair, the other so skinny that the bones of his shoulders all but jutted through his shirt, only confirmed who they were.

"Ed. Scratch," I called out, not raising my voice. "Over here."

I turned back around without waiting for them, not wanting to leave Vlad alone for long with the ghouls. Granted, the odds of Vlad being overcome were about nil, but the odds that he might decide to torch one—or both—of them in my absence were much higher.

To my relief, both Dermot and the other ghoul were still alive when I jogged back to Vlad, though in the few minutes that I'd been gone, the scarred ghoul looked like he'd passed through a volcano. Mencheres must have dropped his power from him, because he was on the ground, Vlad's booted foot over his mouth. Must be why I hadn't heard any yelling even though he'd obviously been burned.

"He doesn't appear to know where Apollyon is," Vlad stated. "I'm not surprised. Apollyon would have to be an idiot to tell where he was to anyone in a group such as this. They report in and receive instructions by e-mail. I have the address and passwords."

Ed and Scratch appeared behind me in the next moment, one of them letting out a slow whistle as they took in the slain bodies that were still held upright, plus the still-alive, burnt ghoul under Vlad's foot.

"Looks like we missed the party," Ed observed.

Vlad's smile was arch. "But you're just in time for the cleanup."

"How come I'm not surprised to hear that?" Scratch muttered, shaking his head. "What a mess, but better them than us."

"Wise outlook," Vlad commented.

The ghoul tapped on Vlad's foot, blinking repeatedly at him. Vlad moved it aside an inch, which was apparently enough for him to talk.

"There are more of us here. In this city, I mean. We're supposed to recruit, add to our numbers, kill some vamps, and then spread out to another city. We're also supposed to leave if we see the Reaper or Bones. That's good information. Good enough for my life, like you agreed," he finished.

Vlad removed his foot all the way, but fire began to dance down his hands. "We already know most of that, so the information's not good at all."

"Vlad," I said, and his brows rose at the sharpness to my voice. "He's done his best to tell you all he knows, so *you* need to let him go.

He opened his mouth, about to argue . . . and then smiled. "Of course."

The ghoul got up, looking in quick darts between Vlad and the promise of freedom behind him, before he began to back away one step at a time.

"Not. So. Fast," I said, drawing out each word with venom.

"He promised to let me live!" the ghoul sputtered.

"*Vlad* promised. *I* didn't," I said, leaping onto his back when he tried to run. Mencheres's power didn't attempt to restrain him, so he flipped over and fought me with furious blows, but I was glad. I *wanted* to beat him into submission. To show him what it was like to be helpless no matter how hard he fought. That was the least I could do for Dermot and all the others like him.

"A vampire made that same mistake once, forgetting I was there and only getting Bones's promise not to kill him," I went on several moments later. Multiple places on my body still stung from the ghoul's blows, but they were healing with every second. I didn't pause to talk more, but swiped my knife through the ghoul's neck with a clean, savage cut, feeling the coldest form of satisfaction as his head rolled to the side.

"He didn't like how it turned out, either," I finished, wiping the blade on the ghoul's shirt. "You know what they say. The devil's in the details."

Twenty-five

WE STAYED A COUPLE MORE HOURS AT the drive-in just to make sure no other, tardier ghouls showed up, and that all evidence of what happened was erased from the scene. It wasn't just out of concern for the police. We didn't want any ghouls to figure out what happened, if more of them used this as a meet-up spot aside from this departed group.

Mencheres insisted that Dermot not go back with us to the town house. His point that no matter how he'd been abused by Apollyon and the other ghouls, Dermot still might be a threat, was too logical to ignore. Stockholm syndrome was a definite possibility, and it wouldn't be right to just assume Mencheres would put the power whammy on Dermot if he wigged out and tried to kill one of us. Plus, we couldn't take him with us on our stakeouts. So, with assurances I wasn't even sure Dermot believed, I sent him off with Ed and Scratch, who swore on pain of death to treat him well and take him to a safe place. Once this thing with Apollyon was over, I now had a new item on my To Do list: Find an undead therapist for the traumatized ghoul, and have someone teach Dermot sign language.

I called Bones back three times, but in each instance, I only got his voice mail. Figures now that I could talk, he wasn't able to. Worry nagged at me, but I shoved it back with all the other things I wouldn't allow myself to dwell on. I hadn't been able to answer Bones's calls before, but that didn't mean I was in mortal danger. He was tough. He could take care of himself. I should stop with the paranoid images of his drying corpse running through my mind.

As an extra precaution in case anyone observed our activities at the drive-in, Mencheres doubled back several times on our way to the town house, then parked a half mile away and carried me as he and Vlad flew the rest of the way. I didn't bother to tell them that I could fly now, too. One, I was tired. Two, I still couldn't fly that *well*, and if I crashed into a telephone pole or something similar in front of Vlad, he'd never let me live it down.

We landed around back, in the darkest part of the lawn, and then went around to the front of the town house. It was about the same size as the place I'd grown up in, but I bet Mencheres hadn't stayed anywhere this small in the past thousand years. He slept on the pullout couch while Vlad and I occupied the two upper bedrooms. I'd just taken my boots off on the patio—remnants of my upbringing, when tracking dirt inside a house was akin to a capital crime—

when Mencheres suddenly jerked his head up to stare at the sky.

"Aliens?" I joked, but tensed anyway, reaching for my knives. Ghouls couldn't fly, but what if someone else menacing had somehow managed to follow us from the drive-in? Our enemies weren't only of the flesh-eater variety . . .

My senses began to tingle like they'd been shot with steroids even as Mencheres said, "Bones."

Vlad barely had time to mutter, "And this had been such a *nice* evening," before the vampire in question dropped out of the sky, landing a few feet away with his black coat swirling around him. Joy and yearning slashed across my subconscious as our eyes met. I went to him, throwing my arms around him, reveling in the strength and vehemence of his answering embrace.

"I missed you, Kitten," he growled. Then his mouth crushed over mine, his kiss more filled with raw need than romantic welcome.

That was fine; I felt the same way. Aside from my compulsive urge to run my hands over him to assure myself that he was really here, relief, happiness, and the most profound feeling of *rightness* zoomed through me, settling all the way to my core. I hadn't realized how deeply I'd missed Bones until that very moment, hadn't let myself acknowledge how everything felt off when I was apart from him. On some levels, it was frightening how much a part of me he'd become. It let me know just how much I'd crumble if anything happened to him.

"Why didn't you answer your mobile earlier?" Bones murmured once he lifted his head. "I tried you several times. Tried Mencheres, too. Even Tepesh. None of you answered. Scared the wits out of me, so I stowed away on a FedEx plane to make sure you were all right."

"You came all the way from Ohio because I didn't answer the *phone*?" I was torn between laughter and disbelief. "God, Bones, that's a little crazy."

And it was, except the part of me that had had images of his tombstone dancing in my head because he hadn't answered *his* phone earlier was nodding in complete understanding. Despite all our protestations, we were so alike when it came to fear over the other's safety, and I doubted we'd ever change.

"Crazy," I repeated, my voice roughening with the surge of emotion in me. "And have I told you lately that your crazy side . . . is your sexiest side?"

He chuckled before his mouth swooped back over mine in another dizzying kiss. Then he picked me up, brushing past Vlad and Mencheres without even a hello, though I doubted either of them was surprised.

We'd made it into the bedroom, already ripping at each other's clothes, when a discreet cough made my head whip around. Bones instantly had a knife in his hand, my bra dangling from his wrist. I'd gotten my own blade out when I realized the person in the room couldn't hurt us if he tried.

"I somehow ended up here, but I can see that this is a bad time, so I'll just check back with you later," the unknown ghost said before disappearing into the wall.

"Not any time soon if you value your afterlife," Bones called out after him.

I let out a strangled sound. If this was what I had

to look forward to until Marie's blood was out of my system, I seriously needed to invest in a *lot* more garlic and pot.

Then Bones dropped his knife and swept me back into his arms, and I forgot to care about any potential ghostly voyeurs.

"You have to leave already?" I murmured, blinking at Bones through the bright slants of sunlight that peeked out from the gaps in the drapes. "But you barely slept."

The grin Bones flashed me was quintessential cat-that-got-the-cream, though that expression was probably better suited to me at the moment.

"I know," he said, the words drawn out with the warmth of remembrance.

I sat up, dragging the sheet with me. "I'm serious."

"Kitten"—Bones paused from pulling on his shirt—"four hours of sleep while holding you is far more beneficial to me than eight hours of endless tossing and turning because you're not there."

I couldn't say anything for a moment. His tone was utterly matter-of-fact, no hint of romantic exaggeration or playful bantering. After all this time, I should be used to Bones's unabashed bluntness about his feelings, but it still struck me. He didn't hesitate to bare the most vulnerable parts of himself without care that I wasn't the only one who could hear him. Me, I layered up in emotional safety nets most of the time, using humor or irony to conceal how deeply certain things affected me.

Not Bones. Badass undead killer he might be, but ever since we started dating, he'd never hidden his

emotions from me, or did the macho downplaying
of what I meant to him in front of others. He wasn't
just stronger than me physically or in power abilities.
Bones also left me in the dust when it came to inner
strength, daring to show his deepest vulnerabilities
without any fear, safety net, or rationalization.

And it was high time I followed suit. Sure, I'd bared
my heart to Bones in the past, but not nearly enough.
He knew I loved him, knew I'd fight to the death
by his side if need be, but there was more to it than
that. Maybe some hidden, fragmented part of me had
feared that if I admitted to Bones how much he truly
meant to me, then I'd be acknowledging to myself that
he had the power to destroy me more thoroughly than
anyone, even Apollyon or the vampire council, could.
All the rest of the world could only kill or devastate
my mind and body. Bones alone held the power to
demolish my soul.

"You once told me you could stand many things."
My voice was raspy from all the emotions battering
against those well-honed inner defenses. "So can I. I
can stand whatever Apollyon dishes out, can take the
bigotry from others over what I am, the freaky ghost
juju from Marie, all the craziness my mother can
throw at me, and even the pain of my uncle dying. But
the one thing that I would never, ever recover from
would be losing you. You made me promise before to
go on if that happened, but Bones"—here my words
broke and tears spilled down my cheeks—"I wouldn't
want to."

He'd been near the side of the bed when I started
talking, but was in my arms before the first tear fell.
Very softly, his lips brushed over those wet streaks,

coming back pink from the drops still shimmering on them.

"No matter what happens, you will never lose me," he whispered. "I am forever yours, Kitten, in this life or the next."

A poignant sort of pain flowed over me, because I knew what he was promising with that statement, and what he wasn't. Bones couldn't swear that we'd never be separated. Being undead didn't give any of us a claim on immortality; it just made us harder to kill. Unless Bones and I happened to be slain at the exact same time, one day, either he or I would know the grief of being without the other. I meant it when I said I wouldn't want to go on if Bones were dead, but hard lessons from the past showed that I'd have to. Or Bones would have to go on without me. No matter how many enemies we defeated, or what impassioned promises we made to each other, this was the harsh reality.

And maybe that reality was what my last few inner shields had been trying to protect me from. Admitting that I'd be irrevocably broken without Bones meant accepting that it would happen. One day, we'd be separated. Not by our will, or even through any potential fault of our own, but through the cold, merciless barrier of death. Unless we died fighting back to back, it *would* happen. I'd put off being as open as Bones was about how he resided in every crevice of my heart because nothing scared me more than acknowledging that harsh, inevitable reality. Now that I finally had, the strangest kind of relief flowed over me, covering even the pain.

Holding back had done nothing to change the truth

of how I felt, or of our inevitable circumstances. I'd only been fooling myself, but even worse than that, I was also cheating the time Bones and I did have together. No one knew their own fate. We could have hundreds of years together. Thousands. Or only ten minutes before a meteor struck the house and vaporized me but missed him, for all we knew. Our time together was finite, and that was all there was to it.

But now, I also finally understood what Bones already knew. Just because death would eventually separate us, that didn't mean it would destroy what we had. *I am forever yours, in this life or the next.* Some things could penetrate even the formidable barrier of death, and love was one of them. Even if death kept me from being with Bones for a while—or him from me—it couldn't keep us apart forever. In the end, *nothing* could, and at long last, I understood that.

"You'll never get rid of me, either," I said, and my laughter came out thicker from tears. "No matter which side of the grave we're on. I'll haunt you, chase you all around eternity, whatever it takes, but it's you and me until the stars burn out."

I barely had time to see his smile before his mouth moved over mine with slow, blistering intensity. It wasn't the skillful way he kissed me that made my chest tighten as though my heart might start up again at any moment. It was the last wall falling down between us.

"Bones," I breathed, long moments later when he lifted his head. "There's something I want to do once this mess with Apollyon is over."

The seriousness of my tone made him pull back slightly. "What's that, luv?"

I whispered it to him, seeing his brows go up, his slight frown, and then at last, his nod.

"If that's what you want."

I stared at him, more of that tightness swelling up in my chest.

"It is."

Twenty-six

FABIAN CAME TOWARD ME. HE COULDN'T have smiled any wider if I was holding out a plate of ectoplasmic cookies, which, of course, I wasn't, because to my knowledge, such a thing didn't exist. I smiled back, giving Fabian an abbreviated version of a hug, which pretty much meant I put my arms in a half circle around the general area where he floated. From my peripheral vision, I saw Vlad roll his eyes, but I didn't care. I hugged friends when I hadn't seen them in a while, and Fabian might not be solid, but he was still a friend.

"Save one for me, too?" Dave asked, appearing behind the ghost.

I laughed as I gave him a big squeeze next, this time feeling the person in my arms. Dave fluffed a handful of hair when he let me go, grinning as he took in my latest disguise.

"With the new black hair, dark eyes, and tanned

skin, you almost look a little bit Latina. Juan would
need to be pried off you if he saw you like this."

I let out a snort. "I doubt it. Juan acts a lot more
respectful since he became a vampire. Hardly tries to
grab my ass at all now. Guess because Bones already
killed him once, Juan doesn't want to provoke him
into a repeat."

Just talking about Juan made me miss him, unrepentant pervert that he was, and that made me miss
everyone else back at the compound, too. It also made
me think of my uncle and mother with a fresh spurt
of anxiety. It was a small offense compared to what
Apollyon intended to do, but I hated him for more
than just using me to attempt to provoke a clash between ghouls and vampires. I also hated Apollyon for
robbing me of spending time with Don in what might
turn out to be the last few months of his life, and for
denying me more opportunities to talk sense into my
irrational, death-tempting mother.

I shook my head, clearing that out of my thoughts
before I started to endlessly stew over my stubborn
family. Dave said hello to Vlad and Mencheres, then
flopped onto the couch, looking tired. He didn't have
long before he had to get back, but he'd said this message was something he wanted to deliver in person.

"The meeting I went to last night was more like
a rally and a seminar combined," Dave started without preamble. "Apollyon wasn't there, but the keynote
speaker was a ghoul named Scythe who sounded just
as fanatic. Preached about how vampires have been
holding ghouls down for millennia, blah, vamps are
evil, blah. Then he started on how you changed over
but still had an occasional heartbeat, so you could still

turn into a vamp-ghoul hybrid. And once that happened, you'd be leading the vampire charge to subject ghouls to slavery."

"That's such bullshit!" I snapped, unable to stuff it back. Then I got ahold of myself. Everyone here already knew that.

"Go on," I said to Dave, in a less strident tone than before.

"I'm not sure how true this is, but Scythe said that the ghoul movement to 'take back their rightful place' was gaining ground all over America. That they'd start the war here, because vampires had a weaker hold here than in Europe. Then, once they'd thrown off the vampire shackles in the States, they'd move on to the rest of the world."

"If Cat is still being used as the focal point behind this fang oppression rhetoric, you'd think more of his followers would question why Apollyon doesn't just unite them together to kill her," Vlad noted, as if he were discussing squashing a bug. If he hadn't proved himself to be a good friend many times over, I'd be insulted.

"Oh, they have an answer for that," Dave said dryly. "Scythe's stating that if anyone kills Cat, then the vampire nation will know ghouls are *on to* them. Which is why ghouls have to rise up now, while the vampires least expect it and the scales are tipped in our favor. Then, Apollyon's first act once he wins the war will be to kill Cat publicly. That way, it will have the maximum crushing effect on the surviving vampires' psyche."

Scheming murderous pricks, I thought in disgusted fury, but kept it to myself this time.

A low growl sounded to my right. I turned, surprised to see it was coming from Fabian.

"Not once did the question of what *my* people would do during all this come up for discussion, did it?" Fabian asked, his voice sharp.

Dave looked as surprised as I felt at that. "Uh, no, no one mentioned ghosts," he answered, sounding both uncomfortable and apologetic.

Fabian's transparent features were as angry as I had ever seen them. "We might not have the same abilities as the rest of you, but ghosts are not without power, and we. Are. Many," he said, emphasizing the last three words.

"Remnants and wraiths I can see being able to tip the scales in battle, but what can the average spectre do?" Vlad asked, sounding a bit impatient. "Your species can provide valuable intelligence and carry messages before a conflict starts, true, but once the fighting begins, your usefulness ends."

Part of me wanted to chastise Vlad for being so cold in his assessment of ghosts, but the other part guiltily agreed with him. Remnants? Scary. Wraiths? Scary. Ghosts? *Not* scary, unless maybe you were a human and you happened to glimpse one in a graveyard. Or you were a kid and one screamed, "Boogie woogie woogie!" while popping up from under your bed.

"There are those of my kind that are more powerful than others," Fabian insisted. "Why do you think humans who aren't psychic have been able to see ghosts? Why some are caught on film or voice recorder? Why some have even attacked people, leaving visible scratches and other injuries? Some ghosts are strong enough to manifest themselves into solid form, sometimes for several hours. Aside from that, when you have enough of my people united in a common purpose, we can manifest enough energy to turn it into an effective weapon."

I was startled. Dave pursed his lips in thought. Mencheres's expression was its usual hooded mask, but Vlad eyed Fabian with open challenge.

"If ghosts can do all that, why do you waste your time haunting old homes and cemeteries, or scaring humans with random strange noises and useless cold spots? You're squandering your worth."

"Vlad, enough," I said shortly. Whatever his thoughts on ghosts' peculiar habits, Fabian was still my friend. I wouldn't just stand there while his whole race was being put down.

Fabian didn't flinch under Vlad's harsh analysis. "You have no idea what it's like, existing between worlds," he said, floating closer instead of backing away. "We are neither the living nor the undead. It takes years to cope with the fact that even though over ninety-nine percent of everyone who dies crosses over to the next place, *you* are left behind. Years to accept that everything you worked for in your life is gone, and the shell of memory is all that remains. Years to recover from hopelessly trying to communicate with loved ones, only to fail time and again because no one except the crazed, psychics, the undead, or other ghosts can see you. Years to accept—even if you don't understand why—that vampires and ghouls will treat you worse than they do vermin, even though they are no more human than you are."

Fabian advanced again, until his finger disappeared

into Vlad's chest. "I'd dare the strongest of your race or any other to say that they've conquered the same hardships my people have overcome. So think again before you question a ghost's worth, or judge those younger ones who are still in the process of becoming tougher than anyone tied to flesh will ever be!"

Stunned silence filled the air once Fabian was finished. I wanted to break out into apologies and applause all at the same time, but I was still recovering from my shock at how my mild-mannered, Casperesque friend had just unloaded a truck full of I-dare-yous onto one of the scariest vampires in existence. Damned if I would ever underestimate a ghost's chutzpah again, or question their fortitude. Being noncorporeal clearly didn't equate to lacking a pair of balls.

I wasn't the only one taken aback. Dave's mouth hung open, and Mencheres gave Fabian a once-over that showed he was considering him in a whole new light. As for Vlad, his expression had changed from bored disdain to speculative interest as he stared at the finger still jabbed half through his chest.

"If there are more ghosts like you who can channel the same impressive anger into something tangible, then you're right. Ghosts would be a valuable asset to have in a fight," Vlad said, inclining his head.

Fabian acknowledged the gesture with a nod of his own, pulling his finger and then the rest of himself back to float by me. I didn't give him a high five—that didn't work very well with ghosts—but I did flash him a discreet thumbs-up. So much for me needing to defend him or his species. I couldn't have done half as good a job as Fabian had.

"All right. If things go even more south with Apollyon, good to know we can potentially add ghosts to our list of allies, if Fabian can act as ambassador between his people and ours," I said, bringing things back to the original subject. "Dave, where was this fun little rally held, anyway?"

He grimaced. "You're really not going to like this part. From the bits of conversation I overheard, Apollyon is the owner of a few large chains of funeral homes and cemeteries, using humans as figureheads for investors and board members. The rally was behind a funeral home that bordered a cemetery. Lots of room there, and they had guards around the area to keep anyone away who wasn't on the guest list."

Damn Apollyon. The short, balding shit was clever. No one would think twice about a large group gathered at a graveyard. They'd just assume someone rich or from a big family was being buried. Most people didn't visit cemeteries for cheery reasons, so it wasn't the place where striking up impromptu conversations was the norm. Not to mention it would take a *really* ballsy person to go up to a group gathered around a gravesite with the opening line of "So what are we talking about, anyway?"

Vlad let out a bark of laughter. "He's found a way to make money from eating, not to mention have a network of secure locations for meetings."

"Make money from . . . *oh*," I said as the rest of what Apollyon was doing became clear. "He's not burying all the bodies brought to him, but *eating* some instead?"

"Not just some," Dave supplied grimly. "Lots. If you're a member of Apollyon's line, either by blood or membership through his extremist group, then your food's supplied to you for free. If not, Apollyon has an underground supermarket for ghouls who would rather buy their own food than go out hunting and gathering for it."

I couldn't throw up anymore, but I thought I might dry heave. Most of the times, ghouls ate raw meat of the animal variety, like uncooked steak or pork roast. But at least a couple times of year, they needed to add some *Homo sapiens* to their diet in order to maintain their strength. Don supplied Dave's extra dietary requirements from bodies donated to science or left unclaimed at hospitals. It didn't take much. One corpse on ice parceled out in small amounts could last a ghoul a year or two, easy.

But taking money from grieving families to bury their loved ones, then turning around and selling those loved ones like so much deli meat while burying an empty casket instead? That was just . . . wrong.

"Apollyon makes those pension-stealing Wall Street crooks look like amateurs," I said, shaking my head.

"That's damn straight," Dave muttered.

"It does give us a new way to attempt to track him," Mencheres noted, logical as always. "I'll have some ghouls in our line start investigating places rumored to sell human meat. Perhaps we can find one connected to Apollyon. In the interim, Dave, tell me where this funeral home is. I want to go there."

"Why?" I asked. "I'll have Tate start watching it from satellite and tapping into their phone lines and Internet to see if we can luck out and snag Apollyon that way, but all of us showing up there is too risky."

Mencheres gave me a faint smile. "I agree. That's why I'll be going alone."

"Haven't you had enough of risking your life to play lone hero lately?" Vlad asked, making an exasperated noise.

"One vampire stands a far better chance of avoiding notice than three," Mencheres pointed out. "I agree that everything Cat outlined should be done, but that's not enough. If I'm close, I can listen to the thoughts of any humans they might employ, as well as scent the area to see if Apollyon's been there—and before you tell me you can do all these things, of the three of us, I am better equipped to escape should my presence be detected."

I'd love to argue with him, but he was right, and the tight line of Vlad's mouth said that he knew it, too.

"When are you intending to do this?" I asked, glancing out the window. It would be dark in a couple hours, and we were supposed to be cruising the bar and club scene as usual, hoping Apollyon or one of his close aides was in a partying mood.

"Now," Mencheres said, nodding at Dave. "Direct me."

Dave gave him the location of the funeral home/ cemetery, and Mencheres walked away without another word, heading up the stairs to weapon up, I guessed.

"You'll call us when you're done, right?"

"Yes," his voice floated down.

Dave glanced at his watch. "I gotta get back. Don't want them swinging by my apartment early and wondering why I'm not there."

I gave him a final hug, resisting the urge to tell him to be careful. He was a smart, tough soldier and he already knew that.

"I'll see you guys soon" was what I said to Dave

and Fabian, hoping I sounded confident and not like it was a prayer. Fabian might be able to slip away unscathed to warn us if Dave's spying was discovered, but even at our fastest, we might not be able to rescue Dave in time, and he knew it.

"Say hi to Tate and the rest of the guys," Dave said.

"Will do."

I kept my smile until they left, and then it dropped from my face like a fallen bridge. Vlad turned away, saying something about checking in with his people.

He wasn't the only one who had to make a phone call. I sighed, then picked up my cell to call Tate and give them the location of the latest place to put under surveillance—and hope he had no awful news to relay about my mother or uncle.

Twenty-seven

I STARED OUT THE WINDOW, LOST IN MY thoughts, barely noticing the blur of buildings that we drove past. Most of Memphis had recovered from the terrible flooding last year, but here and there, you could still see signs of the water's ravages. The people had bounced back, though, reopening businesses and rebuilding homes. Ghosts might have proved to be a surprisingly tough bunch, as Fabian pointed out, but my species—or former species, I guess—was pretty resilient, too.

I frowned when Vlad turned the corner and went down a long street that didn't look like it was any-where close to the bar we were supposed to go to.

"You're not lost, are you?"

He glanced at me, one side of his mouth ticked up in a sly smile. "Field trip," he said, taking the next right.

I took one look at the wrought-iron arch at the end of the road and shook my head.

"A cemetery? We agreed that Mencheres was doing recon on Apollyon, not us!"

"We're not here looking for Apollyon or any other ghouls," Vlad replied evenly. He parked at the farthest spot from the entrance before turning to fully face me. "We're here because you're going to try that new trick you picked up from Marie."

For several seconds, I was speechless, torn between wondering if I should lie and say I didn't know what he was talking about, or demand to know who told him. I couldn't imagine that Bones would have said anything to Tepesh. They certainly weren't close.

"What do you *think* you know about that?" I settled on at last, giving him a hard look. No way would I start babbling out a confession, even if he was drilling me with the ol' Dracula knowing stare.

"I know you didn't start wearing garlic and weed just to make a bold fashion statement, and that your sudden popularity with ghosts didn't start until after you saw Marie," Vlad said, his mouth twisting. "Hadn't quite worked it all out until this morning, when I heard you mention being able to stand the 'freaky ghost juju' from Marie during that unutterably sappy conversation you had with Bones. Then I realized what was going on. Very impressive, being able to absorb powers from ghouls, too."

"Are you crazy?" I hissed, looking around. "What if this cemetery is crawling with you-know-who's people and they overheard you?"

He snorted. "It's not. I'd feel it if there were ghouls here. I'm a lot older than you, so my range is stronger. The only dead things around for a mile in any direction are you, me, and everyone buried under the dirt."

That mollified me, but I still remembered the warning Bones had relayed from Marie about what would happen if we told anyone that I'd drunk her blood. "It's not just the dead or undead we need to worry about overhearing," I said, jerking my head toward the window.

"If you see a ghost, just order it not to say anything," Vlad replied inexorably. "Don't think that's escaped my attention, either, Reaper."

Aw, fuck. Well, what did I expect? Despite the garlic and ganja armor, some of them still made their way to me and I'd had to send them off with a firm instruction not to come back. With staying under the same roof as Vlad for the past week, he had to have overheard, even if I'd tried to make my orders really soft.

"This can't become common knowledge," I said finally.

Vlad let out a single laugh. "To use a phrase from your generation, *no shit.*"

"I think that expression's older than my generation," I muttered, but let that drop. Vlad knew and that's all there was to it. At least he wasn't the gossiping type, so I still had a decent chance at this not getting around. But what he wanted me to do was out of the question.

"You don't understand what you're asking for. It's not as simple as holding a séance. It's too dangerous."

Those coppery green eyes bored into mine. "I know very well what Marie can summon, and if you can now also call forth such creatures, that would give vampires a critical edge if we are unable to kill Apollyon and prevent war from breaking out."

"Calling them forth isn't what scares me," I said, a shiver of remembrance running through me. "Controlling them once they're here, or sending them back, *that's* the problem."

"This is far too important for you to refuse simply out of fear," Vlad retorted.

"You just don't get it." I swiped a hand toward the cemetery for emphasis. "Those things—Remnants, Marie called them—are like ghostly land mines, and you're asking me to stomp on them to see if I can direct the blast radius! It's not fear for me that I'm saying no. They didn't hurt me last time and probably wouldn't again. It's fear for you if I do it and fail."

Vlad held up his hand. Flames covered it, indigo and orange intertwining across his skin without singeing a single hair.

"The power I have is only valuable because I can and will use it. Apollyon's right; Marie's new lack of allegiance to vampires *is* a game changer, but we now have the ability to counter the ghoul nation's most devastating weapon through you, but not if you refuse to wield that power."

I remembered the icy, ravenous feel of the Remnants, the mental maelstrom of their voices in my head, and shuddered. "I'll wield it, or try to, only as a last resort. You don't know how strong the Remnants are. I could raise them, lose control of them, and then end up watching them eat allies and enemies alike. Only a fool throws a risky Hail Mary pass in the first quarter of the game."

Vlad's brow arched insolently. "No, only a fool would attempt to see if their best weapon works during a battle instead of before it."

."There are days when you really push my buttons, Tepesh," I snapped.

"And there are days when I wonder how you've survived as long as you have," he countered. "You won't get a better chance to test your abilities than right now. Bones isn't here, so your biggest concern is gone, and you can risk my life because I accept the danger, and because friends might be rare, but they're not irreplaceable. Now, let's get in the graveyard and get started. Before Mencheres calls and then lectures us into an early grave about how im*pru*dent this idea is."

Vlad's face had been granite-hard during the first half of his speech, but then his lip curled almost impishly at that last sentence. I was torn by anger at his disdainful comment about my survival skills, dismay at how casually he assumed I'd react to his death, and amusement at how an over six-hundred-year-old Master vampire could still sound like a naughty kid planning to outwit his babysitter.

"You have got to be one of the most unusual people I have ever met, and considering all the strange ones I know, that's saying a lot," I managed, shaking my head.

His grin was shameless. "If you're just now realizing what an original I am, Catherine, you're even later to the game than I imagined."

"Your arrogance deserves its own zip code, Drac," I said, laughing despite myself.

"And you're stalling. Get out and let's get started."

My flash of good humor vanished under an onslaught of nervousness. "Maybe we *should* wait for Mencheres. With that power of his, he might be able to help if things get out of hand—"

"Not when it comes to anything from the ground," Vlad cut me off. "Grave magic is immune to Mencheres's telekinesis. That's why he couldn't do anything to the zombies that New Year's Eve except grab a sword and start hacking away at them like the rest of us."

Good point. I hadn't ever wondered why Mencheres hadn't tried to stop that attack with his power. Probably because I was too busy thinking, *Holy shit, we're all gonna* die*!*

And some of my friends had died. Nothing good ever came out of being close to magically raised creatures from the grave, in my experience. That brought up another concern, a less deadly but far more embarrassing one. I cleared my throat, glancing away from Vlad.

"You know, Marie said it wouldn't happen that bad again, but just in case . . . if I do this and safely put the Remnants back, then all of a sudden start coming on to you, I don't mean it. It's just the aftereffects of being connected to the hungers of the dead. Not me suddenly having a crazed desire to jump on your jock."

Vlad threw back his head and roared with laughter. Pink tears gleamed from his eyes before he reined himself in to just a few lingering chuckles.

"I'll be sure to thwart any jock-jumping attempts you might make on me or anyone else," he replied at last, his lips still twitching.

I sucked in a deep breath and then blew it out, trying to center myself before I made a leap into the other side, metaphorically speaking. I had no idea how to raise the Remnants, but I assumed I'd start with trying to tap into the connection I felt to ghosts and work my way up from there.

"You sure you want to be close by when I do this?" I asked, shooting a worried look at Vlad. "At best, you'll get hurt. At worst, I won't be able to stop them from killing you."

His expression was a mix of utter ruthlessness and reckless challenge, making me wonder if he'd looked that way when charging on horseback into battle all those centuries ago.

"I've lived on the razor's edge of death most of my life. Save your coddling for children, Cat; it's wasted on me."

Damn arrogant Romanian price. I hoped those weren't his last words.

"All right." I began to pull out all the packets of garlic and pot that I had stuffed inside my clothes. "Let's try this."

ᴛ**wenᴛy-eighᴛ**

Crickets chirped in a continual cadence around us, most of them hidden in the
grass. Mosquitoes, though I could see them buzzing
nearby, left me and Vlad alone. Guess they didn't like
undead blood, which was probably a good thing. The
world had problems enough without hordes of immor-
tal mosquitoes being added to the mayhem.

Vlad lounged on a headstone, watching me silently.
I'd chosen to go to the older section of the cemetery,
not just because it was farthest from the road and
any random passersby. It was also because, quite
irrelevantly, I thought it was prettier. The simple
upside-down U-shaped headstones and crosses reminded me of the cemeteries around where I grew
up. They were the first place I tried when hunting
for vampires as a teenager, but I never found any in
them. It didn't take long for me to realize that vam-

pires tended to hang out in places where the *living* gathered, instead of surrounding themselves with the inedible dead.

No other vampires or ghouls might be here except us, but we weren't the only supernatural beings lurking in the dark. I felt the tingles in the air, hanging like an invisible fog, marking the presence of residual energy from nonsentient ghosts. Every once in a while, a stronger pulse would ride the air, and I'd glance toward its source just in time to glimpse a faint silhouette before it disappeared. This cemetery had more than just residual ghosts, but I'd worry about them later. After I found out if I could do what I came out here to do.

"While I'm young . . ." Vlad drew out.

"You haven't been young since the fourteen hundreds, a few more minutes aren't going to make any difference," I muttered, but then tried to focus on that buzz of energy in the air. Maybe that was the door that led to wherever the Remnants slumbered, when they weren't being yanked into this reality. I tried to drop all my emotional shields, leaving myself open to the magic that I knew still resided in my blood from Marie.

Flashes of silver zoomed right for me from all sides, so fast I wouldn't have had time to draw my knife even if that would have done any good. In the next instant, I was staring at five ghosts, two of them male, the other three female, one of whom was a child. All looked back at me expectantly.

"Yes?" the ghost with the old-style bushy mustache asked, as if growing impatient that I hadn't said anything.

"Ah, sorry to disturb you," I began, feeling very weirded out by the ghostly little girl. She had on a cap with strings and a hazy gown that hung to her feet. A nightgown, I realized, one whose style hadn't been common for a hundred years or more. I'd never seen a child phantom before, and it made me unsure how to respond. It seemed wrong to order a little kid away without an explanation, especially when I'd probably woken her up.

Behind the spectral figures, Vlad whisked his wrist in the universal gesture for *hurry it up.*

"I didn't mean to call you," I went on, before he said anything rude to them. "I'm, uh, here for something else. Sorry I bothered you. Please, go back to whatever you were doing, and don't mention we were here tonight."

Without a word, the ghosts dispersed, the little girl vanishing just as quickly as the others. I fought the urge to call them back and ask if anyone took care of her. We *were* on a timetable, and Vlad might set my clothes on fire if I started questioning whether the little girl floated out here alone, or under appropriate ghostly guardianship.

But after a solid ten minutes of standing there with my eyes closed, leaving myself open to the unearthly energy in the air and trying to will the Remnants into being, I opened them with a sigh.

"It's not working. We need to try something else."

Vlad arched a brow. "We? I can't help you with this, Cat."

"Yes you can," I replied, coming toward him. "Nerves, anger, or fighting seem to flare up my borrowed powers. I'm nervous about this, but clearly not nervous enough. So hit me. Hard. See if that gets me mad enough to do the trick."

Bones had kicked my flying abilities into gear by

throwing me off a bridge—but there weren't any
bridges here. If Vlad and I had a fair sparring session,
that might prove counterproductive because I'd probably enjoy testing myself against the Master vampire.
But not defending myself while getting pummeled
would go against all my instincts as a fighter, and I
was betting pain would instinctively trigger my anger
even if I knew the logic behind it.

I'd been on my feet when I made the pronouncement, but was on my ass in the next second, my chest
burning from a punch that felt like it crushed all my
ribs. Looked like Vlad didn't need me to cajole him
into doffing his chivalry long enough to comply!

"That's a good one," I managed, grimacing at the
pain of my bones reknitting themselves together. "Do
it again."

Vlad's brown hair fell across his shoulders as he
leaned down to pull me to my feet. "As you wish."

This time, I was braced, but all that meant was I
stayed on my feet instead of landing on my ass when
Vlad unleashed another sledgehammer, this one into
the softer area of my stomach. Technically, body shots
were easier to recover from than a blow to the head,
so he was being courteous in that regard, but techni-
calities faded into insignificance at the pain blasting
through me. At least it wasn't followed by the sound
of my ribs snapping like the last time.

"Goddamn, that hurts," I muttered, bending over in
reflex.

A snort ruffled the top of my hair. "I assumed you
weren't looking for something that would tickle."

So saying, Vlad let fly another blow, this one to my
side. I staggered back, anger flaring.

"You can't even give me a second to recover in between? It's a *wonder* you're still single, Tepesh!"

"Getting pissed now, though, aren't you?" he replied, without the slightest hint of remorse. "Quit bellyaching, Reaper. I've seen you in battle. You can take far worse than this."

Yeah, well, in battle it was kill or be killed, so adrenaline kicked in, acting like morphine for the pain. This, on the other hand, just hurt seven ways from Sunday. But he was right. The pain and frustration over not letting myself fight back was making me angry. In the past, that was a good sign when it came to accessing my borrowed powers.

"If this is the best you can manage, I suppose it'll have to do," I said, to egg him on. I'd need a rougher attack than this to get me good and steamed. "Just thought you should know, though—Bones hits *so* much harder than you do."

He gave a bark of laughter before another blow sent me flying into a tree before slumping to the ground. Now my entire front and back hurt. I was definitely getting riled, yet still nothing happened as far as Remnant activity. Either this wasn't working or I had to get a whole lot madder, fast.

I shook myself off as I sprang up, watching Vlad approach with far more slowness than he'd use if we were sparring for real.

"That last one was better, but quit punching like a girl," I said. "Take off the leash. Just don't knock me into any of the headstones. This is a nice cemetery. Breaking them would be disrespectful."

Vlad let out something that sounded like a sigh. "You asked for it."

I fought my instinctive urge to defend myself when I saw his arm wind up. I didn't even let myself brace, the thought flittering through my head that it was a damn good thing Bones couldn't see the two of us right now, or he'd be furious.

Then all mental reflections cleared my head at the exact same instant that Vlad's fist landed there. Stars exploded in my mind, followed by a flash of searing pain and blackness. When I could see again, I was vaguely amazed that little blue birdies doing a slow circle above me weren't the first things that met my vision.

"Again," I said, wondering if it was actually possible for me to throw up. From the throbbing in my head, it might be.

The next blow took me across the jaw. My teeth snapped together hard enough that I was surprised I wasn't chewing them. Blood dripped from my mouth. Vlad saw it, gave a slight, dismissive shrug that made me want to thump him, and raised his fist for another strike.

It never landed. I felt like ice flashed through my veins even as a shield of transparent bodies formed over me, deflecting Vlad's blow as if they were made of solid diamond instead of only vaporous air. He stared at them with grim triumph as that shield of Remnants grew into a wall—and then fell on top of him.

"Good, it worked," Vlad gritted out even as his whole body was smothered by them. "Magnificent weapon. This hurts . . . absolutely everywhere."

Voices echoed all around me, some as low as growls and others in pitches so high they sounded

like nails on a chalkboard. Vlad was right; it obviously worked. Now came the *really* hard part. I'd
raised them, but I had to get them off him. It was
hard to concentrate with them bombarding my mind
with more voices than I could ever count. If I had
any hope at controlling them, I needed to use the
same techniques I'd developed while learning to
keep humans' thoughts from overwhelming me.
*Focus on one voice. Tune into it. Make everything
else fade into the background.*

"Vlad, talk," I urged him. It was better to stay focused on *his* voice instead of getting lost in the myriad
whispers of the grave. I scrambled to my feet, only
then realizing that I'd been on the ground with his
last blow.

"Rather busy . . . at the moment," I heard amidst the
whirl of other sounds.

"I need your voice," I insisted, shivering convulsively. I was so cold. So tired. So *hungry.*

Vlad began to sing, words hoarse from his obvious pain. It took me several moments to feel in control of myself enough to focus on him alone—and to
be amazed that Vlad knew the lyrics to "Run This
Town." I shook that off as I stared at him. His entire
body was covered in Remnants, and I tried to ignore
the tie I felt to them. The icy, ravenous hunger that
threatened to blind me to everything else.

"Get off him," I said to the sinuous, writhing forms.

Nothing happened. Not one of them even paused in
their assault on him to look at me.

"Get *off* him," I repeated, putting all my fear at
what would happen if they didn't into my voice.

Still the Remnants slithered over Vlad, coiling

on and through him. His body arched in a way that was all too familiar, telling of his agony even if he wouldn't let himself scream. Flames broke out across his hands, but the Remnants didn't move to avoid them, nor did the fire seem to do them any damage when they slithered over them. *Why would they?* my mind supplied in rising fear. Remnants were made of energy and air. Two things that had never been harmed by fire before.

"Go back to your graves *right now*," I tried again, this time desperation edging my tone. Still, they didn't even slow in their movements, or seem to hear me at all. I'd pulled them from the other side, but just as I feared, I now had no control over them. My worst-case scenario was playing out right in front of me as I saw Vlad twist in a futile effort to get away from the Remnants that just kept right on devouring him, growing stronger from his pain and energy while he grew weaker.

Then an idea seized me as I watched the flames on his hands. They did nothing to harm the Remnants, but they would sure as hell hurt *me*.

"Vlad, hit me with a fireball," I breathed. "Passing out last time was what severed my connection with the Remnants, I think."

It was worth a shot. If I was no longer connected to them, maybe they'd automatically go back to where they came from. I had to try something new. My commands were useless and Vlad couldn't last much longer like this.

"No." The single word was filled with pain, but no less emphatic. "You'll learn . . . to control them . . . if it kills me."

"It *will* kill you, dammit," I snapped in growing panic.

"Less bitching . . . more learning," Vlad grated. Then he closed his eyes, as if dismissing me. "I know, I'm delicious. Nummy . . . nummy," he muttered to the Remnants feasting on him. Fire continued to drip from his hands, but he didn't send any of those flames my way. Terror and anger rose in me at the sight of the Remnants moving even faster through his body. They were growing stronger, gaining the energy they'd need to kill him, and he was letting them.

"You're going to die if you don't flame me out of commission! Think of your people!" I yelled, growing desperate as nothing I did, even pulling on the Remnants with my hands, seemed to make them leave Vlad alone.

At that, his eyes snapped open, emerald green and sizzling with both agony and resolve. "I am . . . so *learn*," he rasped.

I let out a scream of pure frustration. Nothing I said would convince Vlad to harm me. Not if he thought he was protecting his people by sacrificing himself.

Fine. If Vlad wouldn't deliver the blow that would take me out of commission, I'd do it myself.

I curled my fist and rammed it as hard as I could into the side of my head. Grass met my vision as I knocked myself over, but one glance at Vlad revealed the Remnants still hadn't budged from him. Son of a bitch. I needed something harder than my hands.

A wide headstone caught my eye, an angel carved into the surface. I sent a mental apology to whoever's grave it covered even as I also cast a fast prayer upward to please let this work.

Then I ran toward the tombstone as fast as I could, my body bent, leading with my head like it was a red flag and I was a bull.

Pain exploded in my mind. That wasn't the only thing that shattered, judging from the shards of granite I saw when my eyes opened. I'd plowed right through the grave marker to land in the grass beyond. I shook my head to clear it, feeling blood running in a few thin lines down from my crown, and swung around to look for Vlad again.

A sharp cry of relief escaped me when I saw all the Remnants had picked their heads up from him. They were looking at me, their deadly assault on him suspended. Vlad began to back away and they didn't move to jump on him again, but kept staring at me in frozen expectation. For a stunned moment, I wasn't sure what had done the trick. It wasn't passing out; they were all still here. Was destroying a tombstone with my head somehow the magic word to them? But then, as I felt those wet trails edging further down my face, it hit me.

Blood. That was their remote control. The Remnants had only appeared after Vlad bloodied my lip, just like they'd only appeared after Marie sliced her wrist with that little mini dagger in her ring. She must have cut herself with it again to draw them off when I wasn't looking. That would have been easy; I'd been staring in horror at Bones more than focusing on her. The fresh blood from my head was enough to get them to stop chewing on Vlad, but it would soon heal like my lip had. I couldn't let them turn on Vlad again. He couldn't take much more.

I didn't bother taking the time to pull out one of my

knives, but slammed my hand onto the jagged, sharp remains of the headstone, inflicting another deep laceration.

"All right, you deadly little ghostlings," I muttered. "Mama says go back to *bed*!"

Twenty-nine

I SHUT THE CAR DOOR, LEANING AGAINST IT for a second, thinking that if life were fair, I could go upstairs and take the longest, hottest shower on record to help chase away the chill that still permeated every cell of me. Instead, we were back at the town house just so I could quickly change clothes. Couldn't quite pull off my happy bar hopper disguise if I went out covered in my own blood.

"You two are back early," a dry voice stated.

I glanced up to see Mencheres framed in the doorway of the town house. Vlad got out, shut his door a little harder than was necessary, and threw the Egyptian vampire a jaded look.

"Car trouble," he said, in a voice that dared Mencheres to inquire further.

"You're back a bit early yourself. Did you find anything interesting?" I asked, trying to divert his attention from the obvious fact that I was splattered in blood while the car looked and sounded fine.

"Nothing Dave had not already confirmed," Mencheres replied, with a slight shrug.

I didn't sigh, but I felt like it. Guess it was too much to hope that Apollyon's address would be spray painted graffiti-style on one of the walls as an appeasement gesture from Fate after the night we had—and it was still early, by vampire standards.

"Don't be disappointed, Cat. I didn't expect to find anything. That's not why I went," Mencheres said, opening the front door for us.

My brows rose, but I went inside, figuring this conversation was best held somewhere other than on the small lawn. Vlad glanced at Mencheres with equal curiosity but also followed me inside. Once the door was shut, I gave a longing glance at the couch but stayed standing.

"Are you going to tell us why you went, then?" I asked.

"Because even if I didn't expect to find anything new, it would be foolish not to make certain," Mencheres said. He leaned against the door frame, the picture of nonchalance. "Besides, if I hadn't left, then you wouldn't have attempted to exercise your new powers, would you?" he added.

"You *knew*?" I blurted, not sure which stunned me more; the fact that Mencheres was obviously aware that I had the ability, or that he'd let me try using it without telling Bones on me. "Did you, um, know because you saw it?" It would be great if his visions were back up to full strength again . . .

The look Mencheres gave me—and Vlad, too, I noticed—was pointed. "No. But I, too, heard you this morning, so I didn't need a vision to predict what Vlad would do if the two of you were left alone long enough. People's natures can be far more telling than even visions at times."

Vlad let out a chuckle. "You sly dog, you set me up! Here I thought I was pulling one over on you, but in reality, you were playing me like a chess piece."

Mencheres flashed him a grin that was full of mischief. I stared, never having seen the normally reserved mega-Master vampire with such a wicked, teasing expression.

"You forget, Vlad, I'm the one who trained you in deviousness. Maybe in a few more centuries, you'll be able to outwit me, but not yet."

Then he focused his attention on me and his expression returned to its normal seriousness. "You were obviously injured trying, but did it work?"

I glanced at Vlad before speaking, noting the curl of his lip that said he'd rather not dwell on how well it had worked.

"Oh yeah. Blood is the key. I should have known, right? It's always blood with the undead. Vampires need it to feed, and it's instrumental with ghouls, because a transplanted ghoul heart might be step two in making them, but it's vampire blood before and after death that's step one and three."

And blood was how Marie had gotten her powers in the first place, as a Mambo whose powers became permanent when she was turned into a ghoul. Looking back, it seems obvious that blood should have been the first thing I tried.

Then again, my logic pointed out, *Vlad hadn't thought of it, either, and he has quite a lot more experience with blood than you*. Maybe I should quit giving myself a hard time and just accept that only hindsight was twenty-twenty, not foresight.

"We now know I can do it, but I feel like hell," I went on. "I'm so cold my teeth would chatter if they still could. And I'm hungry enough that both of you are starting to look really, really good."

Vlad's lips curled. "Is this the part where I'm supposed to remind you that this is just the leftover power talking and you don't really want to cheat on Bones?"

"Not *that* kind of hungry!" I gasped, eyes bulging that Vlad thought I'd just casually thrown out that I wanted him and Mencheres to double-team me. "I meant hungry like drinking you guys' *blood*. Not hungry for . . . you know."

Without thought, my gaze flew to the areas in question before skipping away once I realized what I was doing. Then my cheeks actually tingled with mortification as Vlad let out a long, hearty laugh. Mencheres, more courteous, pretended to suddenly find something fascinating in the door frame, but I saw his lips twitch.

"My dear Reaper," Vlad said, still laughing. "Did you just check out our—"

"No!" I interrupted at once, almost lunging toward the staircase. "I'm tired and still dazed from the Remnants and . . . fuck it, I'm taking a shower. I mean, not a cold shower, because I don't need that"—oh Jesus, I was only making this worse—"because I *am* cold already, and I need to get hot. I mean, warmer. Oh, just shut up!"

This as Vlad continued to laugh the whole time I
went up the stairs. At least he seemed in a better mood
after his near-death experience, even if his new cheer
was at my expense. Arrogant Romanian. But considering I'd been responsible for Vlad's recent brush with
death, maybe he was owed a little masculine mockery.
All things considered, his teasing was the least I could
bear to make it up to him.

As for Mencheres, well, here's hoping he chalked
that up to equality. He'd seen me in less than my un-
derwear before, so if all things were fair, I was owed
that glance.

Besides, it had to be nothing more than a manifes-
tation of the "future twinges" from her power that
Marie had warned Bones about. In my right mind,
I would never check out Vlad or—God help me!—
Mencheres's packages.

And neither of them was wearing tight pants, so it's
not like I could discern anything specific, anyway.

Once I was in my room, however, I didn't jump
right in to the shower. I pulled out my cell phone, pin-
pricks of conscience still needling me.

"Bones," I said as soon as he answered. "I know I
just saw you this morning, but wow, do I miss you!"

Three days later, I was on the couch, scratching my
cat in his favorite spot behind the ears, when a faint
tingle in the air made me look up. I'd gotten better at
recognizing the telltale signs that said a ghost who
was strong enough to get through my stinky force
field of weed and garlic was about to pop up nearby.

"Visitor," I announced, my new way for giving
Vlad and Mencheres a heads-up to stop saying any-

thing possibly incriminating. To my knowledge, my order for silence to other ghosts had worked before, but no need to tempt fate by blathering about which bar we were headed to tonight.

Not that it probably mattered. We hadn't seen hide nor hair of any zealot ghouls since the night at the drive-in. Maybe having some of their group go missing spooked the other ghouls into avoiding popular hangouts. Or maybe the reason we hadn't seen any of them lately was much simpler. All of Apollyon's minions were being supplied with food, so they didn't need to go out hunting for it. Still, we kept going out night after night. Dave said Scythe and the pack of ghouls who drew him into their group were still here. They had to pop up sometime.

A shadowy form passed through the door moments later, still too hazy for me to make out any specific features. Then that outline of fogginess settled into a slim man with brown hair and early twentieth-century sideburns.

"Fabian!" I said, my initial happiness replaced by fear when I saw the grimness in his expression. "Is Dave okay?" I asked immediately.

"For the moment," the ghost almost sighed. "But he's thinking of doing something very foolish."

I stood up, my cat hissing at being jostled from my lap. "What?"

"Letting himself get caught spying," Fabian replied.

Mencheres and Vlad came downstairs. I shot them a bleak look, already starting to pull on my boots. "We need to go get Dave, now," I told them.

"Is he intending to do this in the next hour?" Mencheres asked, putting a calming hand on my shoulder.

"I don't believe so." Fabian gave me a helpless look. "Dave doesn't know I'm telling you. He made me promise not to, until he was caught. But I swore to you that I'd protect him, and I couldn't betray that vow, even though I'm now betraying him by telling you."

"You're *not* betraying him, you're saving him," I replied with all the emphasis of countless past bad decisions. "Sometimes, people think there's no other option aside from sacrificing themselves, but that doesn't mean they're right. Now, why does Dave all of a sudden think he needs to jump on a grenade for us? What happened?"

"He was taken to an unscheduled rally last night where Scythe told everyone he was leaving Memphis because his work here was done. He urged his followers to remain here, staying true to their beliefs, because soon, their movement would spread enough that they could openly act against vampires."

"Fuck," I moaned, to Vlad's grumbled agreement. With every new city these ghouls went to, they continued to infect others with their hatred. Scythe might be higher up in Apollyon's organization, but he wasn't alone in his efforts to spread his leader's paranoia. Worse, we didn't know which area these groups picked to settle in next until vampire bodies piling up pointed the way, and by then, it was already too late. The old saying that the best offense was a good defense didn't do much to soothe me when it came to a game with stakes this high.

I didn't know what Scythe's definition of "soon" was as far as an open uprising. To the undead, "soon" could be weeks, or a few years to a decade. But whatever the time frame, I couldn't allow him and Apollyon to meet that goal. Dave knew how dangerous that would be, too, which was why he was considering something as risky as deliberately getting caught.

"Dave's banking on being brought to an interrogator who might know where Apollyon is. So when you tell me, Mencheres, and Vlad where he is, we arrive in time to save him and nab the bad guys, right?" I asked.

The ghost nodded miserably. "Yes."

Vlad's brows drew together in contemplation even as I snapped, "No way."

"It's an acceptable risk," he insisted quietly.

"No, it's not, because they'd probably just cut off Dave's head and run before asking him even one thing," I shot back. "Apollyon's people don't need answers from Dave. What don't they already know? They know we're after them, they *think* they know where Bones and I are . . . they have no reason to keep Dave alive long enough for us to rescue him. If Dave weren't being so idiotically noble, he'd realize that."

Vlad shrugged. "Then Fabian should return and tell Dave to start his confession with the fact that it's not really you with Bones in Ohio. That should pique their interest enough to want to know more."

"It's still too dangerous," I gritted out.

Vlad's gaze turned hard. "One life risked to save thousands is not too dangerous. If you're too weak to see that, then you have no business being responsible for any of the lives beneath you in Bones and Mencheres's line."

"Really?" I swept out my hand, indicating the room at large. "Then why aren't you with those ghouls who wanted to blow my head off as a preemptive strike to end the war before it started? I'm only *one* life, after all. Wouldn't my death take a lot of steam out of Apollyon's war machine?"

Vlad strode forward, green light spilling from his eyes as he grabbed me. "You are my friend," he said through clenched teeth. "I haven't many of those, yet don't presume for a moment that I wouldn't sacrifice you if I truly felt it was the best way to stop this war from happening."

He let me go just as abruptly, my shoulders still stinging from his biting grip. "But I believe Apollyon would move forward regardless," he went on, spinning around to walk away from me. "He'd only claim you weren't really dead, that it was a trick. And besides, now you're of far more use to the vampire nation alive with your latest . . . ability."

I stared at Vlad. His back was to me, long dark hair still rustling from his rapid movements. It wasn't his stated coldness about my life, or Dave's, that made me sad as I looked at him. It was because, even hundreds of years after the loss of one life had admittedly devastated him, Vlad still couldn't bring himself to admit that sacrificing a life should always be the last resort. Not the first, easiest option.

"If there was no other way, I'd agree this thing with Dave was worth the risk. But we haven't looked at all our options yet, so I say no. And if you still can't see the value of a life, then maybe you should rethink being responsible for all the lives underneath you in *your* line," I replied, calmly but with an undercurrent of steel.

Vlad turned around, nailing me with a stare that should have backed me up several steps. It didn't. I met his gaze with an equally hard one of my own. Hell no would I flinch or apologize when I knew I was right.

"You will understand sacrifice much better when you're older" was what Vlad muttered after several loaded moments of silence.

"It's not sacrifice if it doesn't mean something, and if one friend's life isn't precious to you, then there's no loss involved in offering it up," I countered.

His gaze flicked to my right, where Mencheres watched the two of us with a hooded expression. If I judged him by past actions, I knew Mencheres was ruthless enough to agree with Vlad that the risk to Dave was acceptable without bothering to look at other options first. Hell, if he wanted to, Mencheres could force me to stay right here, waiting helplessly while Dave took that irrevocable step. One snap of his telekinetic power, and I'd be unable to move, let alone leave the house to get my friend.

Of course, one snap of *my* new, borrowed power and I could give Mencheres a whole new topic to ponder. I locked eyes with the Master vampire, seeing from the faint narrowing of his gaze that he knew what I was thinking. The scant space between us seemed to lengthen into a long, ominous road as we stared at each other across the room.

My fangs slid out, concealed by my lips, their sharp tips touching the edge of my tongue. One swipe and I could call forth Remnants with my blood, making both Vlad and Mencheres helpless to stop me from getting Dave. The question was, could Mencheres wrap his power around me fast enough to prevent that tiny movement? And more importantly, did I want to use the Remnants as a weapon against my friends, even if it was to help another friend?

After several moments, Mencheres gave me a slight smile, inclining his head. "The life of a friend is indeed too precious to risk unless it is a last resort. We will stop Dave from doing this while we explore other options."

I still remained tense. Was this a trick? If I retracted my fangs, would Mencheres slap his power around me while smirking about how gullible I was?

Vlad obviously didn't think it was a ploy. He let out a frustrated growl. "Kira's made you soft."

"She opened my eyes," Mencheres coolly refuted. "And you, my friend, protest too much. Before you knew of her new *ability*, you could have snatched Cat away to kill her with adequate vampire and ghoul witnesses. Then Apollyon wouldn't be able to refute her death. Bones would kill you afterward, and I myself would be furious with you, but your people would be protected and the war stalled. So if you truly believed the life of a friend wasn't precious enough to protect, you wouldn't be here scowling at me now."

Vlad muttered something in a language I didn't recognize. Whatever it was, it didn't sound like "Well played, sir!" and the glare he threw the other vampire warned that Vlad might combust at any moment.

"Aww, who's really a widdle softie on the inside?" I teased him, feeling some of the dread leaking out of me. It would be tough, true, but we'd find another way to bring down Apollyon, Scythe, and all the other hateful warmongers under them. Hadn't Bones repeatedly told me in the past that there was *always* another way?

"Actually, Reaper, the thought of your death isn't bothering me a bit at the moment," Vlad ground out.

I ignored that. He could huff and puff all he wanted, but Vlad kept proving that he was only brutal when the circumstances required it. Despite his frightening reputation, loyalty was Vlad's strong suit, not viciousness. I turned to Fabian, who'd stayed silent the past several minutes.

"First, we're going to get Dave. And then"—I glanced at Mencheres—"you and I get to reunite with our spouses, because with Scythe and the gang pulling out of Memphis, there's no reason for us to stay anymore."

I'd gotten on both boots and was busy stuffing them—and other parts of me—with weapons when my hip pocket vibrated in a familiar way. I pulled out my cell phone, answering, "Yep?" without bothering to look at who was calling.

"Cat."

He only said my name, but something in Tate's voice made me freeze as abruptly as if Mencheres had unleashed the full force of his power upon me.

"Is it Don?" I breathed, my chest tightening in a painful way. *It can't be. I just spoke to him a couple days ago!* my denial screamed.

"Yeah," Tate replied shortly, but his tone sounded as raw as I felt. "Go to the Marine Safety office in Memphis. A chopper's waiting for you."

I had to swallow twice before I could answer him. "I'm on my way."

I hit end with fingers that felt nerveless, looking up to meet Mencheres's dark, compassionate gaze. He'd obviously overheard the call.

"Go," he said. "Vlad and I will retrieve Dave and meet you there."

Vlad gave me a short nod of confirmation. I stopped piling on weapons and went upstairs. On the dresser was my red diamond ring. It was so distinctive that I hadn't been able to wear it while out ghoul hunting, but I put it on now, taking comfort in its familiar weight. Then I grabbed the pet carrier. I knew I wasn't coming back, and aside from my wedding ring and my cat, everything else was replaceable.

Thirty

YOU'LL GET THERE IN TIME.
I chanted that to myself the entire way in the car and in the air. Even though the compound wasn't far away—just on the opposite side of Tennessee, in fact—I was still stiff with fear that I might, indeed, be too late. The chopper landed a little less than two hours after Tate's call. Barely a tick of the clock, all things considered, but it still seemed like the seconds dragged by with pitiless disregard for my urgency.

A vampire waited for me on the roof, dark hair whipping around from the rotor blades. Not Bones, though I'd called him and he was on his way. It was my mother who wordlessly took my hand when I jumped out of the helicopter, keeping pace with me as I strode inside the building. My mental shields were up as high as I could crank them, because I didn't think I could stand it if I overheard a stray thought telling me that Don was already gone. I couldn't even bear to look at my mother as we went straight to the elevators, let alone ask the question that burned a hole in my throat. I was too afraid of what the answer might be.

"He's still alive, Catherine," she said quietly.

I choked back the sob of relief that threatened to claw its way out, managing to nod while tears blurred my gaze. The elevator doors opened and I went inside, part of me registering that the last time I'd been in an elevator was when I was ambushed by ghouls at the Ritz.

"Is it his cancer worsening, or did something else happen?"

Something else *better* have happened, I added silently. I'd called Don every few days to check in on him, plus got regular updates on his health from Tate. No one had even hinted to me that he was going downhill. If Don had been steadily growing worse over the past few weeks and everyone lied to me about it, I'd stop speaking to every last fucking one of them, my mother included.

"He had a heart attack a few hours ago."

I closed my eyes, absorbing the swell of pain as it came. Heart attacks were lethal enough all on their own. Add one to Don's already-ravaged health, and I knew what that meant.

Cool fingers squeezed around mine. "He's still hanging in," she said. "He knows you're coming, too."

"He's awake?" I was surprised, but how else could he know I was on my way?

She glanced at the ground, shifting uncomfortably. "He was when I last saw him."

Even amidst my fear, worry, and grief, I caught an edge in her voice that I well recognized. Defensiveness. The elevator doors opened on the second sublevel where Medical was, but I didn't budge.

"What aren't you telling me, Mom?"

She let go of my hand to gesture to the pet carrier. "It's not sterile for an animal to be in the same room with Don. All that hair. I can take your cat to your old office while you—"

"*What* aren't you telling me?" I repeated, slapping a hand on the elevator door when it started to close.

"Crawfield."

Both our heads whipped up, but Tate's indigo glare was only for my mother as he approached the elevator.

"Get off this floor, Crawfield. I told you not to come within a hundred yards of Don again. Cat." Tate's voice softened. "Come with me."

"Not until someone tells me what's going on, and as we all know, I'm in a hurry," I growled. My mother was forbidden to come within a hundred yards of Don? What the hell had happened?

"She directly violated Don's medical orders," Tate said, his gaze now flashing emerald at her.

"And he'd be dead now if I hadn't!" My mother stopped glaring at Tate to give me a pleading look. "That's the only reason I gave him the blood—"

"Which you had no right to do. You knew he had a DNR," Tate snapped.

Fresh tears filled my eyes as I put together what happened from the fragments of their argument. "Don had a 'do not resuscitate' on his medical orders, but you gave him some of your blood when he had the heart attack to bring him back?" I rasped, looking at my mother through a haze of pink.

She dropped her gaze. "I knew you'd want to see him one last time."

I let go of the cat carrier to wrap her in a fierce embrace, hearing her surprised "oof" even as Tate let out a disgusted noise.

"You can hug her all you want, but she's suspended indefinitely, so get off this floor, Crawfield, before I throw you off."

I let her go to round on Tate. "You can't even stop being a dick under *these* circumstances? What is wrong with you, Tate!"

My voice was loud. The medical staff paused in their activities to glance our way before quickly going back to what they'd been doing.

"I'll take your cat to your office, like I said," my mother muttered, stepping back into the elevator and hitting the close button.

Tate took my arm, leading me down the hall, and it was only because I didn't know if Don was awake and could hear us that I didn't send him flying along the polished sterile floors.

"Regardless of the circumstances, she defied orders," Tate stated, keeping his voice low. "If she wants to be on the team, then she needs to learn to obey orders even if she disagrees with them."

"Some things are more important than *orders*," I hissed back, stopping before we got too close to my uncle's room. "Don might be nothing more than a boss to you, but he means a little more than that to me. At least my mother recognized that, even if you refuse to!"

"Don't you dare," Tate breathed, coming closer until we were nose to nose. "Don't you *dare* stand there and pretend you're the only one losing a family member here. I grew up passed from foster home to foster home until I turned eighteen and joined the army. Spent the next five years trying to forget everything that happened before enlisting. Then Don took me under his wing when I was twenty-three. First fucking person to ever truly give a shit about me, to look up my birthday and send me a card. To remember that on the holidays, I'd be alone unless he stopped by pretending to talk about work. All this was before you ever met him." Tate's voice thickened with emotion. "I'd kill or die for that man, don't you ever think I wouldn't."

"Then why are you letting him just *die*?" I demanded, the last word cracking with the grief frothing inside me.

"Oh, Cat." Tate sighed, his entire body drooping as though something inside him had magically deflated. "Because it's not my choice. It's Don's, and he made it. I don't like it, I don't agree with it, but I sure as hell have to respect it."

And so do you hung heavy in the air, even if he didn't say it. I glanced down the hall toward my uncle's room, hearing the beeps from the EKG machine that weren't the steady rhythm they should be.

"I'm going to ride your mother until she learns that she can't ignore orders again, but, Cat . . ." Tate raised his hand as if he were going to touch me, then dropped it. "Despite the fact that she shouldn't have done it, I'm glad you got here in time," he finished, looking away with a shine in his own gaze.

My anger deflated with the same abruptness with which his posture had slumped. It would be easier to hold on to it, I knew. Easier to whip myself into a rage over this and every other thing Tate had ever done to piss me off, but that would only be trying to camouflage my grief over losing someone I loved. Tate loved Don, too, I knew that. Knew it even as I flung the "boss" comment at him before. Aside from me, Tate was probably hurting the most right now, but he was handling his pain the way he always had—by being a good soldier.

And I was handling my pain the way I always had—running from it with denial and anger. Of the two of us, I had the least amount of room to throw stones over coping mechanisms.

Slowly, I reached up, brushing my hand across Tate's cheek and feeling the light stubble that said he hadn't shaved today; very unlike his military regimented, impeccable grooming habits.

"Don loves you, too," I whispered.

Then I walked away, leaving Tate to go into my uncle's room.

Thirty-one

I knew how critical Don's condition was. Understood that, if not for my mother's intervention earlier, he'd already be dead now. But somehow, I hadn't truly accepted that he was dying until I walked into his room and the final shreds of my denial were ripped away from me.

It wasn't the bluish paleness of Don's features as he lay, eyes closed, on the bed. Not the hospital gown he'd previously refused to wear, the EKG machine that showed his shockingly low blood pressure, or the heavy scent of what I now knew was cancer. It wasn't even his erratic heartbeats that drove home the reality that this would be the last time I would ever see my uncle. No, it was the rolling tray pushed into the corner of the room—naked of a phone, laptop, or any files—that tore through my heart with all the pain of a thousand silver blades.

You just talked to him a few days ago! a voice

screamed inside me. How could it come to this so *fast*?

I shoved back the sob that threatened to break free and went over to his bedside, very softly running my hand over his arm. I was afraid to disturb him by letting him know I was here, and afraid not to. He was hooked up to an EKG, but aside from the tubes in his nose, he breathed on his own in small, shallow puffs that didn't give him enough oxygen, judging from his pallor.

I sat there in silence for half an hour, watching him, thinking back to the first time I met Don, all the way to the last time I saw him before now. We had both good and bad history between us, but the mistakes of the past faded underneath my belief that Don had always tried to do what he thought was right. That hadn't always made him a good uncle, but it made him what we all were—flawed people who tried to do their best under rough circumstances. I had no grudges over our past. Only gratitude that he'd been in my life at all, and a wish that he didn't have to leave it now.

"Cat." The faintest smile ghosted across Don's mouth as he woke up and saw me next to his bed. "Didn't think I'd get to see you again."

I took in a deep breath. It was that or I'd lose the fragile hold over my emotions that kept me from breaking into uncontrollable tears.

"Yeah, well, you wouldn't, except I hear you're having obedience problems with your new recruit," I said, managing a smile even though it felt like my face would splinter.

Don let out a small, pained laugh. "Turns out your mother obeys orders just as well as you did."

His wry comment served to underscore our history, intensifying my grief at the thought of losing him. The only emotion my father and I shared for each other was mutual loathing, but Don had found his way into my heart even before I knew I was related to him.

"You know what they say about the acorn and the tree," I replied. Then my composure cracked and a few tears slipped out despite my best effort to hold them back.

Oh, Cat, don't cry.

Don didn't say it out loud, but I heard in from his thoughts as clearly as if the words were shouted. His hand drifted over, patting mine before his eyes closed.

"It'll be okay," he whispered.

And I heard the other thing he didn't say, but it echoed across my mind with more clarity than I thought I could stand.

So glad the pain will be over soon . . .

"Don." I leaned forward, stroking his hand pleadingly. "You said no before, but it's not too late if you've changed your mind. I can still—"

"No," he interrupted, opening his eyes. "I've lived longer than I should have as it is. Promise me you'll let me go, and that you won't bring me back." *I'm tired, so very tired*, his thoughts sighed.

A piece of my heart broke, but I held his gaze and nodded as I forced the words out, whisking away another tear that slipped down my cheek.

"I promise."

Good girl. Proud of you. So proud.

I got up and began to pace so he couldn't see that more tears rushed out at hearing that from him. I'd been in countless battles before, but letting him go would take the kind of strength I didn't know if I had.

"You don't know how much I'm going to miss you," I whispered, keeping my back to him, trying to wipe away the tears that wouldn't stop flowing no matter how hard I tried to stuff them back.

He grunted softly. "I'll miss you, too." *Love you, niece. Wish I would have gotten to know you sooner. Shouldn't have waited so long . . .*

A choked noise escaped me hearing that. I stabbed my fingernails into my palms, hoping the slight physical pain would distract me enough to control my raging emotional anguish. It didn't. My heart constricted, aching from an injury that no amount of supernatural healing abilities could soothe.

Moments later, I heard a familiar booted stride and felt power in the air that I'd recognize anywhere. God, Bones had gotten here *fast*. That only further hammered away at my fragile control. He'd come quickly because he knew how devastated I'd be, and I loved him more for it even as it reminded me of how much I'd hurt when Don was gone.

Then Bones was beside me, his dark gaze raking the room to take in everything in an instant, hard arms reaching out to pull me to him. I allowed myself a few precious seconds to sag in his embrace, not needing to pretend I was strong with him, before turning around to give Don a forced cheerful smile.

"Look who else made it."

"I see that." Then a pained cough came over my uncle. Bones took my hand as his heart had several ominous pauses in between beats. "You turned out to be a better man than I expected," Don rasped once he'd regained control.

Bones stared at my uncle, his gaze steady and serious. "So did you, old chap."

"Bones and I talked," I said, trying to smile so I wouldn't burst into tears at the knowledge that this was their way of saying goodbye. "Remember your offer to give me away as a bride? Well, we'd like to take you up on it."

Don's mouth twitched in a wistful smile before his features tightened, his thoughts revealing that more pain flared in his chest. I glanced at the EKG machine even though I knew what it would say. My mother's blood had brought him back, but it wouldn't be for long. His heart was failing right in front of my eyes.

"'Fraid I won't be around for your wedding, Cat," he murmured, eyes fluttering closed.

"Yes you will," I said, so strongly that Don's eyes reopened and stayed open. "Because we're going to renew our vows here and now."

"Cat." His face pinched with sadness. "You were planning a big wedding once things were . . . settled down. You don't have to ruin those plans . . ."

He paused to close his eyes, his breathing and heart rate dipping for a moment. I bit my lip, squeezing Bones's hand until a cracking noise let me know to loosen my grip.

"These are hardly the right circumstances," my uncle finished a few moments later, waving vaguely at the machines by his bed.

I thought back to when I was a little girl and how I'd imagined what my wedding day would be like. I'd pictured wearing a white dress, of course. Imagined my grandfather fussing over his tie like he always did when he was forced to wear one, and my grandmother replying that yes, it was straight, with that little roll of her eyes. My mother would be there, smiling because she was so happy for me, and I'd have friends who would be helping me get ready to walk down the aisle. My bouquet would be roses and wildflowers, my hair would be up, and I would look at my husband-to-be through a filmy white veil that would only be lifted once we were pronounced man and wife.

Of course, I'd imagined all that back when I didn't believe in vampires, let alone realize I was half one. Bones had wanted to give me a close version of that dream, somehow knowing I'd still held on to it, but the lives we led kept interfering with making that white wedding fantasy a reality.

My wedding would never play out like that dream from when I was a child. It wouldn't be now, either, in the hospital wing of a secret government facility that policed the activities of the undead. My wedding had been on a blood-spattered arena, witnessed not by friends or family, but by hundreds of vampires I'd never met before. My bridegroom hadn't lifted a white veil from my face at the pronouncement from a minister that we were married. Instead, he'd cut his hand and held it out to me, swearing by his blood that I would forever be his wife, should I choose to accept him as my husband.

That was my wedding day. Pretty much the exact opposite of everything I'd ever dreamed, but I wouldn't try to substitute it with something else. The image I'd had of myself as a child was someone I'd never be, and it was only recently that I realized it was okay to be *who I was*. That bride might have worn a slutty black dress instead of a beautiful white one, or had blood in her hands instead of holding a bouquet, but no woman had ever been as lucky as I was the day Bones held out his hand and declared me to be his wife.

"This isn't about circumstances," I replied, continuing to fight back tears as I tried to sum up everything I'd only recently learned. "It's about family."

Don hadn't been there on that day. Neither had my mother, and my grandparents had been dead for years by then. But both of them could be here for this. It wasn't a new ceremony for my sake, but a reenactment of the previous one for theirs.

"Will you do it?" I went on.

Don's eyes misted. Through his thoughts, I heard how much the request meant to him even though he only spoke a single word in reply. "Yes."

"Tate." I turned toward the doorway, knowing he'd lingered in the hall this whole time. "You think you could bend the rules to let that disobedient new recruit back up on the floor for a little while?"

A grunt escaped him; half laugh, half disbelief as he filled the door frame. "Jesus, Cat."

"Actually this won't be a religious ceremony," I replied with a faint smile, "but feel free to offer blessings anyway."

Tate's gaze moved over Bones and then down to our clasped hands. "Since when have you two ever cared about my blessing?" he asked dryly.

"I never asked for it and I don't need it," I replied in an even tone. "But you're my friend, Tate, so I do care."

I watched his face, waiting to see if he'd take the olive branch I'd extended, or throw it back at me like

he had so many times in the past. Those dark blue
eyes met mine, emotions skipping across his expres-
sive features like waves on a pond. First regret, then
resolve, and at last, acceptance.

"I hope you're very happy," Tate said, the words
quiet but sounding sincere. Then, to my surprise, he
walked over and held out his hand, but not to me. To
Bones.

Bones accepted Tate's hand and shook it without letting go of mine; easy enough since I held his
left hand with my right one. When they let go, Tate
glanced at me, smiled slightly, and said, "Don't worry.
I won't bother asking to kiss the bride."

Then he looked over to Don, whose eyes had closed
during this exchange even though I could hear from
his thoughts that he wasn't asleep. His chest hurt too
much for him to sleep, and he had a new pain radi-
ating down his arm that he recognized from a few
hours ago. Still, I knew what his answer would be
even before Tate asked, "You up for this?"

My uncle didn't know I could hear his thoughts.
Didn't know that I picked up on every word of his
thinking this was a far better way to die than before,
when he'd been alone, hearing only the steady flat
line of the EKG machine before everything had gone
black, then awoke to Tate screaming at my mother for
what she'd done. I heard all of this, and though my
throat burned from stuffing back the tears that relentlessly came, I said nothing. Did nothing even though
the very blood running through my veins could possibly prevent the next heart attack that I knew was
coming.

This was his choice. I hated it—oh, so much!—

because it was taking from me the only real father I'd ever known, but Tate was right. I had to respect it.

"Let's do this," Don replied. His voice was raspy with pain, but the smile he flashed me was genuine despite that.

Tate picked up the phone by Don's bed, telling whoever was on the other line to "get Crawfield, now, and bring her up here."

To distract myself from falling all to pieces as I heard Don's heartbeat become more erratic and listened to his mind try to shelter him from the increased squeezing in his chest, I began to explain the intricacies of a vampire marriage ceremony.

"So, if a vampire couple wants to get married— which they'd better be damn sure about, because with vampires, it's till death do you part or *nothing*—it's kinda like those old handfasting ceremonies. One of them, usually the guy first, gets a knife, slices it across his palm, and then says . . ."

By the time my mother arrived, I'd repeated all the words and described my prior wedding to Bones, leaving out the more grisly details. She looked at the four of us with slight confusion, but Tate didn't give her a chance to say anything. He grasped her arm and took her into the hall, telling her in a voice too low for Don to overhear what was about to happen.

I was glad Don's eyes were closed again, because that meant I didn't have to fight the tears that burst out of me. Tate liked the idea of witnessing my re-dedication of vows to Bones even less than my mother would. Yet here he was, sternly telling her to act pleasant, dammit, and not ruin this for Don because he didn't have much time left.

That was excruciatingly evident. My uncle's breath-ing was increasingly labored and he was thinking that it felt like he had a car pressed on his chest, but he was fierce in his will to last long enough to do this one final thing. The EKG machine began to make warning noises, as if I couldn't tell from his thoughts and his skipped heartbeats what was happening. More tears coursed down my cheeks in a steady stream that wet my top and stained the floor an ever darkening pink where they fell.

I took my uncle's hand, hating how much cooler it felt with his rapidly decreasing circulation, and squeezed his fingers gently.

Bones covered my hand with his own, his strength feeling like it overflowed from him to permeate into my flesh. Such a stark contrast to my uncle's rapidly fading mortality and the approaching chill in Don's fingers.

"Donald Bartholomew Williams," Bones said for-mally. I startled at the "Bartholomew" part. I'd never heard Don's full name before. *Figures Bones knows it*, a part of me thought hazily as I tried to suppress my sob over the increased skips in my uncle's heartbeat. Bones extensively researched Don after finding out he was the man who'd blackmailed me into working for him all those years ago.

"Do you give your niece, Catherine, to be my wife?" Bones went on, brushing his fingers over Don's.

My uncle's eyes opened, lingering on me, Bones, and then Tate, who still stood in the doorway. Even though I knew how much pain he was in and the effort that it took was palpable, Don managed to smile.

Then his hand clenched around mine, agony blasting through him that I heard in the sudden scream of his thoughts. His whole body stiffened and his mouth opened in a short, harsh gasp—the last one he'd make. Don's eyes, the same gray color as mine, rolled back in his head as the EKG machine's beeps became one horrible, continuous sound.

Tate crossed the room in a blink, gripping the bed rail so hard that it crushed under his hands. That was the last thing I saw before everything blurred into reddish pink as the sobs I'd held back broke free to overwhelm me.

Yet even in the throes of the fatal heart attack, my uncle's will proved stronger than the frailty of his body. He'd sworn to himself that he would live long enough to give me away, and he would not be denied, even if Bones and I were the only ones who knew it.

Don's dying thought was one single, protracted word.

Yesssss.

Thirty-two

Bones held open the door and I stepped inside what was technically our home, even though we hadn't stayed here much in the past year. My cat didn't share my lack of enthusiasm at our arrival. As soon as I opened the door to his crate, Helsing sprang from the carrier onto the back of the couch, looking around with an expression that could only be called wide-eyed relief.

To be fair, he'd lived here longer than we had, what with how we'd had to leave him with a house sitter for months last year. Or maybe he was just glad to be out of that cage. I couldn't blame him. Denise had been stuck in a pet carrier for hours after she'd shapeshifted into a feline, and she didn't recall the experience with fondness.

I looked around at our living room, thinking I should start taking the furniture coverings off the sofas and reclining chairs. Or get some dusting spray and several cloths, because, wow, I could write my name in the mantel over the fireplace or on any of the end tables. But I did none of those things. I simply stood there, looking around, mentally calculating which place would be the best to put Don.

Not on the end tables or the mantel; my cat occasionally leapt onto all the above and I didn't want to be sweeping up my uncle's remains if Helsing accidentally knocked Don over. Not the kitchen table; that would be inappropriate. Not the closet; that was rude. Not upstairs in my bedroom; I didn't think Don needed a bird's-eye view of what Bones and I did in there. I wasn't about to put Don in any of the bathrooms, either. What if the steam from the showers got him all wet?

"None of this will work," I said to Bones.

Hands closed gently over my shoulders as he turned me around to face him.

"Give it to me, Kitten."

My grip tightened on the brass urn that I'd held all the way from Don's memorial service in Tennessee to our home in the Blue Ridge. Leave it to my uncle to insist on being cremated. Guess he didn't trust that one of us wouldn't yank him out of the grave if he just allowed himself to be planted in one piece. No chance of that now, with ashes being all that was left of him.

"Not until I find the right place for him," I insisted. "He's not a plant that I can just stick on a ledge near the sunshine, Bones!"

He tilted my chin up until I either had to look at him, or grind my jaw against his hand in a show of stubborn refusal. I chose the former even if the latter was more of what I felt like doing.

"You know what you're holding isn't Don," Bones said, his dark gaze compassionate. "You wanted to bring his remains here so that nothing happened to them while we were traveling, but that is no more your uncle than this coat is me, Kitten."

I looked at the long leather jacket Bones had on, its edges slightly frayed from extended wear. I'd gotten it for Bones for Christmas when we were first dating, but hadn't given it to him personally. I'd been gone by then.

"No, that jacket isn't you," I replied, feeling an all too familiar stinging in my eyes. "But you pulled it out from under a cabinet anyway because at the time, it was all you had left of me. Well, this is all I have left of Don."

His thumb caressed my jaw while his other hand slid down until it rested over the urn.

"I understand," he said quietly. "And if you like, we'll build an entire new room just to have a space exactly as you want it for this. But in the meantime, luv, you need to let it go."

Very lightly, he tugged on the urn, making it easy for me not to let him pull it from my grip, if I didn't want to. I looked down at the small brass container and the pale hands—mine and Bones's—that encircled it.

It. Not Don. I knew that logically, but the part of me that was having the hardest time saying goodbye to my uncle didn't want to acknowledge that what I held was nothing more than ash surrounded by metal. It had been four days since his death, yet I still felt like I was moving around in a dream. Even attending his memorial service and giving the eulogy felt more

surreal than rooted in reality, because Don couldn't
really be gone. Hell, I could swear I'd glimpsed him a
few times in my peripheral vision, looking as mildly
exasperated with me as ever.

Bones tugged again and I let the urn slip from my
hands into his, blinking back the tears from the relin-
quishment that was more symbolic than the transfer-
ring of an item. He leaned down, brushing his lips
across my forehead, and then disappeared up the
stairs. Maybe it was a good thing that Bones was
putting Don's remains away instead of me. With my
current emotional state, I'd probably think the only
safe place for his ashes was tucked inside my clothes
next to the garlic and weed.

I rubbed my hands together, bleakly noting how
empty they felt without the surrogate for my uncle that
I'd clutched the past several hours. Then I rolled up
the sleeves of my memorial-appropriate black blouse.
I might not have control over much else in my life,
but I could get the goddamn dust off the furniture, for
starters.

My ferocious scrubbing of the house in an effort to distract myself from grieving over Don turned out to be
beneficial in more ways than one. Mencheres called,
saying he was on his way over because he had important information to relay. From the way Bones said he
sounded, it wasn't wonderful important information,
like Apollyon being found dead with a "Happy early
birthday, Cat!" note pinned to his corpse. Frankly I
didn't think I was up for any more bad news, but since
life had no pause button that I knew of, I was about
to be dealing with Mencheres's news, up for it or not.

At least the house was sparkling and the musty scent was gone from the air. Of course, that could also be from the new plants Bones went out to procure while I was doing my imitation of Martha Stewart. Now I was the dubious owner of several fragrant garlic bulbs and a few fluffy pot plants. I didn't even want to ask where Bones had gotten the latter from. Sniffed it out and dug it up from a local illegal field? Or bought it from a friendly neighborhood drug dealer?

God, I couldn't wait until the effect from Marie's blood was out of my system. If I never smelled garlic or weed again, it would be too soon. The only upside of our new decor was that it meant I could take the packets off, and not having dozens of little porous baggies under my clothes was a welcome relief.

"They're here, Kitten," Bones called out from downstairs.

I didn't hear anything yet, but I knew his connection to Mencheres was unusually acute because of their shared power, so I took him at his word. I wouldn't have time to put on makeup, but I didn't think anyone would notice. Or care. I was showered, in clean clothes, and my home was neat. Those were the three most important things when having visitors over.

Unless those visitors were hungry, of course.

"We don't have any blood," I said to Bones as I came down the stairs.

His gaze swept over me, pausing at certain points with appreciation. My dress was hardly sexy, being a plain black cotton number that hung to my feet and had three-quarter sleeves, but either it hugged the right places or Bones was showing the effects of a week of celibacy. To say I hadn't been in the mood since Don died was to put it mildly.

"I rather doubt they'd expect us to," he replied. "They know we just arrived."

Right. Plus, this wasn't a social call. "He's probably coming over to tell me we need to put Plan Dave into action," I muttered. "We were supposed to think up another way to swipe a few of Apollyon's higher-ups without having Dave reveal that he was a plant, but that got pushed by the wayside."

Bones raised a brow in a way that said, *Perhaps*. He'd heard about that. Dave told Bones shortly after Don died, fueled by grief into wanting even more to strike a blow against Apollyon, but Bones talked him out of it. Still, I knew he thought the idea had merit.

I was even more opposed to it now than before, though. I'd just lost my uncle. I didn't want to lose a good friend next, and Dave was reeling from Don's death like the rest of us, which made him sloppier. That was the cold hard truth. I wondered if my uncle had any idea the profound effect he'd had on the people around him. Knowing Don, I doubted it. He wasn't much for grandstanding.

A car came up the winding driveway in the next few minutes, the sound almost loud compared to the relative quietness of the woods around us. The seclusion of having a cabin on fifteen acres of mountaintop property was what had drawn us to this place to begin with. Now that I could read minds, I appreciated the lack of close neighbors even more.

"Grandsire, Kira, welcome," Bones said once they were at the door.

I noted the elegant leather satchel Mencheres carried with a mental sigh. Of course they'd spend the night. He was coming all the way out here to deliver information; it would be beyond rude for us to hear him out, and then send them on their way. Plus, he probably wanted to strategize, and I couldn't blame him for that, either. No matter what upheaval might be going on in my personal life, there was still a war we had to prevent.

"Hi, guys," I said, giving both of them a hug to make up for my initial, selfish wish that they weren't staying.

"I'm so sorry about your uncle," Kira whispered, patting me when I let her go. "If there's anything we can do . . ."

"Thanks," I said, forcing a smile. "The flowers you sent were beautiful." All the arrangements had been, but I'd had them sent to a local hospital after the memorial. None of the burly team members were keen on the idea of taking them home, and I didn't have room for the dozens of floral sprays, bouquets, and wreaths.

"It was the least we could do," Mencheres replied with his usual reserved courtesy. "I regret to impose on you at this time of sorrow. However—"

"It's fine," I interrupted with another mechanical smile. "I know the bad guys don't call a time-out just because someone dies. I appreciate you handling things for the past few days, but it's time for Bones and me to get back in the mix."

I gestured for them to sit down, doing the polite hostess thing by asking if I could get them anything to drink. As Bones predicted, neither of them asked for an authentic version of a Bloody Mary, but just took water instead. That, at least, I had plenty of.

Mencheres waited until I was seated to dive into why they'd come. "I have found out what happened to Nadia Bissel," he stated.

I just stared at him blankly. "Who?"

Bones also cocked his head in puzzlement. Glad I wasn't the only one who felt lost.

"The human female you were seeking," Mencheres amended. At my continued confused look, he sighed. "The one who worked with the reporter you are friends with and who disappeared while investigating rumors of vampires?"

"Oh!" I said, the light bulb finally going off in my memory. I'd forgotten all about sending Nadia's picture and information to Mencheres so he could circulate it among his allies, looking for a clue as to what happened to her.

"She's dead?" I asked in resignation. Poor Timmie. He'd held out such hope that she was okay.

"No," Mencheres said, surprising me. "On the contrary, she's quite well, according to what I discovered."

"So why do you have that uh-oh tone to your voice?" I asked warily.

His lips curled. "My uh-oh tone is because you indicated your friend had more than a platonic interest in Nadia, and she is now the lover of a powerful vampire who has no intention of sharing her."

"Oh," I repeated, more thoughtfully this time. Then, "His *willing* lover?" Some vampires weren't up on the whole "no means no" concept.

"*Her* willing lover," Mencheres corrected.

Well. Timmie's chances with Nadia just went from slim to never gonna happen. I was glad she was alive and not being held against her will. Considering I'd thought Mencheres had come to bear more grim news about Apollyon, this was almost cause for popping the champagne, if I'd had any. Timmie's heart might be bruised, but there were far worse things that could have befallen Nadia. She'd gone looking for vampires and apparently found a whole lot more than just proof of their existence.

"Your sources are good? There's no doubt Nadia's with this vampire of her own free will and not just tranced into staying?"

"I know the vampire Nadia is with," Mencheres stated. "It would be very unlike Debra to force a human into staying with her, even one who'd discovered our race. Debra could have easily sent Nadia away with no memory of her discovery."

"Unless Nadia is like me," Kira said, with a slight smile. "Erasing my memory didn't work out so well for you when we met."

Mencheres let out a growl so edged with passion that I had an urge to glance away. "It worked out extraordinarily well in the end," he murmured to Kira.

Her soft laugh was also filled with things that were best left behind closed doors. Technically, they weren't doing anything but sitting on the couch together, but with the newly charged air around them, I felt almost like a voyeur in my own home. I looked away to study my fingernails, as if struck by an urgent need to get a manicure.

Out of the corner of my eye, I caught Bones's slight grin. He knew how this would affect me, but the sudden heat coming off the two of them did nothing to discomfit him, of course. Mencheres and Kira could start boinking like rabbits right in front of Bones, and he'd probably just warn them that the sectional they were on tended to flip over during such activity.

If Mencheres and Kira wanted to take this upstairs to a guest room, they were welcome to, but if they were staying down here, I was defusing the mood.

"Not nice for Nadia to disappear without telling her friends she was okay, though," I said, clearing my throat.

Mencheres rescinded the energy he'd been emitting until the room felt back to a PG–13 level, instead of R heading into NC–17. "Debra is what you would refer to as old school," he replied, pulling his gaze away from Kira to look at me. "She would not want Nadia contacting people from her former life, especially those who had an interest in exposing our race."

Her former life. I almost let out a snort. That was the damn truth, because once a person became involved in the vampire world, nothing about their life would ever be the same again.

Then I glanced at Bones's profile, noting his curly hair, richly defined cheekbones, dark brows, and lips that were firm enough to be masculine and full enough to be sinful. Nothing about my life had ever been the same once I plunged into the vampire world, too, but looking at him, I wouldn't want it any other way. I hoped Nadia found half as much happiness in her undead relationship as I'd found in mine.

"I'll call Timmie, give him the news," I said, rising.

"Poor bloke can't catch a break when it comes to women," Bones noted.

I met his dark brown gaze with my first real smile in the past several days. "He just hasn't met the right one yet, but once he does, he'll forget everyone else."

His smile became full of promise even as his power seemed to encompass me like a slow, sensual fog. "Indeed," he agreed, his tone now deep and silky. "The right woman is well worth waiting for."

Now it was Kira who cleared her throat at the decided shift in the atmosphere. I went upstairs to my room, still smiling in a lingering way, to call Timmie and give him the news that was both good and bad.

Thirty-three

I HUNG UP HALF AN HOUR LATER, BLOWING out a sigh. Timmie had taken the information about Nadia well enough, albeit needing to be talked out of seeing her in person so he'd *know* she was all right. I negotiated it down to a phone call. Timmie had no idea how strong vampire territorialism was. If he showed up reeking of lust and unrequited love for Nadia around the admittedly "old school" Debra, he'd be lucky to walk away without a permanent limp, if he walked away at all.

" . . . saw them myself several years ago, though Marie only used them to threaten me instead of having them attack me," Bones was saying.

That perked my ears up. I'd gone in my room and shut the door so my conversation wasn't distracting to everyone below. Talking Timmie out of doing something dangerously dumb had tuned me out to what they were saying, too. Had the conversation turned to Remnants? Bones never told me he'd seen them before, let alone that Marie had threatened him with them.

I hurried downstairs just as he finished with, "Who's to say she doesn't use them often, and most people don't live long enough to tell the tale?"

"I imagine it takes quite a lot out of her to raise and control them, which would preclude Marie from making Remnants her most common weapon," Mencheres stated before raising an inquiring brow at me. "You were very tired afterward, as I recall."

I sat next to Bones with an affirmative grunt. "At least Marie was right and their effect wasn't as overwhelming as it was the first time."

I'd still felt tired and cold everywhere for a few hours after raising them with Vlad, but I was able to keep control of myself the whole time. Nothing like when I first drank Marie's blood and then went nuts for two days.

Bones turned to stare at me. "The first time? You raised them *again*?"

Oh crap. With everything that happened, I hadn't had a chance to tell Bones what I'd done in the graveyard that night with Vlad. Now he thought I'd been hiding it from him.

"I did a trial run of raising Remnants a little over a week ago," I said, raising my hand at the whiplash of disbelief I felt across my subconscious. "Before you get pissed, I didn't deliberately go behind your back. It just happened. And no, I didn't have a case of the sluts again."

"And you neglected to mention this to me why?" he asked, a hint of anger brushing my senses.

"Because the next time I saw you was when Don died," I replied steadily. "And it hadn't been the sort of thing I'd wanted to casually mention to you over the phone before that."

Bones let out a breath in a slow hiss, that anger ebbing to something milder, like disapproval.

"You knew about this?" he asked Mencheres.

An oblique shrug. "Afterward."

I concealed my snort with the utmost difficulty. Sure, he'd had it *confirmed* afterward, but Mencheres knew damn well beforehand what Vlad and I would do, as he'd admitted once we got back. Still, Bones wouldn't be able to pick up the slightest hint of subterfuge in Mencheres's bland charcoal gaze. *Note to self: He tap-dances around giving a straight answer with impressive skill.*

"All right," Bones said at last, sounding resigned but no longer mad or disapproving. "Well, what was it like this time, Kitten?"

"Still very freaky," I admitted with a shudder. "It took some trial and error, but we found out they're summoned and controlled by blood. After I sent them back, I felt tired, freezing, and hungry—for food," I added with a pointed glance at Mencheres, who merely blinked in an innocent way. "Still, nothing as bad as the first time."

Even though I didn't want the memory to come, it did anyway. *Cold all through me. Such incredible hunger. The smash of voices in my mind, intertwining into a roar of white noise . . .*

Except for one voice, oddly enough. It tugged at the edge of my memory, honey-coated and Southern Creole, dancing amidst the chaos that night when

I'd first been exposed to the true depths of Marie's hold over the dead. That's right, Marie had asked me a question I hadn't registered at the time because I'd felt like I was suffocating underneath the power I'd absorbed from her. Now, however, her question was as clear as though she were whispering in my ear this very moment.

Haven't you ever wondered how Gregor escaped Mencheres's prison?

Such an odd thing for her to ask. Mencheres snatched me away from Gregor, erasing the entire time from my mind and locking Gregor up as punishment. Yet somehow, Gregor had escaped a dozen years later and came after me, claiming I was his wife, not Bones's. At the time, finding out how Gregor had gotten out hadn't been first on anyone's list of priorities. Not with the trouble Gregor caused on the loose.

To be honest, I hadn't thought about Gregor much since I blew his head off with the pyrokinesis power I'd temporarily absorbed from Vlad. Why, of all things, would Marie ask me if I knew how Gregor got out? She knew I didn't know how he'd slipped Mencheres's prison. No one knew, not even Mencheres. Plus, that was the last thing I'd care about, being crazed from the connection to the dead that I'd absorbed from her . . .

"Holy shit!" I burst out, shooting upward so fast that the couch flipped over from my momentum.

Bones was on his feet, gaze darting around and a knife already in his grip. I waved that away with an almost feverish swipe of my hand, stomping over hard enough that I should have left dents in the floor.

"Gregor." I seized Bones by the shoulders, barely

noticing that his eyebrows shot up at that name. "He escaped from Mencheres's prison, something no one should've been able to do with how smart and powerful granddaddy pharaoh is, right? But Gregor got away, leaving no sign how he did it. Don't you see? We thought he must've hatched a clever getaway plan himself, but the fucker didn't do a *thing*!"

Out of the corner of my eye, I saw Mencheres and Kira exchange a concerned glance with Bones.

"Kitten," he said, in the same tone I'd heard Bones use on trauma victims when he thought they were only a harsh syllable away from a complete mental breakdown. "You're upset over everything that's happened recently. It's natural to fixate on something from the past when the present feels overwhelming—"

That made me laugh with a maniacal sort of amusement, causing his brow to furrow even more.

"Luv, perhaps—" he tried again.

"No one can hide from death," I cut him off, deep satisfaction filling me as the last piece of the puzzle fell into place. Marie said that, but I hadn't pondered it as promised. For the past several days, I'd been too numb with grief to think about anything but losing Don. Before that, I was busy chasing my tail trying to find leads on Apollyon, plus also trying to mute my new connection with ghosts—and still being so pissed at Marie for what she'd done.

No one, not even our kind, she'd stressed. *Death travels the world and passes through even the thickest walls we protect ourselves with . . . When you truly understand what it means, you'll know how to defeat Apollyon . . .* God, she'd given me all the pieces. I just hadn't put them together.

"Marie said that before she sicced those Remnants on you and blackmailed me into drinking her blood," I went on, my voice rising. "I thought she was just threatening me in a cryptic way—you know how she loves to be all freaky and mysterious—but she was trying to help us."

Gregor hadn't gotten himself out of Mencheres's prison. *Marie* had found him by using the one thing that no one could hide from: ghosts. She probably used Remnants to break him out; not even Mencheres's guards could have protected themselves against those. Marie might have hated Gregor, but her loyalty wouldn't allow her to abandon her sire.

It fit with her ruthless practicality as well. Marie had wanted to be free from Gregor. That wouldn't happen as long as he was imprisoned, and Marie had admitted she knew why Mencheres locked him up. So with letting Gregor out—and him coming straight for me—Marie knew Bones would try to kill him. He hadn't, but I'd done it, accomplishing her objective for her, all without her being in direct violation of her oath to her sire.

The devil's in the details, I'd told that ghoul at the drive-in. Yes it was, and the clever voodoo queen appeared to be a master at details. The same loyalty that wouldn't let Marie kill Gregor herself also wouldn't let her ally herself against her fellow ghouls in a brewing war, but yet again, Marie had found a way around that. She'd forced me to drink her blood, giving me the same power she had. Helping us against Apollyon in a way that couldn't be traced back to her, considering how we'd been sure to keep quiet about what occurred between Marie and me in the cemetery.

"God, that woman's a *hell* of a lot more devious than I gave her credit for!" I exclaimed.

Bones glanced behind me, with just the barest inclination of his head. I walked away from him, muttering, "Don't worry. You don't need to have Mencheres break out the invisible straitjacket again. I haven't gone crazy. I just didn't understand until now."

He still looked like he was debating having Mencheres lay the power whammy on me, so I sat down by Kira in a very deliberate manner, folding my hands in my lap. There. Didn't I look calm and sane?

"Apollyon is as good as caught," I said, meeting his concerned brown gaze with a purpose that felt like it radiated through me. "He just doesn't know it yet."

THIRTY-FOUR

"ALL THE GARLIC AND WEED'S GONE?" I asked Bones as he came in the front door. Aside from the garlic, it occurred to me that I sounded like a teen trying to clean up from a big party before her parents got home.

"Far away," Bones replied. "Took it flying and then dropped it in a lake. It'll sink, or some lucky sod will have a grand day fishing."

I'd already scrubbed myself enough to take off a layer of skin, let alone all remaining stench from the herbs, and thrown out my clothes that had touched them. I was as ready as I was going to get.

"All right," I said, looking at Bones, Mencheres, and Kira. "Time to raise the dead."

I went onto our wraparound front porch, staring up at the sky to try and clear my head. The stars really were much brighter out in the country as compared to the city. Still, I wasn't here to admire the pretty twinkling lights. I was here to put a big ol' supernatural WELCOME sign above my head, summoning the very beings I'd tried to repel for the past several weeks. Even though I was in a sparsely populated area, I knew the dead were close by. The lack of human voices bombarding my mind made it easier to focus on the hum I felt in the air that had nothing to do with the three vampires joining me on the porch. This was something else, coming from the ground up.

I closed my eyes, trying to picture the trails of spectral light I'd seen when the other side of the grave first opened to me back in New Orleans. Something that felt like gooseflesh danced across my skin, but it wasn't cold out, and I wasn't afraid. I was calm, because I *knew* they were close. *Come*, I thought, seeking them with the power that resided in my veins. *Come*.

Behind me, Kira let out a hiss even as Bones said quietly, "Four of them just showed up, luv." I kept my eyes closed, smiling so those who came would know they were welcomed, and continued to pull on the power inside me. Before, I'd had to be angry, or afraid, or in pain to activate the power I'd borrowed from Vlad and Mencheres, but this was something different. Stillness was what called to the residents of the grave, not seething emotions.

"Five more," Bones said, a question in his voice I didn't answer out loud. No, I wasn't done. More were close by. I could feel them.

A chill blew through the warm summer air. Not frigid. Pleasant, like the kiss of frost on a fevered brow. I invited it to come nearer, and it accepted, the coolness settling over me with a slow, sweet lethargy.

It grew inside me, urging me to release myself to it. I didn't fight it, but surrendered, letting it settle all the way through me.

"Eight more," Bones said, almost a growl.

I heard him, but still didn't respond, falling into the white emptiness that attached itself to the center of me. The more I let my fear, grief, and stress slide away from me, the bigger that inner sphere grew, replacing those emotions with cool, blissful nothingness. It was such a relief to let my burdens fall to the ground, swallowed up by the soothing white emptiness. How had I ever lasted so longer under the weight of the pain? Now with it finally gone, I felt like I could fly.

Bones said something else, but I didn't hear what this time. Wave after wave of peace crested over me, insulating me from everything except the cool, restful silence inside me. This was bliss. This was freedom. I reveled in it, never wanting it to end.

A thread reached down into my consciousness, tugging me back. Bones's voice, sounding harsh in worry. It chased away some of that beautiful nothingness, replacing it with concern. It was so calm and peaceful where I was . . . but I didn't like hearing him that way.

His voice came again, more urgent this time. Sandbags of distress seemed to form on top of me, holding me down from that floating, freeing emptiness. They formed a path that I followed, each step piling on every painful emotion I'd let go of before, but I didn't turn around. Bones was at the end of this road. That was more important than all the blissful barrenness behind me.

All of a sudden, I had more than his voice. His face

was only inches away, dark brows drawn together as he said my name, louder, strong hands shaking my shoulders.

"I'm right here, no need to yell," I murmured.

Bones closed his eyes briefly before speaking again. "You turned white as chalk and then crumpled to the floor. I've been calling your name trying to rouse you these past ten minutes."

"Oh." I rubbed my face against his. "Sorry."

At the feel of wetness, I touched my cheek and then looked at the pink glistening drops on my fingers.

Tears. "I was crying?" Odd. I didn't remember feeling sad.

"Yes," Bones rasped. "You were, and yet the whole time, you were still smiling."

Eesh. That sounded kinda creepy. "Did it work?" I remember him rattling off some numbers before, but I didn't know if those ghosts were still here. I was on the porch floor, and Bones's body blocked out most of what was around me.

"Oh, it bloody well did," he replied. Then he sat back, lifting me up with him. The rest of the porch and surrounding yard came into view.

I couldn't control my gasp at the dozens and dozens of transparent forms that lined up around our house. I could barely even make out all their faces, there were so many of them floating by each other. Good God! It was like being back in New Orleans. How was this possible? I'd only summoned five ghosts the last time I tried this with Vlad and that had been in cemetery, for crying out loud!

"Are these the Remnants you guys were talking about?" Kira asked, sounding rattled.

"No." Amazement was still in my voice. "They're regular ghosts."

One of the hazy forms zoomed up yard and onto the porch. "Cat!"

It took a second, but then those indistinct features solidified into someone I recognized.

"Hey, Fabian," I said, trying to lighten his concern with a joke. "I see you got my page."

He reached out, his fingers passing through my cheek. "Your tears were like a rope that pulled me to you," he said.

Wasn't that ironic? It was blood that raised and controlled the Remnants, but maybe tears did the same for ghosts. That had to be the wild card. I'd bled in the cemetery with Vlad, plus been angry, frustrated, and sad, but I hadn't cried. Yet ten minutes of tapping into that stillness inside combined with tears and now I had a veritable army of spectres on my lawn.

"I'm all right," I said to Bones and Fabian since both of them were watching me with concerned expressions. "Really," I added. "Now that we've got a good crowd, let's do this."

I stood up, going to the end of the patio that overlooked the area where the ghosts were the thickest, though more were coming, from the rustling back by the tree line.

"Thank you for coming," I said, trying to sound confident. "My name is Cat. There's something very important I need to ask you to do."

"'Ello, mistress," a vaguely familiar voice boomed out. "Not thought to see you again."

I cocked my head at the ghost who flitted between the others to the front of the group. He had graying brown hair, a barrel belly, and he obviously hadn't shaved any time soon before he'd died. Something about him nagged at my memory, however. Where had I seen him before . . . ?

"Winston Gallagher!" I said, recognizing the first ghost I'd met.

He cast a disappointed look at my empty hands. "No moonshine? Ah, yer a cruel one, to summon me here without a drop of nourishment."

Never let it be said that something as simple as death could cure alcoholism, I thought irreverently, remembering all the moonshine the ghost had co-erced me into drinking the night we met. Then my eyes narrowed and I covered my hand in front of my crotch as I saw Winston's gaze fasten there next.

"Don't you even *think* of poltergeisting my panties again," I warned him, adding in a louder voice. "That goes for everyone else here, too."

"This is the sod?" Bones started down the porch stairs even as Winston began to edge away. "Come back here, you scurvy little—"

"Bones, don't!" I interrupted, not wanting him to start using slurs that might offend the other living-impaireds gathered here.

He stopped, giving a last glare to Winston while mouthing, *You. Me. Exorcist*, before returning to my side.

I shook my head. Vampire territorialism. It had *no* sense of appropriate timing.

"As I said, there's something very important I need you to do. I'm looking for a ghoul who's trying to start a war among the undead, and he'll have a lot of other pissed-off, vampire-hating ghouls with him."

It would be a huge task, but if Marie found Gregor through ghosts with no clue where he was in the world, then I should be able to find Apollyon a lot easier with what I knew.

"Ride the ley lines," I said, feeling like a warped version of General Patton rallying my troops. "Tell your friends and get them hunting, too. Search all the larger funeral homes that are bordered by cemeteries. Find the short ghoul with the black comb-around that goes by the name of Apollyon, and then come right back and *tell me where he is*."

"Not you, luv," Bones said at once. "Fabian. Have them report to Fabian, who will then relay it to you."

Good point. I trusted Marie's power enough to believe that every ghost I personally spoke to wouldn't betray me, but I was enlisting others who'd never met me. No need to have this plan backfire by leading Apollyon right to me instead of vice versa.

I gestured to the ghost at my side. "Wait. Report back to Fabian, my right-hand man. He'll stay here so you'll be able to find him."

Fabian's chest puffed out at my declaration, a beaming smile spreading across his face. I rested my hand over where his shoulder would be, meeting the gaze of every ghost who stared at me.

"Now go," I urged them. "Hurry."

†HIR†Y-FÍVE

A SILVERY BLUR FLÍ††ED OVER †HE O†HER cars in the parking lot before diving into our black van. We were only a couple miles away from the Lasting Peace cemetery and funeral home in Garland, Texas. It had taken Marie Laveau twelve years of sending out ghosts to find Gregor, but Fabian received information of Apollyon's whereabouts in six days.

In fairness, the world was a big damn place, and Mencheres had had Gregor in an old, reinforced mine tunnel in Madagascar—hell and gone from Marie's home base of New Orleans. I, however, had narrowed Apollyon's location down to only one country *and* a type of business. Still, they had done an amazing job. No one would disparage ghosts while I was around, that was for sure.

Fabian's features solidified from the random hazy swirls, but his mouth was turned down in a frown.

"I think you should get more people."

"How many are there?" Bones asked him.

"At least four score," Fabian replied. "They're having a rally in about an hour."

"Is Apollyon still there?" I pressed.

Fabian nodded. "You could capture him afterward, once the others leave."

Bones exchanged a glance with me. *Or Apollyon could leave with the other ghouls.* Then we'd need to have the ghosts hunt him for us all over again.

"The bulk of the ghouls—do they look like visitors for the rally, or guards?" Bones asked, tapping his chin.

Fabian looked confused. "How would I tell?"

"You can tell by how many of them are armed," Vlad said, with pointed emphasis on the last word.

"Ah." Fabian's brow smoothed. "A few of them had large weapons with bullets that crisscrossed around their torsos."

I made a mental note to familiarize Fabian with modern artillery so he'd be able to give better descriptions.

"Machine guns?" I asked, miming holding one and making a series of rapid staccato noises.

Bones's mouth twitched, but he dipped his head so I wouldn't see his clear amusement over my "GI Jane does Pictionary" imitation.

"Yes, those," Fabian said. "Some of the other people could have knives on them, but those were the only weapons I could see."

Vlad let out a snort. "I didn't come this far to run now."

I felt the same way. Still, I had to assume the machine guns were armed with silver bullets and at least some of the ghouls would have silver knives. Most of them might not be armed, but eight to one was still eight to one.

"Mencheres, use your power to keep any humans from getting hurt. One side of the cemetery borders a business district, and I can't have Tate send troops to block it off because that would tip Apollyon to our presence. So keeping people out of the way is your top priority."

"As opposed to restraining Apollyon?" he asked, polite disagreement in his tone.

I met his charcoal gaze. "If you rip his head off, that looks very impressive for you, but it won't do me much good. You guys keep telling me if I don't smack people down hard enough when they come after me, then more will follow. Well, I'm the one Apollyon used as a scapegoat all this time, so I'm the one who has to take him down."

Silence met this pronouncement. I braced for arguments, especially from Bones, so I was surprised when he coolly nodded his head.

"Don't use your power to restrain the other ghouls, either," Bones stated. "We'll take them in a match of strength on strength."

I looked around at the occupants of the van. In addition to Mencheres, Kira, Vlad, Spade, Denise, Ed, and Scratch, we'd picked up a few new additions in recent days. Bones's sire, Ian, grinned at the prospect. Gorgon, Mencheres's old friend, just shrugged, and the blond Law Guardian, Veritas, who was as old as Mencheres even though she looked like Barbie doll's younger sister, only appeared bored by the topic. No one voiced a word of objection.

Eleven vampires and a shapeshifter against whatever Apollyon had at that complex. That might not sound like good odds, but I knew how deadly this bunch was. Also, if we gathered too many vampires together, we ran the risk of Apollyon getting tipped off.

"All right." I gave everyone a steady, unblinking glance. "Apollyon wants a war? He's going to get one, but not between our two species. It'll be between his best and our best."

Bones met my gaze, dark brown eyes glinting with green.

"We go in an hour," he stated, the promise of violence caressing each word. "Gives the rest of them time to arrive."

And all of them being there meant less chance of any ghouls stumbling across the fight and then summoning backup for Apollyon. I smiled at Bones, feeling the mixture of anticipation and purpose that always filled me before a fight.

"I can't wait to crash the party."

His answering smile was edged with the same lethal expectancy.

"Neither can I, Kitten."

The sharp wind made me squint as I stared down at the cemetery Bones flew us over. The majority was only lit up by residual illumination around the perimeter gates, with two exceptions. One was the funeral home. Exterior lights shone on the LASTING PEACE sign out front, emphasizing the somber yet elegant design of the two-story building. The other area that had lights was on the edge of the southern

burial plats, bordering against the unplowed acres
set aside for future graves. I looked down at the
small, illuminated platform, one ghoul standing in
between the two portable floodlights, and couldn't
bite back my scoff.

Apollyon didn't have those lights set up on either
side of him so his followers could get a good view of
him gesturing emphatically during his rhetoric about
how Cain was really a ghoul and vampires originally
derived from flesh-eaters instead of the other way
around. Ghouls could see in the dark. How arrogant
did Apollyon have to be, to insist on being lit up like
a rock star during what was supposed to be a secret
undead rally? And was that an Armani suit he had
on? In my boringly functional, all-black leotard with
multiple weapon holsters, I was clearly underdressed
for this shindig.

Bones abruptly tilted us downward and all thoughts
of clothing left my mind. Fabian was right; a crowd
of around sixty gathered in a loose diamond-shaped
formation, listening to Apollyon with rapt attention,
while about two dozen guards armed with machine
guns roamed around the assembly. We'd also seen
about four or five guards near the main entrance of the
cemetery, but I wasn't worried about them. Mencheres
would handle them, and Denise and Kira would make
sure no latecomers showed up.

I gripped my two katana swords as Bones bulleted
us toward the thickest cluster of armed guards. Goal
number one was to take out the guns before the guns
took us out. I had a split second to enjoy the look of
shock on the guards' faces as either Bones's power
level preceded us, or they saw a big dark form hur-

tling right for them. And then we plowed into them with a tremendous crash.

The impact was like smashing into a group of trees, except these trees shouted and fought back. I hacked away with my two swords before even coming to a stop, knowing Bones had already rolled to the side to stay well clear of my blades. Limbs and heads separated underneath my ferocious slices as I used the shorter swords like extensions of my arms, swinging away at anyone in front of me no matter if they were armed or not. If they were here, then they were on Apollyon's side, which meant they'd kill me if they could.

More gunfire and shouts let me know that the rest of our welcoming party had landed. As much as I wanted to look around and check on Bones, I didn't, keeping my attention on hacking my way to the ghouls who were now spraying the crowd in an effort to take out the intruders. Flashes of white-hot pain arced into my side, making me roll in defense even as I continued to swing my blades at anyone unlucky enough to be near me. Dammit. I'd been hit.

All the tumbling made my hair come loose from its bun. Dark strands interrupted my vision as I rolled to avoid another barrage of bullets, seeing the grass explode in mini pops where I'd just been. Acting on instinct, I flung my sword, hearing a scream before I jumped up, my side still burning, to see a ghoul fall backward clawing at his face, my sword hilt where his nose used to be.

I ignored the pain and vaulted forward, tackling him before he could raise the gun again. A hard swipe across his neck and he wasn't moving anymore. Another swipe took out the trigger on the gun. No need leaving it functional so a bystander could pick it up and start shooting away.

Pain exploded in my neck in the next instant, blood filling my mouth. I grabbed the dead ghoul, using his body as a shield, coughing even though I didn't breathe. That searing matched the pain in my side, but it faded quicker, and the red on my clothes let me know what happened. I'd been shot in the throat.

Somehow, that pissed me off more than the bullets still burning their way deeper into my side. I kept ahold of the corpse, balancing his body in front of me as I charged at the ghoul who continued to fire at me. Those bullets struck his fallen comrade instead, and I had time to let out a savage snarl before I threw the body on him, knocking him over. I followed immediately with my sword, slicing through the arm he raised in defense and then his neck, putting all my pain and anger behind the blow. His head rolled a foot away from his body.

I didn't stop to celebrate but swung around. Just in time, too. A duo of ghouls bored down on me, one shooting, one holding out a knife. I had time to fling myself upward, making the bullets intended for me hit empty air instead, before I landed behind them. My sword ripped through both their necks with the momentum from my jump, blood splattering me as they fell, headless, to the ground.

"Kitten!"

My head jerked up just in time to see a flash of silver above me. I flung myself down, the sword that had been about to cleave through my neck catching me in the side of the head instead. At once, my vision went red and agony exploded in my skull. Every inner impulse screamed at me to hunch defensively and clutch my wound, but the part of me that remembered all the brutal training Bones put me through knew to strike out instead. I swung my blade where I'd last glimpsed the ghoul's legs, putting all my strength into the blow. I was rewarded by a scream and a thump, something heavy landing on me. The blood in my vision made it hard to make out specifics, but I kept swinging, knowing from each new scream that I was hitting my mark even if I couldn't see what that mark was. Sizzling pain erupting along my back had me arching in reflex and redoubling my efforts. The ghoul wasn't done fighting yet.

After several rapid blinks, my gaze cleared enough to see him. His arm was missing. So were his legs at the calves, but he had a silver knife that he kept stabbing into my back, seeking my heart. Instead of rolling away from him, I lunged forward, head-butting him with all my fury. He jerked back in a dazed way, but the sudden stars in my vision and urge to throw up let me know that my head injury wasn't done healing yet. With pain crashing through my skull and my side throbbing like I had heat-seeking missiles doing the tango in my guts, I brought my sword down toward his neck.

He kicked me with his stumps at the same time, knocking my aim off. Instead of cleaving through his neck, my sword buried deep in his shoulder. I tugged but it wouldn't come free. The ghoul let out something like a snarl and a laugh.

"Missed me," he chortled viciously, raising his gun.

My other arm whipped forward and the ghoul's laugh died in his throat. He fired, but the bullets went wild, probably because he now had two silver knives in his eye sockets. He should have never taken the time to taunt me before he fired. I had plenty of other weapons aside from my sword.

He reached for the knives—another mistake. I wrenched the gun from his hands and used it to shoot my way right through his neck, letting out a scream of deadly triumph. Then I yanked my sword free, whirling around to defend against the next attack.

None came. Although I still heard spates of gunfire, they were far less frequent than before. The cemetery was littered with bodies, and those still standing looked like they were trying to run more than attempting to fight. For a split second, I was surprised. Yeah, I knew our group was tough, but . . .

A flash of yellow and black caught my eye, moving with the speed of some sort of cartoon Tasmanian devil. It plowed into two ghouls who had been firing at Ian. In the next blink, there was nothing more than a crimson pile of body parts on the ground, a lithe blonde with two swords standing over them.

Veritas? I didn't have a chance to goggle at her before she was off in another crazily fast blur, heading for an eruption of gunfire over the hill. Within moments, that gunfire stopped.

"Am I the only one who has wood over that little vixen?" Ian asked cheerfully even as he cleaved his sword right through the center of a ghoul. That shook me out of my momentary stupor and I started chasing down the next spate of gunfire I heard. My side still felt like it had been set on fire, but I pushed it back.

I didn't have time to dig the bullets out, and nothing else would make the burning stop.

I continued to run toward the sounds of gunfire, clearing the crest of a small hill. At the bottom was a large memorial fountain, but that's not what made my body seize with a fresh spurt of adrenaline. It was the sight of the short, expensively clad ghoul backed up against the fountain, three guards surrounding him in protective formation as they fired at the vampires who cut off their escape.

"Apollyon!" I yelled, running down the hill in a straight line toward him. "You remember *me*, don't you?"

Even with the distance, I saw his eyes widen. "Reaper," he mouthed. Then louder, in a scream at the ghouls protecting him, "That's her, that's the Reaper!"

The gunfire changed direction, but I'd expected that. I dove to my right, all but one bullet missing me. It slammed into my side with the impact of a torpedo, but I kept rolling, knowing the gunfire wouldn't cease. Unlike the movies, in real life, the bad guys didn't quit shooting to check and see if you were dead. Those bullets chased me, but I scrambled up and kept moving, headstones exploding around me as those were struck instead of me.

A scream preceded one of the guns going quiet. Then another one. Even as I kept running, I smiled. I knew Vlad, Spade, and Gorgon had only needed a few moments of distraction to pounce. Apollyon and his guards should have known that, too, and never focused all three of their guns on me.

I whirled around, heading back toward the bottom of the hill. Vlad had one of the gunmen in a merciless grip, flames erupting all over the ghoul. Spade wrestled with another ghoul, but I wasn't worried about him, because at some point, he'd managed to knock the gun away. That left Ed and Gorgon fighting with two more ghouls who'd joined the battle, but my attention wasn't focused on them. It was on the stocky ghoul running flat-out for the gate bordering the cemetery. On the other side of that gate was a small business district, mostly deserted this time of night, but with lots of buildings and apartments that Apollyon could hide in.

"Oh no you don't," I growled, running faster. That sickening pain increased, the burning in my side feeling like acid eating all through me, but I couldn't concentrate on that now. I had to focus on the air around me, picturing it as something with form that I could mold and bend to my will. Bones's words echoed in my mind. *You have the ability. You just need to sharpen it.*

My feet lifted off the ground, but I didn't fall. I *flew*, leaning into the air, letting it take me faster than I could run before. Wind rushed through my hair, streaming along my body, lifting me as though it understood my need and wanted to help. The distance between me and Apollyon grew shorter, his steps seeming so slow and clumsy in comparison to the way I arced above the ground. I streamlined my body, my hands out in front of me, aiming for the back of his Armani jacket like it was a bull's-eye and I was an arrow. *Thirty feet. Twenty. Ten . . .*

When I barreled into him, my velocity plowing him to the ground hard enough to tear up the dirt, I was smiling even though a fresh deluge of pain blasted through my side. And when I came up, twisting so Apollyon was in front of me, relief made me almost immune to the strikes he got in before I had his neck locked in an iron chokehold.

"You move and I'll rip your head right the fuck off," I told him, meaning every deadly word.

Apollyon was either smarter than I gave him credit for, or he really did fear me, because he stopped struggling at once.

"What are you going to do with me?" he hissed, the words garbled from the grip I had around his throat.

I let out a pained laugh.

"I'm so glad you asked."

Thirty-six

By the time we reached the fountain, Spade had killed the ghoul he fought with, nothing but charred remains were left of the one I'd seen with Vlad, and two headless bodies were on the ground near where Gorgon and Ed stood. I didn't see Bones, but I knew he was okay. I could feel our connection, strong as ever, his emotions washing over me with intensity and purpose. Now that I had a sufficient amount of vampires close by, I let go of Apollyon, giving him a hard shove that had him bracing against the edge of the fountain to keep from falling.

"Let's talk about what I'm going to do to you," I said, picking up a sword someone had left discarded on the ground. Movement on the top of the hill drew my attention for a moment, making me pause, but then I continued. "I think I'll take your idea of celebrating a victory with an execution, only with a small reversal of who loses their head."

Apollyon bared his teeth at me. "Even if you kill me, my people will fight yours to the death," he snarled. "Your victory will be naught but ashes and—"

He stopped at my laughter, his face almost mottled in its fury. I didn't say anything, but instead, pointed behind him toward the hill.

He turned, his mouth sagging a little at what he saw. Someone, I wasn't sure who, had rounded up the remaining ghouls and brought them out in a group onto this section of the cemetery. At a rough estimate, there were a little more than twenty of them, and their hands were folded on top of their heads in the universal gesture for surrender.

"Looks like your people know a losing battle when they see one," I said, relishing the stunned look on the ghoul leader's face. That quickly changed as he glared at them, his rage palpable in his expression and the harsh scent wafting off him.

"How dare you betray me this way!" he thundered at them.

I tapped him on the shoulder with the tip of my borrowed sword. "Hate to interrupt," I drew out, "but you and I have still some business to conclude."

Apollyon looked at the sword and then at me before glancing back at the surrendered ghouls. I didn't take my eyes off him or relax my grip on the weapon. I wouldn't swing until he was ready, but neither would I give him a present of dropping my guard. I already knew Apollyon didn't fight fair or we wouldn't be here now.

Therefore, I was somewhat taken aback when he spread his arms out, palms open. "Go on, Reaper, strike me down with flames! Or freeze me with your mind. Show my people the power they so recklessly refuse to stem."

Even his last moments would be filled with hateful rhetoric, I thought in disgust.

"Give him a sword," I said to Bones, who'd come out from behind the group of ghouls, Veritas at his side. He was blood-spattered and his clothes were torn, yet he moved with a lethal precision that said he could have fought all night. It shouldn't surprise me at all that he'd think to bring the ghouls out here to witness their leader's fall.

"I don't need any unusual power to strike you down," I told Apollyon once Bones thrust a sword into the ground near the ghoul's feet. "I've got silver bullets in my left side and they hurt like damn and wow, but pick up that sword and I'll *still* beat your ass, I promise you that."

Apollyon looked at the blade and then back at me. "No."

"No?" I repeated in disbelief. "I'm offering you a fair fight, jackass! You'd rather I just hack your head off and call it a day?"

Apollyon turned toward Veritas, dropping down on one knee. "I surrender to the Guardian Council of Vampires."

"You sniveling little shite, pick up that sword before I rip your head off with my bare hands," Bones thundered at him.

Apollyon's expression was twisted with a crazed sort of triumph. "You can't kill me if I surrender to a Guardian. None of you can!"

I regarded him with amazement. *This* was the person who'd been responsible for bringing vampires and ghouls to the brink of war in the fourteen hundreds? And who'd made a damn credible effort to do it again in the twenty-first century?

I'd seen a lot of villainous instigators in their final moments, but while none of them had relished their own deaths, few had ever groveled as much as Apollyon was doing now. He even edged closer to Veritas in a sort of hop-crawl, until he was clutching the blond Guardian's red-stained pants. I couldn't believe a person who'd devoted so much of his life to the pursuit of mass genocide could be so spineless in the face of his own defeat. It reminded me of history's accounts of Hitler's final hours. Looked like both of them were cowards at heart.

"This is who you were following?" Vlad asked the other ghouls, voicing my own inner scorn. "I'd kill myself in shame if I were you."

Veritas looked at Apollyon, her ridiculously youthful features hardened into an expression of pure contempt.

"You think to find mercy from me?"

She snatched at Apollyon's single long piece of hair, ripping it away from his bald spot and using it as a lever to tug his head back. I almost lost it right there, because damn, that was *cold*.

"You repeatedly seek to destroy my people, and you think I will grant you asylum?" she all but growled.

"You must," Apollyon said, his voice cracking at the last word.

Veritas straightened to her full five feet six inches, but with her sizzling power and imperial presence, she might as well have been nine feet tall.

"Malcolme Untare, you who have renamed yourself Apollyon, for inciting others in your species to murder and insurrection, you are hereby sentenced to death."

He let out a shriek that Veritas ignored. She leaned in until her mouth brushed his ear, and only my close proximity let me hear what she whispered.

"You miserable worm. Jeanne d'Arc was my friend."

Then she kicked him, avoiding his grasping hands to stride away with a "Die on your knees or take the fight she offered you. I care not which," thrown over her shoulder.

My mouth gaped at this tidbit about my famous half-breed predecessor, but I snapped it shut. *Note to self: Don't get on Veritas's bad side. She holds a grudge for* centuries.

Then I looked down at the ghoul, feeling my former hatred ebb. For all the lives he'd been responsible for ending and his blind, centuries-long quest for power, in the end, Apollyon proved to be too pathetic to hate. He wasn't even worth killing, but if I let him live, my current and future enemies wouldn't see it as mercy. They'd see it as a weakness they could exploit. With a clarity I'd lacked before, I understood why Bones did what he did with my father, and why Vlad let his ruthlessness be seen more readily than his finer qualities. It wasn't out of sadistic enjoyment or to pick fights. It was to prevent them.

"Pick up that sword," I said to Apollyon, enunciating each word. "Or I'll kill you where you kneel."

I wouldn't take any enjoyment out of it, but I'd do it because it had to be done. Veritas had already sentenced him to death on behalf of the vampire ruling body. If I walked away, it wouldn't save his life. She or someone else would just kill him.

"No," Apollyon said, almost a whimper. Then he scrambled forward and tried to run.

I caught him before he'd made it even a dozen feet, letting him hit me with all the power in his stocky body. He only had his hands, and I still had a really long blade.

"Apollyon had all of you getting your hate on because of a lie that I'd become a half vampire, half ghoul," I called out to the ghouls who watched us with grim enthrallment. "Because if someone's unusual, then you should be afraid of them, right?"

Apollyon tried to tackle me to the ground, but for all the years he had on me, he obviously hadn't spent them learning how to fight—and I'd had one hell of a teacher. Despite the pain still arcing down my side, I swiveled at the last moment, leaping onto his back when his momentum still had him charging forward. Then I brought my sword against his neck.

"You all want to know why I have abilities other new vampires don't?" I said, digging that blade in. "Because I don't feed from humans; I drink vampire blood."

And then I yanked it toward my body, cutting my hand to grip the naked edge for maximum balance, feeling more satisfaction from that public admission than I did seeing Apollyon's head separate from his neck. All my life, I'd had to hide what I was. First as a child when I didn't even know why other kids weren't like me, then when I hunted vampires in my late teens and mid-twenties, and finally, my oddities this past year as a full vampire. Well, I was done hiding, hating, or apologizing for the parts of me I hadn't chosen and couldn't change. If some people had a problem with my differences, that was just too fucking bad for them.

"That's right, I eat *vampires*," I said again, louder this time. I pushed his body away and stood, shaking the blood off my sword as I faced the remaining group of ghouls.

"World's freakiest bloodsucker, right here," I went on. "And you know what? If that makes some of you uncomfortable, too bad. If it makes some of you so uncomfortable you want to start shit with me about it, step right up and see if I don't eat the hell out of you next!"

I'd meant that last part as a threat, but somewhere in my impassioned declaration of independence from hiding what I was, I'd neglected to think through my phrasing. I saw Bones raise a brow, a muffled snicker broke out from Ian, and then Vlad laughed loud and hearty.

"With that sort of invitation, Reaper, you might want to suggest the line form to your right."

"That's not . . . I meant eat them in a *bad* way," I sputtered.

"I think you made your point, luv," Bones responded, his face carefully blank even thought I caught a faint twitch to his mouth. Then his expression hardened as he looked at Veritas, who'd turned around to watch me behead Apollyon. "And I second it," he said, all traces of humor gone from his voice.

The Law Guardian stared at me. I didn't regret a moment of my public declaration—aside from perhaps my wording—but I knew her response carried more weight than my vampire audience or the score of surrendered ghouls. She also spoke for the highest ruling body over vampires.

At last, Veritas shrugged. "That does make you the world's freakiest bloodsucker, but there's no law against a vampire feeding from other vampires." And then she turned away.

I let out a laugh that died in my throat as movement at the back of the gate caught my eye.

Marie Laveau walked slowly into the cemetery.

Thirty-seven

I DIDN'T BLINK AS I STARED AT MARIE. To anyone who didn't know better, the sight of one lone ghoul strolling up shouldn't have looked frightening at all. But I knew that Marie could summon a wall of Remnants to fight for her before I could even whisper, "Oh shit." Could I raise my own army of them fast enough to counter such an attack from her? Or should I focus my energy on trying to control the ones she raised, if it came to that? I'd assumed Marie gave me her power so that, in a roundabout way, she could help me defeat Apollyon, but had she been on his side all along? Had everything I thought about her been wrong?

"Why have you come here?" Veritas hissed at her.

I held up my hand, ignoring the incredulous look the Law Guardian gave me as I shushed her.

"Majestic, so nice of you to come by," I said, sounding a lot calmer than I felt. "I hope you found the place because of your ghost friends telling you about what was going down. Not because you're just showing up late to the hate rally."

Her deep brown eyes met mine, face absolutely expressionless. She walked forward, gaze flitting around the cemetery to look at the fallen bodies of the ghouls around her. Those still living who'd crouched back in fear minutes before now began to edge toward her.

"Apollyon is dead?" Marie asked, no hint of what she was thinking in her buttery smooth voice.

"Very," I replied before Veritas could speak. "Most of his top lieutenants are dead, too."

Marie was now ahead of all the other ghouls, only a few dozen feet of headstones separating her from the line of Master vampires.

"And your plans for the others?"

I glanced behind her again, anticipating a seething mass of Remnants appearing at any second. We hadn't had a chance to formally discuss among ourselves what we were doing with the surrendered ghouls, but I didn't wait to consult anyone before I answered.

"We're letting them go."

"You have *no* authority to make those decisions," Veritas snapped.

"What a shame." Marie's voice sliced across the air, that sweet Southern twang gone and filled with the echoing tenor of the dead instead. "If Cat were correct, then I would have no cause to attack you to protect my people. I want peace. Don't force me to war."

Veritas stared at Marie, her pretty, deceptively young-looking features hard. I only hoped she'd had run-ins with Marie in the past to know that the voodoo queen's new spooky voice was a warning that she was about to unleash all kinds of pain. If not, I didn't have time to convince Veritas about how ferocious Remnants were. I'd only have time to try to raise my own, or this would turn into a bloodbath with the casualties heavily on our side this time. Marie had her hands clasped in front of her in a deceptively casual gesture, but I knew that just meant the sharp point in her ring was pressed to her flesh.

Only Mencheres's power could be fast enough to stop her from drawing her blood to summon the Remnants. Even though I saw him walk up out of the corner of my eye, relieved to see Denise and Kira were also with him, I didn't dare look over at Mencheres for fear any gesture would antagonize Marie into acting. Plus, if Mencheres froze her, he'd better kill her, too. She'd never let such a thing slide, especially with witnesses. And if we wiped out Apollyon, his lieutenants, *and* Marie Laveau all in the same night, we'd start the war ourselves.

"Cat has no authority to make those decisions," Veritas repeated. Beside me, Bones tensed even as I mentally braced to start counter defenses against a horde of diaphanous killers. "But she is correct nonetheless," Veritas finished.

It took everything in me not to let out a loud whoop of relief. Some of the tension leaking off Bones into my emotions lessened as well, even though not a fraction of his posture eased.

"They'll make us slaves," one of the ghouls called out bitterly, to a chorus of grim sounds of agreement.

"No they won't," Marie said, managing to sound both strident and comforting at the same time. "Peace does not mean vampires will ever rule over us. They are not strong enough to do so. As long as I live, the ghoul nation will *always* be equal to vampires in strength."

I didn't see Marie's fingers move, but I felt the snap of power in the air right before the Remnants appeared behind her, looking like a transparent version of hell's army. Their numbers were staggering, their energy moving over me like icy waves along my skin. My bullet holes had long ago closed, so some part of me roared that I needed to draw my own blood, now, if I had any hope of holding them off. But Marie didn't send the Remnants after anyone. She had them pile behind her instead, building up into a wall that rose higher than the trees and widened to reach the far side of the cemetery, easily five times the number I'd raised with Vlad.

If this was a dick-measuring contest, I found myself thinking numbly, *then I was Pee Wee and she was John Holmes.*

"Hail to our queen!" one of the ghouls called out, echoed almost at once by another cry of "Hail!" More ghouls repeated the salutation, until all of them practically trembled with their shouted allegiance.

Marie bowed her head at the acknowledgments, and then the wall of Remnants collapsed, disappearing into the ground. This time, I saw the flick of her finger that preceded her drawing the necessary blood to send the lethal apparitions back to their graves.

I quit looking at Marie to glance at Bones. He shook his head in a cynical way that mirrored my own thoughts. By getting rid of Apollyon and his top henchmen, we'd cleared the way for Marie to step in as queen of not just New Orleans, but the entire ghoul nation, judging from this reaction. If she'd taken on Apollyon herself, she might indeed have weakened their species through civil war as his supporters battled hers. But with him gone, she was now her people's loyal savior and protector.

Hail, my ass.

I met her hazelnut gaze, noting the satisfaction in her eyes, before tapping the side of my mouth in silent warning. Marie might be the queen of the flesh-eaters now, but she and I shared a secret that could bring her down. Her people wouldn't be cheering her so adoringly if they knew she'd shared her power with a vampire, giving me the tools necessary to bring down Apollyon. And if she tried to use her new position as a springboard for a war against the vampire world, she'd soon find herself fighting ghost for ghost against every spook I could rally using her borrowed abilities *and* the help of my friend Fabian.

But when Marie inclined her head at me in a polite way, not an antagonistic one, I felt a twinge of hope. Marie was many things, but rash and stupid weren't among them, so she'd know all this. With the incredible powers that many Master vampires had, plus what I'd absorbed from Marie and now knew about ghosts and the vital role they could play in battle, the two species were pretty evenly matched again, even with Marie's abilities.

The scales had been tipped when Gregor's death made Marie's allegiance to ghouls alone, but maybe balance was what Marie intended all along when she forced me to drink her blood, using the one form of threat I could never refuse: Bones's life. I could only hope that evening the scales for the sake of peace had been her plan . . . and be ready in case it wasn't.

I inclined my head at her in the same respectful manner, but still kept my finger near my mouth. A slight smile creased her face before Marie turned away. Both our messages were sent and received.

"Come," Marie said to the surviving ghouls. "We will leave together. You have nothing to fear from them. We are at peace now."

As one, the ghouls began to follow Marie when she turned to walk out of the cemetery the same way she came in. I wondered if they picked up the warning note in her smooth voice when she said that we were at peace. I had, and once again felt a twinge of hope. If any of them went behind Marie's back to start with vampires again, they'd find out the wrath of the voodoo queen was just as frightening as what I or any other vampire would do to them.

"She used no spell," Veritas murmured in surprise.

I gave her a brief, jaded look. "That's because she doesn't practice black magic; she *is* black magic," I said, repeating Marie's words from that day.

"Can we trust her?" Veritas asked Mencheres, so low I could barely hear her.

He cast a thoughtful look at where Marie exited the cemetery before bestowing a single glance my way.

"We can trust her not to be foolish," Mencheres replied at last. "Beyond that, we will have to see."

I looked at the direction in which the voodoo queen disappeared with my own shrug. Time would tell Marie's true motives. Until then, we had to pick up the pieces and move on.

Speaking of pieces . . .

I cast a glance around at the remains of the battle. Shriveling limbs, bodies, and blood stained the ground in various dark patches. What a mess. We'd have to burn most of the areas where the battles took place, both to hide the evidence of undead blood and just in case any of Denise's blood had been spilled. I'd call Tate and have him keep the local cops back once we started the fires. It still felt strange to know Tate was the one I'd be speaking to about containing the scene, instead of hearing Don's voice on the other line when I phoned in the details.

Even thinking of my uncle seemed to conjure his image out of the corner of my eye; wearing a suit and tie, gray hair impeccably combed, tugging on his eyebrow like he did when he was annoyed or reflective. Several times over the past ten days, a mirage of my uncle would appear in my peripheral vision only to vanish as soon as I turned around. Grief did funny things to people, I supposed, but I didn't turn yet. I had bullets to dig out of my body and a whole lot of other unpleasant things to do, but just for a few moments, I wanted to pretend that Don was still with me.

"Lucifer's bloody ball sack, I don't believe it," Bones hissed.

I did turn then. As expected, the image of my uncle vanished, but I was surprised to see Bones staring at that same spot behind me, his mouth dropped open like . . .

Like he'd seen a ghost.

"No," I breathed.

Bones met my gaze, and one look in his eyes told me everything.

"Son of a bitch," I whispered, my emotions swirling faster than a blender set on high as disbelief gave way to realization. Then I strode toward the area where Bones had been staring.

"Donald Bartholomew Williams," I called out loudly. "Get your ass back here *now*!"

Dear Reader:

I hope you enjoyed *This Side of the Grave*.

If you can't wait to find out what's next for Bones, Cat, and her uncle, here is an excerpt from *One Grave at a Time*, the next novel in the Night Huntress series, available Fall 2011. Just before the scene you're about to read, Cat received a call from Tate asking her to come to the compound to meet the new "operations consultant," cryptically adding for her to bring Don along, too.

Thanks, and happy reading!

Jeaniene Frost

"Cat Crawfield . . . Russell," I intro-duced myself to the older man after a minuscule pause. Okay, Bones and I weren't married according to human law, but by vampire standards, we were bound together tighter than a piece of paper could ever make two people.

A wave of pleasure brushed against my subconscious, drifting out from the shields Bones had erected around himself as soon as our helicopter landed. He liked that I'd added the last name he'd been born with to my own. That was all the officiating I needed to decide that I'd be Catherine Crawfield Russell from this day forth.

Even though I hadn't needed Don's reaction to deduce that Jason Madigan was going to be a pain in my ass, years of strict farm-bred manners made it impossible for me not to offer my hand. Madigan looked at it for a fraction too long before shaking it.

Yep. Not enough calluses to come from anything other than pens, mouse pads, or phones, just like I'd thought. And his hesitancy revealed that our new "consultant" had a prejudice against women or vampires, neither of which endeared Madigan to me any further.

Bones stated his name with none of my hand-offering compulsions, but then again, his childhood had been spent begging or thieving to survive the harsh circumstances of being the bastard son of a prostitute in eighteenth-century London. Not being endlessly drilled about manners and respecting your elders like mine. He stared at Madigan without blinking, his hands resting inside the pockets of his leather coat, his half smile more challenging than courteous.

Madigan took the hint. He dropped his hand from mine and didn't attempt extending it to Bones. The faintest expression of relief might have even crossed his face, too.

Prejudice against vampires, then. Perfect.

"You were right, weren't you?" Madigan said to Tate with a joviality that rang false. "He did come with her."

For a second my gaze flicked to Don. Good God, could Madigan *see* him? He was human, but maybe Madigan had some psychic abilities . . .

"With vampires, if you invite one spouse, the other is automatically included as well," Bones replied lightly. "That's an age-old rule, but I'll forgive you for not knowing it."

Oh, Madigan meant Bones. I stifled my snort. What he said was true, but even if it wasn't, Bones wouldn't have stayed behind because some stuffy suit wanted to pull a power play.

"What's up with the ID check on the roof?" I asked to steer things away from the staring contest between Madigan and Bones that the consultant would lose. No one could out-stare a vampire.

Madigan shifted his attention to me, his natural scent souring ever so slightly underneath its preponderance of chemical enhancement.

"One of the oversights I noted when I arrived two

days ago was that no one checked my identification when I landed. This facility is too important to be compromised by something as simple as sloppy security."

Tate bristled, hints of emerald appearing in his indigo eyes, but I just snorted.

"There are three security checkpoints on the ground, but if you're arriving by air, they would have double-checked the identity of the aircraft, the crew, and the flight plan, so whoever's inside is who they're supposed to be. Besides"—another snort—"if anyone got here by air that *didn't* belong, you think they'd be able to get away with their aircraft in missile range and several vampires able to track them by scent alone?"

Instead of being offended by my blunt analysis of how useless a roof ID check was, Madigan just stared at me in a thoughtful way.

"I heard you had difficulty with authority and following orders. Seems that wasn't exaggerated."

"Nope, that's true," I replied with a cheery smile. "What else did you hear?"

He waved a hand dismissively. "Too many things to list. Your former team raved about you so much I simply had to meet you."

"Yeah?" I didn't buy that as the reason I was here, but I'd play along. "Well, whatever you do, ignore what my mom has to say about me."

Madigan didn't even crack a smile. Uptight prick.

"What *does* an operations consultant do, I wonder?" Bones asked, as if he hadn't been busy using his mind-reading skills to filch on Madigan from the moment we arrived. I'd have done the same thing myself, but my mental snooping abilities weren't active at the moment.

"Ensures that the transfer of management in a highly sensitized Homeland Security Department is as smooth as it needs to be," Madigan said, that smugness back in his tone. "I'll be reviewing all records over the next few weeks. Missions, personnel, budgets, everything. This department is too critical to only *hope* that Sergeant Bradley is up to the task of running it."

Tate didn't so much as twitch a brawny muscle, even though the implied insult had to burn. For all the issues I'd had with him in the past, Tate's competence, dedication, and work ethic had never been among them.

"You won't find anyone more qualified to run this operation now that Don's gone," I said with quiet steel.

"That's not why he's here," Don hissed. He'd been quiet for the past several minutes, but now he sounded more agitated than I'd ever heard him. Did becoming a ghost give my normally urbane uncle less control over his emotions, or did he and Madigan have a nasty history together?

"He's the head of a *really* covert branch of the CIA, so if he's here, he's after something more important than auditing Tate's job performance," Don went on.

"I'm particularly interested in getting caught up on your records," Madigan said to me, oblivious to the other conversation in the room.

I shrugged. "Knock yourself out. Hope you like stories about the bad guys—or girls—getting it in the end."

"My favorite kind," Madigan replied with a glint in his eye that I didn't care for.

"Are Dave, Juan, Cooper, and my mom in the Wreck Room?" I asked, done with playing these stupid subtext word games. Seeing them would distract from the urge I had to check Madigan's ass for a large bug. If I spent much more time with him, my temper might overcome my common sense, and that wouldn't be good. The smartest thing would be to play docile and let Tate find out if Madigan was really sniffing around this operation for ulterior motives.

"Why do you want to know their location?" Madigan asked coolly, as if I had nefarious intentions he needed to protect them from.

My smile hid the fact that I was gritting my teeth. "Because since I'm here, I want to say hi to my friends and family," I managed to reply, proud of myself for not ending the sentence with *dickhead*.

"Soldiers and trainees are too busy to drop what they're doing just because a visitor wants to chat," Madigan stated crisply.

My fangs jumped out of their own accord, almost aching with my desire to tear the snotty expression right off Madigan's lightly wrinkled face. Maybe some of that showed in my face, because he followed that comment with, "I must warn you, any hostile actions toward me will be taken as an attack against the United States itself."

"Pompous prick," Don snapped, striding over to Madigan before stopping abruptly, as if remembering there wasn't a single thing he could do to him in his current state.

A thread of warning edged into my furious emotions, Bones's silent reminder for me to get control of myself. I did, forcing my fangs to retract and my eyes to change from sizzling green to their normal shade of medium gray.

"Whatever would give you the idea that I'd attack you?" I asked, making my voice as innocent and surprised as I could, while mentally folding him into the shape of a pretzel.

"I might be new here, but I've extensively studied reports on your kind," Madigan said, dropping his patronizing G-man façade for an instant to show the naked hostility underneath. "All of them show that vampires' eyes change color right before they attack."

Bones laughed, a caressing sound that was at odds with the dangerous energy starting to push at his walls. "Bollocks. Our eyes turn green for reasons that have nothing to do with intent to kill—and I've seen vampires rip throats out without the slightest change in iris color. Is that the only experience you've had with vampires? Reports?"

The last word was heavy with polite scorn. Madigan visibly stiffened.

"I've had enough experience to know that some can read minds."

Bones's smile widened.

"Shouldn't concern you. Men with nothing to hide have nothing to fear. Right, mate?"

I waited to see if Madigan would nut up and outright accuse Bones of prying into his mind during this conversation, but he simply adjusted his wire-rim glasses as though their location on his nose was of prime importance.

Wasn't going to cut the crap, then. Fine. I suppose it was naive of me to hope that he'd be a straight shooter. Life wasn't that easy.

"Your mom and the others will be done with training in an hour," Tate said, the first words he'd spoken since we'd come into his office. "You can wait here, if you'd like. Madigan was just leaving."

"Are you *dismissing* me?" Madigan asked with a touch of incredulity.

Tate's expression was bland. "Didn't you say right before Cat got here that you'd had enough of me for the day?"

Faint color rose in Madigan's cheeks. Not embarrassment, from his scent spiking with hints of kerosene. Carefully controlled indignation.

"I did," he replied shortly. "You'll have those reports for me in the morning? I assume staying up the rest of the night should be no hardship for someone like you."

Oh, what an *asshole*. My fangs did that *let me at him!* thing again, but this time, I kept them in my gums, while also stifling the nosferatu green from leaping into my gaze.

Then Madigan turned back to us. "Cat. Bones." He said our names like we should apologize for them, but I just grinned as though I hadn't already eviscerated him in my fantasies several times by now.

"*So* great to meet you," I said, holding out my hand again only because I knew he didn't want to touch it.

He took it with the same faint pause he'd shown last time. I didn't squeeze once I had him in my grip, but oh, it was tempting.

As soon as I let him go, Madigan swept out of Tate's office, trailing a cloud of aftershave and irritation behind him.

"I'm following him," my uncle said flatly. "And I'm not coming back with you later, Cat."

I glanced at Tate, who gave me a barely perceptible nod. In truth, I was relieved that he didn't attempt to argue. Don could snoop on Madigan a hell of a lot more effectively than Tate or anyone else. Maybe Madigan was here because Uncle Sam *was* just being paranoid at a vampire in charge of an operation that hunted and concealed evidence of the undead. If so, Madigan would waste a lot of taxpayer dollars by scrutinizing this operation only to come to the conclusion that Tate was an outstanding replacement for Don. His record was spotless, so I had no fear of Madigan unearthing any skeletons in Tate's closet—real or metaphorical.

But that wasn't why I was glad my uncle was focusing more on Madigan than on finding his way to the eternal doorway of the other side. If Madigan had a more sinister reason for being here, Don could alert us faster than anyone else. I had faith in Tate, Dave, and Juan being able to get themselves out of here if Madigan's dislike of the undead took a more menacing turn, but my mother, for all her bravado, just wasn't as tough as they were.

And this wasn't a regular building that she could just bust through a wall to escape from. The fourth sublevel was built to contain vampires against their will. I should know. I designed it back when I was capturing vampires so Don's scientists could make a synthetic wonder drug called Brams. That drug, derived from the healing compound in undead blood, had kept several members of our team alive after they'd sustained grievous injury. Then Bones joined the operation, and Don got over his fear that raw vampire blood—far more effective in healing than Brams—would turn anyone evil who drank it. Bones donated enough of his blood for

Don to parse out to injured team members as needed, and the vampire cells on the fourth sublevel had remained empty for years as a result.

But that didn't mean they couldn't be put back into use, if Don was right and Madigan was here for other reasons than a routine evaluation . . .

Or maybe I'd had so much shit happen lately that I assumed the worst about everyone now, whether I had valid reason to or not. I gave my head a shake to clear it. For all that Madigan pissed me off, it wasn't too long ago that Don had had the same prejudice about vampires. Hell, it was less than eight years ago that *I'd* thought the only good bloodsucker was a dead bloodsucker, too! Yes, Madigan's attitude screamed Suspicious Bureaucratic Bastard, but hopefully spending some time with Tate, Juan, Dave, and my mother would make him realize there was more to supernaturals than what he'd read in the pages of classified murder reports.

"So what do you think of him?" Tate drawled, that former tightness now gone from his tone.

"That he and I won't be BFFs," was all I said. No need to say more when the room could be bugged.

Tate grunted. "I'm getting that vibe, too. Maybe it's a good thing that . . . circumstances are what they are."

By Tate's careful allusion to Don's condition, it was obvious that he also was taking no chances over our words being played back to Madigan later.

I gave a concurring shrug. "I suppose everything does happen for a reason."

At Avon Books, we know your passion
for romance—once you finish one of our
novels, you find yourself wanting more.

May we tempt you with . . .

- **Excerpts** from our upcoming releases.
- **Entertaining extras,** including authors' personal photo albums and book lists.
- Behind-the-scenes **scoop** on your favorite characters and series.
- **Sweepstakes** for the chance to win free books, romantic getaways, and other fun prizes.
- Writing **tips** from our authors and editors.
- **Blog** with our authors and find out why they love to write romance.
- **Exclusive content** that's not contained within the pages of our novels.

Join us at
www.avonbooks.com

AVON

An Imprint of HarperCollinsPublishers
www.avonromance.com

THE NIGHT HUNTRESS NOVELS FROM
Jeaniene Frost

✠ **HALFWAY TO THE GRAVE** ✠

978-0-06-124508-4

Kick-ass demon hunter and half-vampire Cat Crawfield and her sexy mentor, Bones, are being pursued by a group of killers. Now Cat will have to choose a side...and Bones is turning out to be as tempting as any man with a heartbeat.

✠ **ONE FOOT in THE GRAVE** ✠

978-0-06-124509-1

Cat Crawfield works to rid the world of the rogue undead. But when she's targeted for assassination she turns to her ex, the sexy and dangerous vampire Bones, to help her.

✠ **AT GRAVE'S END** ✠

978-0-06-158307-0

Caught in the crosshairs of a vengeful vamp, Cat's about to learn the true meaning of bad blood—just as she and Bones need to stop a lethal magic from being unleashed.

✠ **DESTINED FOR AN EARLY GRAVE** ✠

978-0-06-158321-6

Cat is having terrifying visions in her dreams of a vampire named Gregor who's more powerful than Bones.

✠ **THIS SIDE OF THE GRAVE** ✠

978-0-06-178318-0

Cat and her vampire husband Bones have fought for their lives, as well as their relationship. But Cat's new and unexpected abilities threaten the both of them.